# VERONICA MIXON

# THE LONG ROAD HOME

Vinci Books

vinci-books.com

Published by Vinci Books Ltd in 2026

1


A CIP catalogue record for this book is available from the British Library.
Paperback ISBN: 9781036733711
The EU GPSR authorised representative is Logos Europe, 9 rue Nicolas Poussion, 17000 La Rochelle, France contact@logoseurope.eu

## By Veronica Mixon

Loblolly Mystery Series

*The Town I Call Home*

*Loblolly*

*The River House Inn*

*BlueRidge Crossing*

*The Long Road Home*

Savannah Sleuths

*Beyond the Shadows*

*Between the Mourning Doves*

*Behind the Iron Fence*

*Below the Wisteria Veil*

*Beside the Hollow Oak*

*Beneath the Silence*

Savannah Mystery Series

*Changing Fortunes*

*Changing Tides*

*Changing Winds*

*Changing Sands*

*Changing Lanes*

Savannah Women Series

*Three Faces in the Mirror*

*In a Father's Footsteps*

*Who's Watching Maddie?*

# Part I

# Chapter One

## MAGGIE

My doctor advised rest. My boss, Claire, insisted I take the month off, let the inflammation calm, and come back when I could work without pushing through pain. Katrina—the other half of my work team—worried about me, about our projects, about everything, really.

Resting my hand sounded like excellent advice. I understood it intellectually. I simply couldn't seem to comply.

Rest had never come easy to me. I'd been juggling too much for too long to know what to do with days of sudden nothingness. So I worked. Or tried to. Just a few pages of a favored script Katrina and I couldn't seem to get quite right. I told myself a light pass through a stubborn script wouldn't interrupt my recovery. In fact, a familiar exercise to remind my hands what they were meant to do seemed entirely reasonable.

I'd used that logic on my doctor. He'd been unimpressed, shaking his head and repeating, hand rest—only rest.

Nevertheless, here I was, staring at the cursor blinking

on my laptop screen like a sentence waiting to be finished. I'd already tried writing by every means other than typing—hours of voice dictation, recording into my phone, playing the sentences back, editing, then playing them back again—until they sounded more hollow and stiff than when I'd started.

What this experience revealed was simple: my creativity didn't live in my voice—or even solely in my head. It evolved in motion, traveling from brain to fingers to keyboard, clean and uninterrupted. I saw the scene in my mind, and the words appeared on the page. No shortcut. Or at least none I'd found that carried the same easy magic.

Or so it seemed.

I was a script doctor, for all practical purposes—a writer who fixed what wasn't working in stories for directors, actors, and, occasionally, the studio itself. Sometimes a project arrived as little more than a kernel of an idea, and Katrina and I worked it until it blossomed into a full story—or an entire series.

A staff position at a film studio was one of the most coveted jobs in the industry. Hundreds—thousands—of writers would give years of their lives to sit at my desk. I was acutely aware of that fact. Especially now, when I felt it in the furtive glances from directors and producers, in my boss's softened voice, in my partner's wide eyes when she came to me with a story that needed our touch—and my blank mind had nothing to offer.

Writing was all I'd ever wanted to do. I didn't know anything else. And this job—this job and my daughter, Poppy—were all I had in this country I now called home. I couldn't afford to lose focus. Or my income. My contract wasn't forgiving; results were expected on schedule, pain or not.

I inhaled a deep, yoga-style breath and tried a mind-over-matter trick I'd read about years ago in some long-forgotten magazine. I imagined my hands typing in sync with my creative instincts. Just like always. Imagine it. Don't think. Just do.

My left hand hovered over the keys, steady and automatic. The right followed, slower but cooperative—until the fourth finger hesitated, curled inward, and refused to strike the key. Pain flared sharp and sudden, racing up my arm like a live wire. I tried typing the sentence again. Same result. Again. Same.

The mind trick had sounded so simple in the magazine.

"This," I muttered, "is exactly what Einstein meant by the definition of insanity."

One finger. One small, uncooperative digit, quietly dismantling my career, my routine, and—if left unchecked—my bank account.

Dr. Moreau called it focal dystonia, a condition that affected a small percentage of writers, musicians, and other fine-motor professionals—rare, unpredictable, and cruelly precise. "It's not just pain," he'd said in his gentle Parisian English, showing me diagrams of nerves and neural pathways as if science could soften the truth. "It is also a misfire. The signal breaks down." He tapped his temple. "The brain forgets what the hand once knew."

Which was a clinical way of saying my body had stopped honoring the contract we'd worked under for over three decades.

I'd read everything on my new condition—articles, case studies, interviews with professionals who'd quietly disappeared from publishing houses, writers' rooms, concert halls, and coding labs. Apparently, I wasn't the only one whose creativity depended on a near-magical connection between brain and fingertips. Musicians. Programmers. Surgeons. Anyone whose work lived in that narrow space where thought became motion. Most never returned to the same work. A few adapted—dictation, editing, teaching. Other lives.

I told myself I'd beat the odds. I'd rest. I'd heal. I'd come back. I was very good at telling myself things.

But sitting in my apartment in the hush of a gray Paris morning, staring at a half-repaired script I could no longer move through, I understood how easily something you love can simply shut its door—and how impossible it is to write your way back once the rhythm is gone.

The phone rang.

I stared at it, half expecting another check-in from my boss Claire—polite, measured, faintly edged with concern about deadlines—or my writing partner Katrina, wired and anxious, afraid she couldn't manage the department without me. Both reactions would have made sense. Neither would have surprised me.

When I saw my mother's name, I hesitated. Not because I didn't want to talk, but because I didn't want to worry her. I hadn't told her the full story about my hand. She still believed this was a brief slowdown—a few days off using up holiday and sick time—not a fracture running through my whole working life. But if I didn't answer now, she'd only call again.

"Maggie," she said, breathless, "I hate to bother you, but I wanted to run an idea past you."

Her voice carried that gentle Southern lilt I missed every time she called—soft as the hush of pecan leaves after rain. I leaned back, closing my eyes, and for a moment I was twelve again, listening from the porch while she called me in for supper. Somehow, it was always when the world felt most unsteady that I wanted her voice the most.

"Now don't get alarmed but I fell," she said.

The image of her alone at the farm recalibrated my worry instantly. I sat forward. "You fell? Are you hurt?"

"No. No. Don't get ahead of yourself," she warned. Then she explained she'd taken a fall in the orchard—nothing serious, she insisted, just a bruised hip, a twisted ankle and a lot of swelling—and her doctor wanted someone nearby. "I just need help for a few weeks," she added, her voice dipping lower. "I wondered, since you've taken a leave from the studio—"

"Yes." My heart lifted, the word leaving my mouth before my better judgment could catch up. "It's the perfect time to come home. It might take me a few days to wrap things up—can you find someone to help until I get there?"

---

I'd have to talk to Claire, invoke the clause in my contract that allowed for a ninety-day medical leave. Unpaid—but I had savings. I could make it work.

---

"Sue Ellen will check on me before and after work," Mama said. "I'm just relieved you can come. And I can't wait to spend time with Poppy."

After we hung up, I sat at my desk, the phone still warm in my hand. It felt like the perfect answer to what Claire had delicately referred to as my creative slowdown. I might argue the phrasing, but the result was the same. And if it walked like a duck, as Mama would say…

A short change-of-scenery trip home to Loblolly—just long enough to visit Mama and line up help at the farm—made perfect sense.

I briefly debated whether to let my ex-husband Julian know we were leaving, then decided there was no need. A man who hadn't bothered to call his daughter in over six months didn't deserve updates.

He'd left three years earlier—the final act in a slow unraveling that began with late nights and quiet glasses of wine that turned into bottles. He'd never found his footing in Paris. Whether it was the instability of freelance work or the three hundred rejections for his great historical novel, I never really knew. What I did know was that I'd stopped accepting invitations—dinners, weekends away, all the ways people pretend they aren't lonely.

I blamed deadlines, motherhood, the constant pressure to deliver. The truth was simpler: it was easier to stay home than to pretend we were still in love. To pretend my husband hadn't found his companionship in a bottle of wine—and eventually, in a more understanding woman's arms.

Maybe I should've fought harder. Demanded more. But fighting for a marriage requires wanting to save it. And for me, if I'm honest, that desire had slipped away long before the end. Maybe it had never fully existed. Julian had been my easiest choice, and I'd accepted his proposal with relief. It solved my problems—until it didn't.

Now the apartment felt like a museum of my mistake—Poppy's toys neatly stacked, my laptop closed, Julian's old notebooks still tucked onto a shelf like proof of a life we'd both abandoned.

Once upon a time, I'd believed my life was mapped out for good—graduate school, Paris, a coveted internship at

Aurore Films & Télévision that turned, exactly as planned, into a permanent position. As long as I worked hard and stayed sharp, I thought I'd earned the fairy tale.

But fairy tales don't account for broken marriages or failing hands.

Maybe it was time to go. A few weeks in Georgia wouldn't fix everything unraveling in my life, but it might help me remember who I was before the noise. And Poppy—sweet, curious Poppy—would finally have room to run and get to know her Nana instead of another Paris park with a nanny who knew her routines better than I did.

I told myself it would just be a visit. A brief leave while I healed.

Yes, I had become very good at telling myself things.

What I didn't yet know was that this trip would pull me into a new story—one shaped as much by endings as by beginnings.

# Chapter Two

ASA

Asa Griffin measured time by the sound of the delivery truck backing into the alley behind Griffin's Market. The beeping started before sunrise, a steady rhythm that meant another day was beginning, whether he was ready or not.

He'd already stocked the produce bins and checked the orders when the side-door bell jingled. Only friends and family used that entrance.

Sheriff Caleb Benton stepped into view, Pine County clay dust clinging to his boots.

"Morning." Caleb tipped his hat and went straight for the coffee urn in the back corner. "Heard you got a new shipment of those Honeycrisp apples."

"Up front by the registers," Asa said, wiping his hands on a towel. "Best we've had this season."

"I'll let Tally know. Seems Lola's getting a little picky about her apples these days."

"I'll save my favorite girl a few." Lola—Caleb's recently adopted daughter—was as cute as a bug, all upturned nose and bright-eyed determination.

Caleb filled his cup half decaf, half full strength, added two sugars, and leaned against the counter with the easy confidence of a man who rarely seemed in a hurry. "Ran into Barb McAllister's neighbor at the pharmacy yesterday," he said, casual as weather talk. "Sounds like Maggie's in town for a few weeks. Took some time off from her fancy Paris career to help Barb out, since her mama will likely be on crutches for a while."

Asa's hand stilled on the counter.

"That so?"

"Your Aunt Sue Ellen mentioned over coffee this morning that Maggie's got her little girl with her—uh..." Caleb snapped his fingers. "What's her name?"

"Poppy," Asa said before he could stop himself.

Caleb's brow lifted just enough to show he'd noticed. "Right. Cute kid, from what I hear."

Asa busied himself rearranging a basket of tomatoes. "Glad someone's going to look after Barb. Heard she took a bad fall."

A quick zap of guilt ran down his spine. His Aunt Sue Ellen had hinted more than once that he ought to stop by and check on Barb—a widowed woman living alone likely needed a few things seen to. He'd agreed to swing by.

He just hadn't found the time yet.

"Jackson and Joleen are throwing a get-together at the River House a week from Saturday," Caleb said. "Figured they'd give her a few days to settle in before folks start descending. Jackson said he's calling you with an invite, but I told him I'd beat him to it. Thought you might appreciate a little warning."

Asa huffed a quiet laugh. "A party, huh? Y'all thinking we can pretend it's senior year again? You, me, Jackson—

and Maggie McAllister Black back in town like nothing ever happened?"

---

Caleb grinned, but Asa caught the flicker of concern behind it. "Something like that. Just don't be surprised if folks start talking."

---

"They always do." Asa reached for another crate, pretending not to hear the edge in his voice.

Caleb finished his coffee, set the cup down, and gave Asa's shoulder a friendly squeeze. "See you at poker night—Jackson's place this week."

Asa gave a noncommittal grunt and kept stacking tomatoes.

When the door closed behind Caleb, the market felt too quiet. Asa stood in front of his display, listening to the hum of the coolers and the faint creak of the sign outside as it swung in the breeze.

Most folks figured he'd stayed single because he'd never really gotten over Maggie McAllister. Asa chalked that up to small-town boredom—people needing a story to fill the quiet.

He hadn't given Maggie more than a passing thought in years. When she did surface, he'd gotten good at pushing the image aside.

But hearing she was back stirred something he'd thought was safely buried.

He walked to the front window, where sunlight fell in long stripes across the floor, and let his gaze drift past the garden center toward the oak trees lining the edge of the city park. An image surfaced, and this time he let it flow unbound—Maggie at eighteen, barefoot in the bed of his daddy's truck, laughing as the last of the summer light caught in her hair.

That was the day before she told him about Emory. About leaving. About how they'd make it work.

They had. For a while.

He'd stayed close to home for school—community college first, then the state school in the next county—so he could commute and help his dad with the business. He and Maggie wrote letters and called every week. She came home when she could. He visited Atlanta. Then the letters slowed. The visits stopped. And somewhere along the way, Asa quit trying to figure out why.

After Emory came Stanford. Then a fellowship in Paris. The whole town had been proud of their star, and when her name started appearing in film credits, that pride only grew. Then, they spotted her on the Oscar's red carpet. Imagine, they marveled—one of their own writing movies and television.

And Asa? Asa stayed right where he was. He ran his father's store and grew it into something solid, something the town could rely on. It wasn't the life he'd once imagined, but it was honest. Steady. It was his.

He told himself Maggie's visit would be short-lived. Just long enough to help her mama. Then she'd head back to Paris, to that elegant life she'd built.

That suited him just fine.

Rekindling a polite, platonic friendship was one thing. Anything more was off the table. He and Maggie had already come to that understanding—on his one trip to Paris, more than a decade ago. They'd shared the decision that whatever they'd been wasn't meant to survive adulthood. They'd closed that door cleanly.

Or close enough to count.

Asa Griffin would not let Maggie McAllister drift back into the quiet corners of his life.

That chapter was finished.

# Chapter Three

## MAGGIE

The rental car's dashboard hummed the entire way down the two-lane road, as if it were trying to sing me back to a life I used to know. Pecan trees lined the road on both sides, leaves thick and deep green, the branches already weighted with small, pale-green husks. Heat shimmered in the open spaces between rows, sunlight and shade stitched together like an old quilt someone had loved hard and long. Everything looked smaller than I remembered—simpler, quieter—like the world had been turned down a notch while I was gone.

"This is it?" Poppy asked from the back seat. Her nose pressed to the glass, breath fogging a circle. "Nana's farm?"

"Orchard," I said, because that's what Mama would say. "It's Nana's orchard."

"I'm going to find the biggest pecan," she decided, feet drumming the seat. "The very biggest. I'll take it back home and show my class."

"Just don't eat anything you find on the ground without asking." I gave the kind of warning I'd once promised myself I'd never say in exactly that tone. Parenting has a way of borrowing your mother's voice while you're not looking.

A weathered sign hung by the gravel drive: MCALLISTER PECAN ORCHARDS. The paint had cracked into tiny rivers. I remembered the day my father hammered it into the post, Poppy still a maybe-one-day idea, Paris still a far shore.

I told myself we were here for just a few weeks. Long enough for Mama to heal. Long enough for my hand to stop acting up. The road curved, and the roofline of the farmhouse rose ahead—white clapboard with blue shutters, a row of porch rockers waiting for company.

We rolled to the end of the drive and parked. The screen door creaked open before I could reach for the car handle.

Mama stood framed by sunlight, a single crutch tucked under her right arm like she'd been born with it, chin up, lipstick on—the way she meets every fortune or misfortune, well dressed and unamused.

My mama, known in these parts as Barbara McAllister, had always been trim and sharp-edged, all posture and opinions, her silvering hair swept back as if she were perpetually expecting company. She wore blue jeans and a soft chambray shirt, silver hoops in her ears, and the solitary diamond on a gold chain my dad had given her on their thirtieth anniversary. I couldn't remember that necklace ever leaving her neck after the day he fastened it there. The boot and crutch hadn't softened her one bit. If anything, they'd made her more determined to look unbothered.

"There she is," she called, and I knew from her voice she'd been watching since we turned off the highway. I'd dropped a pin so she wouldn't have to pace back and forth on crutches, but of course she'd been waiting anyway. "My girls."

Poppy was out of the car and up the steps before I could grab her shoes. Mama caught her one-armed and laughed—the kind of laugh that finds its way under your ribs whether you want it to or not.

"Careful," I warned, pointing at the boot on Mama's foot.

"I'm fine," Mama said, which in our family can mean anything from *I am genuinely fine* to *I am hanging off a cliff and would appreciate it if you wouldn't mention it.*

She held Poppy close and cocked her head. "Let me look at you, Maggie." She assessed me with the maternal attentiveness of a lost chick returning to the nest. "Paris air looks good on you."

"Airport air," I said, stepping into her hug. She still smelled like furniture polish and cinnamon. Under that, the faint, clean note of Ivory soap. Home had a scent profile; I hadn't realized how much I missed it until it curled around me.

Inside, not much had changed. The coffee table was still losing its quiet battle with stacks of magazines, and a rose porcelain figurine I didn't recognize had appeared beside the lamp—unlike anything else in the house, so almost certainly an impulse buy or a gift from a friend. The old upright piano waited in the corner like it always had, closed and patient, and I had the passing thought that maybe Poppy could take a few lessons while we were here. Something to keep her busy. Something harmless.

My attention shifted to the small writing desk by the window. The new computer I'd sent Mama for her birthday sat there untouched, the screen dark, the keyboard pristine

—so pristine it might as well have come with a museum placard.

Mama caught me staring. “That thing,” she said, settling into her chair with a sigh, “is supposed to let me see Poppy whenever I want. Face… something.”

“FaceTime,” I said.

“Well, FaceTime’s got more buttons than sense,” she declared. “I tried turning it on once and thought I’d broken it.”

I smiled, picturing Mama’s face the first time Poppy popped up on the screen, full of chatter and missing teeth. Project number one, clearly. “It’s not hard,” I said. “We’ll figure it out. Together.”

Mama gave the computer a long, wary look, then glanced back at me. “If you say so. But if it starts talking back, I’m unplugging it.”

I saluted. “Got it. Turn off the talking minions.”

Poppy’s attention lasted exactly four minutes indoors. She slipped out the door like a wind-up toy, the screen door slapping in her wake.

“Poppy, shoes!” I called, but the orchard had already swallowed her laughter and woven it between the trees.

“Let her run,” Mama said, waving off my concern. “This farm will be hers one day. She needs to fall in love with it.”

I knew that came from love, not strategy—but it mixed with my guilt and landed heavier than she meant it to. This was only Poppy’s second time here. The first, Daddy’s funeral, had been a blur of casseroles and condolences, five days when she was still small enough to sleep through grief. Mama talked about *one day* as if it were already penciled into the calendar. I didn’t have the bandwidth to explain that Paris had been built around different assumptions.

"I'm going to grab something to drink—care for anything?"

"Fresh pitcher of iced tea on the counter. I'll have a glass with you," Mama said.

"Be right back."

I snuck a peek out the window, watched Poppy at the fence staring down my old mare Sugar. My heart turned soft. I'd missed Sugar and looked forward to giving her some attention soon. I placed ice in two glasses, poured in tea, and carried them back to the living room.

I made myself comfortable on the sofa, kicked off my flats, and sipped. The tea was strong and sweet and almost certainly compliments of Miss Sue Ellen, who'd probably dropped off an entire homecoming meal with the hope Mama would stay off her feet.

My hand flattened on my knee, thumb pressing the place where the tremor starts when I'm tired or worried or pretending I'm neither. "How's your foot?"

"Doctor says the fracture's clean. Four to six weeks." She wiggled her toes inside the boot. "I don't like being useless."

"You're not." I meant it, but the words barely grazed her. Mama's definition of useful was a moving target no one could keep up with.

She tipped her head. "Your friend Katrina called this morning."

It was the kind of line she might plant in the garden and walk away from, knowing I'd trip over it sooner or later.

I picked at a thread on my jeans. "She's just checking in, making sure I arrived okay," I said with ease, as if I really believed that was the only reason.

"My doctor suggested a month's rest from work." I

wiggled my fingers. "Can't work without these, and I still have a rogue digit that refuses to cooperate."

"A short visit will do you good," Mama said.

I could tell from her tone she was looking forward to our time together—the longest stretch we'd had since I left for college.

A month didn't seem short. Two days, maybe three, might be short. Even a week could be stretched if you said it fast enough. But a month? That was a lifetime in my world—especially when your name appeared neatly on writing schedules mapped out for an entire season. Missing even one rewrite meant freelance writers would be waiting in the wings, ready to claim my chair.

Suddenly the sweet tea turned my stomach queasy, and I popped off the sofa. "I think I'll put on a kettle for hot tea," I said. "I brought a few of my favorites from Paris. I think you'll like them."

I rummaged through my tote, then headed for the kitchen. A moment later, she followed—like she always did when something between us hadn't been said yet.

"Three weddings called this week." She repositioned a chair and sat at the breakfast table overlooking the orchard and the barn.

My gaze caught Poppy busy picking wildflowers from the overgrown middles between the pecan trees. I should warn her not to go too far.

"Brides asked if we'd still host events. I told them yes, then I told them no." She sighed. "Pride makes promises my body can't keep."

"I can help," I said, my eye still on Poppy. She started wandering back toward the house, and I turned away to finish making our tea.

"I know you can help." Mama's voice held a note of

thanks. "And that would be wonderful. But these weddings are six months away."

"But you'll be better by then."

"Lord, I hope so. Weddings bring in a good bit of money, but the work's become more than I can handle anymore."

"Can't we hire help?" I asked. "I can interview, walk them through your program. I can meet with brides while I'm here. We can make storyboards like we used to. It'll be fun."

She smiled. "Let's take it one day at a time." Then, "How's Julian?"

The kettle whistled. I was grateful for the choreography of mugs and honey and lemon. My left hand did most of the work. My right hovered like a guest unsure where to sit.

"Julian?" Odd question—she never asked about him. "I've heard from him twice in the last year. Both times he wanted me to mail something he left behind."

"I never understood why you married him," she said, then added gently, "but I guess you can't help who you fall in love with."

Love sat uneasily between my ribs. I no longer deluded myself that Julian had been about love. He'd been sense. Paris. Order. And when I found out I was pregnant, he'd been the neatest solution to a life spinning faster than I could manage.

Marrying him had been easy.

Maybe cowardly.

"I don't blame him," I said quietly. "Our marriage wasn't built to last. A child can only hold people together for so long."

If Mama agreed, she didn't say. Poppy burst in, demanding our attention, then wound down as the afternoon folded into early evening and I reheated the supper Miss Sue Ellen had dropped off.

Later, the porch pulled us outside. Crickets stitched the dark together. The swing remembered my weight. Mama studied me once more before turning in.

"You don't have to pretend with me," she said softly.

"I'm not," I said—and she let me have that.

When the door clicked shut, the orchard sighed. I set my phone face-down and let the sounds of home fill the spaces I realized the city never had.

Paris would wait.

But Loblolly, I would soon realize, had plans of its own.

# Chapter Four

## MAGGIE

Two days later, Mama declared it was high time Poppy got a proper tour of Loblolly. The roses needed fertilizing, and since she was out of Miracle-Gro, she sent us into town on the errand—with instructions to give Poppy a tour of all the important places: the bakery, the bookstore, the grocery (a nudge that was not happening), and of course the diner.

I agreed easily. It gave me a reason to stop at the feed store and pin a note to the bulletin board. We needed help. The farm was showing its age, and some of the work—fencing, the barn roof—was beyond what I could manage on my own.

But first stop—Loblolly's diner.

It hadn't changed in twenty years—same black-and-white tile, same chipped Formica counter, same sense that news traveled faster than the coffee got poured.

Morning light streamed through the wide front windows, glinting off chrome napkin holders and catching in the steam rising from coffee cups. The place smelled like bacon, syrup, and pancakes sizzling on a hot griddle—

familiar and comforting. Poppy's fingers were sticky around mine from the strawberry jam slathered on a half piece of toast Nana had let her sneak to tide her over before we left the house. We settled on two barstools, and I fished a napkin from my purse and handed it over.

"Wipe your hands, sweetie."

She dutifully swiped at her fingers. "Can we get pancakes?" She perused the chalkboard menu on the wall like she was negotiating a major life decision.

"Pancake, as in one. They're the size of a dinner plate. And you'll have to add bacon and orange juice and eat the bacon before you finish your pancake." I gave her my no-arguing Mom stare to nix the inevitable debate.

"Deal." She swiveled her stool and looked down the long row of booths against the window.

Within two steps of us entering the diner, the hum in the room dipped three levels. Not gone—just shifted. As if the room had a universal pause between thoughts.

I'd grown up with that sound. Loblolly was small enough that any change in its orbit registered—a new car, a for-sale sign taken down, a girl who'd once left town with a full-ride scholarship to a prestigious school and a boy wrapped around her heart now coming back with another man's child by her side and Paris in her rearview.

"Maggie McAllister Black, well I'll be," Sue Ellen Griffin called from behind the counter, hand already reaching for an extra mug. "I thought Tally was pulling my leg when she came through here runnin' her mouth about you bein' back."

Her voice broke the pause. Conversations picked up again, but now they curved around us.

I managed a smile. "Hey, Miss Sue Ellen."

Poppy brightened. "Hi! I'm Poppy."

"I know exactly who you are." Sue Ellen came around the counter, apron already smeared with grease and something that looked suspiciously like blood that I hoped was ketchup. "Your mama's sent more pictures to your Nana than the church bulletin. Come here and let me see you proper."

Poppy slid off the stool and stood before her willingly, preening under the attention like every ten-year-old who knew a compliment when she heard one. Sue Ellen gave her a quick hug, then steered her back to her barstool.

"Sit here and we'll catch up on your life. You look like you could use caffeine and carbohydrates," she said, grabbing a mug with one hand and pouring coffee with the other. "You came on a good morning."

"Good how?"

Before she could answer, the whispers drifted over from the nearest table.

"Is that Maggie?"

"She came back for Barb. Bless her heart."

"Heard she's been livin' in Paris. Paris, France, not Paris County. Imagine that."

"Wonder if she brought that handsome husband—"

"Huh, heard he was more slick than handsome."

I wrapped my hands around the warm mug Sue Ellen set in front of me. The heat sank into my fingers but did nothing to get rid of the prickle racing up the back of my neck.

"Mama," Poppy whispered, leaning close, "everyone is looking at us."

"Just smile back," I murmured.

"Pay them no mind, sweetie. They need somethin' to look at 'til the biscuits come out. Besides, your mama's big news in these parts." She topped off my coffee, then placed a glass of milk with a lid in front of Poppy.

"You just missed Tally," she added. "She had her heels in a hurry this morning."

"Tally?" I searched my memory. The name seemed familiar, but I couldn't place the face.

"Caleb's new wife. She opened a bistro down the street." Her eyes glinted with pleasure. "It's big time for Loblolly. You need to bring your mama in for lunch."

"Called and talked to your mama yesterday afternoon. She's blustering about doctor's orders already. Must be feeling better. Said you're planning to stay awhile—Lord does answer prayers."

She said it all without taking a breath. I'd forgotten how fast Sue Ellen talked—so unlike most of the locals with their slow Southern cadence. She blamed her Northern roots; never mind that you had to go back three generations to find them. That was always her answer.

"I took a month's leave."

"Mm-hm." She said it like she had an opinion about that. Of course, she had an opinion about most things. This one, she appeared to keep to herself. I took a sip of coffee and waited. She likely knew about my injury, but thankfully didn't go there.

"Can I have pancakes with chocolate chips?" Poppy asked.

Sue Ellen's attention landed back on Poppy. "Baby, you tell me what shape you want 'em in, and I'll let Chet know," she said. "Heart? Star? Dinosaur?"

"Horse," Poppy said promptly.

My throat tightened. "Honey—"

"And a horse it is," Sue Ellen agreed without missing a

beat. "Chet's a regular pancake artist." She reached for the coffee pot again, then paused, her gaze ticking over my shoulder. "Yes, sir, you picked a fine morning, honey. Asa's right over there." She nodded toward the far corner. She'd stage-whispered, which meant everyone in the place had a cocked ear.

Asa. His name rippled through me.

I slowly turned my head. Verified he was in the back corner booth, one arm slung along the seat, newspaper folded in front of him like a prop. I studied him for a few seconds, noted that the years had done what years do—broadened his shoulders, carved his jaw, dusted sun into the lines at the corners of his eyes.

He looked up, and his gaze found mine cleanly, like there'd been a string between us and I'd given it a tug.

He gave me a small nod. Courteous. Controlled. That almost-smile I'd memorized once upon a time.

I could've looked away. I didn't.

"Go on," Sue Ellen murmured. "No sense pretendin' we don't all know each other."

Poppy tugged on my sleeve. "Can we go see the grocery man while we're in town? Lola says he gives her extra cookies."

I scoffed a laugh. What were the chances she'd bring this up at this very minute. Something must be in the air. "The grocery man's name is Asa," I said. My voice came out steadier than I felt. "We… used to be good friends."

"Used to," Sue Ellen repeated, then lifted her chin. "Asa! You gon' sit there and act like you don't see this girl come home?"

He folded the newspaper with deliberate care, set it aside, and stood. Always polite. Always steady.

"Hold your horses, Aunt Sue Ellen. I'm coming," he

said as he walked over. His eyes flicked to Poppy, then back to me. "Maggie."

"Hey," I managed. The word felt too small for the history it had to cover.

"Welcome home," he said.

"Thanks." My throat went tight again.

"How's Barb?" he asked, voice softening.

"Mean as ever," Sue Ellen answered. "Which is how we know she's recoverin'."

I smiled. "She's… doing better. Stubborn. The doctor says rest; she hears rearrange the kitchen cabinets."

"That sounds about right," Asa said. His gaze shifted to Poppy. "And who's this?"

"This is my daughter, Poppy."

"Hey there, Poppy," he said, crouching just enough to meet her eyes without crowding her. "You takin' good care of your grandma?"

"Nana," she said solemnly. "And we just got here. I'm ten."

"Not quite," I reminded her.

She rolled her eyes. "Almost ten. We live in Paris. They have good bread."

His mouth twitched. "Hard to argue with good bread."

"They have chocolate, too," she added, in case he'd missed the important part. "Do you have chocolate in your store?"

"Sure do. You'll have to come see for yourself." He glanced at me. "She got your smile."

"And your sweet tooth," Sue Ellen winked as she pushed Poppy's pancakes across the bar.

Asa hooked his thumb in his jean pocket as if he didn't quite know what to do with his hands. "Didn't mean to interrupt. Just wanted to say I'm glad you made it back for a visit. Your mama's been missing you."

"Thanks," I said. "It's… good to see you."

He smiled faintly. "Imagine the last storm didn't do the orchard any favors. If you need anything—tools, hands, somebody to cuss at a broken fence post—I'm around."

"Tryin' to eat in peace in the corner," Sue Ellen said dryly.

He ignored her, that half-smile deepening. "Weather's supposed to clear this week. Give you a chance to get a good look at what needs fixing."

"I'll keep that in mind," I said.

Under the small talk, something pressed close: the memory of a younger version of us in this same town, making plans like the world would bend to fit them.

"Well," Asa said, straightening. "I'll get out of your hair."

"Bye, grocery man," Poppy said, waving.

"Asa," I said. "His name is Mr. Asa."

"Grocery man works." He chuckled. "Bye, Miss Poppy." To me, a final, "Good seeing you, Maggie."

"You too," I said.

He went back to leave money on the table, and for a heartbeat I wanted to stand, cross the room, and ask him to stop by the farm—to catch up on the lives we'd built apart. Instead, I sat there, as if my chair had claimed me.

He wasn't married. I wasn't married. There was no rule against old friends getting together—but I reminded myself that Asa Griffin was dangerous. Watching him move through the room, memories surfaced, and not all of them were good. Even now, I wasn't sure I trusted my footing.

Asa nodded at a few regulars on his way out, pushed open the glass door, and stepped outside. The bell chimed softly as it swung shut behind him, that little sound lingering with a side of regret.

I used the mirror over the counter to watch him walk down the sidewalk and back toward his store, feeling something in my chest stretch and resist, like a scar tested by a new movement.

Sue Ellen topped off my coffee without asking. "He sold his parents' place and built an apartment over his store," she said, almost to herself. "It's nice enough, but it just doesn't seem like a man should be that married to his work, if you know what I mean."

I did, but knew better than to say so. I loved Sue Ellen, but she took meddling in other people's business—especially the ones she loved—to new heights.

She looked at me, a knowing glint in her eye. "Some things don't change much."

I stirred my coffee, watching the small spiral settle. "No," I said lightly. "Some don't. But others do."

But the truth slipped in underneath, quiet and unwelcome: some things don't die, no matter how far you run, no matter how long you stay gone. Some things just sit in the corner booth, waiting for you to walk back through the door.

# Chapter Five

## MAGGIE

The next day, by midmorning, the smell of blueberry muffins and coffee had given way to the sharper scent of damp earth and hay, drifting in through the open kitchen window where I'd left it cracked to catch the early air. The orchard was waking up slow, same as the rest of us. I'd been sorting through a pile of unpaid bills and feed invoices stacked on Mama's kitchen desk when I heard tires crunching on the gravel drive.

A familiar voice called out, "Delivery for the McAllister girls!"

Mama hollered from the next room. "That'll be Joleen Taylor—Jackson's wife. Volunteered to pick up my grocery order."

I went to the front door and opened the screen just as a woman climbed out of a government-issued SUV. She wore pressed slacks beneath a U.S. Marshal jacket, crease sharp, hair pulled back neatly—not a strand out of place. She balanced two grocery bags on one arm and flashed a grin bright enough to pass for sunshine.

I glanced down at my pajama bottoms and bare feet and decided I was officially underdressed for federal assistance.

"You must be Maggie," she said, stepping up onto the porch. "I'm Joleen. I figured anybody showing up this early on a Saturday better have food."

"That's the rule," I said, smiling as I took one of the bags. "And since you likely saved me a trip into town, you are officially my favorite person today."

She laughed and followed me inside. "Barbara must've ordered half the produce section."

Mama said, shuffling in from the living room, "Thanks, honey. I'll trade out pecans for my delivery fee."

"You know that's a deal!" Joleen leaned down to hug her. "Asa threw in a few extra veggies—and a hug. He says to tell you he's sorry he hasn't stopped by since your accident, but he will soon. Jackson sent his good cheer, and Caleb sent his regrets, same as Asa. Only difference is poker night is what wore Caleb out, but he says he'll be by soon to check on you, too."

Mama chuckled. "Poor Caleb. Jackson take his money again?"

"Nope—Asa this time. Seems Asa's losing streak finally ended."

She settled onto a barstool like she felt at home in Mama's kitchen.

"Asa can't bluff his way out of a paper bag. If I had him in an interrogation room, he'd spill his guts within three minutes. Can't imagine how he managed to beat Caleb." She eyed me with a smile. "Hell of a guy, our Asa."

I ignored the obvious nudge and poured her a mug of coffee. "Poker night, huh?" It warmed my heart to know the three of them sounded just as close as ever.

Joleen took a sip, then leaned back. "Thursday poker nights—Caleb, Asa, Jackson, and Tanner Sutton, our illustrious mayor. Same fifty dollars changes hands. At fifty cents a bet, it's less about money and more about male bonding. If I'm in town, it gives Tally and me an excuse for a girls' night out. You should join us next week."

"That sounds like fun, but I have Poppy—"

Mama waved a hand. "I can manage my granddaughter for one evening."

I knew better than to argue that point—and from the look on Joleen's face, she agreed.

"Okay," I said. "Count me in."

Joleen glanced around, like she was assessing a crime scene. "So—how's it feel to be home?"

I refilled my coffee cup, then Mama's, sliding her mug across the counter with a nod toward the barstool. "You should sit, Mama." I turned back to Joleen. "Truthfully, it feels a little like I never left—and a lot like it's been too long. All in all, I guess it feels familiar. Only now the house is louder, and I'm the one juggling bills and chores."

Joleen laughed. "That sounds terrifying."

"Maybe a little." I shrugged. "Mama and Daddy always handled the business side." I patted Mama's hand. "But I'm insisting she let me take over some of it—and with her help, I'm learning on the fly."

"She's catching on fast," Mama said.

Joleen leaned an elbow on the counter. "And Poppy? Settling in?"

"She adores the farm," Mama chimed in before I could answer.

I laughed. "Maybe a little too much. I'm starting to worry she won't want to go back to Paris."

We chatted about the weather, the party Joleen and

Jackson were throwing the following Saturday to welcome us home. Joleen seemed in no hurry to leave, so I made a fresh pot of coffee and put away the groceries as she and Mama talked about the nothingness of small-town news.

Mama refused another cup when I offered, then rose slowly. "If you girls will excuse me, I'm supposed to keep my leg elevated. I think that's doctor code for 'go take a nap.'"

"You do that," Joleen said. "I'll be gone soon anyway—headed to Atlanta after this cup."

Mama left, and I sipped my coffee. "It's funny—Poppy needed no adjustment time. She loves it here."

"Kids bounce," Joleen said softly. "Gives you one less thing to worry about." Then her voice dropped. "How about you? You adjusting? I hear you're on the mend and had to take leave from your job."

"Temporary leave," I said, then shrugged. "Doctor insisted I rest my hand, so it seemed like the perfect time to help with Mama's recovery. Her doctor's orders are to rest her foot—but her idea of rest is making chore lists. For me. And for herself."

Joleen chuckled. "Most of us have never met a doctor's order we didn't treat like a suggestion."

We talked for a while—about Jackson's latest case, about her endless hours. When she mentioned she and Jackson had been talking about starting a family "if life ever slows down," I caught the fatigue behind her smile.

"I suspect you'd make a great mom," I said.

She shook her head. "You have to be home for that, Mags."

My childhood nickname landed like a hand on my shoulder. Jackson must still use it. "I travel too. Spend more nights in hotel rooms than my suitcase can handle. Half my life is spent on a movie set, and our studio doesn't have private lots like Hollywood—we do location shoots all over Europe."

I started to ask her about her travel—then realized Poppy hadn't run in to greet our guests. Not like her. And then the quiet hit me. She wasn't in the house. The hair on my neck prickled.

I lifted a wait-a-minute finger. "I'm not sure where Poppy is."

"Poppy?" I called.

Nothing.

I checked the hallway, then the porch. Her coloring book still sat on the table, a half-finished mermaid smiling up at me. My stomach dropped.

"Poppy!"

Joleen was off the barstool and on my heels. "You check the bedrooms. I'll see if she's with Barb."

We searched the house—nothing. Joleen met me in the living room and said Mama was dozing, undisturbed and no Poppy. Outside, I stood on the porch and searched the orchard row by row. Leaves murmured in the breeze, but no little girl ran up and down the rows.

"I'll grab the four-wheeler," Joleen said, already heading for the shed.

I jogged toward the barn—then slowed to a stop when I heard a laugh. Small. Bright. Carried on dust and sunlight.

"Found her," I called, my voice catching. My racing heart eased, and I stepped inside.

The stall door stood half open. And there, in the middle, was my daughter—barefoot in the straw, holding a bag of carrots, talking like she'd met her best friend.

Sugar.

My old mare stood patient and regal, gray threading her muzzle, eyes soft and wise as ever. She let Poppy stroke her neck, listening as if she understood every word.

Poppy held out a carrot. "You're the prettiest horse in the whole world," she whispered.

Somehow my lungs remembered how to breathe again, and I said, "Poppy McAllister Black, what on earth are you doing?"

She turned, startled but unashamed. "Feeding Sugar. She was hungry."

Her angel face stole the last of my worry. "Baby, you don't go into the stalls without an adult. Horses can scare easily. She could've—" I stopped. "You just can't go into Sugar's stall without me yet."

"She didn't spook," Poppy said matter-of-factly. "She's not scared of me."

Joleen leaned against the doorframe, a grin on her lips. "Well, looks like you've got a natural."

"I've got a heart attack," I muttered, pulling my daughter to my side. "I know Sugar seems gentle, but you could've been hurt."

"But I wasn't." Her upturned face was so earnest. "Sugar loves me."

Sugar nudged my arm, as if agreeing—or more likely, nosing for another carrot. I rubbed her forehead automatically. "You're not helping," I told her.

Back in the kitchen, Joleen was still smiling. "You know, Asa runs a 4-H riding program at the middle school. He trains the kids for the state competition. You should ask him to teach her—she's already got the bug."

"I can train her."

"Sure," Joleen said, one brow raised. "Because you've got so much free time on your hands."

I groaned. "I just hate asking Asa for a favor."

"You say that like asking is a bad thing."

"It is," I said, though my heart wasn't convinced. "It's complicated."

Joleen shrugged back into her jacket and winked. "Oh, I know the history. Probably more than you'd like me to know. It's a small town—and you're a celebrity."

"Gotta run," she added before I could ask exactly what she meant. "I've got a meeting in Atlanta today."

I decided to leave gossip alone. People talk. I knew that better than most. "I'm not a celebrity," I said, walking her out.

"To us you are. And it's good you came home to help Barbara." She paused, eyeing the house. "But you're going to have your hands full. Between your mama's rehab, the orchard, the farm repairs, and now Poppy's sudden horse obsession—girl, you need help. A good place to start is someone who knows his way around a saddle." She smiled. "And this farm."

When she drove away, I turned toward the barn. Sugar stood near the fence, head lowered, watching Poppy walk back to the house.

Daddy used to say horses remembered the sound of love.

Maybe he was right.

From the porch, I watched Poppy hum to herself as she gathered a fistful of wildflowers. And I realized that both of them—horse and child—deserved the chance to grow a bond, even if only for a little while.

The orchard—our lifeblood for so many years—stretched all the way to the road and deserved love too.

So for now, I'd give my attention to this farm, my Mama, Poppy, and yes, even Sugar—reclaiming what had always been mine and sharing that life with my daughter.

Asa Griffin flitted across my mind. I sighed. Don't play with that fire, Maggie. That blaze burned out a long time ago.

# Chapter Six

## ASA

Thursday nights in Loblolly had their own rhythm. Some men went to the pool hall next to Tally's Bistro, some went to the dock for a little nighttime fishing, others ended up at the VFW hall. But for Asa, Caleb, Jackson, and Tanner, Thursday night meant poker. Tonight their game was in the upstairs room of Jackson's detached garage—half game room, half sanctuary, or as Jackson liked to call it, his man cave.

The old ceiling fan spun slow, stirring the scent of good whiskey, cigars, and microwave popcorn. A deck of cards lay on the scarred oak table, its edges soft from years of use.

Caleb dealt, his sheriff's badge still clipped to his belt buckle glinting in the lamplight.

"All right, gentlemen. Ante up. Let's see who's buying breakfast at the diner tomorrow."

"Not me," Tanner said. "The mayor doesn't buy his own biscuits."

Jackson smirked, the corners of his mouth hidden

behind his neatly trimmed beard. "Last I checked, mayors don't get paid enough to justify bragging."

"I get paid in public appreciation," Tanner said. "And free pastries if I time it right."

Asa tossed in two nickels. "You get free pastries because my Aunt Sue Ellen has her eye on you as one of the last bachelors in town she's not related to. Now that you and Stella are sparking, that's likely to change real soon."

That earned a round of laughter.

For a while, the conversation rolled easy—talk of rain patterns, the new diner cook (Chet's nephew from Michigan, who couldn't make grits to save his life), and the eternal debate over whether the high school football team would ever win district again.

Then Caleb leaned back, tipping his chair. "Hear Maggie McAllister's trying her hand at keeping up the family farm. At least until Barb gets her strength back."

Jackson nodded. "I haven't seen her yet, but since we're throwing her a coming-home party Saturday night, I'll have the pleasure soon." He said it while side-eyeing Asa, who gave no reaction.

"I call." Caleb tossed a chip into the pot. "Stopped by to pay my respects, and I have to say—Mags looks good. Not too much city polish and still has those killer brown eyes."

Tanner peeked at his cards. "That girl always could stop traffic on a dirt road."

Asa kept his expression even, though something in his chest gave a small, familiar pull. "Farm's her home," he said simply. "Stands to reason she'd come back when her mama needed her."

Caleb grinned. "Just like high school—still defending her honor."

"I'm not defending her. Just stating the truth." Asa

shrugged. "Besides, her honor speaks for itself. Doesn't need my defending."

Jackson chuckled. "Now that sounds like defending to me."

"Man can't win around here," Asa said, matching the bet and tossing another coin into the pot.

"Not when you're bluffing with that face," Caleb said. "You get the same look every time you're hiding something —like you swallowed a lemon and liked it."

They laughed, and the moment softened.

"Sue Ellen says Maggie's doing her own rehab," Caleb said, tossing in another chip. "Something with her hand. She's on leave for a month or so, hoping it heals. Turns out, in her job she needs her fingers to type."

All eyes cut to Asa, who kept his gaze steady on the cards in his hand. "Well, she is a writer."

"Ever heard of recording devices?" Tanner said.

"Maybe it's affected her creative process," Asa said, trying to keep the irritation out of his voice. At least, that's what his Aunt Sue Ellen had explained when he'd said the same.

"Yep, sounding a little defensive. Maggie being home is definitely getting under your collar." Jackson threw in a chip. "I call."

The fan whirred overhead, slow and hypnotic—the kind of sound that made men nostalgic for things they didn't talk about.

Asa laid down a pair of queens.

Caleb cursed under his breath and mucked his hand. Jackson folded. Tanner pushed his cards forward with a shake of his head.

"Next deal's mine," Caleb said, gathering the cards and

shuffling with practiced ease, putting the conversation back where it belonged—on the game.

"Any of you bums gonna help me set up at the River House Saturday morning?" Jackson asked. "Joleen and Tally are planning a full-on barbecue with music, and it seems half the town wants in on the fun."

Caleb leaned back. "I've got a county meeting that morning that I can't squeeze out of, but I should be there after lunch."

"I can help, but not until after three," Tanner said. "Showing property at noon."

Jackson looked at Asa. "You?"

Asa checked his cards. "Yeah. I can help."

Nobody spoke for a moment.

Then Tanner broke the quiet. "Man acts like he's being asked to preach Sunday's service."

"Maybe if the preacher's had any luck at cards," Asa said.

That got them laughing again, easy and full.

Around ten, the door at the top of the stairs creaked open. Joleen stepped inside wearing jeans, scuffed brown boots, still wearing her badge and her Marshal's jacket.

"Well, look at this," she said, smiling and waving her hand to move the smoke in the air. She walked over and raised the window higher, then turned the overhead fan up a notch. "Four grown men pretending fifty cents is high stakes."

Jackson stood, grinning like a man caught with his hand in the cookie jar. "Hey now, we're keeping the local economy alive."

"Sure you are." She kissed him lightly. "I'm going to turn in, sweet-ums. Some of us have to get up early and protect the nation."

"I thought you were planning a party," Tanner said.

"That, too." Joleen pointed to her chest. "I am woman, bringing home the bacon and frying it up and all that jazz."

Jackson rolled his eyes. "You've never fried bacon in your life."

"It was a metaphor, darlin'." She blew him a kiss.

"I'll be in soon," he said, smiling at her with that soft look only a man truly in love wears.

Caleb tipped his hat. "Nice to see you, Marshal."

"Evenin', Sheriff." She gave Tanner and Asa a friendly grin. "Mayor. Grocer."

"Marshal," Asa winked. "I have to say, never seen a woman in uniform look better."

She laughed and glanced at Jackson. "Hear that? I have an admirer."

He gave Asa his best stink-eye. "No poaching!"

Asa raised both hands in surrender.

Joleen all but cackled. "I'll leave you men to your big-stakes drama. Whoever wins, don't spend it all in one place."

She left, but Jackson's grin lingered. "That woman runs circles around me."

Tanner snorted. "She runs circles around all of us."

Caleb stretched his legs, reaching for the last beer. "Well, gents, I'm calling it. Some of us gotta keep the peace in the morning."

"Translation," Tanner said, "you're broke."

They ribbed each other as they packed up the cards and change, the kind of banter born from decades of shared ground.

When the others headed out, Asa said goodbye to Jackson and lingered a moment on the deck, finishing the last of his one cigar for the week. Below him, the garage lights cast a warm glow over his truck in the drive. The night hummed with crickets and a whippoorwill calling from the pines.

He thought about Maggie—about how she'd looked at the diner, the small smile, the curve of her shoulders, the knowing in her eyes that said there'd always be a spark between them.

He'd told himself his feelings had died when she chose Paris over him.

But as he stood listening to the quiet settle over the night, he couldn't help but wonder if he'd been fooling himself all these years.

# Chapter Seven

## MAGGIE

The bell over the door chimed, and we were immediately washed in the scents of rosemary, lemon, and butter. Tally's Bistro—new since I'd left town—smelled like the place where good intentions met real hunger. Today, the air felt like a postcard from two lives at once: Southern cafés I'd left behind and Paris kitchens I'd only just escaped.

Warm wood tables. Old brick walls. Sconce lighting.

A chalkboard menu greeted us, curved in looping script: trout almondine, cornmeal-dusted okra, lemon tarts with blueberry compote.

Mama wanted a new dress for the party tomorrow night and insisted we come early enough to have lunch at Tally's Place. She said she wanted me to meet Tally before the party—said she was *our kind of people.* Since she'd married one of my best friends from high school, I had to admit I was curious.

A tall blonde stepped out from behind the host stand, her apron dusted with flour, hair pinned back in a practical twist.

"Maggie McAllister in my restaurant—now there's a headline I didn't expect today."

She hugged my mother carefully, mindful of the boot on her foot, then folded me in like we'd known each other for years.

"I warn you, I'm from West Virginia and we hug people," she said. "Besides, I feel like I already know you—your mama talks about you all the time." She laughed and rolled her big blue eyes toward the ceiling. "The whole town's talking about you coming home all the way from Paris."

Tally leaned around me and grinned. "Now who's hiding back there? You must be Poppy. I've heard all about you, too."

Poppy peeked out, wide-eyed. "You've heard about me? From who?"

"Everyone," Tally said with a wink. "Everyone in town wants to meet you. That's why we're having a party tomorrow."

Mama waved a hand, encompassing the room. "Thanks to Tally, we feel like we're in the big city," she said, pride tucked into the corners of her voice.

Tally shook her head, though her dismissal carried its own quiet pride. "It's the brick," she said. "And butter. Brick and butter will make any restaurant a winner."

Her gaze softened as she took in Mom's crutch and my face. "I'm going to sit you two by the window—best light in the room." Then she turned to Poppy. "But I have a very special table for *you*. And someone I want you to meet."

At the first table past the hostess stand, a girl about Poppy's age sat with a fistful of crayons. Her blonde hair—just a shade darker than Tally's—was woven into a crooked braid. Her head bent, tongue caught at the corner of her mouth in the serious way of small artists.

She glanced up. Her eyes were a perfect copy of Tally's —only instead of sparkle, they held curiosity.

"This is Lola," Tally said, pride unhidden now. "She's working on illustrations for next week's lunch specials. We usually rotate artists, but she's been on a tear lately. Seems to have a real knack for drawing."

Poppy pressed closer to me, then tipped onto her toes for a better look at Lola's board.

"Bonjour," Poppy said shyly. Then, braver, "Je m'appelle Poppy."

Mama leaned over. "Why's she speaking French?"

I chuckled. "She's nervous—and that's her native language. She forgets not everyone speaks two."

Lola's eyes widened like someone had lit a sparkler behind them. "Hi," she breathed, then tested the word carefully. "Bon… jour."

Poppy grinned. "You speak French."

Any trace of shyness vanished as she scrambled into the seat beside her new friend.

We stood there a moment, watching them find their footing—crayons sliding across paper, giggles forming their own language. Every now and then, a French word floated up like a soap bubble—*bleu*, *citron*—and popped into laughter.

"Well, look at that," Tally said, one hand on her hip. "Worked like a charm."

"What did?" I asked.

"Last night, Caleb taught Lola ten French words so she could show off when she met Poppy."

I laughed. "Didn't know Caleb spoke French."

"Doesn't," Tally said, watching the girls huddled

together like old friends. "He used Google and something called Duolingo. Entertained us all night with his fake accent."

She grabbed a couple of menus. "Lola and I will keep an eye on Poppy. I've got the perfect table in the corner for you two."

My heart softened. It was just like Caleb to think ahead —to make sure Poppy felt welcome before she ever walked through the door.

---

From our table by the window, Main Street spun its daily web: shop doors propped open, a man in a straw hat checking his watch, someone unloading flats of marigolds beneath a striped awning across the way. On the sidewalk, a small display of flowers and plants sat in tidy rows, simple and unassuming, quietly beautiful.

"Asa's selling flowers at the grocery store now?" I asked.

"Sometimes," Mama glanced out the window. "If he's selling them, you can be sure they'll be top notch."

---

Later, as the room filled and the rhythm of the town settled around us, I watched Tally move through her restaurant—rooted, content, belonging in a way I couldn't yet picture for myself.

For the first time since coming back, I felt a small tug of loneliness. Not the Paris kind, full of echoing rooms and practiced solitude—but the kind that settles in when life keeps moving smoothly without you. It was a bit of a surprise to see how Loblolly had thrived in my absence. The town felt fuller, more alive, and nothing like the small place I'd carried with me all these years.

When we finally rose to leave, I glanced through the oversized window.

Across the street, beneath the striped awning of Griffin's Market, a man rearranged the plants and flowerpots. He turned and lifted his face to the light.

Asa.

My heart gave a quick, traitorous flip.

Tally followed my gaze but didn't say anything—which was the kindest thing she could have done. Mama pretended not to notice, too.

Poppy tugged my sleeve. "Can we come back for dinner?"

"For dinner?" I searched her face and realized she didn't want to leave her new friend. Not yet.

"You'll see Lola at tomorrow's barbecue," I said. "But right now, we need to shop for Nana's new outfit."

I cleared a path for Mama toward the door, though my eyes drifted back across the street and lingered a beat longer than they should have.

I told myself it was curiosity. Nothing more.

The lie was thin, and I knew it.

Apparently, Loblolly did too.

I could take Joleen's advice—call him, ask about riding lessons for Poppy. Keep it practical. Harmless.

I could call him for any number of reasons.

The real question was whether I trusted myself not to want more once I did.

# Chapter Eight

## ASA

By the time Asa got back to the Riverhouse, the lights were already on—warm and gold against the dark bend of the river. The party bulbs he'd strung along the porch swayed in the evening breeze like lazy fireflies. He heard the laughter drifting from the inn the moment he stepped out of his truck.

He'd been roped in all afternoon, setting up tables and chairs, moving ice chests and whatever else Stella, Joleen, and Tally had instructed. He'd gone home only to shower and change—and to talk himself out of simply grabbing a beer and sitting on his deck.

His gut was jumping like a swarm of grasshoppers had invaded his stomach. No use denying it. The thought of spending the evening with Maggie in the room played havoc on his nerves.

Suck it up, Griffin. You'd never live down the gossip of missing the party. No choice but to just suck it up.

Loblolly celebrated everything—births, marriages, championships in any sport, male or female—and evidently, the return of one of their own from Paris. And when Loblolly celebrated, it usually happened here. Stella, the inn's owner, only served breakfast, so Tally's Bistro teamed up with the Riverhouse chef, a man everyone called Colonel from his time in the service, to cater this feast.

"Name's Colonel Sanders," he'd say to any newcomer. With a twinkle in his eye, he'd add, "No kin to the chicken fellow."

Inside, the air was thick with music and the smell of barbecue, garlic bread, Tally's famous lasagna, and Colonel's little artichoke appetizers everyone always fought over. The whole place glowed. Tables lined the walls beneath platters stacked high, while groups stood or sat with heaping appetizer plates, bottles of beer or wine glasses in their hands, swapping news and laughter. Lola and Poppy danced near the DJ as if the floor had been built just for them. Asa hadn't realized how much he'd missed a good Loblolly gathering until this one.

"Thought you'd bailed on us. What took you so long?" Jackson called from near the buffet.

"Traffic," Asa said, knowing full well everyone knew the worst traffic in Loblolly involved a tractor and a stubborn dog disputing road rights.

Joleen broke away from a cluster of guests and pulled him into a hug. "Thanks for helping set up. Jackson owes you one of those single malts you love, and I owe you dinner—which, with my schedule, might mean Christmas." She leaned back, studying him. "Wow. You look good. New shirt?"

Heat crept up his neck. It was a new shirt, though he had no intention of admitting it. "Heard you gave up chasing bad guys for the weekend."

Jackson slid up to them, slung an arm around her shoulders. "That's right. She can't stay away from me."

"Now that's the truth," Joleen said, swatting him. "But don't let it go to your head, Judge." The smile on her lips was real; the shadow in her eyes, not so much. She looked preoccupied—or maybe it was just the lighting. Or a particularly troublesome case. She never talked about her work.

Jackson had confided a few weeks ago that he and Joleen were trying to start a family, but her travel schedule made it nearly impossible. Since her last promotion, she was gone three weeks out of four. Asa had caught the flicker of worry in Jackson's eyes when he'd said it. The man loved her more than she probably realized—loved her enough to want her safe. But he knew from experience that worry could rub a person raw, both the worrier and the one being worried over.

Caleb and Tally appeared from the direction of the kitchen, and Lola and Poppy abandoned the dance floor to greet them, Poppy chattering as if she'd been part of their family forever. After a few words, she made a beeline for the band.

Tally spotted Asa and grinned. "Grocery man, you're looking good tonight. You might find it hard to stay out of trouble."

"Don't start rumors you can't support," he said.

Caleb chuckled. "He was born to find trouble—just got better at hiding it."

"Some of us grew up," Asa said.

"I could be your wingman," Caleb offered.

"That so?" Tally lifted a brow.

Poppy spotted Asa and ran over. "Hey, Mr. Grocery Man!"

Asa laughed, returning her greeting with a high five. "Well, hello, Miss Poppy."

She twirled away, her frilly purple dress flaring around her knees.

His eyes scanned the room, seeking her mother.

"Poppy came with us," Tally said, then turned away, as if giving him a minute to adjust to the idea that he'd been that obvious.

Caleb laughed and slapped his back, then went straight for the appetizer table. Tally went straight to hugging half the room.

Asa stood in the middle of the room, surrounded by friends and family. It should've felt easy—and mostly, it did. Joleen chatting with Tally about new menu ideas, Caleb spinning a story that had Jackson doubled over, people clapping shoulders, the air full of joy and community.

But there was a face still missing and that made him edgy. He wanted the initial greeting done and over. Move past it. He told himself he'd come for Joleen and Jackson—to show up, to be part of things just like always.

Then the door opened.

Maggie stepped into the foyer, and the real reason he'd dragged his tired butt off his balcony waltzed in.

"Mama!" Poppy raced across the room. "You look so pretty."

And she did. The light haloed her hair, deep chestnut and touched by the sun, and for a heartbeat the whole room seemed to take notice. She wore a pale gray pants suit, the fabric falling in smooth lines that moved with her, settling against her frame and reminded him of water gently rushing over a rock, then finding its level.

She bent to hug Poppy, whispered something that made the girl laugh, then urged her to run ahead—straight back to Lola. She straightened to her full height, assessed the room and chose to move in more slowly, answering greetings with a soft, polite smile, eyes alert, measuring the space the way she always had.

Barbara McAllister stood near the front, cane propped, lipstick perfect, already holding court like she'd organized the whole event herself. Tanner Sutton leaned in as if to kiss her cheek but whispered something that made her swat him away, half offense, half humor.

Asa couldn't seem to take his gaze off Maggie. A small knot tightened in his chest. She moved easily now—hugging Joleen, laughing with Tally, teasing Caleb about something Poppy had said. She still had that gift: stepping into a room and adjusting to its shape, it was like she'd never been gone.

When her eyes finally met his, she stopped.

Just a breath. Just enough.

No scene, no drama. Just recognition—clear, steady, sharp as the first cold wind of autumn.

He gave her a nod. She gave one back. That was it.

But in his chest, it carried more weight than he wanted to admit. He chastised himself for seeing something that probably wasn't there—like some high school fool who hadn't learned the difference between memory and hope.

The DJ eased into a low, bluesy tune. Folks drifted toward the porch. Joleen raised a glass and made a toast about second chances—health, work, family. The crowd cheered, glasses clinked, laughter spilling out the open doors toward the water.

Across the room, Stella tapped a spoon against a glass and called the room to attention. "Before the Colonel opens the kitchen, I want to say welcome home—at least for a little while—to Maggie McAllister. We're glad you're here."

She raised her glass to Maggie. "You know we love any excuse to have a party."

Everyone chuckled. A few said amen to that.

She paused just long enough for the room to settle, then nodded toward Caleb. "Now, I believe we have an announcement."

Caleb cleared his throat and held out his hand for Tally to join him. He raised their clasped hands. "Well, we're expecting," he said simply. "This December."

The room erupted—applause, cheers, a rush of congratulations. Tally laughed, glowing, her free hand resting instinctively at her middle.

After the noise settled, she leaned into Caleb and elbowed him gently. "Wonder why no one seems too surprised?"

Caleb grinned. "We don't exactly keep secrets well in this town."

His Aunt Sue Ellen snorted. "That's one way to put it."

Names were debated loudly, opinions offered freely. Tally smiled through it all, then held up her hands.

"Okay, knock it off. I know you all already knew about the baby, so quit pretending this news is a surprise. But there's something you don't know—because I didn't tell my husband yet. He couldn't keep a secret to save his life."

She turned to Caleb, eyes bright, and rubbed her hand over her abdomen. "It's true I'm pregnant, and for that I'm very thankful for our first baby together. And now that I'm over the shock, I'm also thankful for his or her brother or sister."

Caleb's ear to ear grin slowly faded. "Wait. What?" Confusion swamped his face. "What are you saying?"

Tally reached into her back pocket and pulled out a piece of paper and slowly unfolded it. Held up one of those pictures of a baby in the womb that looked like a peanut. Only this one had two red arrows.

She followed the red arrows. "Baby one." Her finger slid sideways. "Baby two."

"Twins," someone yelled. Another person whistled.

The applause and laughter erupted, loud and unrestrained.

Someone said something about twins running in families. Someone else joked about lightning striking twice.

Caleb stood in place as starstruck as any kid he'd ever seen.

Tally shook her head, laughing. "I am a twin, but my sister Harper and I are what the doctors call a fluke of nature," she said. "Identical twins just… happen."

"And this?" Caleb pointed to the sonogram.

"This," Tally said, "is what happens when you're over thirty-five and your doctor decides your ovaries need encouragement."

Caleb let out a low sound somewhere between a laugh and a groan. "Encouragement."

"Yes," Tally added, grinning, "apparently I dropped two eggs. So while it's a wonderful thrill, it's not exactly a mystery why we'll be welcoming two babies before Christmas."

That only seemed to make everyone laugh harder. No one tried to smother the joy. It took another fifteen minutes before Stella could finally herd everyone toward the buffet table.

Asa clapped when he should, smiled when required, tossed in a word or two. But his attention kept sliding back to Maggie by the window, Poppy dancing with Lola, and Barb standing more than she ought to—her color looked much too pale, her eyes too bright. He moved closer.

Searched the room for his aunt. She was the only one who could ever make Barbara McAllister do anything.

Barb was pushing herself. He'd seen that look before—pride holding a body upright long after sense said to rest. His mama had been the same.

From his position a few feet away, he could see the sheen at Barb's hairline, the way her fingers tightened around her cane. He found Maggie, who turned in his direction as if they had an electrical current sizzling between them. He nodded toward Barbara, and Maggie rushed over. Barbara waved her off with that familiar don't-you-dare-fuss-at-me look.

Asa shifted closer, just in case.

He and Maggie exchanged another knowing look. He gave a small nod—got her.

"I'll get her a glass of water," Maggie said as she passed. "Please talk her into sitting down. She won't listen to me." She squeezed his arm, then asked for a favor. It was the smallest kind of trust, and silly to think it mattered. Still, he could've sworn she exhaled, like she'd handed something over—just for a moment. And for reasons he didn't quite name, his heart answered.

Onstage, the singer slid into another slow number. Someone called for a refill. Kids squealed by the railing. Under the porch lights, everything looked almost the same as it always had.

Asa stood with one hand near Barb's elbow, ready if she needed him. She didn't—at least not yet—and that, too, felt like a kind of balance.

Then the DJ eased into *My Girl*. His and Maggie's song in high school.

Across the room, Maggie walked toward them, a glass of water in her hand. She paused, as if the song had registered. Her eyes found his. They held there, quiet and steady.

Barb leaned closer, and he reluctantly pulled his attention from Maggie to her mother. “Sweetheart, would you mind finding me a chair?”

He moved quickly to find one, and the quiet moment loosened.

Asa heard the song in the back of his mind, along with Barb’s laughter and the low hum of the night settling in around them. Maggie was back in Loblolly. And somehow his life felt off kilter. It was silly. Still, he had the feeling the night wasn’t finished with him yet.

# Chapter Nine

## MAGGIE

The Riverhouse shimmered against the river like it was lit from within—porch lights swinging, laughter spilling through open doors, and the sweet smoke of barbecue drifting across the water. For one night, Loblolly felt like I remembered. People needed something to celebrate, and apparently my mother, along with my childhood friends, had decided that tonight I was that something.

Poppy met me at the door, tugging at my hand, eyes wide as she took in the crowd.

"Look, Mommy—Miss Tally says all these people are here for us."

I smiled, kneeling to her level. "That's right. And do you know what that means?"

She blinked. Blinked again. Clearly stumped.

"It means you have to introduce yourself to everyone here and thank them for coming."

"Everyone?" Her eyes rounded as she scanned the room. "Will you come? I don't know their names."

"You know who'd be a big help? Lola."

"Yeah, Lola! She knows everybody." She hugged Mama, then dashed off to find her new bestie.

Mama looked the picture of recovered health—pink cheeks, lipstick perfect, scarf tied at her throat. Our shopping trip yesterday had been a bust, so she'd decided to wear the long jean dress she'd found in Paris on her first visit, along with flats with rubber soles. Her cane rested neatly beside her. She looked beautiful, rosy cheeked and bright eyed, a woman who'd outrun death and decided to throw it a party.

Tally had brought in a DJ from Atlanta who was halfway through a blues number that somehow made heartbreak sound hopeful. People were dancing, talking, drifting between tables lit by mason jars and candles. Every so often, I caught a glimpse of Asa across the room—shoulders relaxed, sleeves rolled, that calm expression that steadied everyone around him.

He laughed at something Caleb said, but his gaze found me now and then—searching, though for what I had no idea. We never talked about anything deeper than the farm or Mama or the weather. I tried to pay him no mind, but it was next to impossible for some annoying, completely baffling reason.

The buffet line wound past the door. Poppy and Lola quickly abandoned their guest-greeting plan in favor of standing on tiptoe to study the desserts. Jackson was retelling a story from poker night, Tanner heckling him about "selective memory." The noise was comforting and familiar.

Sue Ellen swept across the room in her usual rush, carrying two champagne flutes. She handed one to Mama, one to me, then linked her arm through Mama's.

"You'll excuse us—we've got catching up to do."

"Well," Mama said, "this might require more champagne."

"No worries. There's more where that came from."

I touched Mama's shoulder. "Maybe you should switch to water after this glass."

"Oh, don't start, Maggie." Mama smiled the kind of smile that dared you to reason with her. "You're not the parent here."

"You're supposed to be taking it easy."

"I am." She winked. "I'm going to sit down with my friend and gossip."

It wasn't worth arguing. Not tonight.

Off they went, leaving me scanning the crowd for a familiar face that didn't come with searching blue eyes.

Those searching blue eyes moved to intercept Mama and his aunt Sue Ellen with an easy smile.

"Evenin', Barb. You're looking mighty pretty," I heard him say.

"Flattery will get you everywhere, Asa Griffin," she winked.

"So I've been told." He glanced in my direction and nodded—as if he'd read my mind and knew Mama drinking champagne and roaming the room was pushing her luck. Or at least I hoped he'd read my mind. He'd been pretty great at that back in the day. If so, at least one other person was watching out for her tonight.

Just then, Poppy darted back across the room, breathless with excitement.

"Mr. Asa! Look at the horse I drew!"

She thrust a napkin sketch into his hand. Asa bent to her level, studying it with exaggerated seriousness. "Well now, that's a fine-looking mare." His voice warm as honey.

Poppy laughed—quick and bright—and Asa chuckled with her, low and gentle.

For the smallest moment, something tugged behind my ribs. Their cocked heads were so similar it left a soft ache beneath my breast I couldn't place.

Maybe it was the easy way Poppy sparkled around new people.

Maybe it was how naturally Asa met her excitement.

Maybe it was simply being home again, in a place where everything felt strangely familiar.

I shook it off, the feeling already slipping away.

I spent the next thirty minutes chatting, laughing, talking, enjoying the camaraderie of old friends. I moseyed over to Mama and Sue Ellen and offered to get Mama a glass of water. I'd no sooner poured the glass, turned, and *My Girl* drifted from the DJ's speakers.

My gaze instinctively found Asa. When his eyes met mine, something old and familiar sparked—steady and dangerous. Before I could stop myself, I stepped in his direction.

"Mama," Poppy called. "This is your song."

The look on Asa's face said a million things all at once.

Mama leaned toward him, asked something, and his gaze slid away to her. He nodded and pulled out a chair, leading her to sit.

Relief Mama asked for Asa's help, disappointment that the moment between us had passed.

Asa turned back, searched the room until he found me, in the ten steps to his side, I lost myself in his blue eyes.

"How's the store?" I asked, reaching for safe ground, just like always.

"Steady."

Our conversation drifted like a leaf between currents—careful, casual, full of unspoken history.

"You seem happy," he said after a pause. I smiled, but something drew my attention sideways. Suddenly, time fractured. Mama swayed, her eyes blinking fast, mouth forming my name.

"Mom!"

Asa lunged forward, catching her before she hit the floor. The sound of shattering glass vanished beneath the rush of voices—chairs scraping, someone calling for help, Tally ushering a crying Poppy away.

I dropped to my knees, folded her in my arms. "Mama, can you hear me?"

She tried to speak, but only the thinnest whisper made it past her lips. Her skin had gone ashen, damp with sweat.

"Ambulance is on its way," Caleb said, his calm voice reaching past my panic.

"Don't make a fuss," Mama murmured.

"You're not giving orders," I said, clutching her hand. "Just breathe. Don't you leave me, Mama." I rocked her in my arms. "Please, Mama. Don't leave me."

What felt like an eternity later, sirens rushed down the inn's long drive, painting the trees in red and white. I kissed Mama's forehead, smoothed her hair, barely breathing myself.

When the paramedics lifted her onto the stretcher, I followed, dimly aware of Asa's voice beside me.

"You go with your mom. I'll meet you at the hospital."

I climbed into the ambulance, glancing back through the blur of faces.

"Poppy."

"I'll see to her," Asa said. "Just go."

The ride to the hospital was a blur of motion and sound

—the cry of sirens, lights flashing off dark windows, the sickening hollow between heartbeats.

"She was fine," I said again to the attendant in the back. "She was laughing three seconds before she collapsed."

My declaration was met with silence as the medic called in blood pressure and heart-rate numbers.

By the time we reached St. Joseph's, the world had narrowed to the squeal of gurney wheels and the slam of double doors. Someone told me to wait; someone else pointed me toward Admissions.

I stood at the counter, hands shaking, trying to remember her insurance carrier, her birthdate, her medications. I knew nothing except her birthday and her doctor's name. I'd been gone so long I didn't even know the names of her pills.

Everything slipped through my mind like water.

The nurse's voice was kind but efficient. "Take a breath, sweetheart. We'll need her ID, insurance card, and a list of any maintenance meds."

"We left our purses at the Riverhouse," I explained. "I don't even have my phone. I don't have anything."

"That's all right," she said gently. "We'll get her started while you figure it out. Stay close by."

I sank into one of the plastic chairs in the waiting area, hands twisting in my lap, the smell of disinfectant and burnt coffee stinging my nose. For the first time since the porch lights blurred behind the ambulance, I felt completely, uselessly still.

Then the automatic doors hissed open.

Asa jogged in, hair mussed, shirt damp with sweat, clutching both purses to his chest—Mom's leather bag and my smaller one. "Figured you might need these," he said, handing them to me before sliding into the chair beside me.

Relief broke through the fog. "You're a miracle."

"I can't take the credit. Joleen and Stella sent them. They'll be here once the inn clears out."

I took Mom's purse to the desk. The nurse copied the cards and handed me a clipboard.

"Fill out what you can. The doctor will update you soon."

My hand shook too much to write. Asa took the clipboard. "Tell me what to put down."

Together, we filled out the form. His neat print took me back to high school for a moment, remembering the sweet notes he used to leave in my locker.

We finished, I returned the form and then my mind cleared enough to ask him, "Where's Poppy?"

"She went home with Tally and Caleb. Lola's keeping her busy. The ambulance scared her."

"And my tears didn't help."

"That's what small towns are for," he said. "Someone always steps in when you can't."

We sat side by side, not touching, not talking, but his presence steadied me. The room buzzed softly—the hum of a soda machine, the murmur of a night nurse, footsteps echoing in the hall.

"She's strong," Asa said quietly. "She'll pull through."

"I can't lose her," I whispered. "Not like this."

"You won't," he said—not with bravado, but conviction.

The silence afterward wasn't empty. It was full of everything we couldn't say.

"She pushed herself too hard," he said.

"If I'd made her sit—"

"Maggie." His voice anchored me. "You couldn't have *made* her do anything."

"She's all I have."

He met my eyes. "You've got more people in your camp than you think."

Others arrived then—kind faces, quiet chatter. Stella and Tanner, Joleen and Jackson, Sue Ellen. They stayed for hours, but eventually everyone left except Asa.

"I'll be okay," I said. "You should go home. You have to open the store early in the morning."

"I'm not leaving you."

Four hours later, the doctor emerged.

"She's stable," he said. "A heart attack." He explained the it was moderate, requiring two stents. She would need medication and strict rest for at least three months.

Three months.

"She can't run the farm anymore." I said.

"No," Asa said gently. "She can't."

"I'll sell the orchard," I heard myself say. "I'll take her to Paris."

"She'll never go."

"She has to."

"She won't," Asa said softly. "This land is her heartbeat."

"Then what am I supposed to do?"

He met my gaze. "Stay. For a while. See where it leads."

His words, released so easily from his lips, settled deep—quiet and undeniable.

Later, they moved Mama to recovery. Asa walked beside me. We sat together, his arm resting along the back of my chair—not touching, just close, a quiet promise I didn't ask for but didn't refuse.

"She's not going anywhere," he said. "Too stubborn."

A shaky laugh slipped out before I could stop it.

"I'm not leaving," he assured me when I suggested he needed sleep before opening his store.

The monitors above Mama's bed beeped—steady, faithful. Eventually, dawn eased through the blinds, the sky pale and patient.

Ninety days.

I could probably manage ninety days.

Deep in my bones, something shifted—and ninety days suddenly felt very small.

# Chapter Ten

MAGGIE

The afternoon sun broke through the windows of the farmhouse, but the quiet inside was heavy as dust. That is, if there'd been a speck of dust.

The house smelled of Mama's lemon cleaner. I'd scrubbed for hours, room to room, until I couldn't keep my eyes open anymore. It had been a long time since I'd cleaned a house myself, long enough to forget the labor of it. But no matter how much I wiped and polished, the years showed through. Shelling nuts on the porch and at the kitchen table had left a faint sweetness behind—something no cleaner, candle, or diffuser could fully erase.

No matter. It smelled like home. And I hoped Mama would agree.

Somewhere between the aching muscles and the stubborn scent of the past, it dawned on me that Mama would need help—real help. Someone to keep up the house. Someone else for the heavier work on the farm. I could hire people to check in, schedule regular cleanings. But the only way to truly look after Mama was if she was with me in

Paris. I had to convince her. I wasn't above recruiting her friends to help.

Before I left, I did one last walk-through. It was probably my imagination, but the house felt watchful—waiting. The clocks ticked softer than usual. Even the floorboards seemed to hold their breath beneath my steps. Outside, the breeze slipped through the porch screens with care, as if whatever storm had passed, what was needed now was rest.

Or maybe it was just me, feeling the weight of being in the empty house.

In Paris, there was always sound to lean on—voices drifting up from the street, the hum of the elevator, traffic arguing with itself outside the window. It had been a while since I'd had to sit with this kind of quiet.

I had spent the early morning signing Poppy up for school—she was over the moon to find she'd been placed in the same class as Lola. But by the time the noon sun angled through the farmhouse windows, the house was spotless—and silent. That would soon change.

I locked the door behind me and headed to the hospital to meet up with Asa. He'd volunteered to help me bring Mama home and get her settled.

Releasing her took the better part of two hours, most of it spent listening to instructions: new meds added to old meds, a revised schedule, and endless rules about what she could eat, how much she should rest, and which exercises were "permissible." I was ready for a nap before we even got her in the car.

But as it turned out, that was the easy part.

We pulled into the farm's driveway, and of course, Mama refused the wheelchair Asa rolled out from the porch.

"I'm not an invalid," she informed us—in that I-used-to-change-your-diapers tone that could stop me in my tracks faster than any doctor's order.

I took a deep breath and searched for calm, got all the way up to mild angst before stepping in front of her. "Mama, I don't want to argue about every blessed order the doctor gave before letting you out of the hospital." I pointed at the chair. "Now sit—or I'm going to ask Asa to carry you inside."

She looked at the wheelchair as if it had wronged her personally. The effort to climb out of the car and into the chair turned her three shades of pale, but her jaw stayed fixed in that stubborn line I'd known to steer clear of my entire life.

I had tried to make the house cheerful—fresh flowers on the table, curtains washed and pressed—but in Mama's current mood she hadn't seemed to notice, or at least, if she did, she chose not to comment.

"Doctor said rest," I reminded her as Asa rolled her down the hall toward her bedroom.

"Take me into the living room," she ordered.

He looked at me, rolled his eyes, and tried to hide his grin—but he obliged her demand.

He rolled to a stop, and she pushed herself out of the chair, hobbling straight to the picture window overlooking the orchard.

"Mama. Your doctor said you need rest," I said.

"The doctor also said I'd never dance again after I fell out of the hayloft in '82," she shot back. "He was wrong about that, too."

The refusal had nothing to do with the wheelchair. It was our conversation on the drive home. I'd dared to suggest she sell the farm and move to Paris. Her reaction had been… memorable.

Too soon, I realized. Not wrong—just too soon.

I bit back a sigh. "The orchard isn't going to fix itself, Mama—"

"You don't think I know that?" She turned, steadying herself against the chair. "You're right, it won't. But sitting around whining about the state of the trees won't fix it either."

Her words might have stung less if they hadn't been a direct reproach for my refusing to agree to stay and fix what was broken.

"Mama, listen. The farm needs more than pruning. The barn roof leaks, the pump's half-dead, and the taxes alone—"

"Then sell it," she snapped. "You've wanted to ever since you came home. If legacy and land mean nothing to you, just call Tanner Sutton and let him or one of his real estate agents sell it all."

I looked at her—really looked. Past the flush of her face, the defiance in her eyes, all the way down to the fear flashing in her beautiful hazel eyes. Fear of losing the last piece of Daddy—and of her parents and his parents. When Mama and Daddy married, the union had combined two three-generation family farms. My mama and daddy had lived next door to one another their entire lives. Born on this land, the land her grandparents and his had left to their children and their children to theirs. I stared into the face of fear of what waited for her if she left this land.

Fear.

Fear I understood.

I softened my voice. "I just don't want you to spend the rest of your life struggling. If you don't want to sell the farm, then please consider leasing the orchard. That way you can come back to Paris and spend time with Poppy and me. I promise we'll come home for visits. It's time to let someone else worry about making this land pay for itself."

For a heartbeat, something flickered across her face—fatigue, maybe, or temptation—then it was gone. "I don't need Paris. I need purpose. You've got a life there, Maggie. Go live it. Hire a man to keep the orchard up—I'll manage."

"Mama, it's not that simple. The farm isn't turning a profit. Without major work—"

She waved a hand, cutting me off. "I'm tired. I think I'll lie down."

That was her cease-fire signal. End of discussion.

Asa left soon after our argument. I couldn't tell which side of the heated debate he walked on, and really, it didn't matter. Facts were facts.

With the house clean, Poppy in school, and Mama resting, I spent the rest of the afternoon reading over a script Katrina had emailed, begging for my overall thoughts. A prescription from the doctor, she'd teased. I read the first five chapters, understood there was a problem, and even narrowed down the issue in an email that I voice-transcribed back to her.

Within two minutes she texted back. "I know that—how do I fix it? I'm out of ideas."

My mind went blank. It was a good script, with well-known actors signed on. If we didn't fix it—and fast—that caliber of talent would move on. We had a narrow window, but my thoughts stalled, as stubborn as Mama's will.

I sat at the computer, but blanked. Rose and walked to the piano, lifted the lid, and sat. One of the exercises for my hand was simple stretching—slow, careful movement to ease stiffness without forcing it. I let my fingers move over the keys more motion than music, warming up the way I'd been taught.

I pulled the beginner book from the bench and played softly, my thoughts drifting back to childhood, to the year Mama insisted I practice an hour a day.

"You said you wanted to learn," she'd told me. "Your daddy took you at your word and bought the piano. We pay for lessons. You owe us the courtesy of doing your best for five years. After that, if you don't like it, you can quit."

Somewhere along the way, I'd learned the value of showing up, even when talent alone wasn't enough. God knew I didn't have a musical bone in my body.

Katrina's email surfaced again—and this time, an idea followed. I turned it over once, felt it settle. It might work.

The door creaked open behind me. Mama stood in the doorway. At least she was using her cane. That was something.

"You can play the piano," she said, "but you can't type?"

"I'm not really playing," I said. "Just stretching my fingers. It might help."

Maybe the block wasn't just about my hand. Or maybe ideas came easier when my mind was busy elsewhere. I scanned the room for my phone, wanting to catch the thought before it slipped away.

---

Asa had taken to stopping by every day or so after he closed the store, checking to see if we needed anything. After putting Poppy to bed, we'd sit on the porch and talk about nothing important.

One night, after a particularly tough day with Mama, I finally admitted what had been circling my mind since the day we brought her home from the hospital.

"I found her crying in her room this morning," I said. "She's scared of the unknown—and I know how that feels. I can't leave her with a dying farm."

He rocked once, slow and thoughtful. "You saying you're staying?"

"For now." The words settled heavy but certain. "She refuses to go back to Paris with me. So, if I can get the orchard producing again and hire a farm manager, she'll be okay. Most of the damage is neglect—broken fencing, overgrown brush, a leaking roof, no marketing plan. Those are things I can fix."

"And your job?" he asked gently.

I stared out at the dark silhouettes of the pecan trees and admitted what I'd been avoiding. "I petitioned for another two months of medical leave. My boss reluctantly agreed, but made it clear that after that, she'll have no choice but to replace me. And that means that if my hand doesn't heal, I'll have to find another way to make a living."

I took a breath. "Writing is muscle memory, too. Every day I don't use it, I feel it slipping. I'm lucky—I have a steady income doing work most writers only dream about. But my heart won't let this place die. Not while Mama's still breathing."

I shrugged. "So I'll have to do both."

He nodded, like that was an answer he knew was coming.

The porch light cast a soft pool around us. In the distance, a barn owl called—low and haunting—as if reminding me that night doesn't last forever. I took a deep breath and reached for my cell.

I pulled up notes and hit the voice icon to make a verbal list. "One. Call someone about the irrigation system. Two—find out who sprays for blight. Three—prune the lower grove before winter."

The list grew, practical and steady, each line pulling me a little closer to the results Mama wanted;.

Asa glanced over, smiling. "Looks like the beginning of a plan."

"Looks like the beginning of staying for now," I said.

"Make sure to add 'teach Poppy to ride.'" He smiled when I looked up, surprised. "I hear she loves Sugar, and I'd love to teach her how to care for her properly—and to ride. If that's okay."

I sighed. One thing to mark off my list. "Thank you. She asks every day if she can ride Sugar, and caring for Mama and the house, attempting to work a few hours with Katrina, I simply haven't had the time to teach her."

Honestly:, I was happy that Poppy would get her wish—but knowing Asa would spend more time at the farm made me even happier. I knew I was on thin ice. My dependence on Asa's friendship was growing, and he'd shown no interest in being anything but friends. So I had to tamp down the flame—the one that had grown from a flicker into a steady blaze—and focus solely on the farm. Lord knew I had enough to keep me busy without adding romance into the mix.

Inside, the lights in Mama's bedroom flickered off. The house creaked, settling into its bones. And somewhere between the sigh of the pecan trees and the hush of the night air, I swore I could hear the farmhouse exhale—like it finally believed it wouldn't be abandoned.

"I brought a bottle of that wine you said you like," Asa said. "Would you care to open it? It's a nice evening."

"That sounds just about the perfect way to end this day."

Even as I spoke the words, I wondered how many nights like this would pass before friendship stopped being enough—and what it would mean once it did.

# Chapter Eleven

## MAGGIE

The days that followed slipped into a rhythm of their own—sunrise, sweat, and sore muscles. There was something strangely comforting about the work—overseeing the painting of the barn before the wood softened too much to be saved, scrubbing years of mildew off the north porch, helping a few locals looking for work clear brush from the orchard until the air smelled of nothing but sap and old memories.

I had no control over how long my hand would take to heal—so I focused on the things I could control. I spent my nights working on a marketing plan for our crop—a plan beyond simply selling to the co-op. A plan that would bring in more money, one I hoped Mama would endorse.

And, in the late hours, I tried writing longhand. But the effort of physically writing took too long and my scribbling couldn't keep up with my thoughts and the writing magic never materialized.

As the days wore on, I found myself more absorbed in the farm and less in my writing, making little time for the piano—even though it was where my script problems often untangled themselves without effort, ideas slipping into place while I played.

Maybe that's why Katrina's emergency emails were coming less often now. She sent word last week our boss had hired a temporary partner to bounce ideas off, and I assumed it was going well. I told myself I was happy about that.

---

The orchard had been half asleep, but not beyond saving. The trees had gone shaggy from neglect, branches heavy with gray moss that fluttered like ghosts when the wind caught them. A few had stopped bearing altogether, but most still offered a decent crop of pecans that rattled in their shells. With the proper nutrients, the next crop should outperform last year's. At least, that was the plan.

When I stood beneath the trees, sweat streaking my temples, I could almost feel their quiet endurance. They'd weathered storms, drought, and human indifference. They just needed tending—a bit like Mama, truth be told.

For the first time that I could remember, the farm wasn't profitable. But I understood now why Mama had let the farm decline. She simply ran out of money. That's where I came in

Asa stopped by most evenings after closing up the store. He brought things I didn't ask for—nails, replacement hoses, a tool I didn't know I needed until I used it. And though I told him not to fuss, I never turned him away.

He'd trailered his mare, Junebug, to the farm the previous weekend, backing the trailer up to our old paddock with a grin that said he knew he was overstepping—and planned to do it anyway.

"Easier if she stays here for a while," he'd said. "Less hauling, more riding. Poppy will learn faster if she can watch me do what I'm asking of her, and I don't want to drag Junebug back and forth every time I give her a lesson. Once Poppy finds her balance, we can take short trail rides as a little reward."

He started teaching Poppy to ride in the pasture behind the barn. From the porch, I'd hear her laughter carry across the field—pure, unfiltered joy that loosened something tight inside me.

"He says I'm a natural, Mama!" she'd shout, perched proudly on Sugar's back while Asa walked beside her, one hand steady on the reins, the other resting lightly on her knee.

"She's got good balance," he said when I wandered over. "Better than most grown-ups I know."

"That's the polite way of saying she's stubborn," I said.

He grinned. "Guess she comes by it honest."

Poppy straightened in the saddle at that, proud as a peacock. She mimicked the way Asa adjusted his shoulders, lifting her chin the same way he did when he focused.

Something tugged low in my chest—soft and fleeting, gone almost before I noticed it.

Nothing recognizable. Just a quiet ripple, like a memory brushing past without introducing itself.

I shook it off, blamed the sun, or maybe fatigue.

Or the simple sweetness of watching the two of them fall into an easy rhythm. She seemed to cherish his attention. Every little girl needed a male role model in their life.

Mama had started joining me on the porch again, propped up in her chair with her leg elevated on a stool.

She'd sip sweet tea and issue gentle orders—when to stop trimming, where to replant, what she'd do if she "had two good legs under her."

I'd smile and nod, pretending to argue but, in the end, agreeing her ideas were best. It felt good to have her voice back in the air.

One afternoon, Asa stayed to fix the sagging hinge on the back door. When he was done, Mama insisted he stay for supper.

"Since you're working up an appetite, you might as well enjoy Maggie's cooking," she said, her tone half invitation, half decree.

"Now wait a minute," I protested. "You did half the cooking yourself."

"Supervision isn't cooking," she said, waving me off. "I just made sure you didn't burn the gravy."

By the time supper hit the table, the house smelled like gumbo and cornbread and something close to peace. At Mama's instruction, Poppy set out the newer dishes—the ones with blue rims she always saved for company. Mama bragged on my gumbo as if I'd invented the recipe.

"Takes a delicate hand to get the roux right," she said, nodding toward me.

"Delicate?" Asa lifted his brows. "I've seen her swing a hammer like she's breaking up concrete."

"Only because it was concrete," I said, and for the first time in weeks, Mama laughed—a sound that filled the kitchen like sunlight through clean glass.

We lingered long after the food was gone, after Poppy went up to take her bath and finish the last of her homework. The three of us talking about nothing important—the weather, the state of the roads, a new family moving into the old Miller place. It felt ordinary, and that ordinary felt sacred.

Later, Poppy returned for her requisite cookies and milk before bed, and Asa offered to help with the dishes.

Mama shooed him toward the porch. "Go on," she said. "You've done enough for one day." Insisting it was high time she taught Poppy how to properly clean the table and load the dishwasher, and they didn't need me looking over their shoulders either.

So, at her behest, I joined Asa on the porch a few minutes later.

The night was mild, the kind of Southern evening that wrapped itself around you like a quilt. Fireflies blinked in the grass. The scent of gumbo still lingered, mingling with the honeysuckle climbing the porch columns.

"I'm not sure who has a bigger crush on you, Mama or Poppy," I said, settling beside him on the porch steps.

He chuckled. "Your mama could outstare a federal judge, but yeah, I admit she's taken a liking to me over the years. Now, Poppy? That's no crush—that's true love on both parts."

I laughed, agreed it to be so, and we sat in easy silence, listening to the crickets tune up in the field.

"I brought another bottle of that wine you like," he said after a while. "Would you like to open it? It's a nice evening."

"That's becoming a bit of a habit," I said.

"Can't think of a better one," he smiled, and my heart did a soft somersault.

Turns out he'd packed the bottle of wine and two stemmed glasses in a picnic basket. His basket had a special cool compartment for the wine and he poured our glasses.

"Wow, fancy!"

"I can do fancy," he said with a straight face.

I grinned and let it stand.

The wine was light, cool, and crisp, the kind that reminded me of summer evenings in France—but tonight it tasted lighter. Maybe it was the air, or the company, or the sense that I didn't have to be anyone other than who I was in this moment.

Inside, I heard Mama humming as she and Poppy stacked dishes in the dishwasher. For once, the house didn't feel heavy with expectation. It just… breathed.

By the time Asa left for home, Poppy was already asleep. I walked through the quiet rooms, turning off lights, then drifted to the living room. The moonlight stretched across the desk like a spill of silver.

I opened my laptop, scanned the last emailed script Katrina had sent. My right hand trembled. I read the first three chapters, had an idea and tried to forget my hand and simply mesh with my creativity flowing through my fingers. My typing was uneven, stops and starts, but eventually I saw some of the old magic come to life.

The yearning to write was still in me, stubborn as ever. It wasn't ambition so much as instinct—like breath or heartbeat. Writing and creating stories had always been the language that spoke when words failed me.

But now, I couldn't tell if writing again would heal me—or if my writer's block reared its head, would it break me all over?

I sat there long after the house grew still, the wine gone warm inside me, my fingers resting on the keyboard that had once felt like home.

Who was I if I didn't write?

The question drifted through the quiet, unanswered, like a string of words held just beyond hearing.

# Chapter Twelve

## MAGGIE

It was early enough that the morning mist still clung to the pasture when I stepped outside with Poppy to feed Mama's pet chickens. She always kept a small flock for fresh eggs, swearing they made the best pound cakes. And Mama was famous for her pecan-filled cakes. But I'd forgotten to bring the hens into the barn to roost last night, so they could be anywhere this morning—finding them was a little like playing hide-and-seek.

We stopped in the paddock. "Let's be real still and listen for their clucking."

The world was soft and muted, and the pecan trees in the distance looked suspended between night and day. Poppy had just roused from bed when she followed me out the door, her hair still wild from sleep, wearing her pajamas tucked into the rubber farm boots Mama had insisted she needed for chores. The feed bucket looked too big for her small hands.

"The chickens are either by the fence line or the old stump." I nudged her with my elbow. "What's your guess?"

She paused—really paused—her eyes lifting toward the pasture with that slow, thoughtful beat. And it hit me that Asa always took his time before answering anything. She was definitely spending too much time with him if his mannerisms were wearing off on her. The contemplation made her seem older for a moment, as if she were weighing more than the two simple choices I'd laid out.

"Fence line," she said finally. "The sun hits there first."

A small, quiet flicker went through me. Nothing big. Just a soft tug somewhere deep, like a note vibrating faintly under a well-written sentence.

I brushed it off and quickly filled the silence. "I bet the chickens are mad at me for not bringing them in last night."

"They'll be hungry," Poppy added.

We walked toward the barn with Poppy humming a tune. At first, I didn't place it—simple, rolling, something that could've been from a commercial. I wondered if she might be musically inclined and reminded myself to make some inquiries about piano lessons.

Then she pursed her lips and whistled the next line.

Not a squeak.

Not a beginner's puff of air.

A clear, practiced whistle.

I stopped mid-step. "Sweetheart," I said slowly, "I didn't know you could whistle?"

She grinned and puffed her chest, strutting like a peacock across the yard. "Mr. Asa taught me yesterday! He said some people can just do it and some can't, but I can. Listen—"

She whistled again, the notes bright in the cool air.

It startled me. I'd never been able to whistle more than a weak hiss, and Poppy had never shown any interest in trying. Kids learned all kinds of things quickly, I reminded myself. Especially around people they looked up to.

Still… for some reason, it hit me as almost remarkable. Could Julian whistle? I had no idea.

Before I could give it deeper thought, a truck rumbled up the drive, snapping the morning wide open. I turned and watched as a Loblolly Lumber flatbed stacked high with cedar posts rolled up the drive, with Asa's blue truck bringing up the rear.

He climbed out, toolbox in hand, his calm energy already settling over the farm. Somehow, that steadiness of his reached me before his words did.

"Morning," he said, pushing his cap back. "Figured we'd get an early start."

"Early start on what?" I asked, baffled. I hadn't ordered lumber. Why was another white van pulling in behind Asa's truck? And why wasn't he at his grocery store on a Saturday morning—his busiest day? And, why hadn't he mentioned this visit when he left last night after sharing a bottle of wine on the porch?

"Poppy needs a proper round pen if she's gonna learn to ride correctly." He nodded toward the lumber truck easing to a stop behind him. "If we get started early, we should be able to knock it out in one day."

"What…" My stomach dipped. "Asa, I really can't—"

He held up a hand before I could finish. "If you want Poppy to learn how to ride, this is the quickest way." He turned and walked back toward the front porch. "I could really use a cup of coffee. I didn't have time to make a pot of coffee this morning."

"Asa," I said again, firmer, rushing to catch up with him. "Between the farm repairs, Mama's car on the verge of giving out, and the ancient farm tractor that might die any minute, I can't afford anything extra right now."

He leaned one arm on the porch railing, his smile easy. "Then it's a good thing you're not paying for it. Call it an early birthday present for Poppy."

"Her birthday's not for three months." My voice came out thin as an out-of-tune high note.

"Guess I'm just getting a head start for once."

Before I could argue, Poppy barreled up, grinning like she'd won the lottery. "Mr. Asa! Do I have a lesson this morning?"

"Not a lesson." He crouched. "But I heard a certain someone needed a place to practice her riding. Can't have you learning circles in the open field forever."

Poppy gasped. "A real ring? For me?"

"For you," he said, tapping her nose. "But you're gonna have to help me build it."

She nodded so hard her curls bounced. "I can help! Mama, can I help?"

I laughed despite myself. "Looks like you've already been recruited." I nodded toward the white van pulling in. "More men you're using?"

"Saturday's the only day I could talk Lloyd Penner out of his crew. Best construction crew in three counties."

Five men piled out. Now I could see how a round pen could be finished in one day.

---

The crew unloaded posts while Asa and the foreman laid out the ring with practiced precision, measuring each section like he was outlining a short story. Within an hour, they'd set all the posts and watered them in, then started on the fencing.

Poppy hadn't gotten around to changing into play clothes or brushing her teeth. Mama did insist she shove down a piece of toast, which she did so fast I wondered if her stomach noticed. She followed Asa around, carrying nails in her pockets and handing him tools—though she sometimes forgot which was which.

"You're mixing up the wrench and the pliers again," he told her gently.

"They both look grabby," she said, shrugging.

He laughed and rested his hole-digger against one of the already set post. "Well, I can't argue with that logic."

Watching them together, something in the air shifted—warm, familiar, unsettling in a way I couldn't quite name. I chalked it up to the sun or gratitude or the simple truth that seeing your child adored is enough to undo anyone. Especially when her father hadn't bothered with more than a couple of phone calls in three years.

When the posts were finally all set and the lumber stacked, I brought out a pitcher of sweet tea and lemonade, a platter of oatmeal cookies I'd made when I couldn't sleep a few nights ago, and a stack of plastic cups. Asa leaned against a post, sweat glistening at his temples, and took a long drink.

"Did you ever have one of these growing up?" Poppy asked, tracing the smooth wood.

I shook my head. "Not a chance. We made do with an old rope and a patch of grass. This"—I swept a hand at the growing circle—"is pure luxury."

"Your mama's right," Asa said, tightening a bolt. "Round pens teach balance, patience, trust. You learn to read the horse, and the horse learns to read you."

"And if I want to jump?" Poppy tilted her head and squinted—exactly the way Asa did when he asked a question he didn't know the answer to.

If my heart hadn't already been racing at the idea of her learning to jump, it might've leapt clean out of my chest at that expression. A perfect, uncanny echo of his.

I swallowed, forcing myself to focus on her words, not the odd little jolt beneath them. Kids copied the adults around them all the time. That was all this was. I was reading too much into it. Wanting a solid male figure in Poppy's life didn't mean I should go assigning Asa Griffin to the role. He was just being kind. He'd always been kind—with kids, with horses, with everyone.

"You want to learn to jump?" He winked at me, then turned to Poppy with a straight face. "Then you master this first. Every good jumper starts in a ring. If you can stay steady here, you can handle anything on a jumping course."

She nodded solemnly, like he'd just handed her a key to adulthood.

The smell of cedar and dust hung in the warm air, and I couldn't help thinking how right it all felt—the hammering, the laughter, the small, ordinary acts of kindness that stitched this place back together. This ring reminded me of the weekends I'd spent in the stands, watching Asa master his horse, winning more first-place ribbons than the bulletin board in my room could handle. Where were those ribbons now, I wondered. Likely in the attic with all my other memorabilia.

When the last rail went up, Asa wiped his hands on a rag and turned to me. "There. She's got herself a proper training ring."

I looked at the sturdy circle, sunlight glinting off new wood. "It's beautiful," I said softly. "You didn't have to—"

He met my eyes, something unspoken passing between us—tender and careful, like a first step on uncertain ground.

"I wanted to," he said simply.

Behind us, Poppy was already trotting slow circles with Sugar, her giggles carrying on the wind.

Inside the house, Mama watched through the kitchen window, a knowing smile tugging at her mouth.

"Stay for supper?" I asked.

He smiled. "Wouldn't say no to a home-cooked meal." He nodded toward Poppy. "Looks like she's primed for a quick lesson."

---

By supper, the smell of fried catfish and hush puppies drifted through the open windows. Mama had insisted on cooking, though I'd done most of the lifting and she most of the instructing. When Asa and Poppy knocked the dust off their boots and stepped inside, we waved them straight to the table.

"You can't work a man all day and send him home hungry," she declared.

"I wouldn't dare try," I muttered, setting hush puppies beside the coleslaw.

Mama smiled at me as if she knew a secret and motioned for him to sit beside me. "I told Maggie her gumbo last week was good, but this—this is comfort food."

Asa smiled over the rim of his tea glass. "I'm starting to see where she gets her bossiness."

Mama's laugh came quick and light. "Oh, she didn't inherit that from me. I'm as gentle as a lamb."

"That's one way to look at it," I said, and Poppy giggled so hard she almost spit her milk.

We talked about the orchard, pecan market prices, and how the new ring might help Sugar not tire so easily—though if Poppy got serious about jumping, we'd need a new horse. Nothing deep, nothing heavy. Just the kind of talk that felt like breathing.

After supper, Mama insisted on showing Asa the new flowerbed she'd designed from her chair. She bragged on my "green thumb," though she'd told me exactly what to plant and where.

"Don't let her fool you," she told him. "That girl could make dirt grow daisies."

Asa grinned. "I believe it."

Her matchmaking was more than a little obvious, but it made her happy. And Asa didn't seem embarrassed, so I let it be.

The porch light glowed amber when Asa and I stepped outside. Poppy chased fireflies in the yard, her laughter echoing in the dark.

"Girl needs a dog to play with," he said. "Might have to see about a puppy for her birthday."

"You've already built her a round pen for her birthday, and I don't need the burden of training a puppy on top of everything else." I leaned against the porch post, watching her cupped hands catch the flicker of light. "Maybe one day—but not now."

"Feels different around here," Asa said quietly.

I nodded. "Yeah. Feels alive again."

He looked at me a long moment. "Maybe it's not just the farm that's waking up."

The words caught me off guard. I glanced away at Poppy. "Maybe."

He didn't press—just smiled that easy, patient smile. "She's a lucky kid, you know. Not every little girl gets a mama willing to rebuild the world for her."

I swallowed hard. "Sometimes it feels like she's rebuilding my world for me."

He chuckled. "Yeah. That's called love."

I cut my gaze in his direction, and his ears pinked. The word must've slipped out. But I knew what he meant.

The backdoor slammed, and inside, Mama and Poppy laughed about something, and I thought maybe that sweet sound was enough for now—but beneath the calm, a worry lingered I couldn't quite define.

The farmhouse might've found its rhythm again.

But mine still skipped a few beats.

# Chapter Thirteen

## ASA

Asa stacked the last crate of tomatoes by the front display and straightened, rolling his shoulders to work the stiffness out of them. The store was quiet in that early-morning way he liked best—lights on, doors still locked, the hum of the coolers steady and dependable. It gave him time to think. Too much time, if he was honest.

He reached for another box, lining up a display of peaches beneath the hand-painted sign Mama Ellis had made years ago. Local. Fresh. Honest. He'd kept it even after she passed. Some things didn't need improving.

His thoughts, unfortunately, did.

Maggie had been standing in his mind since dawn—her laugh on the porch, the way she watched Poppy ride, careful and hopeful all at once. The same way she'd watched him later while they shared a bottle of wine he'd brought, just to stretch their time together. A habit he'd fallen into, and one he wasn't sure he should continue.

He recognized the look she'd passed him last night. He'd seen it in Paris too, during those two weeks he'd flown across the ocean and done the bravest, dumbest thing of his life.

He'd told her he loved her. Told her she was it for him. That he didn't think he could live without her. Then he'd stood there, waiting for her to say she was choosing him.

She hadn't. But she also hadn't pulled away. That had been the problem.

She'd said she loved him too—but she'd said it like a truth she couldn't act on. Like something precious she had to set carefully on a shelf while she went on living the life she wanted to build. Her career. Her writing fellowship that looked like it was going to be a permanent position. Paris. She'd tried to explain that her writing was like her breath, something she couldn't live without. And that her boss believed in her. And how hard that was to find in such a competitive industry. She couldn't pass up the opportunity to write for a renowned studio.

She hadn't asked him to stay.

Hadn't asked him to wait.

And she sure as hell hadn't offered to come back to Loblolly.

So he'd said the words he'd hoped might force a choice—that their relationship had to come to an end. That they should go their own way once and for all.

Asa lined up jars of green beans, labels facing forward, his hands moving on muscle memory. Maggie never did anything halfway. If she said she loved you, she meant it. But loving someone and choosing them were two different things. He'd learned that the hard way.

If she hadn't been willing to leave it all behind back then, over the last twelve years she'd worked too hard and come too far to toss it all aside now. He respected that—

even admired it. He just hadn't known how much it would cost him to have to accept it all over again.

Back then, when he'd come home, he'd told himself that loving her meant letting her go. That if she ever came back, it would have to be because she chose to—not because he'd made it easy, or tempting, or safe.

Now here she was again. Back on the farm. Back in his orbit. Close enough to touch.

Too close.

But the thing was, she wasn't back for him. He needed to remember that.

He shifted to the dry goods aisle, stacking flour and sugar, the same brands he'd ordered for years. Outside, the delivery truck pulled away, tires crunching gravel. Life moving forward, whether he was ready or not.

Maggie wasn't staying. She'd talked about plans and repairs for the farm, and it was all about now. She hadn't said she was giving up Paris. Hadn't said she was giving up her fancy job. And she sure as hell hadn't said she was choosing him.

He couldn't ask. Wouldn't ask.

He'd already put his heart on the line once. He knew without a doubt it wouldn't survive another leaving.

Asa paused with a case of green apples in his hands, the smell sharp and clean. Poppy's laugh floated into his thoughts, bright and unguarded. The way she trusted him without question. The way she looked at him like he was something solid.

That was the part that scared him too.

If Maggie went back to Paris—no, *when* she went back—he wasn't sure who he'd miss more: the woman who'd always felt like unfinished business, or the little girl who'd quietly carved out a place in his life he hadn't known was empty. He set the apples down carefully and wiped his hands on a towel.

---

Jed, his assistant, clicked the lock open, and the bell above the door chimed.

Customers would come in soon. Needing milk. Needing bread. Needing the ordinary things he knew how to provide.

Asa took a steadying breath and stepped behind the counter, resolved in the only way he knew how to be.

He would wait.

If Maggie came to him—truly, freely—he'd be here.

But he would not chase a woman who hadn't decided where she belonged, or worse, had decided where she belonged—and it was an ocean away.

No, not again.

# Chapter Fourteen

## MAGGIE

By midmorning, the sun had settled into that hazy warmth that makes a person second-guess outdoor chores, but I was already knee-deep in the new vegetable patch behind the barn. Mama had been on me all week to get an early fall crop planted—"the soil won't wait forever," she'd said—and since she was napping, I figured I'd surprise her by getting it tilled and ready before she woke.

Gardening had been my favorite chore growing up—a stretch of quiet hours where my hands worked the soil and my mind wandered freely, unburdened by rules or expectations. It was the one place I could live inside stories without the pressure of writing them down perfectly, or at all.

In my head, everything worked. The pacing never lagged, the dialogue landed exactly as it should, and no one ever questioned motivation. My male character was brave and fearless in the uncomplicated way heroes are when they've never been tested on the page; my female even braver, because she didn't need permission to be. Together they rode horses through open country, survived dangers I didn't yet know how to name, and always arrived exactly where they were meant to be.

I didn't understand then that this was storytelling in its purest form—instinctive, fearless, and blissfully ignorant of technique. I only knew that the rhythm of pulling weeds and turning earth gave my imagination room to stretch, and that the stories came easily because no one was watching. Years later, after I'd learned about structure and stakes and the thousand ways a sentence can go wrong, I would miss that simplicity. But I've come to realize I was practicing even then, learning to trust the voice in my head long before I learned how to put it on the page.

The earth was dark and soft beneath my hoe, smelling of last night's rain and the hope of renewal. I'd just finished clearing the last of the crabgrass when tires crunched on the gravel drive.

Tally's little white Tesla rolled into view, glinting in the sun. She waved from behind the windshield and climbed out, her long curls tamed beneath a bright pink head scarf that somehow looked fabulous with her aqua tunic and yoga pants. She had a manila folder tucked under one arm.

"That's exactly what I should be doing," she called.

"Gardening?" I brushed dirt from my knees. "You have a bistro to run."

"A bistro that needs fresh herbs. I tried growing them on my patio, but it turned into a disaster."

"I'm planting a whole row of herbs," I said. "We'll have plenty to share in six weeks."

"That would be fabulous."

"If you're here to recruit me for another PTA committee, I'm gonna need a signing bonus."

She laughed—though not her usual belly laugh. More a small sound that faded quickly. "Not just another committee. This is official business—homeroom mother business. Halloween party planning."

"Ah. Vital work." I laughed, then gathered my tools and placed them in a plastic bucket. "Let me wash up, pour some lemonade, and catch my breath."

A few minutes later, we settled on the porch—my bare feet on the rail, two tall glasses sweating on the table between us. The orchard shimmered beyond the yard, gold and green, most of the weeds finally under control thanks to Asa hiring a crew who filled in when work got slow. Turns out six men working a couple of hours in the afternoon could whip an orchard into shape pretty fast. For a while, Tally and I just sat, the easy silence of two women who genuinely enjoyed each other's company.

"So," I said eventually. "What's the grand plan for this party?"

She smiled faintly. "You'd think organizing twenty-three second-graders for cupcakes and juice boxes would be simple, but…" Her voice drifted off.

"But it's not," I teased—then stopped. She had that faraway look. From my limited interactions with her, it seemed very un-Tally. "What's wrong?"

She blinked, as if trying to shake something loose. "It's nothing."

I lowered my feet from the banister and turned toward her. "We may not have known each other long, but I'm a good listener. And a vault." I drew an X over my chest. "Promise."

Her fingers traced the condensation on her glass, then wiped it away, only to start again.

"I'm just trying to figure something out." She attempted a smile, the kind that didn't quite hold. "It's complicated."

"I'm good with complicated," I said gently. "I've had a bit of practice."

She shifted in her chair, the movement small but restless, and looked past me toward the orchard. The night breeze lifted a strand of hair she didn't bother tucking back. Whatever she was carrying didn't read as frustration—it sat closer to the surface than that. Uneasy. Alert.

"It's my ex-boyfriend," she said. After a pause, "Royce." Just saying his name seemed to cost her something.

"What about him?" I asked.

"I thought he was out of my life." Her hand finally stilled on the glass. "But last week, he found me."

I slid my feet to the floor, turned in her direction. "What do you mean by found you? Found you how?"

"He called the restaurant. Asked for the owner, Tally Benton." Her fingers moved to her lap, curled, then loosened again. "So he knows I'm married. Knows I own the place." She swallowed. "He told my hostess he was passing through Savannah—and wanted to see his daughter."

She hesitated, eyes dropping for a moment. "He's never laid eyes on Lola. Not once." She raised her gaze, focused her gaze at the orchard. "And now he's tracked me to Loblolly and playing an interest in Lola."

"Maybe if you just talk to him—"

She shook her head. "No. I know him. He'll breeze in and act like there's no bad blood between us. He wants something, and he'll use Lola to get it." Her eyes glistened. "He's underhanded. He's quick to say he loves you. But I have photos that prove what kind of love he's capable of." She exhaled unsteadily. "Back in Savannah, Joleen insisted I file them with the restraining order."

"If you have a restraining order—"

"Expired years ago. And Royce never cared about that kind of thing anyway."

A cold pull settled beneath my ribs. "Have you told Caleb?"

She nodded. "Yes. He's furious—said he'd handle it if Royce came sniffing around. But you know Caleb. Calm on the surface, storm underneath. And Royce usually makes it ugly when he doesn't get his way."

"Does he know Caleb adopted Lola?"

"He doesn't even know Lola's name. After he bolted, I never tried to find him." She rubbed her arms. "Caleb and I went through all the legal channels after we married—filed for abandonment, finalized everything. Lola was three then. He's been her daddy ever since. She knows nothing about Royce, and I want it to stay that way."

I took her hand. "She has everything she needs, Tally. A daddy who adores her and a mama who'd fight the devil himself to protect her."

She squeezed back. "I just can't shake the feeling he's here to cause trouble. Maybe he's broke. Maybe he's jealous. Royce could always smell other people's happiness like blood in the water."

The orchard seemed to still around us.

"Do you want me to ask Asa to keep an eye out?" I offered. "He knows everyone in the county."

"I already did," she said. "Him and Jackson. Caleb pulled a couple mugshots too." Her shoulders sagged. "I'm sorry to dump all this on you. Normally I'd talk to Joleen, but she's out of town."

"You're not dumping anything. I'm glad you told me. Text or call anytime—day or night."

That earned a soft laugh, and for a while, we talked about

normal things—school projects, what treats to make for the Halloween party, how the year was flying by. When she finally left, the worry in her eyes had eased but not disappeared.

"Call me if he so much as sends a text," I said walking her to her car.

"I will. Thank you." She hugged me tight, like a friend—which I realized we were. I stood in the driveway until her taillights disappeared. The orchard rustled softly in front of me. But the peace I'd felt earlier had shifted.

Later that evening, while setting the table with Mama, I said, "Tally's worried her ex-boyfriend Royce might come around. Caleb's says he'll handle it, but she's scared Royce will stir up trouble."

Mama shook her head. "Some men can't stand to see what they threw away turn out just fine without them."

"Yeah, I know men like that." I shrugged. "Honestly, I know a few women who fit that bill as well."

"Tally's lucky to have Caleb. And you're lucky to have Asa and this farm keeping you steady."

I didn't bother correcting her. After all these weeks of talking and eating and easing back into each other's orbit, Asa hadn't once reached for more. It stung, but I couldn't fault him. I'd broken his heart before—more than once.

Mama seemed convinced we'd slipped easily back into our old rhythm. But I knew Asa well enough to recognize restraint when I saw it. He was holding himself in check. And I understood why.

After supper, once Poppy was in bed, I sat on the porch steps, letting the evening wind cool the day from my skin. A night bird called from the orchard, low and sweet.

Tally's worry had stirred something in me—an uneasiness I usually kept tightly pressed down.

My situation was different, yes. But familiar enough to make my heart thump uneasily.

Julian had never been abusive or reckless. Just… careless. Careless in that effortless, drifting way of men who assume the world will always catch them.

When he ran off to Switzerland with the wealthy widow, he'd promised to *see Poppy often.* That promise never materialized.

Years earlier, when I'd found myself pregnant in a foreign country—tired, overwhelmed, and staring down choices I never imagined—I'd let Julian's certainty steady me. I allowed myself to lean into his vision of our future because it was easier than unraveling the alternative. He offered marriage, stability, a clear path… all the things that made sense when nothing else did.

And when he offered to stay home with the baby so my career wouldn't derail, I'd clung to that practicality like a lifeline.

Maybe that's why I let it slide when I suspected he had affairs.

Why I never pushed for child support.

Why I handed him the divorce terms he wanted.

I knew Julian well enough to understand that responsibility—real responsibility—only registered with him when it aligned neatly with the *now* life he wanted. He could be attentive, even devoted, for a time. But permanence seemed to make him restless. Long term commitment, at least with me, asked more than he was willing to give.

Lately, I'd wondered if, offered the chance to step away cleanly from Poppy's life—no expectations, no obligations—he'd take it without blinking.

The idea should have made me furious.

Instead, it left me tired. Bone-deep tired.

And—if I was honest—relieved.

Not because I didn't want Poppy to have a father. She deserved a steady, devoted one. But Julian didn't seem capable of that kind of long-lasting love. Maybe that's why I was a little off-kilter with Asa in Poppy's day-to-day life—and why Tally's news this afternoon hit too close to home.

This morning—completely out of the blue—Julian had texted.

*Heard you and Poppy are in Loblolly,* he'd written.

*How long are you staying?*

I'd stared at the screen, unsettled more by the casual familiarity than the question itself. Small talk had never been Julian's style. He didn't check in. He swept through, made declarations, then disappeared again.

Still, I'd answered lightly. Vaguely. Nothing he could grab hold of.

And the thought of him breezing back into Poppy's life like Tally's ex was trying to do—full of charm, spinning stories of European villas—made me wish Julian would remain aloof and out of her life. Lord knew he could turn a woman's head when he wanted to. And Poppy adored her Papa.

I stared into the darkness beyond the fence, cicadas humming their endless tune.

Tally had Caleb—a man who'd stood up and stayed. She had roots now, and fears that made sense. Mine were different. Julian seemed to have no desire to be in Poppy's day-to-day life, and I doubted he ever would.

Julian would never trade his jet-setting life—or his Viscountess—and show up in Loblolly. He'd seen Poppy three times in two years, and calling those visits *brief* was generous. A coffee. A hug. A promise to call. Always late, always somewhere he needed to be.

Whatever the text meant, it wasn't a prelude to anything important—likely just boredom until the next fun thing came along.

---

Poppy never asked about him anymore. It was beyond me how a parent could abandon their child without a backward glance. I'd long ago swallowed my anger and thanked God for the life we'd made in Paris.

Yet under the slow rise of the moon, I knew the truth: peace—like a well-written love story—was fragile. One wrong chapter, and everything could come undone.

I took a slow sip of wine and adopted one of Mama's favorite quotes:

*Some worries, like weeds, weren't worth watering.*

So I let the thought of Julian go—for now—and listened to the steady hum of crickets and the whispering orchard. On the edges of my mind, memories of Asa lingered, comforting and distant all at once.

Then, unbidden, a moment from this afternoon surfaced—Poppy in the passenger seat of Mama's car, her face tilted toward the trees as we passed through the orchard.

"This farm feels like it remembers me."

An odd way for a child to describe coming home.

Especially since Asa used to say almost the exact same thing about his family's land.

*There you go again, Maggie McAllister—connecting dots that aren't there.*

Kids say poetic things all the time. All. The. Time.

Still… my heart fluttered with the wishful idea.

For a foolish, breath-long moment, I let myself wonder

how different everything might have been if Asa and I hadn't been quite so careful during those two whirlwind weeks in Paris. If timing and distance and responsibility hadn't gotten in the way.

But I shut the thought down the way I always did—cleanly, firmly—because wanting something that deeply when the man himself was now in the same town felt dangerous. My heart wasn't built to survive that kind of dreaming.

The night wrapped around me like an old quilt worn, familiar, and for this moment, having Asa in our lives, steady and kind to both me and my daughter—even if only as a friend—was enough.

# Chapter Fifteen

## MAGGIE

By the time the sun lifted over the pecan grove the next morning, Mama had me—and my first cup of coffee—out in the orchard, leaning on her cane like a field marshal inspecting her troops.

"Those lower branches need pruning," she said, eyeing the row nearest the house. "You let them droop that way and you'll invite blight."

"That's why I had Jed spray for blight last week." If she heard me, she didn't care to admit it.

I stood a few yards behind her, coffee in hand, watching her fuss and scold as if the trees could hear her. "You know they can't apologize, right?"

"They don't need to apologize," she said, squaring her shoulders. "They just need to do better."

It had become her routine since she'd shed the crutches—a slow shuffle through the orchard each morning, one hand on her cane, the other brushing the limbs as though the bark itself held conversation. It wasn't hard to see the truth of it—the orchard had become her therapy.

She lectured those trees like old friends who'd let her down and were now working to earn back her trust. And to my surprise, the more she talked, the stronger she grew.

"Watch yourself." I jumped forward, grabbing her arm to steady her. "The ground isn't even. I stepped in a gopher hole the other day."

"I'm fine," she said, swatting me away. "I've been working this land and pruning trees longer than you've been walking."

"Not since your fall and heart scare," I reminded her. She didn't like me to call it a heart attack—she preferred scare, as if not naming it lessened its weight. It didn't matter; my nagging did no good. Fussing over these trees she thought of as children gave her purpose.

I kept within a step or two as she walked. She rewarded my attentiveness with a sideways glare that used to silence entire classrooms when she taught high school English. "Don't crowd me."

"I'm not."

"And don't sass me either, young lady. Recovery isn't about rest—it's about motion."

I sighed, but my chest swelled with affection. Truth was, she was getting better. Seeing her reclaim her life gave me pride and peace—and most of all, hope that she'd be back to normal soon. Somewhere deep inside, I knew my days of indecision about the future were numbered. And to be honest, nowadays, that gave me the most unease.

When Mama tired and went inside for her morning rest, I sat down at my laptop. For weeks, I'd avoided it—afraid the magic I'd always found in writing had died. But this morning, something inside me whispered that it was time to try again.

I laid my fingers across the keyboard. My right hand still

trembled, stubborn and stiff, but I started with a simple email to Katrina. Slow. Asking how things were. If she'd made all her deadlines. How her love life was coming along.

My finger didn't work perfectly, but it didn't curl and send shooting pains either. At first, it stumbled, and I struck the wrong key, but as I kept going, my fingers began to feel natural and move without thought. My words tumbled out, a little faster than my fingers could move—but it was progress.

For the first time since the doctor issued his diagnosis, my troubled finger didn't feel foreign. I spent the rest of the day, off and on, at my computer, looking over the last script Katrina had sent, one she said she still hadn't figured out. I took long breaks but always came back, stretching my fingers, excercising my hand just as the doctor had ordered, before sitting down to work.

Not perfect. Not yet.

But close enough to remind me who I was.

I just needed a daily regimen—mornings for farm chores, free time in the afternoons and evenings devoted to my writing.

---

The next morning, after Poppy left for school, I called Katrina.

"Maggie!" Katrina exclaimed, her French accent lilting through the line. "Mon dieu, it is so good to hear your voice! Comment ça va, ma chère?"

"I'm healing," I said. "Better every day. I've started writing again. In fact, I worked late into the night on the problem script you sent me a couple of days ago."

I could almost hear her sigh of relief. "Ah, tu me rassures," she said—you reassure me. "I was beginning to worry you had given up on writing for good."

"For a while, I wondered, too," I laughed. "But it seems my hand and my heart had other plans."

"You must not rush," she said. "But can I tell Claire you are back at the keyboard. She will be ravie—so delighted! We have a new series on the drawing board as you say, and I have three scripts on my desk in need of your special touch. Not to mention the actors." She sighed, "Peter and Violet, claim no one can capture their voice like you. Violet cried yesterday—threw one of her tantrums. You remember—you were the only one who could calm her."

"I know." I hesitated, the weight of returning settling heavy on my chest. Paris again. Writing. Demanding schedules. Demanding actors. Demanding producers. I'd dreamed of returning for months, waking with excitement coursing through my veins from the perfect fix I'd dreamt about. "I'll let you know in a few days if my hand stands up to the rigors of daily work," I said. "Send me a few easy scripts and let's see what I can do."

"Mon Dieu—easy scripts. There are none—you know this better than me. Oh, ma chère amie," Katrina replied softly—my dear friend. "If you are writing again, then perhaps the worst is behind you, yes?"

"I hope so," I said.

"So, I'll let Violet know to expect you soon. Anything to dry her tears."

When our call ended, I sat staring through the window at the orchard. The trees swayed in the breeze, gold light spilling between them like forgiveness. Maybe Katrina was right. Maybe the worst really was behind me.

I set my cell aside and turned from the window, opening the ledger on the kitchen table. Reality rushed in at tsunami force.

The farm budget I'd worked out was a patchwork of optimism and subtraction. Roof repairs, irrigation parts, replacement trees, fertilizer, fuel—it all added up. The balance at the bottom of the page glared at me, a merciless reminder that I would run through most of my savings by the end of the month.

I leaned back in the chair, rubbing the ache between my eyes. The farm had no debt, but keeping it afloat while Mama recovered meant every dollar I'd tucked away in Paris was bleeding out faster than I could replenish it. Julian had taken half our savings and stock portfolio in the divorce, even though he'd contributed nothing to those accounts. And I'd even bought out his half-interest in our apartment. I'd agreed to his demands just to end it—to be rid of him and start fresh. I thought I'd be fine. I could always make more money. No problem.

How foolish I'd been.

I flipped to the next page—my personal accounts. The Paris apartment seemed a guilty indulgence. I loved that space: the high ceilings, the balcony overlooking Rue de Turenne, the late afternoon light that turned the walls to honey. It had been my refuge after long hours away on location—a quiet pocket above the city noise.

But sentiment didn't pay bills.

If I sold it, I could finish the renovations here, buy Mama a new car, and have enough left over to cushion Poppy and me in Paris for six months. When we returned, we could simply rent—a smaller place, maybe closer to her new school.

I smiled at the thought. A fresh start. Our own space. No ghosts trailing through the rooms.

Loblolly was beautiful—grounding, even—but it wasn't forever. I could already feel Paris tugging again, soft and persistent as a story I couldn't shake.

That evening, I made dinner while Mama sat at the table shelling last year's pecans from the freezer. Poppy had requested her favorite pie, and Mama was quick to oblige her only grandchild.

"Some call shelling pecans slave labor," she teased—a familiar complaint from my childhood.

"You love shelling pecans," I said, repeating her response to my childhood bellyaching, as she called it. "You just like to complain while you do it."

We both chuckled at the memory.

We ate our dinner by the open window, the warm air thick with honeysuckle, Mama's pie cooling on the sill. The sweet scent of desert carried me back to childhood summers—bare feet on cool kitchen tile, cicadas buzzing outside, Mama humming while the ceiling fan turned slow and steady.

We talked about replanting the wildflower strip—her idea—and hiring help for harvest season—mine. Her face had color again; her hands moved with purpose as she spoke. The orchard was healing her as much as I ever could.

After she went to bed, I poured a glass of wine and took it out to the porch, settling into one of the rockers. The night hummed with crickets—steady and sure. I'd always loved that sound, the unseen life in the orchard continuing even when you weren't listening.

The numbers from the farm ledger kept floating through my mind, colliding with thoughts of Paris—the apartment, the office, the smell of espresso drifting from the café below my balcony. It was a world away from this one, but it was still mine.

If Mama hired a farm manager, she could spend part of the year in Paris with us. I could already picture it—her seated by the window, complaining about the traffic but secretly loving the attention of the local grocer who would call her Madame Barbara. She'd grumble, of course, but she'd come alive there too.

Poppy would adapt quickly—she always did. New school, new friends, a nanny to help keep our lives running smoothly.

We'd make it work.

I stared out across the fields where the moonlight painted the orchard in shades of silver. The branches swayed gently, like old hands waving approval.

It all made sense. Paris had been our life. Loblolly was just a pause.

So why did it ache to imagine leaving?

My mind wandered to Asa—the easy way he filled the porch with laughter, the steadiness of his voice, the quiet kindness that slipped in when no one else was watching. The thought made something inside me twist.

I needed to be honest with myself. If Asa had wanted more, he'd have said so by now. He'd had every chance.

He just wanted friendship. That's all.

And friendship was fine—safe, predictable, uncomplicated.

Still, as the night settled deeper around the farmhouse, I couldn't help hearing his voice in my head, that slow drawl when he'd said, *Maybe it's not just the farm that's waking up.*

I took a long sip of wine, ignoring the way my heart tightened.

"We were not in high school, and Asa was no longer head over heels about me," I said aloud, as if the orchard needed convincing. "And that's okay."

The trees made no argument—only the soft rustle of leaves, steady and forgiving.

Inside my head, the faintest thought began to rise, an idea for the new series Katrina had emailed about. A farm, a second chance love affair. It sounded all so familiar.

I suddenly pictured the scene and watched it come to life in my mind, and it felt like breathing again. I held onto it, surprised by the quiet thrill of it. For weeks now, my thoughts had been crowded with worry—Mama's heart, the orchard, the fear that my life was slipping out of alignment, that I'd somehow stepped off the track I'd worked so hard to build.

But maybe nothing was broken. Maybe I'd only paused.

Paris waited for me. My career, Katrina and Clarie, even my beautiful apartment all waited. The life I'd built page by page—long days, early mornings, the travel and the temperamental actors—all brought me a particular satisfaction of belonging to something exacting and alive. It wasn't a fantasy or a postcard version of success. It was real, solid, earned. A life any writer would be proud of.

Loblolly would still be here. The farm. My friends, new and old. I'd come back for breaks, for holidays, for the quiet that refilled me. And on holidays, I'd bring Mama home—let her sit on the porch, let Poppy run the fields she loved so fiercely.

The thought sent a small, unmistakable tingle through my chest—excitement, not fear. The idea of stepping fully back into my life, of going out more, meeting people, letting the Parisian life I'd carved out for Poppy and me carry us forward again. With Mama there, it could be bigger and better than before.

The orchard sighed, the wind moving through its branches like applause.

And for the first time in a long while, I let myself believe that both of us—the farm and me—might just be coming back to life.

# Chapter Sixteen

## MAGGIE

Friday morning came bright and soft, the kind of light that made the kitchen tile look newly scrubbed even when it wasn't. It was a school holiday—a teacher workday—and I'd agreed to watch Lola for Tally. Poppy was ecstatic.

I had a batch of warm blueberry yeast rolls and bacon cooling on a paper towel when I heard a car door shut and Poppy's delighted "Lola!" float down from her bedroom upstairs. No doubt she was hanging halfway out her window, waving.

Joleen knocked on the screen door and stepped into the foyer—hair twisted up, sunglasses pushed onto her head, Lola's backpack slung over her shoulder. Lola barreled straight past her, meeting Poppy at the bottom of the stairs. The two of them launched toward the backyard as if they were training for a relay. Sugar's optimistic whinny drifted from the pasture, as if she knew she'd be adored today.

"Morning," I said, wiping my hands. "You came bearing chaos, I see."

"Free-range chaos," Joleen said, smiling. Then the smile

softened at the edges. "Lola spent the night with us—insisted on showing Jackson how to make chocolate-chip pancakes shaped like hearts. He pretended disdain to eat chocolate for dinner and then made a second batch after she went to bed."

"That sounds like him."

"It does." She took in the kitchen—the cooling racks, the colander of blueberries, the butter softening in a small dish—and let out a breath that sounded like she'd been holding it since yesterday. "You got a minute?"

"Always." I slid a plate of rolls onto the table. "Eat first. Confess second."

She bit into one, eyes closing. "Okay, that's illegal."

"I won't tell if you won't."

She set the roll down and folded her hands like she was in a courtroom about to ask for leniency. "I need female perspective."

"Okay." I picked up a roll and pinched off half. "I can do that."

"I got the call. The promotion I've been waiting on—the D.C. division. It's everything I've worked for." Her voice didn't lift on the last word; it sank. "This promotion is big but requires travel three weeks out of four. It's a once-in-a-career thing."

"And yet, from your tone, you seem to have reservations," I said gently.

"Maybe." She glanced out the window, where Lola and Poppy were already dragging the mounting block toward the fence for an improvised stage. "There's another piece."

I waited.

"You know the big case Jackson had—the one that ended yesterday? The woman who laundered money through her boss's business?" Her jaw tightened, anger and pity braided together. "Her husband died, and evidently she reworked the company accounts when one of her kids got sick and she couldn't afford to keep the lights on. Then when she needed more—or maybe simply got used to having more—she turned into the cartel's errand runner. Now the feds have her cold on racketeering. Mandatory minimum—fifteen years."

My stomach dipped. "Kids?"

"Three." She released a long sigh. "A nine-year-old girl and twin boys—two. No family, or at least none willing to step up for the kids."

"That's terrible. Truly. But what does it have to do with your promotion? I'm not connecting the dots, unless …"

She nodded. "Yeah. Last night Jackson mentioned we could foster the kids for a while to keep them out of the system. Just until we can find a family who can take them permanently."

The timing felt cruel—everything arriving at once, demanding answers that didn't belong in the same hour.

"Wow. Three kids at one time—and twin boys." I chuckled. "It's a lot."

She rubbed the space between her brows as if staving off a headache. "He tried to sound casual, but I've been married to him long enough to know when he's moved past thinking to deciding. He wants to step in. He offered to hire a full-time nanny so I wouldn't have to adjust my travel schedule or turn down the promotion."

"And you?" I asked. "What do you want?"

"I want—" She stopped. "I want both. The job and the temporary family. I actually want to start our own family, but that gets complicated with all my travel."

I sat with that for a moment, remembering what it was like to worry that a baby might change your career. "You can have both. My job requires traveling to locations all over Europe. I've traveled Poppy's entire life. It does require a nanny to shift chaos into order, but if Jackson's willing …"

"See, that's the thing. I don't want the version of having kids where I kiss a forehead on Sunday night and reappear Friday with a suitcase and exhaustion. Raising three kids, even temporarily, on the weekends won't cut it. Not a nine-year-old who just lost her mother to prison and her father to death—and not for toddlers who won't understand anything except who shows up when they cry." She paused. "It sounds small, but it isn't. It's the whole thing—who is there when the door closes."

The backyard erupted in laughter. We glanced through the window at Lola bowing with grave theatrics and Poppy clapping like a tiny impresario. Joleen watched them, and the look on her face told me she already knew the shape of her own answer, even if she didn't like its edges.

"Jackson pretends not to push me," she said quietly. "He says it like it's an invitation—*We could*—only if you want to. But I can hear the wanting under it. I can feel mine, too."

"Ambition, marriage, and family life," I said. "It's a tricky braid."

She huffed a small laugh. "Says the woman deciding between a coveted writing position, motherhood, and a farm."

I smiled faintly. "I had a call from my writing partner, Katrina, yesterday. She knows I'm writing again. She won't be able to keep herself from checking in every day. She's ecstatic, and her excitement pushes me to keep pushing myself."

Joleen turned back to me, eyes bright. "Mags, that's … that's awesome."

"It's something," I said. "I'm starting to create again, so that's good."

I knew the balance she was trying to establish. I was living inside it.

She reached for another biscuit, broke it open, but didn't eat it. "The thing is, like you, I love my work. I'm good at it. The promotion means I'd be at the table where decisions shape which high-level cases to take on—not just clean up whatever lands on your desk."

She rubbed her thumb along a butter smear on her plate. "But these kids … I lay awake last night thinking about their breakfast and their lunch boxes. Who will feed them? Who will stand in the bathroom doorway and coach tooth-brushing? Who will tuck them in at night or rock the two-year-olds when they're too tired to sleep? It sounds small, but it isn't. It's the magic of life."

"You can be brilliant at both," I said. "But maybe not at the same time."

She smiled—the kind of smile that acknowledges a truth and forgives it. "Jackson said something like that. He also said if I wanted the job, he'd take point at home without blinking."

"And you believe him," I said.

"With my life," she replied softly. "That's what makes it harder. He'd give up his dream to make sure we have a family."

The girls tumbled back inside, all elbows and declarations, claiming thirst. We handed out lemonades in plastic cups and endured a detailed recounting of Sugar's opinions on stage hustles. After the parade moved outdoors again, quiet folded around us.

"I'll figure it out," Joleen said at last, standing. "I just …

needed to say it out loud to someone who wouldn't make it about a scoreboard."

I hugged her. "You'll make a good decision because you'll make it with thought and a heart filled with love."

She squeezed back, then let go with a briskness that said if she stayed she might not keep the tears swimming in her eyes from falling, and headed for the door. "Caleb's supposed to pick Lola up mid-afternoon. Tell Asa his pen thingy"—she pointed toward the round pen—"looks amazing. Not sure what it's for, but it looks great."

"You're such a city girl," I said, laughing. "Thanks for dropping off Lola—and call me anytime to talk."

It dawned on me that I had no friends in Paris who stopped by for coffee, morning rolls, and a chat about their lives. I wasn't sure what that meant, but I did know my heart felt fuller.

When the house settled again, I cleaned up plates and thought about braids—how you blend strands and hope they hold without strangling the scalp. The kettle ticked as it cooled. The orchard light shifted, that late-morning gold that makes everything look both finished and beginning.

The phone rang.

Katrina's name lit the screen.

"Bonjour, Maggie," she sang. "I promised to be brief, and for once, I will keep it. How is the hand this morning?"

"Better" I said. "I'm actually typing slowly for an hour without pain."

"Très bien. Delacourt asked for an update last night in person." Delacourt was the head of our studio. "I ran into him at a dinner party. He is a man of few words and many eyebrow movements, but both went up in the hopeful direction."

I laughed. "I remember that direction."

A small pause, and her tone shifted subtly, like a bow angling on a string. "A small note, *ma chère*. Not urgent, but … relevant. Julian rang the office."

The name brushed past my ear like a cold draft from a door I thought was shut.

"What did he want?"

"He asked—very casually—if I had heard whether you planned to return to Paris any time soon. He mentioned running into a one of your friends who told him you had writer's block and couldn't work." Katrina's voice was silk wrapped around steel. "Not such a great friend if that was the story they're telling. I told as much to Julian, then told him you had an injury that is healing, and any plans to return to Paris are yours to share when you are ready."

My fingers tightened on the counter's edge. "Thank you."

"You're welcome. I do not like when men collect information they haven't earned." A beat. "If you wish, I can be … less polite next time."

"No," I said, letting out a breath. "Polite is fine. Distance is better."

"Then distance he shall have." Her lightness returned. "Write, rest, and call me when you're ready to collaborate on the problem series. If you keep this pace, you'll be back at your desk within a month."

"From your mouth to God's ears," I muttered.

We said our goodbyes, and I set my phone down as carefully as if it were glass already cracked. The kitchen ticked and hummed the way old kitchens do. Outside, the girls' voices rose and fell, the swing's chain squeaking on its appointed note.

I pulled the ledger toward me, pencil sharpened to honesty. The numbers were still numbers—glaring and undeniable. I confirmed that by month's end, my savings would be dangerously low. The repairs had eaten more than I'd originally planned. The orchard was coming back to life, but it was thirsty and still had a ways to go.

Sell the Paris apartment. Renovate the last of the farmhouse. A car for Mama that didn't beg for mercy every start. Return to Paris and find a smaller place to rent—something sunlit and simple near Poppy's school. I'd have to hire a nanny, so things might be financially tight for a while. But we'd have our own apartment, our own rooms, our own things—a beginning that didn't carry the echo of old choices. And I had to somehow convince Mama to come along.

And just like that, my imaginary little apartment was growing: a nanny's room, a guest room, a bedroom and bath for Mama.

I wrote the numbers in a neat column and circled them. Then I flipped to a clean page and wrote, in smaller letters: *farm manager*. I could hear Mama arguing all the way from the front room, but I'd noticed how her voice softened at supper these days—the way she said *we* more often than *I*.

We could find someone steady. I could convince her to split her time between Loblolly and Paris. She could come back with us, complain about the price of butter in euros, and charm the fromagerie into a discount within a week.

Mama in Paris wasn't impossible. Only unfamiliar.

The screen door clacked, and Poppy's head popped in. "Can we take the basket to the porch and have snack like a picnic?"

"Absolutely," I said. "Apples and peanut butter?"

"And four cookies," she bargained.

"Two," I said.

She grinned. "Deal."

I packed the basket and watched her carry it out, careful with the balance, serious as a waitress. Lola crowned her with a pecan leaf and pronounced her Queen of Snacks. The title seemed accurate.

The rest of the day unspooled in small, good ribbons: the sound of Sugar's hooves in the paddock, a breeze that kept the worst of the heat honest, Mama's voice from the sofa instructing me to "stop fussing with the hammock she'd asked me to put up and sit in it like a person." I tested it. It held.

Joleen came back for Lola later, said Caleb had gotten tied up at the station. Her eyes looked clearer—the decisive kind of calm that follows a storm that's chosen a direction.

"You look as if you've wrestled your indecision into submission." I said, handing her Lola's backpack.

"I have," she said. "I told the D.C. director I needed seventy-two hours to decide on the promotion. And I told Jackson we should go meet the kids."

"Both good calls," I said.

"At least I'll know which ache I'm choosing," she whispered, more to herself than to me. "I figure if it's meant to be, I could ask for a ninety-day leave. That should be enough time to find a suitable home for the kids. Jackson agreed it should be enough. So that's our new plan."

After she and Lola left, the house went loose and quiet again. I found myself at my computer without deciding to be there. My left hand was almost normal—not perfect, but close. The story I'd been coaxing all week found a new curve. It wasn't perfect yet, a little stubborn. I respected stubborn.

When the last sentence formed, I let my hands fall to my lap and stared out at the orchard. The light had gone molten, the trunks lit on one side as if the day had pressed a kiss on each.

Julian's name tried to enter the room again. I set it outside and locked the door. It rattled once. Then went quiet.

Returning to the studio, working with Katrina—it all looked possible. So did selling the apartment in Paris. So did loving the farm enough to stay. And so did letting go.

I thought of Asa then. Uninvited, but unavoidable—the round pen, the way he steadied Poppy's knee without making a sermon of it, the quiet he brought into a room as if he'd traded for it somewhere and wanted to share. A soft hope uncoiled, then folded itself back up.

The phone call he'd made that afternoon—asking if I wanted to see the new movie, maybe grab a bite to eat. Chastising me for never leaving the farm, saying I needed a break. Chastising meant friendship, nothing more. I'd said yes immediately. Now, I needed to temper my heart, remind it that friendship was solid and good and peaceful.

Be honest, I told myself. If he wanted more, he'd have said so by now—or maybe he was waiting for permission I hadn't given.

*Friendship is good,* I answered. *It doesn't ask for what it won't keep.*

# Chapter Seventeen

## MAGGIE

By midafternoon, the heat had eased into something almost merciful. The air still held the day's warmth, but a thin breeze moved through the pecan trees, rattling their leaves just enough to sound like distant applause. As a child, I imagined the trees were my personal audience for storytelling. I'd walk through the orchard, making up places and people, whole lives from nothing—it seemed at my story's end a breeze would stir the branches, the leaves rustling like applause.

"I've missed the farm. Until Poppy and I came back, I didn't realize just how much."

Mama and I sat on the porch with a big metal bowl between us, snapping green beans for Sunday lunch. She always made them the night before so we could eat as soon as we got home from church. The soft pop of the stems as we broke them set a quiet rhythm, steady and familiar, easing my nerves into something closer to peace.

Out in the new round pen, Asa worked with Poppy and Sugar.

"Sit deep, sweetheart," he called, his voice carrying just enough to reach us. "Let your heels drop. There you go."

Poppy's shoulders softened, her little body following Sugar's motion like she'd been riding her whole life instead of a handful of weeks. Every now and then she'd throw her head back and laugh—pure, unfiltered joy drifting across the yard.

Mama flicked a snapped end into the discard bowl. "That man's got a gift with horses."

And with little girls, I thought, but didn't say.

Sugar circled the pen, her chestnut coat glistening. Asa walked in the center with the lunge line loose in his hand, posture relaxed but attentive, as natural there as breathing.

"You're smiling," Mama said lightly. "That's not your usual 'the roof is leaking' expression."

"I smile," I muttered.

"Mm-hm." Snap. "Now and then."

In the ring, Poppy's posture shifted. Sugar picked up speed, and my spine locked.

"Careful," I whispered, though I knew Asa had it.

He lifted a hand, his voice low and even. "Breathe, Poppy. Let your breath catch up."

The words struck like a stone in still water. He'd said the same thing to me a hundred times in high school—before an exam, waiting for acceptance letters for college, my driving test, my valedictorian speech on graduation night.

And Poppy… she listened to him. Her little body eased. Her shoulders dropped. Sugar calmed.

"You're braver than you think," Asa said gently. "Just let your breath catch up to you."

Poppy straightened, nodded slowly—the exact way Asa always did when weighing something important.

A strange jolt shot through me.

Too small to name.

Too sharp to ignore.

Mama paused mid-snap. "You all right, sweetie?"

"Fine," I rushed my answer.

"Mm." She didn't seem convinced.

Asa moved Poppy and Sugar through more exercises—circles, halts, transitions. Then Poppy brought Sugar to the rail, stopped the mare, and lifted her arms for Asa to help her down.

She wrapped her arms around his waist without hesitation. He ruffled her hair with a soft smile that unspooled something tight in my chest.

Too much.

All at once.

Mama set her beans aside. "Let's go in. Let those two cool Sugar down without an audience."

We carried our bowls into the kitchen, the air thankfully cooler inside.

Mama didn't move toward the sink. Instead, she pulled out a chair and sat slowly.

"Maggie," she said gently, "sit down a minute."

I hesitated. She waited.

I sank into the chair across from her.

She studied me carefully. "You look the way you did when you were nineteen and didn't know whether to run toward something or away from it."

"That's oddly specific."

"It's also true."

The walls felt thinner then, like everything I'd been holding back was pushing to be heard.

I swallowed hard, my hands fidgeting in my lap. "Mama, remember when Asa came to visit me in Europe?

What if I told you there's a chance—a very small one—that Asa could be Poppy's father?"

The kitchen went still.

No gasp. No drama. Just quiet truth.

"I'd say I've been waitin' to hear you say that."

And once that door cracked open, everything spilled—Paris. Julian. The timing. Asa always careful, always using protection. Not so with Julian. The fear. The wanting. The avoiding.

And the clues I'd tried so hard not to see in Poppy's mannerisms.

"Oh, Mama," I said softly. "She's so much like him."

I listed all the ways Poppy reminded me of Asa.

Her pauses.

Her nods.

Her little phrases.

Her way with Asa.

Her way with horses.

Her way of belonging to this land.

Mama let me talk until the ache softened, until the truth felt less like a betrayal and more like a crossroads.

"Well," she said softly, "I can't say that I haven't noticed the same. But I wasn't sure if it was me noticing—or just wanting it to be true."

That gentleness splintered something inside me.

"And Maggie…" she added, her voice low. "Maybe it's just me wishin' it to be so. But Poppy—she does seem to have a lot of Asa's ways in her. His softness. His steadiness." She stopped, took a long breath. "…But she's also got a lot of you in her, too. A lust for life—and a heart she sometimes guards too close."

Mama reached across the table and took my hand.

"The thing that's dawned on me these past weeks," she

murmured, "is that she seems to have none of Julian in her. Or at least none that I can see."

A helpless sound escaped me. This couldn't be happening.

Mama sat back in her seat, turned toward the window. She had a clear view of Poppy and Asa finishing up.

"Now maybe that likeness to Asa is just her admirin' him and modelin' him—children do that. But in my heart…" She hesitated. "…it doesn't ring true."

My stomach rolled so hard I thought I might be sick.

"Mama," I whispered, "what have I done?"

Her eyes softened, full of a mother's knowing.

"I think, sweetheart, it's more what you haven't done."

Tears ran down my cheeks, and Mama handed me a paper napkin.

"You just said Julian talked you out of endin' your pregnancy," she reminded gently. "And I'm grateful to him for that. But you were barely twenty-two—raw and scared—in a foreign land, chasin' a dream few ever reach. And Julian looked you in the eye and reminded you that he had rights as the baby's father. Assumed it was his child. Painted a picture of how your future would unfold. Family. Security. And you bought his future because…" She tilted her head. "…because maybe you wanted to. It was easier."

Tears stung my eyes.

"Believing his version simplified your problem," she continued. "You wanted your life as you'd imagined it. A career. No questions. No scandal. No mess."

I covered my mouth with both hands as a wave of nausea rolled through me.

"But I never would willingly keep Asa's child from him," I choked out. "But if what we suspect is true, that's exactly what I've done, and —"

"I know," she whispered. "You didn't intend it. But intention can't erase the truth you have to face now."

The room blurred. I pressed my palms to the table.

"Why is it that back in Paris, I didn't see Asa in Poppy? I didn't notice all the mannerisms that are so obvious now. But here… when they are together, it's so obvious."

"That's reasonable, don't you think?" Mama asked.

"If Poppy is Asa's," I said, my voice shaking, "I've robbed him of nearly a decade with his daughter. I've robbed my daughter of the father she should've had. How do I look Asa in the eye after that? How do I live with it?"

I dragged in a shaky breath. "And Mama… it's not just Asa I keep thinking about."

She tilted her head. "Who else, baby?"

"Julian." The word scraped out of me.

Mama's expression didn't sharpen or harden—it softened, like she'd known this piece was coming too.

"For all his faults," I whispered, "he loved Poppy. He was a devoted father in the beginning. You remember… how he held her? How he'd pace the floor with her at two in the morning? He hired the nanny when I couldn't keep my head above water. Made sure our days ran smooth when I was drowning in rewrites and traveling and exhaustion."

Mama nodded slowly. "He did."

My voice wavered. "What would this truth do to him, Mama? To learn she isn't biologically his? After giving her his whole heart those first five years?" Tears burned behind my eyes. "Whatever happened later—however careless he got—his love for her in those early years was real. And I'm about to break something in him that can't be unbroken."

Mama reached across the table, her voice gentle. "I know, honey. I know. And you're right—it'll hurt him something fierce."

A tear slipped down my cheek. "He may have failed her the last five years... but that doesn't erase what he gave her in the first five. His love wasn't perfect, but whose ever is?"

"No one's," Mama murmured. "And that pain you're worryin' over? It just means you have compassion. And guilt—but it's the compassion you need to remember moving forward."

I let out a small, broken sound. "How can I live with what I've done?"

Mama squeezed my hand. "You live with it by tellin' the truth when the time is right," she said. "And by rememberin' you were just a child yourself when all this began."

"I was twenty-two. By all rights an adult. I keep going over it," I whispered, pressing a hand to my stomach. "My cycles were never regular—I'd skip months at a time. My doctor even took me off birth control for three months to try to reset everything, said all the stress from work and meeting deadlines was throwing my body off.

"And Asa and I... we were so careful in Paris. Every single time. But after he left—after I realized whatever we were could never survive the real world—I was so lonely I could hardly breathe."

I stopped, pulled that time back into my memory.

"So when Julian came back into town and wanted to pick up right where we'd left off... I let it happen. At least he took my mind off the ache of losing Asa. Julian wasn't careful, not always, even when I told him I wasn't protected. And I let myself believe it didn't matter because my timing was messy and my body was unpredictable and..." My voice cracked. "Because wanting something to be simple is not the same as it being true. But I wasn't a child. I was an adult."

"It's true, you were. But you were also scared, and it's

not a crime to want an easier, uncomplicated life." She patted my hand. "The irony is that you didn't get it in the end."

A cold shiver rippled straight through me.

"Wanting something easier doesn't excuse ignoring the truth, or at least the possibility of the truth."

"No," she agreed. "It doesn't. But it explains it. And the Lord knows we all need a little explainin' for the things we wish we'd done different."

Outside, Poppy laughed—bright, breathless—and Asa's voice followed, warm as a summer afternoon.

The sound of his voice knotted my insides.

"If you could know for sure," Mama asked, "would you want to?"

My heart answered before my voice did.

"Yes."

Fear followed immediately.

"If she is his," I whispered, "it changes everything. And oh, Mama—" I buried my face in my hands. "He'll never forgive me."

"And if she isn't his child," Mama murmured, "it changes nothin' about the love already here. Between him and Poppy. Between you and Asa." She held up a hand. "Don't deny it. The room sizzles when you two are in it."

Silence drifted between us.

Outside, Asa's low whistle floated back. Poppy's laughter followed. A truck door thumped shut. His engine rumbled, then stopped.

He wasn't leaving.

Just repositioning.

Mama rose, standing beside me at the window.

"Whatever the truth is," she murmured, "it's already walkin' this land with you."

Her hand rested warm on my arm.

"You can think how to tell him," she said softly. "But you must. And you need to get ahead of it, Maggie. Because that child…" She paused, her breath catching. "…in my mind, that child is Asa Griffin's. To me it's as plain as day."

That evening, long after Poppy had gone for her bath and Mama had gone to lie down, I found myself standing on the porch, replaying every moment from the ring. Every gesture. Every shared laugh. Every tiny echo of Asa in my daughter's face.

The orchard hummed softly around me, steady and familiar, while the truth I'd buried—maybe not on purpose, but buried all the same—pressed closer than it ever had.

And somewhere down the road, Asa was heading home with thoughts of his own.

Thoughts that would collide with a truth he didn't yet know he was walking straight toward.

Because Mama was right.

With every passing day, I felt more certain that Poppy was Asa's child.

# Chapter Eighteen

## ASA

Asa's week had been slammed. The busiest time of the month, and two employees were out with the flu. He'd been running checkout, stocking shelves, and keeping the whole damn store from tipping over. He'd missed two of Poppy's riding lessons, and that bothered him more than it should have. He kept reminding himself that soon she and Maggie would be an ocean away, living their lives, and might hardly remember this stretch of afternoons they'd spent together. But reminders didn't always sink in the way they were supposed to.

And maybe that was why he'd finally listened to the small, insistent voice in his head. The one that had been there for years, telling him to stop waiting. The one that said if he didn't speak now, he might lose them both without ever having tried.

He'd managed to carve out a couple of hours for Poppy's riding lesson before Maggie and he went out that evening. He'd finally caved to that voice—and the many louder ones in his ear from friends—and asked her out on an official date. He'd been surprised by her response—almost relieved that he'd finally asked. Which gave him hope that tonight would be their new beginning.

Dinner, a movie, maybe a walk by the river afterward. It had taken nerve just to ask her. He'd even shaved twice to steady himself. Somewhere between counting out the till and locking the back door, he'd decided: tonight he'd tell Maggie what had lived in his chest for twenty years. Tonight he'd stop pretending friendship was enough.

He had to know where they stood—before his heart burst at every turn of her head, every shy smile she slipped him when no one was watching.

When he pulled into her drive, the orchard glowed with late-afternoon sun, the kind that softened edges and made things feel possible. That thought alone was enough to rattle him.

Barb sat on the porch, fanning herself with a church bulletin. Maggie leaned against the rail, laughing at something her mother said, her hair piled on top of her head, a few loose strands catching the light. Lord help him. One look at her and he was seventeen again, wanting her so bad his ribs ached with it.

"Morning, Coach Asa!" Poppy yelled from the round pen.

Coach. Better than Grocery Man, though he couldn't decide which name stole more pieces of him.

"Morning, Champ," he called, stepping into the ring. She sat tall in the saddle—proud and balanced, legs steady. The girl had an instinct for riding, the kind you couldn't teach. His dad had always said he'd been the same way—a natural rider.

They started slow, the usual warm-ups. Maggie's laugh carried across the yard, and every time he heard it, something inside him leaned toward it like a sunflower seeking the sun. He told himself to focus. Just a lesson. Just a few circles. Just another hour of being near a life he wanted too much.

After a while, the heat settled low and heavy. Poppy shifted in the saddle, then drew Sugar to a halt and reached back to fuss with her braid.

She wrinkled her nose. "My hair's driving me crazy," she said, pulling the elastic free.

He chuckled. "Welcome to horse sweat, cowgirl."

She grinned wide at his teasing, gathered her hair, twisted it, clipped it high on her head—and the world dropped out from under him.

A thin streak of white shimmered at the nape of her neck.

Bright. Clear. Unmistakable.

He stepped closer, made sure he wasn't seeing things.

His breath stalled, then disappeared.

All he could do was stare at the nape of Poppy's neck, that small thread of snow-white hair against her skin. A mark he'd seen on his mother, on his aunt, on his grandmother. Griffin women. Always at the nape of the neck. Hidden until you lifted the hair.

A candlewick, his grandfather called it. A blessing. A lineage.

His lineage.

Poppy turned her head slightly. The lock of white glinted in the sun again.

"Did I do good with my loping?" she asked, cheeks bright with pride.

"You're…" He swallowed. "You're a natural."

His voice didn't sound like his. Rougher. Older. Cracked down the center.

He ended the lesson early—something he'd never done. Made up a reason about the heat, Sugar being tired, work calling. Anything to keep from standing there another minute with his insides splitting open.

Disappointment flickered across her face, but she didn't complain. He helped her down, his hands shaking so hard he fisted them to keep the shake from showing. He made an excuse to untack Sugar and give her a quick rubdown to save time, claimed he needed to hurry back to the store. He turned away quickly, fussing with the girth, pretending the saddle needed attention so she wouldn't see what was happening to him.

On his way to his truck, Maggie waved from the porch. "You leaving already?"

Her voice—warm, hopeful—hit him like a blow.

"Yeah," he said. The word scraped out of him. "Got some things to see to."

She came down the steps, barefoot in the grass, a sight so beautiful it hurt. "What time tonight? I can meet you wherever—"

"My place," he said quickly. "Above the store. Come early."

"Early?" she repeated, stepping closer, brows knitting.

He couldn't look at her. Not then. Not before he understood the ground under his feet. Not with the truth pounding at the walls of his chest.

"Yes," he said, already climbing into his truck. "Early."

Before she could ask anything else, he turned the key. Gravel spit beneath his tires as he pulled away.

In the rearview mirror, she stood in the driveway with one hand lifted, shading her eyes, confusion written all over her face.

His chest tightened—hard, sudden—like the world had tilted without warning.

And with it came the unmistakable sense that the ground had shifted under twenty years of memories.

By the time he hit the main road, his pulse still hadn't settled. He pulled off near the old feed store, killed the engine, and dropped his forehead to the steering wheel.

The candlewick.

Paris.

Two weeks that had rearranged his bones.

Three months later, her letter—I've met someone.

A baby born the following spring. He'd never added the months, it hurt too much to think about. Knowing Maggie had found another man.

But now he knew that little girl may have her mother's eyes and quick shy smile. But she had his family's brand.

The candlewick.

A tremor moved through him. His throat tightened until he could barely swallow.

How could this be true?

How could Maggie have kept this from him all these years?

The thought came soft, like a prayer, and sharp, like a blade.

What if he had a daughter?

What if she'd been in the world for almost ten years without him knowing her?

Maggie had to know. His mind tumbled back to those two weeks. They were careful, but…

Did she know? Of course she did. A woman would know such things.

What if she never meant to tell him?

Anger tried to flare, but it didn't stick.

Hurt tried, too, but even that didn't feel right.

What landed—heavy, staggering—was grief.

For the years he hadn't known her.

For the birthdays he'd missed.

For the mornings and nights and little in-betweens he should've had.

And under all that, deeper still—an aching, terrified hope.

If it was true, everything he thought his life was—and wasn't—had just changed.

If it was true, nothing would ever be the same.

He lifted his head finally, staring through the windshield at nothing at all.

Tonight, he'd see Maggie.

Tonight, he'd look her in the eyes and force her to face him and speak the truth bearing down on him.

But first, he needed to get his feet under him. Get a grip on what was churning in his chest.

Because if Poppy was his…

Love, regret, hope—and a kind of hurt he didn't have a name for—were all coming due at the same damn time.

And Maggie—God help him—was the only person on this earth who could answer the question tearing him open.

He just hoped he could hold steady—shove the hurt down far enough—to listen to whatever truth she gave him.

And she would give him the truth. All of it.

Because he damn well deserved it.

# Chapter Nineteen

## ASA

By the time his cleaning lady left, Asa's apartment looked like something out of a catalog—floors shining, counters wiped down, not a thing out of place. Which meant he couldn't busy himself with a broom or a rag or even pretend a stack of mail needed sorting.

The quiet felt wrong.

Too much time to rehash the unbelievable now rooted in his heart as truth.

He crossed his small apartment for the fifth time, then the sixth, hands flexing uselessly at his sides. Every time he stopped moving, that shimmer of white flashed in his mind—a thin candlewick glinting at the nape of Poppy's neck. A mark he'd only ever seen on Griffins. A mark every woman in his family carried. A mark of his bloodline, too unmistakable to explain away.

He dragged a hand over his face and tried to breathe evenly. Tonight was supposed to be simple. Dinner. A movie. Maybe—if he got the right signals and his courage held out—the truth about how long he'd loved Maggie McAllister.

But that plan had cracked open under the weight of a single streak of white.

A knock sounded.

He stiffened, heart tripping once, then he crossed the room and opened the door.

Maggie stood in the golden hue of the porch light, hair wind-tossed, eyes red around the rims like she'd cried on the drive over. She tried for a smile. It trembled.

"I know I'm early…" she said.

The thoughts racing through his head came to a screeching halt. She looked more than upset—devastated. Her mouth trembled, shoulders slumping inward, red rims circling her eyes.

He drew a slow breath, forced his own reaction down, and stepped aside to let her in.

"What's wrong?"

She didn't sit. Didn't even put her bag down. She stood in the middle of the room with her arms wrapped around herself, like she needed help holding everything in place.

His chest tightened.

"Maggie… what happened? Did something happen to Poppy?"

She took a breath that snagged halfway in her throat. "I got a call. Right after you left the farm."

Her fingers trembled as she pushed her hair behind her ear. "It was Julian."

The name landed like a stone in his gut.

Not jealousy—something sharp beneath it that he didn't yet have words to describe.

"He'd just arrived in Atlanta," she continued, "and he

says he's coming here. To Loblolly." Her voice thinned. "He says he misses Poppy."

Asa's mind spun with questions he wanted answered. But instead of grilling Maggie, he motioned her toward the couch. She sat on the edge, her posture still tight, as if her body didn't know how to rest.

"What else did he say?" he asked gently.

"He asked if he could stay at the farm." She let out a small, disbelieving laugh. "I told him no. Told him he could stay at the River House Inn. I even made the reservation so he couldn't pull any tricks and just show up at the farm."

Her composure wavered, her face folding with worry. "I'm a mess. I didn't even think—I just drove here."

Something in his chest loosened—just a notch—at the fact that she'd come to him. She came here. To him. Because she was scared.

He sat beside her, close enough to feel the heat of her shoulder, but not touching. Touch felt dangerous right now—too much truth pulsing beneath his skin.

"Tell me what you're afraid of," he said quietly.

She laughed once—a brittle, exhausted sound. "Because Poppy adores him," she whispered. "She has this dream in her head about what a father should be, and Julian… he isn't it. He never was. Or hasn't been for a long time. But she still imagines him as this perfect, magical version of a dad. And now he just—shows up."

Pain sparked deep inside him—raw, disoriented.

Father.

She said it with absolute certainty.

He swallowed hard, staring at the clean lines of the hardwood floor because looking at her felt too much like being flayed open.

"He hasn't called her in months, Asa. Not on her birthday, not on holidays. They just slip by as if he couldn't be bothered." Her voice shook. "But she still keeps a space for him in her heart."

He had to close his eyes for a moment.

If Poppy was his… that space should have been his.

He forced another breath. "Do you want him to see her?"

"I don't know." Her hands fisted in her lap. "I know she deserves… something. He's her father. But I'm afraid he'll be here all charm and loving, then disappear like always. And that will be worse. She'll be devastated. It's why part of me wants to lock the doors and tell him to stay away forever."

Her honesty was like a knife—clean and true.

"Julian always comes back when he wants something," she whispered. "And I'm terrified he's going to waltz in and turn her inside out again."

He stood, mostly because staying seated felt like trying to hold his body still in a room that was tilting sideways. He walked into the kitchen under the pretense of getting her aspirin. Really, he just needed a second to breathe.

She followed, leaning on the counter, looking smaller and more helpless than he'd ever seen her.

"And what happens when I go back to Paris?" she asked, voice soft as thread. "Will he follow me there? Will he try to play house again? I know he isn't coming because he misses Poppy. I'm certain he's coming because he got dumped. Needs another woman to support his lavish lifestyle."

He set the aspirin and a glass of water in front of her. Their fingers brushed. He felt it like a spark up the nerve of his arm.

But he didn't let himself touch her again.

Not yet.

Not with everything inside him tilting toward something too fragile to name.

"Maggie," he said softly, "what do you need from me?"

She lifted her eyes, and there it was—trust, unguarded and pure.

"I don't know," she whispered. "I just… didn't want to be alone."

His breath hitched.

Because God help him, he wanted to gather her into his arms and promise her everything would be all right.

But he didn't know what all right meant anymore.

"Whatever you need," he said, his voice barely steady. "I'm here."

She studied his face, confusion tightening her features. She pushed her hair back from her forehead, took a steadying breath.

"I should have just canceled our date," she said quietly. "I shouldn't burden you with my problems."

That broke something in him.

"No," he said quickly. "No, Mags."

She looked down, then back up again, like she was bracing herself.

"I didn't mean to bring all this here."

She looked so broken. He couldn't say the words.

Couldn't look into her eyes and ask the question buried in his chest like a live wire.

So he said the only thing that didn't feel like tearing them both apart.

"I just need… a little time to think."

She nodded, even though he could tell from her expression that she didn't really understand.

The hurt flickering through her eyes, fragile as a candle fighting wind.

"I shouldn't have come," she murmured. "I'm sorry. I just wanted…" She blew out a breath, then turned for the door. "I'm sorry."

"Don't be sorry," he said, stepping forward on instinct before stopping himself again. "You can always come here."

But he saw the moment she registered his restraint.

Saw her swallow it.

She walked to the door, shoulders tight, head bowed. He followed, because letting her leave alone felt wrong—even if he couldn't make himself hold her.

At the door, she paused.

Looked up at him one last time.

"Goodnight, Asa."

His voice felt thick. "Goodnight, Maggie."

She descended the steps slowly, her silhouette thinning behind the railing. He waited until her taillights disappeared down the road before closing the door.

Only then did he let himself sink onto the sofa, elbows on his knees, hands wrapped around his head.

Two truths circled like opposing tides in his chest:

Either he was seeing what he desperately wanted to see…

or the truth was bigger than anything he'd ever let himself imagine.

And either way…

Tomorrow, when Julian arrived in Loblolly, everything would get harder.

For all of them.

# Chapter Twenty

## ASA

Asa hadn't slept.

He closed his eyes and tried to slow his thoughts, hoping for enough quiet to rest, but nights grew heavier when the timing of a truth mattered as much as the truth itself. Every time he drifted toward sleep, he saw the streak of white at the back of Poppy's neck. Then Maggie's face when he pulled away. Then Julian's name, lodged in his head—hard and unmoving.

---

By dawn, he stopped pretending rest was coming and put on coffee instead.

Something else his mind had worried over for hours, turning it until the edges blurred: he wasn't sure Maggie realized the truth he was beginning to see. That Poppy might be his.

He searched his memory for that time in Paris, for the conversations that followed—Maggie saying they needed to be careful once things between them turned serious. The timing didn't line up cleanly. Not without gaps. Too many missing pieces to let himself assume he understood.

He knew Poppy was his because of the family brand—the candlewick—but it wasn't something he'd ever spoken aloud. Not common knowledge. And what troubled him most was how certain Maggie seemed. She'd never wavered when she spoke of Julian as Poppy's father. Never hinted at doubt.

That certainty was what kept Asa from driving straight to the farm and demanding answers. It forced him to slow down instead of rushing headlong into something that could fracture everything. He wanted his rightful place, but it wouldn't be as simple as demanding the truth. And Julian's visit—being thrown into the mix now—only complicated it further.

He didn't know what he planned to do when Julian arrived—stand close, maybe. Watch. Protect. Or maybe he just needed to see for himself how this Paris man fit into the world Maggie had built without him.

But he knew one thing with absolute clarity:

He wasn't going to sit around and do nothing while another man walked back into his daughter's life and called himself her father.

For a split second, doubt tried to wedge its way in—quiet, insidious. Then it was gone.

The candlewick wasn't coincidence. It wasn't chance. It was his family's brand.

The only thing still uncertain was how—and when—that truth would surface.

He also knew Maggie would need him, even if she didn't ask. And Poppy—he wanted to be near her, whatever came next. Just in case.

n case what, he couldn't say. And he didn't stop to question the decision. Every fiber in him—bone, blood, instinct—told him he needed to be on that farm when Julian Black made his entrance.

He drank his coffee standing at the counter, barely tasting it. His place felt too quiet—too empty for the noise in his head. By the time he set his mug down, he already knew he wasn't going straight to the farm.

His Aunt Sue Ellen would be up.

It was her day off from the diner, but she'd been waking before five since Asa could remember—long before the coffee pot ever hissed to life at the Loblolly Diner. He could trust her with the news about Poppy. She kept the secrets that mattered. And she'd have an opinion. She always did.

He grabbed his keys and headed out.

Her kitchen light was on when he pulled in, a soft yellow glow cutting through the dark. He knocked once, lightly.

The door opened almost immediately.

"Well, I'll be," Sue Ellen said, already stepping back to let him in. She wore leggings, a Braves T-shirt, and an apron tied at the waist, her gray hair pulled into a loose knot. "Either the world's ending, or you haven't slept."

"Little of both," he said.

She gave him a look that said she'd already clocked everything worth knowing, then turned toward the stove. "Coffee's fresh. Sit. I'll make us a little breakfast."

He did.

Bacon was already in the skillet, popping softly. She cracked eggs into the pan, the scent filling the small kitchen, familiar and steady. She slid a mug across the table without looking at him.

"Now," she said, flipping the bacon. "You don't come calling at this hour unless something's eating you alive. And before you say it—yes, I know Julian Black's coming to town."

Asa huffed a low growl. "Well, that didn't take long."

"Barbara called me last night when Maggie left for your place," Sue Ellen said, sliding bacon onto a plate. "Didn't say much. Just that Maggie was rattled." She set bread into the toaster, then finally turned, one brow lifting. "That's all she said."

He nodded. Took a swallow of coffee he didn't taste.

"I don't know what to do," he said. "He had no right being here. Not really."

Sue Ellen studied him for a long beat, then pulled out the chair across from him and sat. "All right," she said calmly. "You're going to have to give me a little more than that."

He hesitated.

This was the moment—the one he'd been circling since dawn. He'd try everything out on Aunt Sue Ellen first, see how it landed.

"There's something you don't know," he said. "Something no one knows."

Her face shifted—not alarmed, but attentive. "Go on." She finished plating their breakfast, grabbed napkins and utensils from the drawer and sat across from him. Motioned to the plate. "Eat while you talk. You look like you could use more than caffiene."

He set his coffee down before his hands betrayed him. No way to say it other than straight. "Poppy has a white streak of hair at the back of her neck. Small. Easy to miss and unimportant unless—"

Sue Ellen gasped. "That baby girl has the Griffin mark?"

She didn't speak. He imagined the truth rearranging

itself in her mind. Aunt Sue Ellen was his mama's sister, so they weren't Griffin women by blood. But Mama had likely told her over the years, even though Daddy's people lived North of Atlanta and rarely visited, so he doubted it was a common topic of conversation. Still, not likely you'd forget something as odd as this.

"Daddy always called it the candlewick," he said quietly. "His mama and sister had it. Same as my female cousins." He shrugged. "You know how it works. The candlewick passes to the women at the neckline, the men in the beard."

"I can't—" she began, then stopped. Tried again. "Barbara's never mentioned—"

"That's the thing. I'm pretty certain the candlewick conversation never came up." He shrugged. "I mean, why would it? I never gave it a minute's thought as a kid."

"So when you were in Paris all those years ago…" Sue Ellen leaned back slowly, one hand lifting to her mouth. "Lord."

He pressed on, the words tumbling now that they were loose. "I noticed it yesterday. All these weeks working with Poppy, getting to know her." He scrubbed his face with his open palm. "I swear, I've grown to love that little girl. And now that I think back—the way she takes to a horse. The way she loves them sould deep, like I do. The way she took to riding." His voice caught. "Just like me as a kid. I was going to talk to Maggie last night, but—"

"She told you Julian is coming," Sue Ellen finished. She closed her eyes and shook her head. "Lord, what a mess."

When she opened them again, her gaze was sharp and wet all at once. "This changes things."

"It does."

She shook her head. "Not so much changes as clarifies."

She held up a hand when he started to speak. "Let me finish."

He did.

"It's true this changes things. Maggie can't just up and leave for Paris without the two of you coming to some kind of understanding. But she's real tender right now," she said. "She's at a crossroads—with her high-falutin' career in Paris, her mama's illness—and that girl still loves you, no doubt about that."

She sipped her coffee, gave him time to digest her words. "You both need answers, but what she doesn't need is you charging in and demanding them." She exhaled slowly. "But she does need to hear the truth. And Poppy—" Her voice softened. "Poppy deserves this handled like the precious thing it is."

"So you don't think Maggie realizes I'm Poppy's father?"

Sue Ellen's face softened, she reached across the table and cupped his cheek with the hand. "Darlin', it'd take a powerfully mean-spirited woman to raise a child and not tell a man as good as you that he wasn't the father—and then, to boot, let that man's heart get twisted enough to love the child." She tilted her head, holding his gaze, giving him time to sit with it. "That's not the Maggie McAllister I know. Maggie loves you, Asa. She'd never hurt you like that."

She studied him. "I don't know how this all came about, but this is what I think you should consider now that it has and her ex is in town. Don't hide. Don't rush. Stay close. Let Maggie find her footing again. And when you confront her with what you know—and you will—make it clear you're not accusing her of a lie. You're offering to be

Poppy's father in the only way that matters—by showing up."

That settled something deep in his chest.

"And if Julian keeps calling himself her father?" Asa asked.

Sue Ellen's mouth tightened. "Then you have that conversation sooner rather than later. Let's see how long he stays in town. Barbara gives it no more than seventy-two hours. Says his attention span's shorter than a gnat's." She snorted softly. "No idea why he's showing his face now, but he'll find a new shiny toy soon enough."

"So, Barbara's not a fan? I wondered about that."

Sue Ellen smiled without humor. "Barbara isn't a fan of anyone who hurts her family. And mark my word, she'll be overjoyed with this news once she understands you're not trying to take anything from her Maggie. You're offering to stand beside her—and give her only grandchild the father she deserves."

She reached across the table and squeezed his hand. "You've loved our Maggie since she was too young and stubborn to know what to do with it. Don't let fear turn you into someone you're not."

He nodded. Once. "Thank you."

She stood and gathered the plates. "Now go. She's going to need you today."

He paused at the door. "Aunt Sue Ellen?"

"Yes?"

"If this goes bad—"

She turned to face him. "It won't," she said firmly. "It might hurt. But that's not the same thing, Darlin'."

---

The sun was barely peeking over the horizon, the sky still a pale blue, brushing light over the tops of the pecan trees when he made it to the farm. Barb's kitchen light flipped on as he pulled in. She glanced out the window, then waved to him through the glass. He couldn't see her face, but he was certain she'd be a little surprised to see him at this hour.

He took his time exiting his truck, and by the time he'd climbed the steps to the front door, Poppy—still in her nightgown—had it open. Her hair was a wild storm around her pretty little face.

"Coach Asa!" she squealed.

He crouched to eye level. "Thought we'd get a lesson in before it gets hot."

Poppy gasped and spun toward her room, her voice slipping into a Southern-French melody. "Mama bought me new boots—wait till you see!"

She shot down the hall just as Maggie stepped in from the kitchen holding a mug of coffee. Her eyes were soft around the edges—tired but warm.

"You're early," she said quietly, handing him her cup of coffee. "You look like you could use a little caffeine."

"Thanks," He accepted the cup even though he didn't need a fourth cup, but he sipped anyway. "Wanted to make the most of the morning."

Her shoulders lowered a fraction. "Thank you for coming."

He didn't say the words tangled beneath the surface:

I came because you looked scared last night.

I came because I didn't want you facing him alone.

I came because the truth is too big to leave you with.

I came for the truth.

I came for my daughter.

Instead, he nodded, then headed to the barn.

Twenty minutes later, he had Poppy laughing, guiding Sugar in warm-up circles as Maggie sipped her coffee and watched from the porch. For a moment—just a breath—Asa let himself imagine a life of mornings like this.

Maggie eventually went inside, and he continued working Sugar and Poppy in a figure eight.

The roar of an engine hit about the time Poppy brought Sugar to a full stop.

"How was that?" she asked.

"That was almost perfect." He kept his focus on Poppy and ignored the engine racing closer. Definitely foreign. In his mind he saw smooth and glossy and out of place on a farm. Still a ways off yet, but close.

He stepped toward Poppy. "Why don't you hop down."

Poppy's brow pinched at his tone. She thought he was about to correct her—and she disliked doing anything less than perfect.

"What's wrong?" she whispered.

"Nothing, sweetheart. I just want to tighten your saddle."

He lifted her gently, set her on the ground, and stroked Sugar's neck. "Why don't you run inside and see if your mama has lemonade? I'm awful thirsty."

Poppy brightened when she realized she hadn't made a mistake, then took off toward the porch, like he knew she would.

The back screen door slammed behind her just as a black Masarati rolled to a stop beside his truck. Dust curling behind it, sunlight flashing across the hood.

Julian Black stepped out like a star arriving at a film premiere. You'd think there was a roll of red carpet leading to the porch.

Tall. Handsome in a curated way. Linen shirt. Stylish

coat. A scarf—good Lord—a scarf in seventy-degree weather.

Asa didn't move. He simply watched.

Julian's gaze found him and lit with a bright, practiced smile. "Bonjour."

Asa touched the brim of his hat out of habit, not warmth. "Morning."

"Riding? Is Poppy learning horses?" Julian's eyes drifted toward the paddock. "Where are they—Maggie and my little girl? I drove all night."

My little girl.

The phrase wedged like a small, sharp stone in Asa's ribs.

But he only said, "Inside. They weren't expecting you this early."

Julian blinked at the boundary. "And you are…?"

Before Asa could shape an answer, a small voice cleaved the air—

"Papa! Papa!"

Poppy's boots thudded across the yard. Maggie appeared seconds later, breathless and already tense, trying—and failing—to reach her daughter first.

Julian dropped to one knee with the grace of a man who'd rehearsed the moment.

"Ma petite étoile," he murmured.

Poppy collided with him, arms tight around his neck.

Asa kept his face still. His stomach… not so much.

Maggie slowed a few feet away, one hand pressed to her heart. "Julian. You're early."

"For you," he said, catching her hand before she could pull back. He brushed a kiss to her knuckles.

She flinched—barely, but enough—and slipped her hand away.

He smiled as if she'd teased him, not rejected him. Then he whispered something to Poppy that made her glow.

Asa exhaled slowly.

Maggie found Asa's gaze, closed her eyes as if asking for patience.

He saw everything in her expression—fear, shame, exhaustion.

He wanted to walk closer and pull her into his arms, shield her from what was coming. But instead he stayed in place.

Barb stepped out onto the porch. "Julian," she said warmly enough to be polite, but not enough to be fooled. "You're early—and just in time for breakfast."

Julian lit up. "Barbara, you look radiant."

Barb ignored that, looking straight at Asa instead. "Hope you're staying, Asa. Muffins just came out of the oven."

A message.

A warning.

A shield.

"Ah, my little angel, Papa brought his girl a present."

"A present for me?" Poppy jumped up and down. "Can I open it now?"

"Of course, my sweet." Julian walked hand in hand with Poppy to his car.

Asa walked out of the paddock and to Maggie. "You okay?"

She frowned. "He's been here five minutes and she's already building castles in the sky."

"Kids do that," he murmured.

Her eyes shone. "He'll disappoint her. His flame burns out quick."

That twisted something inside him. Julian hadn't only broken Poppy's heart in the past—he'd broken Maggie's, too. And that knowledge burned in a place jealousy couldn't reach.

Before he could say more, Poppy ran forward. "Coach, come on! Breakfast is ready, and Papa says I can open my present!"

He forced a smile. "You haven't brushed down Sugar yet. And we have to give her hay."

For the first time, Poppy looked disappointed at the idea of tending to Sugar's needs.

"Okay." Her shoulders slumped, and she followed him back to the barn while everyone else went inside.

Poppy made a half-hearted effort, her focus drifting toward the house and, undoubtedly, Julian and the present waiting to be opened. Asa didn't blame her. Still, he made her brush.

He kept Poppy a minute longer, had her give Sugar her flake of hay, grounding her the only way he knew how, before walking her through the back door, through the mudroom, and into the kitchen.

Julian immediately settled her beside him at the table and pointed to the present beside him—oversized, wrapped in glossy paper like something from a fancy department store.

Maggie stood nearby, forehead creased, pulled in two directions at once. Asa stepped to her side.

Her expression said enough. She wasn't steering this show.

They'd let Julian have his moment—for now.

Julian's voice drifted from the table. "Maggie, chérie! Breakfast!" He patted the seat next to his, putting himself between her and Poppy.

She hesitated, seemed to weigh her options, then squared her shoulders and walked toward him.

Asa leaned against the wall and took in what looked, at first glance, like an idyllic family morning. Sunlight stretched long shadows across the kitchen floor. Poppy laughed. Julian smiled. Maggie sitting with her hands in her lap, her eyes anything but calm.

Julian was back in the picture.

Poppy was glowing.

Maggie was unraveling.

And Asa stood at the edge of a truth that would change everything.

Someone was going to get hurt.

He just prayed it wouldn't be the little girl whose laugh already lived deep in his bones.

But he couldn't see a way for the truth to come to light without turning Poppy's world upside down.

# Part II

# Chapter Twenty-One

ASA

The kitchen smelled like pecan muffins and strong coffee, but none of it eased the tension threading through the room. Julian had taken over the room with big smiles, dramatic sighs, a hand always landing where it would be seen.

And Poppy… her whole body practically vibrated.

Julian clapped his hands, drawing attention, then slid the shiny wrapped box toward her. "For ma petite étoile," he said, brushing a stray lock of hair from her face as if it were the most natural thing in the world. Maybe to Poppy and Julian it was, Asa reminded himself—until he left her for the jet-set life. "Go ahead. You can open it," he said.

Asa stayed near the counter, hands braced on either side, keeping himself steady. Maggie sat beside Julian, her coffee mug clutched in both hands—a rigidity in her shoulders Asa noticed, even if no one else did.

Poppy slowly removed the paper, then lifted the lid and removed a dark blue velvet box. She opened it, taking out a beautifully carved wooden music box. She carefully lifted the top.

A soft melody drifted out—thin, delicate. A ballerina twirled to the music.

Poppy smiled—then hesitated. Her forehead wrinkled.

Before Asa could register her response, Maggie went still beside Julian—chin lifting a fraction, breath catching in a way only someone watching closely would notice. Here reaction didn't register as shock, more sad than angry.

"Papa…" Poppy said, turning fully toward him. "This looks just like my other music box. The one you gave me when I was six. The one you said was for my birthday that you missed."

Julian blinked—just once—before recovering with a smooth smile.

"Of course. You loved the first so much. So now you'll have another… a collection." He tapped her chin. "A girl like you deserves many beautiful music boxes."

Poppy tried to match his smile. It didn't quite hold. "But shouldn't a collection be different ones?" She turned to Barb. "Like Nana's Santa Claus collection in the cabinet. Each one is different."

"Well, sometimes. But look," Julian said brightly. "This one plays *Clair de Lune*. And it reminded me of you, so I just had to bring it."

Asa's jaw flexed. The lie was thin enough to see daylight through. He'd bet a week's earnings at the store Julian had forgotten about the first box entirely.

Beside him, Maggie exhaled softly—a sound closer to resignation than surprise.

Poppy handled the box with careful fingers. "It's pretty," she said politely. "My other one plays the same song."

Julian didn't seem to notice the shift in her tone. He

pulled her hand to his lips, kissed her knuckles, and launched into a story about spotting the box in a shop window in Paris and thinking of her.

Asa watched Maggie push back from the table, her chair scraping softly against the floor. She picked up her mug and carried it to the sink.

Her breathing was shallow, her eyes too bright, her hands braced on the counter as if she needed something solid to hold her up.

Asa followed a moment later, stopping beside her.

"You doing okay?" he murmured.

She nodded at first—then shook her head, almost imperceptibly. "He's going to break her heart…"

Her voice trailed off. She swallowed and tried again. "He didn't remember he'd already given her that music box."

Asa's chest tightened. He kept his voice low. "Some people remember events," he said quietly. "Some remember only the version that suits them best."

Maggie released a long breath, pinning her gaze back on her daughter.

Julian launched into another tale, hands flying theatrically. Poppy followed every movement, hungry for his attention.

The more he spoke, the more dramatic his tone. "Later, we'll go into town! I'll buy you a dress! Or a bicycle!"

Poppy gasped. "A bicycle?"

Maggie stiffened, eyes snapping toward him. "Julian—" She paused, rethinking. "Poppy can't go to town. She still has chores."

Julian waved the idea away. "Chores? She is a child, chérie, not a farmhand."

Barb's voice cut in like a blade. "On this farm, children contribute."

Julian smiled at Barb, but his attention slid past her almost immediately.

He leaned toward Poppy again, voice conspiratorial. "I'll work on your mama. We will find a way to have our fun, my love. Papa promises."

The glow returned to Poppy's face.

Maggie began clearing dishes, then turned to the sink, her back to the scene at the table.

Asa gathered the rest, while Julian sipped his coffee as if being waited on was expected. The man got under Asa's skin. Simple as that.

A few minutes later, Julian stepped outside to take a call—loud enough to be overheard even from the porch. Though it was in French, it sounded like another performance.

Poppy wandered toward the back door, music box tucked under her arm.

Maggie's eyes followed her daughter… then shifted to Asa. "She still has the other one," she whispered. "She used to play it every night and cry for him. Finally, I put it on the top shelf of my closet. Out of sight, out of mind, as Mama used to say."

The way her throat bobbed when she swallowed told him how raw the memory still was.

He kept his voice soft. "You're trying to protect her. But you can't protect her from disappointment."

"How much disappointment does she have to take?" Maggie said, her breath trembling just enough for him to hear. "Before it becomes cruelty?"

"I get it." He nodded. "But that fight isn't for today."

Her shoulders loosened by a fraction—relief and dread

sitting side by side, as if he'd given her permission to let the moment pass.

Through the window, Julian paced and gestured, performing for whoever was on the other end of the line.

On the porch, Poppy cranked the ballerina. The familiar tune drifted back—thin, pretty, sad.

Asa stepped to the screen door and watched her play with the little music box—shiny, delicate, hollow. He couldn't help thinking it was a fitting emblem of the man who'd brought it.

And in his gut, the truth settled: Julian wasn't here to love. He was here to lay claim.

And as long as Maggie needed steadiness—as long as Poppy needed someone solid—Asa wasn't going anywhere.

Not today.

Not tomorrow.

Not until the truth that lay between all of them finally came into the light.

# Chapter Twenty-Two

## MAGGIE

Tally's kitchen glowed warm and golden—the kind of place where women had been gathering for generations to sort through life's messes. She'd already set out three stemless wine glasses and a plate of rosemary crackers with a cheese–pistachio–hot-honey dip that was beyond delicious. A candle burned nearby—vanilla and something floral drifting through the air.

I hadn't planned on being here tonight. Mama had insisted after Tally called—said I needed a break, that it was a school night, and Poppy would be in bed by eight-thirty no matter how many excuses she managed to invent. She offered to handle bath and bedtime, but I stayed through homework and the bath, then handed Poppy over to her. I told myself a night with the girls might quiet my thoughts about Julian and everything I still didn't know how to manage.

Being here tonight stirred memories—warm, loving ones I hadn't expected. The hum of my new friends chatting helped. I could feel my anxiety easing—not completely, but enough to let me believe this was temporary. Something I could figure out.

Asa and I had spent plenty of after-school afternoons here with Caleb, Jackson, and whichever girl they were dating that week. We studied at this table, ate whatever snacks their housekeeper Jasmine had waiting. Caleb's mother, Senator Benton, was rarely around, but his father—our county judge at the time—would pop in for a few minutes. Mostly, though, Jasmine rode herd on us.

Caleb and Tally had redecorated the public rooms with kid-friendly furnishings; Tally said all the three-and four-generation antiques were now in storage.

"Sit," Tally said, pointing at the tall stool across from her. "I can't drink, but I'm opening a good bottle of wine—maybe two for you and Joleen. We're not playing around tonight."

Joleen slid onto the stool beside me, shrugging off her blazer. "Amen to that," she muttered, rubbing her temples. "My day was… a day."

"Then you both need a glass," Tally said. "Because Maggie's text said she had a situation, which could mean anything from Asa being Asa to a sinkhole opening under the farm."

I tried for a smile, but it wobbled. "It's not the farm or Asa. It's my ex… Julian."

Both women groaned in unison.

Tally poured generously. "What is this—an epidemic of exes? What happened?"

I told them everything—from Julian's too-slick arrival to the way Poppy lit up like she'd been handed a missing piece of her heart. Tally listened with her arms crossed tight, the Benton family steel she'd evidently adopted from Caleb sharpening behind her eyes. Joleen listened differently—

quieter, head tilted, taking in the emotional math beneath the events.

When I finished, silence lingered.

Then Tally slapped the counter. "Just like a man who bolted from his marriage to show up with drama the second another man is interested in the woman he left behind."

"Oh, he doesn't know my background with Asa," I said. "As far as Julian knows, he's Poppy's riding instructor and a family friend."

Tally laughed in disbelief, leaned over the counter, and laid her hand over mine. "Sweetie, if he was in the same room with you and Asa for less than a minute, he got the vibe. Trust me on this."

Joleen reached for my other hand, squeezing. "How are you? Really."

"Scared," I admitted. "Mostly scared."

Tally softened. "Of your ex?"

"Of Poppy," I said quietly. "Of how much she wants him to be the father of her dreams. It's so heartbreakingly obvious how fast he could break her heart all over again. And… of the aftermath I can't pretend isn't important. It was hard enough when she was six. Now that she's almost ten…" I inhaled a long breath. "And I'm scared when he disappears again—which is inevitable—what it will do to her. No matter how much you tell them it isn't so, they always wonder if it's them, if they're not good enough to love."

Joleen's gaze sharpened—not judgmental, just perceptive. "Poppy will have to learn the truth earlier in life than she should. Some people aren't trustworthy with your heart."

I hesitated. Took in her words an searched for a plausible answer. "You're right, but something shouldn't have to be learned. It's as simple as that. My baby will have to learn that her father leaves without a backward glance. Because he will again. Any day now. And he'll break her heart all over again."

Joleen didn't push. She just sipped her wine, steady as a riverbank. "You don't owe us the details. Just know we can carry whatever you hand us."

In other words: *We know you're holding secrets. It's okay.* Somehow that gave me strength, and the knot in my chest loosened a little.

Tally refilled our glasses. "Well, if Julian is who I think he is—stupid, for one, for leaving a woman like you—he has a reason for showing up now. Mark my words."

"I know you don't know him," I said, "but he never walks into a room without trying to be the center of it."

Tally nodded. "Ah. A performer."

"That's the problem," I whispered. "Poppy only remembers the good because I spent three years trying to give her something soft to hold on to. Reminded her of all the good times. And he's playing right into my false narrative."

"He's playing to an audience," Tally said. "Not the same thing as loving someone."

I nodded.

Tally leaned against the counter. "Sounds like Julian feeds on admiration. Poppy adores him with the kind of fierce devotion only a child can hold."

Before I could reply, Joleen's phone buzzed. She glanced at the screen and exhaled softly. "Oh. That's Jackson."

"Isn't this poker night?" I asked.

"It is," Tally said, lifting her brows. "And from that smile, Jo, I'm guessing it's good news?"

Joleen's smile widened, soft and emotional. "Yes." She sipped her wine, then said, "We made a decision today."

She looked between us, breath catching.

"We're fostering the three kids."

Tally's hand flew to her chest. "Joleen."

My mood softened. "Oh, I'm so happy for you." I shook my head in wonder. "Three kids. A ready-made family. That's… well, it's huge."

"It is," she said, voice wavering, cheeks glowing. "The boys are two. The little girl is nine. It's going to be a lot. But it feels… right."

Tally wrapped her arm around Joleen's shoulders and squeezed. "Those babies just won the lottery."

"And you're not doing it alone," I said. "You and Jackson—you're steady. You'll give them the stability they've never had."

Joleen laughed lightly. "Well… with help. I hired a nanny."

Tally blinked. "Already?"

"She was available," Joleen said. "Saffron Tate."

Tally's mouth fell open. "*The* Saffron Tate?"

Joleen nodded, then looked at me and realized I had no idea who she meant. "I tapped Jasmine for a recommendation." She looked at me. "Saffron is Jasmine's cousin. Jasmine is Tally and Caleb's housekeeper—"

"I remember Jasmine," I said. "She's wonderful."

"Saffron retired this year," Joleen said. "Says she's bored. She taught half the kids in this town."

Tally nodded emphatically. "If she's anything like Jasmine, your kids just won a second lottery. I don't know what I'd do without Jasmine. There's no way I could have the Bistro if she hadn't stayed with us after the Senator and Judge Benton moved to New England."

A faint tremor moved through me—memories of Asa, of all of us in this kitchen under Jasmine's watchful eye.

Childhood felt close tonight. Almost too close. Maybe that's why my nerves were jittery.

The words were right there, pressing at the back of my throat. I believed—no, I was nearly certain—that Asa was Poppy's father. And so was Mama. The realization had been circling me for days, gaining weight, demanding air. Demanding to be free. Sitting here with Tally and Joleen, surrounded by familiarity and warmth, part of me wanted to spill it all. To say it out loud and see if it still held its shape.

But I couldn't.

Not like this.

Not before I faced Asa with the truth.

I lifted my glass, took a steadying sip of wine, and let the moment pass.

Joleen nudged my shoulder gently. "What about you? What do you need right now?"

I breathed in deep. "Time. To figure out when—or if—I can tell Poppy anything that might… change the way she sees the world."

After the words escaped my mouth, I realized how cryptic they seemed. But neither woman asked me to explain. I had a feeling both understood the need to hold some things close until the right time.

Tally poured another round. "You'll know when the moment's right," she said, as if reading my mind. "And until then, we've got you."

Joleen nodded. "We're here. That doesn't change."

For the first time all day, I felt like my old self—my earlier anxiety a distant memory.

Tally leaned forward. "All right. We've handled the Julian part, the child-fostering part, and the nanny part. Now I think we need chocolate."

Joleen laughed. "Absolutely."

We talked and laughed, letting the warmth and wine carry us for a while. That's when Tally shared her news—casually, as if mentioning the weather.

"Must be the week for exes. Caleb saw Royce in town today."

The name flickered through me. "Royce? Your ex? What happened?"

Tally's lips pressed thin. "Caleb confronted him. Didn't give an inch. Royce claimed he was 'just passing through.' So far he hasn't approached me or Lola, and Caleb made it very clear that would be… unwise."

"Do you think he's gone?" I asked.

"Caleb says yes. And I'm hoping he's right," Tally said. "But with men like that, you never know if they're just backing off and circling."

"Doesn't matter," Joleen said. "Caleb will keep an eye on Royce. And if Royce has half a brain, he won't test that lawman."

A cold thread wound through my spine. Julian circling—and I wasn't equipped for the swoop-in that felt inevitable. My anxiety returned, sharper this time.

Later, driving home under the soft wash of moonlight, the truth pressed close again.

Poppy was fragile.

Julian was a storm.

And Asa… Asa was steady in ways that made the ground shift under my feet.

Not tonight.

But soon.

If my suspicion was right, the truth would demand to be faced.

First I'd talk to Asa.

Then Julian.

In that order.

Because if Asa wanted a DNA test—and I wouldn't blame him—I'd need one too, just to be certain before speaking to Julian. I had no idea how long results would take. Days, maybe longer.

My life felt unmoored. I'd always craved order; my career demanded it. And now? I felt swept downstream, fighting a current I could no longer outrun.

Beneath it all lived another fear—the one I hadn't yet allowed myself to name.

Asa would be angry when I told him. That was expected. But he would also be hurt. And that was the part that hollowed me out.

How could I explain being so young, so overwhelmed—how easily I'd let Julian, thirteen years older and far more practiced, take control of that chapter of my life?

And how could I live with the possibility that, if my suspicions were right—and they felt more right each day—I'd stolen something from Asa that could never be replaced?

Would he forgive me?

Would he ever understand?

And if our places were reversed… would I forgive him?

The questions followed me home, slipped into bed beside me, and stayed—resting on my chest like a quiet weight, heavy as truth.

# Chapter Twenty-Three

## ASA

Asa's apartment above the store always felt too quiet when he was alone—but once a month, it came alive. Poker night had a way of roughening the edges of the place: leather coats slung over chairs, beers sweating on the table, the low hum of men who'd known each other since they were old enough to swing hammers for summer work. Asa, Jackson, and Caleb had worked summers for Tanner back when he was building houses instead of selling them.

Tonight was Asa's turn to host the rotating game.

Tanner sat at the head of the reversible kitchen-slash-poker table, shuffling cards like he was trying to impress a Vegas dealer. Caleb rested his forearms on the felt, his watch catching the overhead light, while Jackson argued with Tanner over who owed what from last month.

Everything looked normal.

Everything should've felt normal.

But Asa couldn't settle. Chips clicked between his fingers. His knee wouldn't stay still. He had too much on his mind, too much heat under his ribs, and nowhere to put it.

Caleb caught on first.

"You're wound tighter than a coiled garden hose," he said. "What's goin' on with you?"

Tanner didn't look up. "We all know what's goin' on. Rhymes with Maggie."

Jackson snorted.

Asa fisted his hand, raised his middle finger, and slid it over the bridge of his nose. That brought on a round of laughter. They were on a roll, and they'd known him too long for anything he did to stop them now.

Tanner flicked a card across the table. "Ask her out already. I've seen live wires with less spark."

Asa rolled a chip between his fingers. "It's not that simple."

"It's exactly that simple," Jackson said. "She's single. You're single. It's the first time in ten years you've been in the same town. And you light up like a damn porch lantern every time she walks into a room."

Caleb leaned in, deadpan. "If you don't make a move soon, we're takin' your man card."

They all chuckled, but the point was made.

Asa set his jaw. "I have asked her out. It just… didn't go the way I planned."

"Then plan better," Tanner said, dealing the next round. "Invite her somewhere private. No crowds. No interruptions. Just you. Her. A good steak. A better red wine. And whatever it is you've been wantin' to say for ten damn years."

Asa didn't answer.

Because they weren't wrong.

He did want to talk to her. He did want a quiet night. Not the kind full of fear and questions like the last one had become—but something simple. Honest. Something that might give him a foothold before he walked into the biggest conversation of his life.

Before anyone could push further, Caleb cleared his throat.

"Tally's ex—Royce—is in town."

That shut the teasing down.

Tanner looked up. "Doing what?"

"Being an asshat," Caleb muttered. "Showed up at the bistro yesterday demanding to see the owner. Tally was at a PTA meeting at Lola's school, so Sally texted me. I was nearby and handled it."

"How?" Asa asked.

"I moved him outside and told him flat-out no. He wasn't seeing my wife, and he sure as hell wasn't seeing my daughter." Caleb's jaw flexed. "He even tried bluffin' his way, claiming he was Lola's father."

Jackson let out a low whistle. "He's brave or stupid."

"Stupid," Caleb said. "I told him I'd be glad to walk him over to the judge's office for confirmation of who Lola's father was if he wanted. Adoption record's on file." He huffed, sharp and humorless. "Stupid asshat declined."

Jackson barked a laugh. "Asshat ain't that stupid."

"I told him it'd be smart to leave town and not look back."

Tanner cocked an eyebrow. "And?"

Caleb cracked a grin. "He hightailed it to his beat-up truck and headed for the highway."

The table dissolved into the kind of laughter men use instead of applause.

"But did he leave?" Asa asked.

"Yeah, I had one of my deputies follow him out of town, then had another in the next county escort him to that county line north."

Jackson's phone buzzed.

He read his screen, froze, and slowly sat back.

"Everything okay?" Tanner asked.

Jackson swallowed. "Caseworker signed off." His voice turned rough. "Means we can pick up the kids tomorrow morning." He thumbed out a quick text to Joleen.

Caleb straightened. "Ready-made family of five?"

"Three kids, so yeah." Jackson scrubbed a hand over his jaw. "We hired Jasmine's cousin, Saffron Tate, to help with the kids."

"I call." Caleb threw in his chip. "Jasmine mentioned something about that to me as she was leaving today. Can't do better than a kindergarten teacher who practically raised half the town."

Jackson blew a long breath. "God help us, we're officially parents. At least for now."

The loud cheers followed, then Tanner lifted his beer. "Welcome to the club of exhausted men with no personal time."

Caleb laughed. "How would you know?"

"From watching you," Tanner deadpanned.

Jackson chortled a laugh, shook his head, and looked younger than Asa had seen him in years.

As the moment softened into celebration, Asa leaned back in his chair.

This town.

These men.

This life.

And somewhere down the road… Maggie.

And Poppy.

Jackson nudged his elbow. "Your turn."

"For what?" Asa asked, though he already knew.

"For steppin' up," Jackson said simply. "Talk to her. Ask

her out. And do it before that Paris fool talks her into giving him a second chance."

Asa's gut knotted at the thought.

Caleb added, "If you want her, Asa, go get her. Don't sit around waitin' for the universe to send an engraved invitation."

Tanner tossed his cards aside. "Text her now!"

Asa took a slow breath, the decision forming sharp and clean.

"Yeah," he said. "I'll take care of it first thing in the morning."

Because whatever came next—whatever hard truths were waiting—he needed one quiet night with Maggie first.

Just her.

Just him.

No interruptions.

A place to start.

But when the talk settled and the cards were reshuffled, Asa's mind drifted far beyond the table.

He could still see the white tuft at the back of Poppy's neck—the Griffin mark, the thing newborns in his family wore like a banner. His cousins had it. His aunt. And now that he thought about it, his cousin's daughter. He'd grown up hearing his mom say:

"Hard to deny a Griffin girl baby—they come pre-labeled."

And Poppy…

She carried that streak straight from the Griffin line.

Maggie hadn't mentioned it. Nor had Poppy. Neither seemed aware of what it meant.

Like he said to his Aunt Sue Ellen. Why would they? He and Maggie had been kids together. As far as he could remember, the subject had never come up. No reason to talk about his family's brand. What teenager would think to mention something like that? And since he'd never had a beard in high school—where the family mark showed on men—the subject never surfaced. Occasionally nowadays, he'd grow one in winter and someone would comment on the anomaly. He'd always laugh it off. Call it his birthmark. Easier that way.

The more he thought about it, the more certain he became: Maggie truly believed Julian was Poppy's father—believed it deep in her bones.

He saw it now with painful clarity. Every time she defended Julian's place. Every time she apologized for him. Every time she looked torn in two when Julian came up.

He was becoming more and more sure that Maggie wasn't hiding anything. She wasn't deceiving him?

He didn't know what had happened in Paris. He'd left with a mutual understanding that whatever they were couldn't last. They'd gone their separate ways. He'd returned, married a woman he tried to love and failed. Maggie stayed in Paris and married Julian.

But now—when he told her about the Griffin mark—

How would she take it?

And Poppy… nearly ten, tenderhearted, starstruck by Julian's sudden reappearance. What would it do to her to learn the man she'd built stories around wasn't hers by blood? How would she react to learn that the man who taught her how to sit deep in the saddle was her biological father? Just the idea of crushing her made his chest ache.

Julian—whatever else he was—Poppy adored him. Asa didn't know how he'd react, but he could guess.

Dramatically.

Possessively.

Maybe even cruelly.

The truth wouldn't just topple Maggie's world.

It would split Poppy's in two.

And it would strike Julian right at the core of his pride.

Asa pressed his thumb against the edge of a poker chip until it dug into his skin.

This wouldn't be simple.

This wouldn't be clean.

But it was the truth—and truth had its own gravity. It pulled. It demanded. It waited for its moment.

And the time had come.

He couldn't hold it from Maggie any longer. He had to look her in the eyes and say the words that would change all their lives.

He just prayed that when it happened, she wouldn't pull back. That together they'd figure the next move.

Asa drew a steady breath, grounding himself.

Tomorrow, he'd ask her out.

Tomorrow, he'd open the door.

And then...the truth would come. One way or another.

# Chapter Twenty-Four

## MAGGIE

"What's more important than having a night out as a family?"

Julian's words still burned hot behind my ribs. He'd said it so easily—like it was fact, not wishful thinking. Like he could speak it back into existence just by waving his hand and making it so.

"Popcorn, movie, ice cream. Poppy will love having both her parents on an outing."

She would. Of course she would. That was exactly the problem. It would send the wrong message. And her heart wasn't a toy to play with.

This was why I couldn't postpone confessing to Asa any longer.

I had to stop the merry-go-round of claiming rights to a family night.

Stop the endless what-ifs spiraling through my mind.

Stop pretending uncertainty was safety.

I had to stop running from the truth.

When I told Julian I had plans, he asked if they were

with Asa. I didn't answer, but I could tell from his expression he knew he was right. I knew him well enough to see the shadow pass behind his eyes.

"Of course it's Asa," he murmured. "And if that's more important than a family night out..."

He smiled as though it didn't bother him at all.

But I'd seen the crack in the façade.

He never let me miss the cracks.

As I turned off the highway toward town, I kept replaying Asa's call from earlier that afternoon.

*Hey, Mags. If you're free tonight... I thought we should talk about a few things.*

He'd said it in that steady, careful way he used when he was trying not to spook a skittish horse—or maybe he'd learned it was the perfect way to speak to a skittish woman, which I'd been lately.

I'd agreed because we did need to talk, and the quiet of his apartment felt like the right place for me to finally stop dodging what I owed him. I told him dinner sounded wonderful, hung up, and then spent hours wondering what *things* he'd meant.

Julian making a subtle play to reel me back in?

Whether I was thinking of selling the farm?

Whether I planned to return to Paris and the life I'd left behind?

Asa could have wanted to talk about any number of things—just not the one thing I needed to talk about. The truth that had tied my stomach into knots for days.

Tonight, I would stop running. One way or another, I had to say it—and live with whatever came next.

By the time I reached the edge of town, I'd already talked myself out of turning around twice. My fingers tightened and loosened on the steering wheel, unable to decide if they were ready to let go of the secret—or too terrified to face it.

Now here I was, turning off Main Street toward Griffin's Grocery. The store sat on the corner like always, just a little spiffier than when we were growing up—warm brick, green awning, the Griffin logo painted on the window. My gaze found the two lights glowing upstairs, golden behind the blinds, spilling soft light onto the street below.

Asa's world.

My heart squeezed, sharp and tender.

I parked along the side, leaving the car unlocked—this was Loblolly after all. The night air was so still I could hear the coolers humming from inside the store. A streetlamp buzzed faintly overhead. The air smelled of the beginning of autumn—cool pavement, distant woodsmoke, and the citrusy scent from the whiskey barrel flower arrangements flanking the store's front door.

For a moment, I stood looking down Main Street, as if I could steady myself inside the small-town postcard scene before me.

My hair was perfectly styled. My makeup flawless. A careful kind of armor.

I squared my shoulders, locked the car behind me, and crossed the sidewalk toward the store.

I lined up my thoughts.

Simply state the facts.

Ask for a DNA test.

Done.

Simple request, but the words tangled inside me, turning truth into something fragile and unbelievable. He'll never believe I didn't intentionally keep him from his own daughter. Even I struggled to believe how that had happened.

How had I not seen the similarities between Asa and Poppy sooner?

The upstairs door opened, spilling warm light across the landing. Asa stepped out, silhouette steady and familiar.

No smile. No wave. Just steady. Waiting. A quiet knowing, like he could feel my nerves from fifty feet away.

I drew in a breath, forced a small smile, and walked up the side staircase.

"Hey," I said softly when I reached him. "Sorry I'm late."

His eyes moved over my face—not judging, just seeing. "Come on in. You already look like your day's been a lot."

That almost undid me.

Not the words—just the tone.

Dry, gentle, familiar in a way that made tears press behind my eyes again. The way he could read me like no one else ever had.

His apartment smelled like rosemary potatoes, layered with the warm, yeasty scent of fresh bakery bread from the store below. A lamp glowed near the sofa, softening the room.

The table was set—two plates, two glasses, cloth napkins folded in the neat, squared-off way his mother always insisted on.

The steadiness of it made my throat go tight.

"Wine?" Asa asked.

"Please," I whispered, as if the shaky cadence of my heart might otherwise show.

Dinner was easy—like slipping into something I'd worn comfortably for years. He steered the conversation away from Julian—for which I was profoundly grateful—and into gentler territory: Poppy's riding lesson, Mama humming around the living room again, the dented shipment of canned peaches that made the stockroom smell like August exploded.

I laughed—an actual laugh—at the image of Asa trying to mop up sticky syrup in the back while ringing customers upfront.

And for a moment… just a moment… the knot between my shoulders loosened.

But beneath it all, the truth burned a hole straight through me. I couldn't leave without telling him.

After dinner, he cleared the plates, brought out two slices of his Aunt Sue Ellen's pecan pie he said he'd snagged from the diner, and poured Irish coffees into thick glass mugs. The light overhead softened everything—the room, the air, the dread I'd carried for days.

I wrapped my hands around the mug.

"Asa…" My voice wavered. "There's something I need to tell you."

He set his coffee down slowly. "There's something I want to talk to you about too. But you go first. Mine can wait." He tilted his head, studying me with a steady, unreadable calm. "Take your time. Eat your pie. We're not going anywhere."

If he'd rushed me, I would've shattered. But he didn't.

I stared into the swirling cream in my coffee. "Being back home… watching you with Poppy… it triggered something I should've put together long ago." I took a breath that barely went anywhere. "I need you to know my intent was never to hurt you. Not ever."

My breath hitched harder.

"Years ago, when you came to Paris, I'd been off birth control for months. I told you that. And we were careful." I lifted my gaze. "But after you left… I fell apart. I wandered Paris like a ghost, doubting every dream I'd ever had."

I swallowed. "Then Julian came back into my life. And he was easy. I know now it was because I didn't love him—because I knew he couldn't devastate me the way our parting had. That kind of power only comes from love."

The words scraped on the way out.

"And Julian—he said all the right things."

Shame welled, hot and sharp.

"By the time I realized I was pregnant, I'd been offered a permanent position with the studio. I was on probabtion for six months to make sure I could keep up the pace. The travel, the pressure to create… I seriously considered ending the pregnancy." My voice shook. "I truly believed—because we'd been careful—didn't even consider that you—I just knew that Julian had to be the father. So I told him. I thought he had a right to know."

I blinked hard. "Surprisingly, Julian seemed overjoyed with the news of a child. He begged me to reconsider ending the pregnancy, promised I could have everything—a career, a family. That he'd handle all the details."

A bitter breath slipped out. "He made the future look survivable."

Asa didn't move. Didn't interrupt.

Just listened.

"The timing made sense," I whispered. "Since he and I hadn't always been careful. It felt logical that the baby was his. And honestly—I didn't question it. I was too busy surviving. Too busy holding on to the life I'd just been given and wasn't sure yet that I deserved."

My chest tightened. "But now… watching you with Poppy—"

My tears blurred his face.

"I think I made a terrible mistake." My voice broke. "And if I took something from you—something as precious as a child—because I chose what was easier instead of what was true…"

My tears spilled, hot and unstoppable. "I don't know how to live with that."

Asa reached across the table and brushed tears from my cheeks with his thumb.

"Maggie," he murmured. "Look at me."

I did. Barely.

"I'm not angry with you."

I noticed then—small things I might've missed if I'd been less wrecked: the way his fork lay untouched beside the pie, the way the muscles in his jaw held tension he wasn't letting out, the way his hand stayed steady even as his eyes turned fierce with something like protectiveness.

"You should be." My voice cracked. "You have every right. And I know you'll want a DNA test—I agree we need to have one as proof. Whatever you need. I just can't keep living in this uncertainty."

He squeezed my hand—warm, grounding.

"I don't need a DNA test."

Panic flashed. "Asa, I'm not asking anything of you—I just need to know. That's all. Poppy—we don't have to ever tell her. Or at least not right away, maybe—"

"Maggie," he said firmly. "Stop. Breathe. That's not what I meant."

I blinked. "I don't understand."

He exhaled slowly. "I don't need a DNA test," he said. "Because I already know Poppy's mine."

Everything went still.

"But how could you?" I whispered.

"Because." He stopped, took a deep breath. "Last week when she was riding Sugar her braid came loose during the lesson. She lifted her hair to re-clip it, and I saw the white tuft at the nape of her neck."

I frowned. Of course I knew what he meant—the little anomaly her doctor had brushed off as nothing more than a birthmark. "I know it's unusual, but—"

"It's more than unusual," he said gently. "It's my family mark. Fathers pass it to their children. Boys get the white patch in their beard. Girls carry it at the nape of the neck. It's never skipped a generation."

A sound escaped me—half sob, half disbelief. The birthmark I'd always believed was just Poppy's—an oddity, nothing more—suddenly had a lineage. Asa's. My head swam with the weight of it.

"You never said anything about it." I shook my head in disbelief. "So you've known for days?"

"I think my heart suspected even earlier," he admitted. "I've been drawn to her from the beginning—she felt like home. At first I told myself it was because she was yours. But when I saw the mark… everything clicked."

He paused. "Then Julian showed up, and I knew I couldn't wait anymore. We had to talk, that's why I asked you to come tonight."

Something in me broke open—not painfully, but with relief so sharp it felt like grief.

"And you're not angry…?" I couldn't finish.

"Angry?" He sighed, took my hand in his. "What I am is grateful. Very grateful," he said simply. "Would I have loved being a part of Poppy's first nine years? Of course. But I've let go of any anger I felt. I refuse to waste another minute on regret."

My tears flowed freely.

He took my other hand, held them both in his—firm, certain, tender.

"We'll do the test for you," he said. "For Julian. For paperwork. But not for me. I already know."

He was quiet a moment longer, then added—low, practical, like he was already building a plan in his head—"Tomorrow, we'll talk about next steps. What you want. What you need. And what protects Poppy."

We talked softly for a while longer, about what this could mean, if and when she should know. We talked, and talked, and talked. Then reality settled back in.

"I should go," I said. "Julian will bring Poppy home soon, and if he's waiting… I don't want him twisting anything. He has a talent for saying the wrong thing in a way that almost sounds right."

"Yes," Asa said. "I've noticed."

He walked me down the outside stairs, our fingers brushing, then linking, neither of us rushing. At the bottom, he turned me toward him.

"We'll handle this," he said. "Together."

I nodded, emotions thick in my throat. He didn't kiss me goodbye. And though disappointment tugged low in my chest, I understood his hesitancy. We had too much to work out to convolute it with romance.

I climbed into Mama's car, rolled down the window, and he leaned his forearm against the frame.

"Text me when you get home."

"I will."

I pulled away, watching him in the rearview mirror—standing under the streetlamp, one hand lifted in a small wave.

At the end of the block, headlights blinked on behind me.

I ignored the unease crawling up my spine. It was after ten; people drove home at this hour. Small towns didn't roll up completely.

But when I turned onto the road leaving town, heading toward the orchard, the car turned too.

Not close enough to recognize the make and model, even the color.

Not far enough to miss them tailing me.

The road narrowed.

Trees rose up overhead, stitching the sky into darkness.

The car stayed a safe distance.

Unease curled tight in my stomach.

My hand drifted toward my phone where it sat in the cupholder. For one suspended moment, I considered calling Asa—considered turning around, pulling back into town, letting the lights and the people and the normalcy swallow me whole.

But pride is a stubborn thing. So is denial. And I'd already spent too many years letting fear make choices for me.

When I turned into the long gravel drive leading to our farmhouse, the car pulled in behind me and stopped.

In my rearview mirror I could only see the headlights—twin bright eyes watching me.

Then the car crept backward.

Slowly.

Deliberately.

And turned off their headlights, leaving a black night rolling away into the dark.

My skin prickled.

Was it Julian? My gut said yes.

Had he followed me from Asa's?

Had he watched us on the steps?

If so… did he suspect? No, how could he? He knew nothing of Asa's Paris trip. He didn't have the puzzle pieces to put it together. He would simply believe that Asa and I had rekindled our friendship.

Julian only wanted what he wanted. And right now, that was to be back as a family unit. Lord only knew why, because he wasn't happy when we were. But I knew him well enough to know he wasn't likely to give up easily.

The thought chilled me.

The prickling at the back of my neck didn't fade—

Not when I parked under the pecan trees.

Not when I saw the warm light in Mama's kitchen window.

Not even when I stepped inside and locked the door behind me.

Too much had changed tonight for the world to stay simple.

The orchard was quiet.

The house was still.

But something had shifted.

And I had the feeling that tomorrow—ready or not—everything would start unraveling.

# Chapter Twenty-Five

## MAGGIE

By morning, the relief of last night had settled into something quieter, steadier—like a fever breaking, leaving only the ache of what comes next. I woke early, long before the sun reached over the pecan trees. The house was silent except for the hum of the old refrigerator and the familiar creaks of an old house waking up.

I made coffee, wrapped my hands around the warm mug, and opened my laptop at the kitchen table.

DNA tests.

Rapid turnaround.

Legally admissible.

Secure chain of custody.

I clicked the top option—a three-day turnaround with supervised collection at a clinic twenty miles away. Fast. Clear. Binding. Exactly what we needed.

I filled out the form.

My finger hovered over the send button.

My stomach clenched.

I clicked send.

Asa texted before I could send him the link.

Asa: Morning! You sleep at all?

Me: Barely. Just sent the application for testing.

Asa: Tell me where to be, what time, and I'll handle the rest.

I exhaled slowly. That steadiness of his—I didn't deserve it, but I was grateful for it.

I sent him the link.

Me: This one. Three-day results.

Asa: I'm in. Today?

A ripple of anxiety slid through me. Today meant no more pretending. No more avoiding. Today meant letting the truth start its slow march into the light.

Hiding had never protected me—not from heartbreak, not from regret, not from facing the truth.

Me: Yes. Today. We can pick Poppy up from school. The lab needs to swab your cheeks for the chain of custody. I'll tell Poppy it's like a COVID test—she'll remember.

Asa: 👍 Might work. She's pretty curious.

---

I heard the crunch of tires on gravel around nine-twenty. Not Asa—he would've texted. I stepped onto the porch, coffee in hand, and saw Julian climb out of his rental car—sunglasses, perfect hair, the faintest smile curving at the edges.

He waved up at me, all casual charm. "Thought I'd drop Poppy off at school today."

My spine straightened. "Julian, it's after nine. Poppy's bus picked her up over an hour ago."

The words were barely out before it hit me—taking her to school had been his excuse for showing up.

"Well." He shrugged lightly. "That's fine. We can talk about things."

Talk.

A shiver crawled up my back. Last night's drive flashed through my mind—the car that followed me, slowing at the crossroads, its headlights lingering too long.

"Talk about what?" I asked.

He smiled—a slow, practiced effort. "Us."

"There is no us."

He ignored that. "Look, Paris is really where we should have this conversation. Two weeks there. See if it feels right. Poppy would thrive—I'm thinking the new international school. We could travel on her breaks…" He glanced around the farm. "European culture—"

"Julian." I cut him off before he could spin the fantasy any further. "I haven't decided if or when we'll return to Paris. And until I do, Poppy has a life here. Friends. Riding lessons. The farm. Mama."

"But none of that compares to what she could have."

His voice stayed soft, persuasive—but it folded inward in that familiar way, searching for a weak seam in my resolve.

It used to work. Now it just made me tired.

"I'm not moving back to Paris anytime soon," I said. "If at all." I added for good measure. "And I'm not having this conversation again."

He stared at me, something flickering behind his eyes. He slid on his sunglasses, as if to keep me from reading him too easily.

Julian Black—wannabe viscount extraordinaire—did not like losing. But no matter what happened or didn't happen with the Viscountess, titles didn't transfer in marriage for women the way they did for men. Julian would always be Mr. Black.

"Maggie," he said, in that tone that meant I'd drifted away from his chatter.

I tuned back in. "I can't believe you'd consider giving up your career for this place."

A hot line of irritation ran up my spine. "This place? This place is where I was born and raised. This place is where my heart is. This place is where my daughter's heart lives now."

"This is about him, isn't it?" His tone gave him away. "You're letting Asa Griffin cloud your judgment." He inhaled sharply through his nose. "A grocer. Really, Maggie. This is incredible."

I held his gaze. "Julian, I need to get ready. I have an appointment."

"An appointment?" He didn't bother hiding his doubt. "Where?" His head tilted, the smile thinning into something sharper.

I didn't answer.

I didn't owe him that.

I walked inside and shut the door.

---

Once Julian finally drove off—slowly, too slowly—I found Mama, told her the plan, then headed out to the barn to clear my head.

Work was good for me. Repetitive. Steady. It anchored me when emotions threatened to spin in every direction.

Sugar's stall needed mucking, and the irrigation pump hummed with that familiar stubborn rattle that meant the filter was begging for attention. Always something to do on the farm.

As I worked, my heartbeat slowed.

My thoughts did not.

What will Julian do when he finds out?

Will I be able to keep Poppy from being hurt?

Will she feel betrayed?

Should we tell her now? Later?

Will Julian give us that choice?

How do you rewrite a little girl's history without unraveling her life?

The questions came in waves, cresting and breaking until my mind felt waterlogged.

I turned toward the orchard. Morning sun filtered through the pecan trees, turning their leaves to hammered bronze. The land had held my family for generations—roots deeper than mistakes, stronger than regret.

I wasn't hiding behind excuses.

I refused to run.

Not anymore.

By the time Asa arrived, I'd showered, pulled on clean jeans, dried my hair—and made a decision about the part of my life I'd been avoiding almost as much as the truth.

Writing.

If today ended with answers, tomorrow would start with work.

Regular writing.

Daily video meetings with Katrina. Getting back into the rhythm. Sharing the load.

The idea excited me and scared me in equal measure. I had to know if my writer's block would rear its ugly head again—or if that stumbling block was firmly behind me.

I owed it to everyone—Mama, Poppy, Asa, my writing partner Katrina, my boss Olivia—but most of all, to myself. To finally decide whether my future belonged in Paris… or here, among these trees.

Asa stepped out of his truck, jacket slung over his shoulder, face serious, eyes warm.

"You ready?" he asked.

"Yes."

He opened the passenger door—one of those small gestures that shouldn't have made emotion rise in my throat, but did.

We used the drive to Poppy's school—and the ten minutes waiting for her release—to talk everything through again: Julian, Poppy, the truth, the fallout.

"He loves her," Asa said. "Just… not in a way that understands her."

"He lacks boundaries," I said. "And sensitivity. And timing. And reliability."

He huffed softly. "That's a lot of lacks. Can't help but wonder what you saw in him."

I eyed him. "You forget, I know your ex-wife."

He moaned, laughed, then mimicked a stab to the gut. "Fair enough."

"Julian will push," I warned. "He always does."

"And we'll hold our ground," Asa said evenly. "Because you're not the same woman who left for Paris. And now you have me at your back."

My voice softened. "I'm trying not to be the kind of person who always needs others to clean up her messes."

"You don't have to do this alone."

Something steadied inside me at that.

We agreed on three things:

—Take the test immediately. Today. No delays. No excuses.

—I would not tell Julian until the results arrived. No reason to stir more drama.

—Together, Asa and I would decide how—and when—to tell Poppy, if Julian allowed us the space.

She deserved honesty—wrapped in love, not shock.

When Poppy spotted us outside the school doors, she ran straight into my arms. Then she saw Asa three steps back, and her smile could've lit a Christmas tree.

She chattered the entire drive to the clinic—far more interested in telling Asa about her day than the swabs I explained they'd take. I compared it to a COVID test, something she remembered. She barely listened. Instead, she begged for a riding lesson when we got back to the farm.

The clinic was coldly professional. Efficient.

Forms.

Signatures.

Sterile swabs.

Sealed envelopes.

Stepping back outside, the air felt sharper.

"Three days," Asa said.

"Three days," I echoed, as if saying it aloud made the countdown real.

His fingers brushed mine—not a claim, not even a full touch. Just a promise.

I'm here.

Then he lifted Poppy easily onto his shoulders. She squealed, laughter ringing through the parking lot.

As I watched them, a realization settled heavy and clear.

Julian had never—not once—lifted Poppy onto his shoulders.

And for the first time in years, hope didn't feel like a lie.

---

Asa dropped us at the farm, promising a riding lesson the next day. The rest of the afternoon stretched long and quiet. After pecan sandies and milk, Poppy disappeared into her room for homework. Mama downshifted into her afternoon nap.

I tried to concentrate enough to work, but my mind skittered in a thousand directions. So I walked the orchard instead, letting the wind sift through my hair, grounding myself in the rustle of pecan leaves.

That was when I heard Julian's rental car—a low, throaty rumble entirely out of place among the trees.

A Maserati.

A dusty Maserati.

Back roads in rural Georgia seemed a questionable racetrack for an Italian sports car.

Only Julian would rent a luxury car just to drive into a rural county—and pretend the cost had no effect on him. He hadn't worked since before Poppy was born. I assumed he was still living on the Viscountess's money. I wondered how much longer that would last. Or had it already ended, and that was the reason for his sudden appearance in our lives?

He parked in the drive and waved—too cheerful, too insistent.

"Salut, *ma petite étoile!*" he called—*my little star*, the pet name he'd used for me early in our relationship.

He waited for me on the porch, inviting me to sit with him. I took a rocker instead of the double swing he offered.

Two visits in one day. He must be bored in Loblolly with nothing to occupy his time. Good. Maybe he'd go back to Europe sooner.

He recovered from my rebuff quickly, then lingered for fifteen minutes with nothing much to say.

Trying to corner me into a conversation I didn't want.

Trying to resurrect a family that had never truly existed.

Every part of me stiffened at his words.

I didn't take his bait. He didn't ask about Poppy or indicate he wanted to spend time with her, so I refused to reward what I had come to think of as his underhanded behavior by encouraging this conversation.

"This is my writing time," I said, rising from the swing. "So if you'll excuse me."

He clapped his hands lightly. "Oh, marvelous. You know how much I adore being entertained by your brilliance. Use me as a sounding board—throw out ideas, see what sticks." His eyes glistened with excitement.

I tilted my head, studying him. For the first time, his reaction confused me.

"Julian, I have a writing partner. I don't need anyone to toss around ideas with. I'm sorry—I don't have time to visit today."

Because today wasn't about Julian.

Today was about truth.

About choosing honesty and roots and a future built on something real.

Today was about Asa.

About Poppy.

About finally stepping into the woman I should've been all along.

And tomorrow… tomorrow would bring whatever it brought.

I wasn't running anymore.

# Chapter Twenty-Six

## MAGGIE

By the third morning, the waiting had become its own ritual—quiet, tense, impossible to outrun. I woke before dawn, stared at the familiar pine tongue-and-groove ceiling until the room softened into gray light, then pushed myself upright and followed my morning routine.

Up at five for the daily video call with Katrina to map out the script assignments. The six-hour time difference meant long hours, but sleep no longer came easy, and I'd rather be moving than thinking.

Coffee.

Business meeting.

More coffee.

Open the curtains.

Check on Mama and lay out her pills.

Make breakfast for Mama and Poppy.

Walk Poppy to the end of the drive and see her safely on the school bus.

Feed the barn cats.

Feed Sugar.

Feed the chickens.

Spend the rest of the day working on scripts that for the past two days had refused to hold my attention.

Normal tasks.

Normal motions.

Except the truth due in my inbox today—silent, sealed, certain—was anything but normal.

By eleven o'clock, I abandoned work for lack of focus and drove into town in search of flowers for the beds flanking the front door. Anything to keep my hands busy. Julian called on the drive in. I debated letting it go to voicemail, but he'd only call back—or worse, drive to the farm to talk in person.

So I answered.

"I plan to pick Poppy up from school and take her for ice cream. What time does her school let out?"

Not *can I*. Just *I will*.

And honestly, why wouldn't he assume it was fine to take his daughter for ice cream?

"School lets out at two fifty," I said. I'll call now and add you to the approved pick-up list.

"Okay. See you after. Maybe we could have dinner tonight. As a family."

There it was. He never missed an opportunity.

"I'll check with Mama and let you know," I said, buying time—a coward's move, maybe, but the only one I had. I'd figure out how to turn him down later. Right now, I couldn't handle anything more than waiting on the results.

I checked my email again.

Nothing.

What in the blazes was taking so long?

I made it back to the farm by one with four flats of French marigolds and two flats of snapdragons, which the clerk warned might need watching until the nights turned a little cooler.

I unloaded the flats and went to find Mama, hoping she might want to oversee my planting. As soon as I stepped into the kitchen, I heard her humming—soft, steady, and surprisingly strong. A month ago, she could barely make it down the hall without bracing herself against the walls. Today she stood fully dressed, hair brushed, blush and lip gloss applied—the only makeup she ever bothered with—folding dish towels with determined pride.

"Well, look at you," I said, setting her keys in the drawer where she kept them. "You're supposed to be resting."

She sniffed. "Resting is for people who don't have laundry. Or children. Or opinions." She lifted her chin. "Dr. Landers says if I keep improving, he might clear me to drive short distances next month."

"That's wonderful," I said, kissing her cheek. "So don't overdo it and go backward. I found French marigolds and the short snapdragons. Care to oversee my planting?"

Before she could answer, a knock sounded on the back-door frame—three knocks, then a double. Asa's familiar pattern.

He stepped inside with a case of sparkling water under one arm and a brown paper bag in the other.

"Brought these for you, Barbara," he said. "The lemon kind you like."

Mama's face softened. "You didn't have to do that, Asa."

His attention shifted to me, reading every worry I

refused to voice. He held out the paper bag. "Your favorite ribs. Keep you from cooking tonight." His gaze softened. "You holding up?"

I nodded, pressing a hand to my stomach. "Too nervous to eat, I think." I sniffed. "But those ribs smell heavenly."

Mama paused her folding, watching us with a knowing look—but for once, not pressing.

He met her gaze. "Make her eat something."

Then, to me, "I can't stay." He touched my elbow gently before stepping away. "Call me the second you hear anything."

---

The afternoon crawled.

I planted, then reorganized the coat closet. Refolded towels. Wiped down counters that already sparkled. Walked the orchard without remembering leaving the house. Checked my email at least eleven hundred times.

When my cell phone rang—and I saw the clinic's number—I nearly dropped it.

My heartbeat slammed against my ribs.

"Hello?" My voice shook.

"Ms. Black? This is Rhonda from the genetics clinic. I'm calling to confirm your results are complete."

My breath tangled. "Okay."

"The full report is being mailed to the address you provided. It should arrive within two business days. I'll also email a copy. But I can confirm verbally now if you like."

"Yes, please." My hand shook. Just tell me.

A rustle of paper. A pause.

"Results indicate a ninety-nine point nine nine percent probability of paternity for Mr. Asa Griffin."

My knees weakened. The room blurred.

"Thank you," I breathed.

After she hung up, I stood motionless, letting the truth settle into my bones. I'd expected it. I'd feared it. I'd hoped for it.

And still—it hit with a force that emptied my lungs.

I dialed Asa.

He answered on the first ring. "Hey?"

"It's you," I whispered. "Asa… it's you. Officially."

A breath left him—quiet, weighted. "I already knew. But it's still good to hear."

Tears stung my eyes. "I'm so sorry for the years you missed—"

"Stop," he said, firm but gentle. "We're not looking backward. We know for certain now. And that means I get every year going forward."

A laugh—half sob—escaped me. "You and your optimism."

"Somebody's gotta balance out you McAllister women," he murmured.

I exhaled. "Julian's picking Poppy up from school. They're getting ice cream. I'll tell him once they're home. Quietly. Away from her."

"You don't need to be alone with him when he hears this," Asa said, warning threading his voice.

"I won't be. Mama's here. Just… be on standby?"

"I already am."

We hung up, and I leaned against the counter, my hands still trembling.

---

By four o'clock, I stood at the window watching the drive.

By four forty-five, I began checking my phone for texts.

By five o'clock, the knot in my stomach tightened into a painful coil.

School let out at two fifty. Add ice cream and the drive home—it shouldn't take this long.

I dialed Julian's number.

Voicemail.

I tried again.

Voicemail.

"Julian," I said, fighting for calm, "just call me. Let me know you're on your way." I disconnected before I said something I couldn't take back.

At five twelve, with still no return call, Mama placed a hand on my shoulder.

"Honey, why don't you call Edna Caldwell at the ice cream parlor and see if Poppy and Julian left?"

"Great idea." I searched for the number.

"No, honey," Ms. Calwell said gently. "I haven't seen your little girl or your husband today."

"Ex-husband." The correction came automatically.

Then her words registered, and it felt like something in my chest dropped clean through the floor.

I dialed Asa.

"Julian hasn't brought Poppy home," I tried—and failed—to keep the worry out of my voice. "I checked. They never went for ice cream."

Three seconds of silence.

"I'm heading to my truck," Asa said. "I'll be there in fifteen minutes."

I hung up with shaking hands. I turned to Mama and repeated everything, even though she already knew—just to give it the weight of believability.

We were still standing in the kitchen when Asa's truck

spun gravel in the drive. He took the porch steps two at a time.

"I called Caleb," he said. "He wants you to call him."

I dialed and put it on speaker.

Caleb answered on the third ring. "Hey, Maggie."

I repeated everything, tried slowing my words, but there was no need—Asa had already filled him in.

"They're so late," I said. "Julian picked her up. But they didn't get ice cream. No calls. No texts."

"You checked to make sure he didn't pick her up before school let out?"

"What? No—he said after school." My stomach lurched. "I didn't check."

"All right," he said. "Give me a second."

Thirty seconds later, he was back.

"Poppy left class before lunch."

The words didn't compute. They hovered above me, sharp and senseless. He must've picked her up right after he called me. Right after I called the school and added his name to the approved pick up list.

Why would he lie?

Because he controlled with charm, not deception.

Taking her early meant planning.

"Ping his phone," Asa said. "Find out where he's taken her."

"I can't without exigent circumstances or a warrant," Caleb said.

Asa swore under his breath. "Then do something."

"I have an idea," Caleb said. "I'll call you back."

Asa turned to me. "I'll call Stella. Maybe Julian brought her to the River House. Stella's got canoes and kayaks."

Mama snorted. "Julian never struck me as the outdoorsy type."

"It's a long shot," Asa said, already dialing.

I stood frozen—hollow, trembling, unable to think past the roaring in my ears. Julian had never done this. Not once in three years. He missed birthdays. Forgot time zones. Sent vague apologies instead of child support or Christmas gifts. Drifted in and out of Poppy's life like weather—unreliable, impersonal, easy to ignore.

Taking her wasn't his pattern.

The look in his eyes when he'd asked about Asa twisted my stomach. Was this payback? A reminder that he still existed?

Julian didn't love me—not enough for vengeance. And he didn't love Poppy enough to risk his jet-setting life.

Unless that life was already over.

So what was this?

Control. Curiosity. Or the sudden realization that he no longer had a starring role in anyone's story.

"Caleb's the police," I said hoarsely. "Why can't he do more?"

Asa paced the kitchen. His phone rang. He checked the screen and hit speaker.

"I talked to Joleen," Caleb said, brisk. "She has a friend who works under the radar."

"Joleen's on leave," I said.

"She is. But she agreed to make the call. He can ping the phone without setting off alarms. I'll let you know as soon as we have his location."

A tremor rolled through me.

Asa came to my side and took both my hands.

"We're going to find her," he said—to me, then again to Mama. "We'll find her."

Outside, the pecan trees stood unmoving, shadows stretching long across the yard.

But everything inside me was unraveling—thread by thread.

My daughter was out there somewhere.

And whatever peace Asa and I had claimed last night was already slipping through our fingers.

# Chapter Twenty-Seven

ASA

By the time Barbara insisted they sit down to eat, nobody was hungry.

The ribs he'd brought earlier lay on a platter in the center of Barbara's kitchen table, the sauce congealing at the edges. Potato salad, coleslaw, rolls. It could've passed for a Sunday spread, if not for the way Maggie kept checking her phone every thirty seconds, like she could will it to ring.

Barbara had insisted they plate food anyway. "Nobody thinks straight on an empty stomach," she'd said, pushing a fork into Maggie's hand. "You don't have to clean the plate. Just take a bite."

Asa tried. The meat tasted good—smoky, tender—but it sat in his mouth like cotton. He watched Maggie instead. The set of her jaw. The way she worried the edge of her napkin between her fingers. The way her eyes kept drifting to the window, as if Poppy might magically appear at the edge of the pecan grove, backpack bouncing, laughter on her lips.

"She's with Julian," Barbara said quietly, answering the

fear none of them voiced. "And for all his faults, he does love that child. The man's indulgent, not malicious."

"Indulgent doesn't mean harmless," Asa said before he could stop himself.

Barbara gave him a look over the tops of her glasses. "I didn't say harmless. I said he's not the kind that hurts with his hands. That matters."

Maybe it did. Maybe it was supposed to help. It didn't do a thing for the picture in Asa's mind—Poppy's small hand swallowed in Julian's, being led who-knew-where while Maggie sat at home and waited. He recognized it for what it was—a play by design to bring her under his control.

Maggie pushed her plate back. "I can't do this," she said. "I can't just sit here and eat potato salad and ribs until I know where Poppy is and that she's okay. Julian has a Maserati, and on these back roads, anything could've happened—"

"Caleb put out feelers," Asa said. "No report of a Maserati accident in Georgia."

Her phone vibrated against the table.

All three of them froze.

Asa caught the name on the screen first.

Joleen.

He snatched it up and hit speaker. "Jo. Tell me you've got something."

On the other end, he heard the echo of a TV playing, a burst of childish laughter, and the faint clatter of a pot lid. Home sounds.

"I've got something," Joleen said. "I'm standing in my kitchen stirring pasta like a well-adjusted mother of three, but my brain is still wired for fieldwork. So let's multitask. You're on speaker with me and Jackson. Kids are in the living room with Saffron keeping them in check. And I've got about twelve minutes before I have to drain this pot."

Maggie leaned in, knuckles white on the edge of the table. "Do you know where they are?"

Joleen didn't make them wait. "Ping from Julian's phone hit about twenty minutes ago. We waited because we wanted eyes on him before verifying his location—just to be sure it was Julian and Poppy there and not just his cell phone. He's in Savannah. JW Marriott on River Street."

Barbara sucked in a breath. "Savannah?"

Asa's gut clenched. "He took her out of the county."

"But not across state lines," Joleen added.

"Savannah is three hours away," Maggie said, her voice starting to fray. "He promised ice cream. That's not ice cream, that's—"

"A runaway trip," Barbara said softly.

Nobody argued.

"Okay," Asa said, forcing his voice steady. "So we know the hotel. Do we know anything else?"

"I called another friend—one of my best friends and an ex–U.S. Marshal," Joleen said. "Name's Katelyn Parsi. She and her husband own a security firm in Savannah. She knows the security manager at that JW. If I ever had to trust someone to watch my kids without blinking, it'd be her. She has one of her team on River Street right now, eyes on the hotel."

Asa swallowed. "Have they actually seen Poppy?"

"Yes," Joleen said. "Hang on, I'm calling her in."

There was a small chime, then another line clicked open.

"This is Katelyn."

"Hey," Joleen said. "It's Jo again. You're on with me,

Asa, and Maggie Black, Poppy's mother. We're in Loblolly. You're on speaker."

"Understood," Katelyn said. Her voice was calm, level, with that clipped warmth of someone used to talking scared people down off ledges. "My team's got eyes on your guy. Late forties—early fifties, dark hair, polished, European—my guy thinks French from the accent. Checked in as Julian Black, along with a young girl around eight or nine. Dark braids. Blue T-shirt with a pony on it. Says she's his daughter."

"That's her," Maggie said, her voice breaking on the last word.

Asa reached under the table and found her hand. She gripped his like a lifeline.

"All right," Katelyn said. "Here's what I know. He checked in a little before five local time. Two-room suite overlooking the river. Paid with a high-limit card tied to an Italian address. Introduced her at the front desk as 'Mademoiselle Poppy Black, princess of the day.'"

Maggie closed her eyes.

"After check-in, they hit the gift shop," Katelyn went on. "She's now the proud owner of a sequined backpack, a stuffed dolphin, and a pair of star-shaped sunglasses. He bought her a navy dress with gold stars from one of the riverfront boutiques, which she is now wearing at the rooftop restaurant. She's drinking a Shirley Temple with extra cherries. He's working his way through a flight of very expensive red wine, which he seems to know how to appreciate."

A grim, involuntary thought slid through Asa's mind: of course he does.

"He's doting," Katelyn said. "Pulling out her chair, taking pictures on his phone, leaning in close when he talks.

She looks… happy. A little overstimulated, but not scared. No raised voices, no grabbing, no signs of distress."

"So he's buying her," Asa said, the words coming out flat.

"Well, that's one way to look at it," Katelyn said. "From where I'm sitting, it looks a lot like a father trying to play prince for the night. That doesn't mean it's right to cart her off without her mother's knowledge, but it does mean it's not going to hit anyone's abduction radar unless the child asks for help or appears afraid."

"She would never think she needed help," Maggie whispered, more to herself than anyone else. "She would go anywhere with him."

"As far as anyone in that hotel knows," Katelyn said gently, "a girl is on a fancy night away with her dad. That's how this reads from the outside."

Maggie dug her nails into Asa's palm. "He didn't tell me he was taking her to Savannah. He tricked me about the time he'd pick her up. How is that not—"

"Ms. Black," Katelyn said, careful and kind, "I'm not saying it's okay. I'm saying the minute you walk into the hotel and start a fight, the staff and Savannah PD are going to see a custody dispute between two parents with no court orders on record. They will not see a kidnapping. Kidnapping is, quite frankly, a long way off."

The kitchen went quiet except for the faint hum of the refrigerator.

On the other end, a child's laughter rang out again, followed by Jackson's deep voice saying something about keeping sauce off the ceiling.

Barbara sat back in her chair, eyes narrowed in thought. "Julian's indulgent," she murmured. "Always has been. Man knows how to spin a fantasy. Did from the moment he stepped into my kitchen for the first time. But he's never had cruelty in him, Maggie."

"That doesn't mean she won't get hurt," Asa said. He didn't raise his voice, but it came out rough. "A man like that can break a kid's sense of what's real without lifting a finger."

Barbara met his gaze evenly. "Didn't say he wouldn't cause harm. Said he doesn't do it with his hands. Like I said before, there's a difference."

And that, Asa thought, was still a problem. Bruises were easier to prove. But a bruise, Asa was sure, would result in him being behind bars for murder.

On the phone, Katelyn cleared her throat. "Jo, here's my suggestion. I'll keep eyes on them tonight as much as my cameras and hotel staff allow. I'll log room charges, staff interactions, approximate times in and out. If this turns into something bigger, you'll have a record. But unless she signals a reason this isn't a daddy-daughter mini-vacation, I can't intervene directly."

"We appreciate any help," Joleen said. "Can you text me when they head back upstairs?"

"Already planned," Katelyn said. "And Ms. Black?"

"Yes?" Maggie managed.

"For what it's worth, your girl doesn't look like she's been brainwashed. She's watching him. Taking it all in. But I know from experience that kids see through fantasy and make up their own mind what's real and what's not."

Taking it all in sounded exactly like Poppy.

"Thank you," Maggie whispered.

"Hang in there," Katelyn said. "I'll be in touch."

The line clicked as Katelyn dropped off the call, leaving them on with just Joleen.

For a moment, nobody spoke.

Maggie stared at the phone like if she waited Joleen might spit out a different outcome. She looked up at Asa, eyes blazing.

"I'm going," she said. "I don't care what hotel security thinks. She's my daughter. I'm not sitting here while he parades her around Savannah like an accessory."

Every part of Asa agreed. His muscles were already coiled to stand, to grab his keys, to get her in the truck and head east.

"No," Joleen said. The word came through the speaker like a door slamming.

"You show up in that lobby tonight," she went on, "worked up and demanding, and you will be the one they escort outside. He'll be the one staying calm, telling Poppy how 'upset Mommy gets.' Do you really want to hand him that script?"

"What do you expect me to do?" Maggie shot back. "Bake cookies and hope he returns her when he's bored?"

"I expect you not to make your first major move in public with no custody order on file," Joleen said. "Right now, on paper, Julian has the same parental rights you do."

"That is not true," Maggie snapped. "I'm her caregiver. The one who takes her to school. To the doctor. To bed when she has nightmares. He hasn't seen her in three years—"

"In every way that matters, you're her primary parent," Joleen said, her voice softening. "But in the eyes of the law? You and Julian are equal. You've already said that your divorce states shared custody. And you've never filed for primary custody. I'm willing to bet you didn't ask his permission before you brought her to Loblolly."

The words landed hard.

Maggie flinched, color rising in her cheeks. "He wasn't around to ask. For. Three. Years."

"I'm not defending him," Joleen said. "I'm telling you what's going to matter when this turns into paperwork and hearings. That alone could be the reason he states for coming to the States at great expense, you get my drift?" She let that sink in, then added, "This might not go your way if you push at the wrong time."

Asa forced himself to unclench his jaw. "So what do we do? Just sit on our hands while he plays king to his princess?"

"No," Joleen said. "You get smart. You document. You pick your moment and make it count."

She went quiet for a beat, then continued. "Here's what I suggest. Tonight, you don't go to Savannah. You let him have his show. You call him later, when you know they're back in the room. You keep your voice calm. You tell him you know where he is. You tell him you expect Poppy home tomorrow. You don't scream. You don't threaten. You do not give him anything he can twist into 'unstable mother.'"

"And if he refuses?" Maggie asked, voice low.

"Then we start the official process," Joleen said. "You'll need him to keep her more than one night away from you, but in the meantime we can send the paternity report to an attorney in Savannah. I'll set it up. We'll be ready to file for primary custody, defined visitation, a passport restriction. You use this little runaway trip—the early school pickup, the over-the-top spending—as evidence of impulsive judgment and emotional manipulation. And in the meantime, we keep a record of everything."

Barbara nodded, hands folded on the table. "You draw lines," she said. "In ink, not feelings."

Maggie looked like she wanted to argue, to fling her

chair back and bolt for the door. Instead, she stared down at the untouched ribs in front of her, then back up at the phone.

"This feels like doing nothing," she said.

"This is not nothing," Joleen replied. "This is restraint. Emotional reaction is kicking in a hotel door and giving him a story to tell. Strategy is letting him show you exactly who he is while you build the case you'll need to protect her long-term."

Silence settled again, heavier but clearer somehow.

Asa watched Maggie's face. Her eyes were bright, her hands still shaking. But her spine straightened. She hadn't broken. Not yet.

"We'll get her back," he said quietly. "And when we do, we'll make sure he can't pull something like this again."

She held his gaze for a long moment, then nodded once.

"Okay," she said. "We do it your way. For now."

In the background on Joleen's end, a child shrieked with laughter. Jackson's voice rumbled something about chasing the dog in the house.

"I have to drain this pasta and feed my family," Joleen said. "I'll text the second Katelyn tells me they're headed up to the room. Then we'll plan your call, Maggie. You're not doing that part alone either."

"Thank you," Maggie said.

"Hang in there," Joleen replied, then the line clicked off.

Barbara exhaled and pushed the platter of ribs an inch closer to Maggie. "Now," she said, "somebody is going to eat one of these before they turn to leather. No sense planning a custody war on an empty stomach."

This time, when Asa reached for a rib, Maggie reached too. She didn't take a big bite, but she took one. It felt like a small act of defiance against the panic clawing at all of them.

Outside, the late light slanted through the pecan trees, stretching shadows long over the yard. Far to the east, along the curve of the Savannah River, lights would be flickering on above cobblestones and water—casting their reflection on a night designed to feel like a fairy tale.

They couldn't stop the show Julian was putting on tonight.

But they could decide how the story ended.

From here on out, Asa thought, wanting wouldn't be enough.

They were going to need a plan.

# Chapter Twenty-Eight

## MAGGIE

Joleen had warned me this part would feel like chewing glass.

She wasn't wrong.

We'd already covered the script—what to say, what to avoid, what to repeat if he tried to derail me. Joleen synced her phone to mine so she could listen and record, routed Asa's phone through a backup line, and fed me a private channel through the earbud in my left ear in case I needed coaching. Real U.S. Marshal wizardry. Knowing she was riding shotgun gave me a steadiness I hadn't felt all day.

The plan was to call the hotel and ask for his room—Julian had ignored every call and text I'd sent, but Joleen said we'd have a better chance of him answering the hotel phone because he'd assume it was staff.

I sat at the kitchen table, the hotel number glowing on my screen. Mama and Asa stood in the mudroom doorway—silent, steady, their presence anchoring me.

"Okay, let's roll," Joleen murmured in my ear. "Still early enough that Poppy is awake. Ask to speak to her, then finish up with your demand. Remember, this is a power play. Keep it factual. Calm. You expect your daughter home tomorrow. That's it. Completely logical."

Logic.

What an impossible word when my nine-year-old was two hours away with a man who treated theatrics as parenting. It was the only kind of parenting he'd managed after we separated—and I'd let him, because selfishly, it meant I had Poppy to myself except for those brief hours he swung through Paris.

I pressed call.

It rang twice, then I asked the operator to connect me to Julian Black's suite.

"*Bonsoir*," Julian said.

Soft. Self-satisfied. French. Like he was stepping through a velvet curtain onto a private stage and wanted to stand out in the memory of even a hotel clerk.

"It's Maggie," I said.

Silence.

I waited another three seconds, then said, "Would you care to explain why you took Poppy to Savannah?"

"It was Friday, and a beautiful day," he said lightly, and too quickly not to have had his answer perfected with previous thought. "A lovely time to begin a weekend holiday."

If he was surprised I'd found him in Savannah, he didn't show it.

"Where is Poppy?"

"Watching a movie in her room," he said, not a trace of concern in his voice. "We have a two-bedroom suite." When I didn't comment, he added, "We had a full day—shopping, lunch, a walk along the river, then dinner on the rooftop.

Savannah is enchanting. You really should have come with us."

"I don't remember being invited," I said, "or told that you had anything planned beyond ice cream after school."

"Perhaps you'd like to join us tomorrow. We could make a family day of it. It would be… lovely, no?"

There it was—his opening gambit.

Charm first.

Pressure second.

Asa stepped up behind me, quiet but present. Joleen's voice hummed low in my ear.

"Give him the instruction."

I steadied my breath. "Julian, I expect Poppy home in the morning."

A soft laugh.

Patronizing.

"Home? Maggie, *mon cœur*, home is Paris, which would be very difficult to arrange by tomorrow. If you mean your little family farm… I'm afraid that doesn't align with our plans. I've promised Poppy a full day of sightseeing. She's barely had time to enjoy anything. But if you decide to join us, we can turn this father-daughter holiday into a family one."

My throat tightened.

Behind me, Asa muttered something sacrilegious under his breath.

Joleen whispered, "School. Say it exactly."

"Julian," I said evenly, "Poppy has school on Monday. Georgia has truancy laws. Pulling her out early on Friday and missing Monday isn't optional."

He gave a long, theatrical sigh—like I was the one being dramatic.

"Maggie, you have become so rigid. It is a family holiday. A few days of absence won't harm her. In France—"

"We're not in France," I said. Sharper than planned. I tempered my tone. "We're in Georgia. She's enrolled in public school, which has mandatory attendance requirements. She cannot miss another day of school."

A pause stretched—a subtle tightening. I knew from experience this would be the moment his ego shifted from velvet to iron.

"Who is with you?" His tone hardened. "The grocer?"

I didn't answer.

"Of course," he scoffed. "The grocer. Always looming, isn't he? Whispering in your ear. Maggie… mon dieu… is this really the relationship you want for us?"

"There is no us," I said. "Bring Poppy home tomorrow."

His voice cooled instantly.

"I think it's completely understandable for a father to have a weekend trip with his daughter. I'll bring back our daughter after our holiday."

And then the line went dead.

I stared at the phone, pulse hammering, the silence louder than anything he'd said.

Joleen's video feed popped onto the screen.

"He's not bringing her tomorrow, and I'm not sure he'll bring her on Sunday. He's proving a point," I repeated, as if saying it aloud might help my mind absorb it. "And somehow, I've played into his hand."

"You're right," Joleen said, her tone matching her face—cop flat, emotionless. "Doesn't sound like he plans to meet your tomorrow deadline."

Asa exhaled his frustration, jaw tight, fist clenched.

"We're going to need assurance he doesn't stray from Savannah."

"What kind of assurance?" Joleen asked.

"Katelyn's security team," Asa said without missing a beat. "You said they've got experienced ex–U.S. Marshals on staff. I want them to tail him."

Joleen didn't push back immediately, but I could tell she wasn't one hundred percent on board.

"I agree," I said. "Otherwise, I'm going there myself to bring her home."

"Big mistake." Joleen blew out a breath. "Okay, look, I know you need to know she's safe and the first knee-jerk reaction is to go to Savannah, but honestly, it can backfire. Do you believe Poppy is in danger?"

"Not physical danger," I said.

"Then I must remind you once again—he is her father of record."

I'd emailed the DNA report to Joleen in case we needed it for the police, so she knew the truth. I'd asked her to keep it to herself for now.

"Julian has no reason at this point to believe there will be a custody dispute, right?" She lifted her brow and stared us down from ten miles away. "And you said he hasn't seen her in three years. This might just be him trying to compensate for being a lousy dad."

I closed my eyes, choosing my words carefully.

"Before coming to Loblolly, Julian hadn't been part of Poppy's day-to-day life in five years. It's been three years since he even bothered to visit more than an hour or two at a time. We separated when Poppy was turning four."

"Yes, I have that in my notes," she said.

"He filed for divorce, and since then he shows up two or three times a year for hour-long visits when he passes through Paris with his girlfriend. That's the extent of his parenting. If he wants to launch a Father-of-the-Year campaign, fine. But he's not her biological father."

She opened her mouth to speak, and I held up my hand. "Yes, I know he doesn't know that."

A beat of silence.

"You're absolutely sure he doesn't know?" Joleen asked.

"Yes, I'm sure." I said. "I just found out for certain today. There hasn't been time to have that conversation yet."

"If he doesn't know, then it doesn't change the legal facts," Joleen said. "But if it will help you sleep, I'll call Katelyn and order a full-on surveillance."

Which made me wonder if she truly believed there was nothing to worry about.

Within minutes, Katelyn Landers, the ex-US Marshal who now owned a security firm, called Asa to confirm arrangements.

Every time Julian left the hotel, someone would follow.

Every purchase. Every conversation.

I told myself it was precaution. Protection.

But it didn't feel like either.

It felt like a quiet net tightening—around Julian, around Poppy—unseen, unbroken.

And once cast, impossible to pretend it hadn't been deliberate.

"I want daily reports," I said. My voice finally felt steady. "Morning and night."

"You'll get them," Katelyn replied. "And I'll call myself if anything urgent comes in. For now, the smartest thing you can do is prepare for what comes next."

Prepare? Prepare for what?

Another day without my daughter?

Another round of Julian's performances?

I pressed my palms to my forehead. "There has to be something else we can do."

"There isn't," Joleen said gently. "Not tonight. Not without a court order."

We ended our call without me saying more. But Joleen was wrong.

There was something else I could do.

A small, risky seed of an idea—sparked by everything Katelyn Landers' team had observed: the sequined backpack, the new dress, the rooftop dinner. The entire over-the-top show.

Julian didn't know how to love without an audience.

And he hated looking foolish in front of the people he admired most.

"I have one more card to play," I said, pushing my chair back.

Both Asa and Mama stared at me like I'd grown a second head.

"Katrina is an acquaintance of Isabella, the Viscountess," I said. "Julian's girlfriend. Lover. Fiancée—whatever she is to him. If Isabella hears he flew across the ocean to chase after me—possibly dragging Poppy along to make some grand romantic gesture—"

Mama crossed her arms. "You think she'll show up out of jealousy and that will snap him back?"

"I think Julian performs for status," I said. "If the Viscountess believes this trip is about me, if she thinks it's a power play in their relationship—not fatherhood—and if she still loves him, she might reach out. And honestly, the longer he stays, the way he's acting… I don't believe this is about Poppy at all. I think he's waiting around Loblolly for Isabella to make a move."

"And he won't risk losing her or his status as her future husband," Asa said quietly.

"Exactly." I swallowed. "If they fight, he'll rush back to Europe to fix it. And he'll bring Poppy home first."

"Or he'll drag her to London," Asa said darkly.

"He won't," I said, steadier than I felt. "First—I have Poppy's passport. And second, she'd get in the way of their jet-setting life."

"Let's run it by Joleen," Asa said. He dialed and I explained my plan.

She nodded. "It's a gamble. But it won't hurt you legally—and it has the possibility of shortening this circus."

I wasted no time calling Katrina, my hands shaking as I held the phone. The moment I heard her voice, the tears came.

"Maggie? Honey—what's wrong?"

I took a breath and told her. Quickly. Quietly. All of it.

By the time I finished, she'd called Julian every name in the book.

"I'll give Isabella a nudge," she said. "Woman to woman. I don't know her well, but enough to know she doesn't like competition. And as hard as this is to believe, I think she actually loves him. Consider it done."

"Thank you," I whispered.

After we hung up, I leaned forward, gripping the counter. The room felt too bright. Too still. Too full of air I couldn't breathe.

Asa stepped behind me, placing a warm hand between my shoulder blades.

"You did the right thing," he said softly.

I prayed he was right.

I prayed the seed we'd planted would pull Julian back—quickly, cleanly, and an ocean away from Poppy.

Without hurting her.

Because she was the only thing that mattered.

She was in a city she didn't know, wrapped inside Julian's fantasy.

And I was holding the line with nothing but words.

And if this was just another of Julian's life plays, then Act III had begun.

Everything now depended on what cracked first—

Julian's ego.

Or my composure.

# Chapter Twenty-Nine

## MAGGIE

The day after my call with Julian, I couldn't stop reliving the conversation. Why hadn't I argued—demanded he bring Poppy home? Why hadn't I gone to Savannah and taken her back myself? How could I rest everything on Isabella, a woman I didn't even know?

As if he sensed my state of mind, Asa called, reminding me that he closed the story early on Saturday and suggested we have a quiet evening at his place. Maybe watch a movie. Have dinner in. Relax. I thanked him and politely refused, citing Poppy. The orchard. Leaving Mama home alone. I rattled off a dozen reasons why I shouldn't leave the farm right now.

Mama walked into the kitchen and caught the last part of our conversation. She fixed me with one of her looks. "You should take Asa up on his offer. You need a change of scenery. You're no good to anyone running on fumes."

And because she was right—and because I couldn't stop thinking about how unlike Julian it was to hang up on me, and what that meant—I called Asa and told him I'd changed my mind and would love to spend the evening with him.

I ignored the fact that it was barely four o'clock in the afternoon, poured a glass of wine, ran a bubble bath, and vowed not to come out for at least thirty minutes.

Forty minutes later, I slipped into a floor-length ecru lace skirt and cream silk top, braided my hair, touched up my makeup, grabbed my purse, and went in search of Mama.

She was in the kitchen with Sue Ellen, who'd stopped by for dessert, coffee, and a few hours of gossiping. I told Mama to call me if she needed anything. Anything at all. Then I left for town.

---

I parked in Asa's private space behind his store. I had a fleeting moment of homesickness—or maybe the sensation of returning to my childhood, when life felt easier, lighter. I walked to the sidewalk and stood for a moment, taking in the lights of Loblolly's main street glowing warm against the early evening.

On Saturdays, all of Main Street closed early. Many storefronts were already dark—antique lamps dimming, shades lowered over the Honeysuckle Lane Bakery. Across the street, the bell on the Cut Right Barbershop door jingled as a man and his young son stepped onto the sidewalk. Mr. Glower flipped his OPEN sign to CLOSED.

Asa had added window boxes down the length of his building. They overflowed with herbs mixed with marigolds and small decorative pepper plants. A chalkboard sign on the sidewalk promised vine-ripe tomatoes and locally grown sunflowers, and for the first time I noticed the new light fixtures he'd installed. Even though summer dusk was still hours away, the Edison bulbs were already on, mimicking gas lanterns and giving the brick exterior a flickering golden halo.

---

Mama had mentioned that Asa sold his family's homestead after his divorce—that turning the second floor of the store into an apartment was meant to be temporary. He'd kept the land that abutted our farm and built a new barn for his three horses. According to Sue Ellen, if and when he married and started a family, she reckoned he'd rebuild. Right now he devoted his time to his business. It was a subject we'd never discussed.

---

He stepped out a private side door and waved me inside. He'd shed the apron he usually wore when he worked, the same style his dad and grandfather had worn before him. His sleeves were rolled to his elbows, his hair a little messy. He looked like a man who'd had a busy Saturday.

His eyes scanned my face. His smile said it all—*You're here. You're safe. Come inside.*

A little piece of me unlocked.

"I need to do a final walk-through of the store before locking up. It won't take but a minute."

He ushered me down the center aisle, and the familiar scents hit me—fresh basil from the produce baskets, warm bread from the deli counter, and the savory warmth of the specialty meat case, the same one his dad used to stock twice on weekends. Little plastic tubs of Griffin's meat rub were stacked on top—a recipe Asa's family had always treated like a state secret, and one no Loblolly barbecuer would cook a steak without.

"You okay?" he murmured as we walked toward the front door.

"Better. Amazing what a glass of wine and a warm bubble bath can accomplish," I said. "I feel as if I've been granted permission to leave my life for a few hours, thanks to Mom's lecture on self-care. Not her words, but you get the drift."

"She's a smart woman," he said softly. "Come on. Let's go upstairs."

He flipped his sign to CLOSED, locked the front double doors, and led me through the back corridor to the narrow staircase that led upstairs. The door opened, and the quiet of his apartment embraced us—warm lighting, soft music, and the scent of garlic and olive oil drifting from the kitchen.

"You're cooking," I said, surprised. "I assumed we'd order a pizza—or pick up something from the diner."

"Nope, I'm cooking," he said. "Well—halfway cooking, anyway. On Saturdays the deli roasts chickens, so I pulled one and a few other things from the deli case. Nothing better than a warm meal and a good bottle of wine to set the evening right."

Asa was an unfussy cook, confident in the way he moved—pulling roasted vegetables from the oven, slicing a loaf of crusty rosemary bread, stirring a simmering pot of tomato-basil soup that smelled like something from a sunlit Italian kitchen.

"Wine?" he asked.

"Yes," I breathed. "Absolutely yes."

He poured two glasses, handed me one, and nodded toward the small dining table by the window. Traffic passed below in slow, amber glows. My problems felt far away up here, softened.

We ate in companionable quiet. Tomato soup. Roasted chicken with herbs. Pasta tossed with roasted vegetables and basil pesto. Bread still warm from the oven. He kept watching me out of the corner of his eye—not hovering, not pressing, just making sure I was relaxed.

After dinner, he stacked plates in the sink and shook his head when I stood to help.

"Sit. You look like you're being held together by a single thread right now."

"I might be," I admitted.

In the end, I agreed to let him wash as long as I dried. The quiet between us stopped feeling empty and started feeling intentional.

"Movie?" he asked when the last plate was put away.

"What genre?"

"Something that doesn't involve explosions or affairs or people shouting about their feelings."

I huffed a laugh. "So… animated children's film?"

He smirked. "Close enough."

We ended up on the couch under one of his old quilts—muted blues and greens he claimed his grandmother had stitched decades ago. Asa queued up *Casablanca*, the black-and-white glow washing the living room in soft silver.

"Ah," I said. "A love story after all."

"During a war, so… it's allowed." He stretched his arm along the back of the couch—not quite touching me, just letting me decide if I wanted the space or the comfort.

I wanted the comfort.

Slowly at first. Then fully, warmth sinking into my bones. My head rested on his shoulder; his breath was a steady, grounding rhythm. Humphrey Bogart's low voice drifted from the TV, the hazy streets of Casablanca shimmering across the screen.

About half an hour in—just as Sam started playing *As Time Goes By*—Asa's fingers brushed my arm. Not soothing exactly. More… anchoring.

"You've been awfully quiet since the call," he murmured. "How're you really?"

My stomach tightened. "Not well," I admitted. "If I'm honest. It's all so unlike Julian, and I can't reconcile his reasons for all but kidnapping Poppy after three years of not showing up. But one thing I'm sure of—it's not about being daddy of the year."

He didn't push. Didn't rush. Just waited with that steady patience of his that somehow made everything inside me loosen and strain at the same time.

"There's something I need to say," I whispered. "Before it eats me alive."

At that, he paused the movie. Turned toward me. Gave me the full weight of his attention, the kind that made my throat tighten.

"I'm listening," he murmured.

I pulled back just enough to look at him fully.

"I am so profoundly sorry," I said, the words shaking loose. "Not just for misjudging things, not just for making assumptions, but for what my silence and fear have cost you and Julian. I'm sorry for the ten years I let Julian believe he was Poppy's father. Ten years. Every drawing, every school event, every Father's Day… well, at least for the first five years. And now I'm the one who must rip that illusion away. And no matter who he is or how he behaves, that's cruel."

Asa didn't flinch. He just listened.

"And you," I said, my voice breaking, "you were an ocean away, living your life, thinking Paris had been a

moment between us and nothing more. And I told myself that meant something—that your distance made our parting definite. Destiny. That we had something special once, but that it was over. Our lives were to be lived apart."

My breath shook; I forced the words out.

"I kept pretending the timing made everything simple. That because you'd gone back to Georgia, and Julian was the one standing in front of me when I realized I was pregnant, that it could only be him. It made sense. I convinced myself that everything about our time in Paris could stay neatly tucked in the past where it belonged."

My voice cracked.

"Choosing Julian's version of events was logical, especially when Poppy was born so tiny everyone thought she was a premie, even though Mama always reminded me that I'd been a five pound baby, too." A tear escaped, then another. My voice wavered. "It was just easier than admitting that something lasting had happened between us. Easier than reaching across an ocean to tell you I was scared and alone. Just easier—"

Tears blurred my vision. "I accepted a man I didn't love rather !than to make my life work with the man I did."

He squeezed my fingers, but kept his thoughts to himself.

"And that's what I can't forgive myself for."

He opened his mouth, but I shook my head, needing to finish.

"And the worst part? I must've known, deep down, that Poppy was your child. How could I not? The way she thinks before she speaks. The way she observes. The way she has that quiet coil of caution in her body when she doesn't trust someone. The way she holds her mouth when she's nervous. Those aren't from me. And Julian doesn't have a reflective bone in his body. But you..." My face crumpled. "Everything she does that steadies me—she got from you. And I refused to look at it."

My tears came fast, hot, blurring the room into soft watercolor shapes.

"I stole years from you," I whispered. "And I don't know how you could ever forgive me for that."

A long, full silence settled between us before he reached out and gently cupped my cheek.

"Maggie." His voice was soft but unwavering. "We were careful in Paris. So you believed what was most logical. You weren't selfish—you were overwhelmed. And scared. And trying to survive something that gutted you."

"That doesn't make it right."

"No," he said. "But it makes it human."

His thumb brushed a tear from my skin. "Am I sorry that I missed ten years with my child? Of course. But am I angry with you?"

He sat back against the sofa. Sighed. "No. I tried, but it just doesn't stick. So if you're asking me to absolve you," he said, "I do. Not because it didn't hurt. If I'm honest, it still does. But my decision to forgive isn't complicated. Holding it over your head won't give me back the years I missed. Moving forward comes closest, so that's what I hope we will do."

My breath left me in a broken exhale.

"I don't deserve you," I whispered.

"Well, thankfully that's not your call to make," he murmured. "Because you're not getting rid of me so fast again."

He drew me into him then, the move gentle but sure, and I went without hesitation. My forehead settled against his collarbone, the familiar warmth of me sinking into him.

His arms wrapped around my back, one hand sliding into my hair, the other tracing slow, steady lines that felt like they were stitching me back together.

"I'm here," he whispered. "You're here. I'm not leaving. Not now, not after this. Not again. And I hope—with every ounce of strength I've got—that you won't leave either."

"I can't promise—"

He shook his head, brushing his cheek against my temple. "I'm not asking you to promise. I just need you to know what I want this time around."

Slowly—achingly slow—the shaking in my chest eased. My breathing leveled. The tears dried on my cheeks. And when I lifted my head, his expression was a tenderness that nearly undid me all over again.

He brushed his knuckles along my jaw. "Maggie. Look at me."

I did.

"We're in this together now," he said. "Whatever storm is coming, whatever Julian decides to throw our way—we face it side by side. You, me, and our girl who has no idea how loved she's about to be."

A warmth bloomed in my chest—fragile, but real.

I slid my fingers into his, and he pulled me even closer, until the space between us disappeared completely. His lips brushed my hairline, then my temple, then finally my mouth—soft, slow, reverent.

A kiss that wasn't about passion or heat or urgency.

A kiss that said: *you're forgiven; you're safe; you're mine.*

I exhaled into it, something inside me loosening for the first time in days.

We folded into the couch together, the quilt slipping over us like a hush. The film murmured in the background, lost to the shadows gathering around us, and the rest of the world receded until all I felt was his warmth and the steady, grounding pulse of his heart beneath my cheek.

"Will you stay the night?" he whispered, his voice low, close enough to stir the air by my ear.

"Yes," I whispered back.

A quiet night.

A borrowed peace.

The final stillness before the storm found us.

That night, in his arms, for the first time since the truth cracked open, I let myself believe we might survive whatever came next.

I thought the hardest part was behind us.

I didn't realize how much more the truth still had to give…

or how far Julian was from letting go.

# Chapter Thirty

## ASA

Asa slipped out of bed before first light, careful not to wake Maggie.

She lay curled beneath the quilt, her breathing soft and deep, one hand tucked beneath her cheek, the faintest crease between her brows even in sleep. Whatever peace the night had given them, it hadn't erased the weight waiting on the morning.

He stood by the bed for a moment, watching her, letting himself feel what he already knew he couldn't afford. Then he eased from the room, closing the door softly behind him.

In the kitchen, he made a pot of coffee and leaned against the counter while it brewed. The night replayed itself in fragments—quiet laughter, shared warmth, the familiar way their bodies had remembered each other without effort or explanation. Gentle and fierce all at once. Exactly as it had been in Paris.

Exactly why it was dangerous.

He'd wanted her for years. Longer than he liked to admit. Wanted her even during the years when neither of them had the right to want anyone else. That kind of longing didn't disappear just because time passed or lives changed. It waited. It resurfaced. It asked for more.

And last night, he'd given it more.

He loved her. That truth didn't surprise him. It had been there as long as memory, as certain as his own name. What surprised him was how quickly the night had pulled him back into wanting things he wasn't sure they could have.

Maggie McAllister was standing at the edge of several lives at once—daughter, mother, writer, woman still tethered to a world far beyond Loblolly. Barb's health. Her injured hand. Julian. Poppy. None of it was settled yet.

And neither were they.

Asa poured himself a cup of coffee and took a slow sip, grounding himself. The warmth steadied him, but it didn't answer the questions circling his thoughts.

Where did he fit now?

Not just with Maggie—but with Poppy.

That thought tightened his chest. He glanced down the hallway toward the bedroom where Maggie still slept, unaware of the reckoning quietly taking shape in his mind. The truth about Poppy would change everything. It already had. Once Julian knew—once he understood that Poppy wasn't his biological child—Asa didn't doubt what would happen.

Julian would leave.

Men like Julian always did when the story stopped centering on them.

And when that happened—when the air finally cleared and the ground beneath Maggie steadied—that would be the moment for real conversations. Not before. Not now, while everything was still fragile and unresolved.

Asa needed to know where he stood in Maggie's life. In Poppy's. Whether there was a future they were both willing to claim—or whether last night had been a beautiful pause before separate paths resumed.

He couldn't keep sharing his bed without knowing the answer.

No more borrowed closeness.

No more pretending they weren't standing on uncertain ground.

No more letting hope outrun reality.

He would be there for her. Stand beside her when she faced Julian. Protect Poppy however he could. Do the hard, necessary things that mattered.

But the intimacy—the way they'd held each other, the way her presence had already begun to settle into his days—that had to stop until they understood what came next.

Not because he didn't want her.

Because he wanted her too much.

He braced one hand on the counter and bowed his head, letting the decision settle. It felt heavy, but right. A line drawn not out of fear, but survival.

He would wait.

Wait until the truth was told.

Wait until Julian was gone.

Wait until Maggie could choose freely, without crisis or obligation pressing her into something she hadn't fully claimed.

Footsteps sounded softly in the hallway. Maggie was awake now.

Asa straightened, set his mug down, and turned to face the day—knowing the distance he was about to put between them would likely be misunderstood. But even if it was, that was a cost he was willing to bear.

Because he couldn't afford to get any closer.

He was too exposed. Too open. Loving her this intimately would cost him more than he could bear.

And he knew, with absolute certainty, that he wouldn't survive losing her again.

# Chapter Thirty-One

## MAGGIE

I woke in Asa's bed before the sun had fully decided what kind of morning it wanted to be—soft gray light, the faint hum of the refrigerator down the hall, the scent of his laundry detergent lingering on the cotton sheets. Asa was already up. I heard the low clink of a mug in the kitchen, the kind of respectful quiet a man keeps when he knows sleep is thin and fragile.

But I hadn't slept well anyway—not with Poppy across the state in Savannah. Julian assumed that being her father gave him the right to take her out of school and vanish on a self-proclaimed holiday. *I'll bring back our daughter after our holiday*, he'd said, with no clear plan.

He was wrong on so many levels, and the thought of straightening out the entire mess without hurting Poppy—knowing that the problem was my doing—made my head ache.

My phone lay on the nightstand. Dark. No messages. No updates.

The silence sat on my chest, heavier than worry itself.

I slipped out from under the quilt and reached for Asa's robe. He'd laid it on the edge of the bed. Courteous and caring, as always. I slipped it over his T-shirt—my nightgown for the night—washed my face, ran a comb through my hair, and followed the smell of coffee into the kitchen.

Asa glanced over when I entered, his hand wrapped around a steaming mug. "Morning," he murmured, the sound deep and sexy enough to cause a flutter low in my belly.

I smiled and pushed away the memory of last night. He didn't have to open the store until the afternoon, so there was a chance of an encore. I filled the mug he'd left by the coffee urn.

"Any messages?" he asked.

No morning kiss. Not even a warm embrace. I pushed away my disappointment and shook my head. "No calls. No texts. No emails."

I wrapped my hands around my coffee mug, and my phone lit up with Katrina's name. A spike of adrenaline shot through me—maybe she'd been able to reach Isabella and had news. I prayed it would be what I wanted to hear.

"Maggie, I wanted—" The line went staticky.

"I can't hear you."

"Better reception on the porch." Asa said.

"Let me step outside." I opened the sliding door and stepped out on the small covered porch overlooking the park.

"Okay, I'm outside. Better reception." The morning air drifted cool across my skin. A lone mockingbird tweeted in a small birch tree, sounding half-hearted and tired, and somewhere inside me the same sensation flickered—an ache waking slowly over my heart.

"I tracked down Isabella and we had a long chat. I

would have called sooner, but I've been on location. A yacht in the middle of French Riveria with a paranoid star who insisted no photographs which meant they confiscated our phones. She makes Angelina Jolie look low maintenance." Katrina said without preamble. "This is the first chance I've had to call."

A warning bell rang in my head. "What did Isabella say?"

"She told me she already knew Julian had taken Poppy to Savannah," Katrina continued. "She assumed he cleared it with you."

My throat tightened. "He didn't."

"I clarified that for her," she said gently. "She was… disturbed. Julian calls her daily. They've decided to separate, she says they aren't seeing things the same. Julian going to Loblolly seems to bother her more than she wants to admit."

I leaned against the railing. "Why? Does she think he's trying to prove something?" For hours last night, I'd tossed and turned, always landing back on the conclusion that Julian had an ulterior motive for being in Loblolly—something other than simply visiting Poppy. There was too much water under our marital bridge to entertain the idea he actually believed we'd reconcile.

"That's part of what I needed to talk to you about. Maggie, it's the craziest thing, but Isabella—she loves Julian. Loves him. All in. The can't-live-without-him kind of love."

The words hurt. Not because I wanted him, but because the entire situation felt warped—fractured motivations, half-truths, a child caught in the middle.

"They're engaged," Katrina went on, "but she's hesitant to marry. For reasons she wouldn't fully explain, although I gathered from our late-night, one-hour call that she believes her reluctance to set a date is why Julian came to Loblolly. She think he believes a little time apart might force her hand. Not sure why he chose to do that in Loblolly. That part's still a bit blurry."

"He's using Poppy to force Isabella's hand," I said, making no attempt to temper my voice. "That really makes no sense."

"Maybe more than you think. She definitely takes it as a veiled threat of leaving their relationship. And she's angry that he'd resort to emotional blackmail—stubborn enough to pretend she doesn't care. Underneath her anger, I think she's afraid of losing him. She's wavering, and I think now more willing to set a date."

"Which means that when he and Isabella reconcile, he'll disappear again—" Boiling blood rushed to my head.

"But Julian disappearing again—that's a good thing, right?" Katrina said.

Of course she was right. In all honesty, that's exactly what I hoped for. I inhaled a deep breath. Forced my racing thoughts to slow. "It's just that Poppy isn't a prop he can use at will in his love drama."

"I know," she said, her tone consoling and soft. "Isabella said the same. She didn't defend Julian. If anything, she seemed upset that he put Poppy and even you in this position."

I closed my eyes, letting the breeze cool the sudden heat behind them.

"There's more," Katrina continued. "She confided something that might explain her reaction. Isabella can't have children. She claims she never wanted them, but underneath I think she's terrified."

"Terrified?"

"Terrified that if she marries Julian, he'll eventually want Poppy in their lives—or want another child."

I gave that some thought. Felt a little guilty over the relief that Julian wouldn't likely fight me on parental rights if Isabella didn't want children in their lives.

"Isabella isn't proud of her attitude about Poppy being in their life," Katrina said. "It was more confession than complaint."

I let out a slow breath. "This is such a mess."

"Yes, well, Julian has always been a bit of a mess, no?"

I sighed. "There's more. Something I've never admitted —not to anyone, not even myself—until just recently."

I stepped to the far corner of the porch, stood beside Asa's oversized gas grill, and faced the city park. My voice dropped instinctively, though no one was close enough to overhear.

"I'm almost certain Julian isn't Poppy's biological father."

Silence hummed on the line.

"I know it's a shock—"

"Yes," Katrina said. "It is. Does he know?"

Her question knocked the breath from me. "No. It's a long story, but I just got the DNA test."

"Darling, this is a mess. Any chance the father lives in Loblolly?"

"Yes." My mind tumbled back ten years. "Julian and I dated for a few months, but I just didn't love him and we broke it off. A few months later, my old love visited. We had a whirlwind two weeks, but I'd been offered a permanent writing position and Asa's life was in Loblolly. We parted ways."

Memory loosened and spilled:

After he went back home, I drifted through my days in Paris…

then studio came through with permanent contract.

I'd fallen apart after Asa walked away.

I'd felt untethered, questioned whether the dream I'd shaped my whole life around was even mine anymore.

Then Julian appeared—right there on the street—and slipped back into my days like a balm I didn't bother to question. I let him guide me toward marriage when I was too bruised to trust my own compass.

"Maggie," she said softly, pulling me from the spiral. "Listen to me. Really listen. Do you honestly believe Julian Black has an altruistic bone in that beautiful body of his? He tried and failed to make it as a writer, so he attached himself to your rising star. But staying in your shadow? That never suited his ego. He got bored. He moved on. Julian always moves on."

I swallowed the tears that threatened. "That… seems a little unkind."

"Unkind? Perhaps. But is it wrong? I warned Isabella, back when she and Julian first started seeing each other, that he was a handsome vagabond looking for a soft landing—this time preferably into the lap of a wealthy, titled woman. She dismissed it, thought I was biased because of you. And maybe I was. I was furious with Julian back then."

She paused, her exhale long. "But I was wrong—and short-sighted, as you Americans often say. You're much better off without him. And Julian and Isabella—complicated as they are—fit each other in ways you and he never did."

Shame and relief collided in my chest. I pushed it away. There would be ample time to berate myself for the part I played in this mess.

"But here's something you might want to understand," she said gently. "Julian may not be shocked to learn Poppy isn't his child."

My heart kicked. I wanted to believe that. Needed to. But it didn't align with the man I knew. "Why would you say that?"

"Because Isabella says he knew about Asa before he pushed you to marry. About your history and Asa's visit to Paris."

"But I never mentioned Asa to Julian. Never talked about his visit."

She hesitated, then blew a long breath. "Well someone told him. When he came back to Paris after Asa left, he would know it'd be easy to pick up where you two had left off. When you started seeing Julian again, I invited him for drinks and told him that you were in love with another man."

Ice threaded down my spine. He'd never mentioned it.

"Julian manipulated you. Maybe he believed Poppy was his, but he was broke and needed someone to pay the rent."

My hand found the porch railing, gripping it as the weight of her words settled cold beneath my ribs.

"So what are you saying? That he even if he knew Poppy might not be his child, he didn't care? That he loved me so much he convinced himself it didn't matter?"

"He loved your success—and the financial comfort it gave him. And yes, he loved you too, for a while. But when the love isn't shared evenly—" Her sigh was long and weary. "Men can be very good at burying their heads in the sand when the truth doesn't suit the life they want. But eventually, they wake up."

I stared out from Asa's back deck toward Loblolly's park—oak trees swaying, children's swings creaking on the breeze, the old three-tiered fountain catching thin ribbons of morning light—and felt everything in me distill into a single, slicing fear.

"Why didn't you ever say anything before now?"

"Why would I? It's not something I put together until now." She sighed. "Isabella didn't come out and say this, but my impression is her inability to have children is a wound she carries so deep she'd rather cut Poppy out of their world than live with the reminder of what she can't give Julian."

Poppy.

Her wide-open heart.

Her tender trust.

The knowledge that learning Julian wasn't her father would shatter her.

Whatever I'd done to Asa… whatever lies I'd let Julian live with… none of it compared to the hurt I had already set in motion for my little girl. I needed to fix this. All of it. But I had no earthly idea how without blowing up everyone's world.

And worse, Julian still wasn't answering my calls or texts.

"Call me when you hear from him," Katrina said gently. "And you will hear from him. He's not going to keep Poppy indefinitely. Single parenting doesn't fit his carefully crafted persona. But, sweetheart—you shouldn't shoulder this by yourself."

"I'm not. I have Asa," I told her, and for once, that felt undeniably true.

We said our goodbyes, but after I hung up, I didn't move. I stood there, staring at the park—the gazebo framed by pink rosebeds, the old wooden swing tucked inside. The place where Asa and I had once sat on a Christmas afternoon years ago, each of us quietly imagining a future.

It was the day I told him I'd been accepted to Emory on

a full scholarship. The day we faced the truth that our dreams didn't run along the same path.

Standing here on his porch, immersed in the memory almost sixteen years later, it felt as though nothing had changed. Not really. Our lives were still misaligned, each reaching for a future from different directions—me working in Paris, him still running the family business he'd inherited. No matter what emotions tugged our hearts, we lived in different worlds.

The morning felt suddenly too still, too expectant, as if something unseen were gathering just beyond this moment.

Julian was supposed to bring Poppy home this afternoon. Which meant I had only a few hours to figure out how to set right the catastrophe I'd created. I ached for my daughter—her arms around my neck, her bright smile, the way she studied my face when she sensed something was wrong. I wanted time with her before I had to crack her world open.

Suddenly, I wanted to get back to the farm. To sit with Mama, talk this through, let her level me the way only she could—before Julian arrived.

And for the first time since I learned he'd taken Poppy out of Loblolly, a colder thought surfaced, sharp and undeniable: what if Julian suspected the truth—and was afraid? Afraid of losing Poppy. Afraid of what the truth might take from him.

What if he doesn't bring her back?

# Chapter Thirty-Two

## MAGGIE

Julian was due to bring Poppy home this afternoon.

It would be a stretch to say he'd promised. But he knew it was what I expected.

At Joleen's suggestion, I'd left them alone. *Give him nothing to throw back at you in court.* You asked for Poppy to be home Sunday. That's what we want on record. Now it's up to Julian to meet—or break—your implied understanding.

I'd built my whole fragile hope for today on Julian's single, careless, almost promise.

And since speaking with Katrina about Isabella, that promise felt less like reassurance and more like a weight—something sinking steadily beneath my ribs as the hours crept closer.

The porch door creaked behind me.

I turned. Asa stood in the doorway, hands tucked into his pockets, wearing a thoughtful, reserved expression. Nothing sharp or distant—just… something I couldn't quite name. The warmth from last night was still in his eyes, but dimmer, as if the light of morning had thinned it somehow.

As if something had shifted in the space between us while we slept.

"You all right?" he asked quietly.

I nodded, though I wasn't sure that was the truth. "Katrina spoke to Isabella—Julian's fiancée."

His brows lifted a fraction. "Problem?"

"Complicated," I said, the word feeling too small. "Apparently… things are more layered than I ever imagined."

"Layered," he repeated. "An interesting choice of words."

He waited, not pushing, and there was both comfort and ache in that. It struck me again how different he was from Julian—how Asa gave room instead of pressing, how he let silence sit between us without needing to fill it.

I wasn't sure yet what I could say aloud. Some things still needed to settle inside me first.

"I'll explain later," I promised. "It's a lot, and honestly, I'm not sure what's important and what's not yet."

"Okay." He studied my face, a flicker of worry in his eyes. "You need anything before I head downstairs?"

Yes, you.

Time.

A guarantee that Poppy is safe.

"I was thinking…" I said, grasping for something simple, something normal. "If you're not in a rush, maybe we could get breakfast? At the diner? Since it's Sunday and you don't open the store until noon."

His expression shifted—just a breath of hesitation, then a small nod. "I usually catch up on paperwork on Sunday mornings. But yeah, we can do that."

It wasn't reluctance exactly. But it wasn't the easy, automatic yes I'd grown used to from him either. I told myself I was imagining it, that I was reading too much into every pause.

That was the thing about fear: it had a way of tinting everything to its own colors.

"Let me grab my purse," I said. "I should text Julian first. Confirm what time they'll be back at the farm."

My thumbs hovered for a second before I typed:

*Checking in. Do you have an ETA for Poppy being home?*

I hit send. The message went through—marked as delivered, then read. A handful of seconds later, his reply arrived.

*Yes. 2:00.*

I breathed out my relief. Turned to Asa and smiled. "He says he'll be at the farm at two."

Five hours. Just five more hours and I could breathe easy again. I knew in my heart that Poppy wasn't in physical danger, but spending time with Julian would be confusing when he left—and at some point she would learn that Julian wasn't her father. I didn't know how to handle that yet and thought maybe I'd talk to Joleen and Tally, get a recommendation for a child psychologist for guidance.

"So breakfast?" I asked.

Asa nodded, his jaw tightening slightly—or was that my imagination?

The diner sat just down the block from his grocery, the same place we'd eaten a hundred ordinary meals over the years. When we walked in, the bell over the door chimed its familiar greeting, and for a second I pretended we were just another couple out for Sunday breakfast with nothing more pressing to worry about than whether Chet's nephew would overcook the bacon.

"Morning, Asa!"

"Hey there, Stu. We got that delivery of organic tangerines in. I'll save a bag for you, but you need to stop by soon—they're like hotcakes."

"How's your mama?" someone I didn't recognize asked me.

"She's better. Thanks for asking."

Asa placed his hand on my lower back and ushered me to the last booth, nodding and greeting people as we went. He knew everyone. Of course he did. He'd lived here his entire life. I recognized a few faces, smiled, and kept walking.

Asa on the other hand, slowed to answer each greeting with easy smiles—a lift of his hand, a word or two about the store, the weather, the orchard. We finally made it to an empty booth by the window, and the feeling of being half tethered and half untethered swamped me. It was as if my body had made it to the table, but my nerves were still somewhere on Asa's back porch.

He slid into the seat across from me. Not beside me. Not touching me at all.

Last night, we couldn't seem to get close enough. Now, a broad laminate tabletop and a pair of condiments sat between us like boundary markers.

I shook off my worry. Small town. Gossip.

He wouldn't make it obvious that we were together in that way—not his style. Tongues in a small town would wag enough with us here before ten in the morning.

I wrapped my fingers around the menu I remembered by heart. That much hadn't changed.

"Sunday pancakes with a side of bacon?" he asked.

I smiled—he remembered—and nodded. "Yeah. That sounds great."

I slipped my hand over my queasy lower belly. I wasn't at all sure I could handle pancakes, or bacon, or food for that matter. Worry over Julian living up to his promise—made worse by Asa's unusual demeanor, nothing I could quite put my finger on—was enough to make my stomach jump.

Sue Ellen whizzed by, then backtracked and beamed. "Well, well. Look who came to visit me." She winked at Asa, poured coffee into two mugs on her tray, and set them in front of us. "I'll be back for your order."

I added cream and watched it swirl—anything to avoid staring directly at Asa while something quiet and unnamed settled between us.

Sue Ellen returned with her order pad and removed a pencil from behind her ear. "How's your mama this morning?" she asked, the question open-ended.

I smiled. "I haven't talked to her yet." Since Sue Ellen was at the house when I left yesterday, she'd put two and two together and make twenty really fast.

Asa's mouth tipped at the corner as he flashed his aunt a raised eyebrow, his usual warmth intact—something I hadn't personally seen from him this morning. "We'll both have the pancakes with a side of bacon."

She left, and I searched for something innocuous to say. Why did it suddenly seem so difficult to converse? "So you're planning to do paperwork today?"

"Probably for a few hours," he said. "Not my favorite job and I'm behind. I also need to place next week's produce order." He hesitated, then added, "I'll probably work until closing."

It was a thoughtful response. Solid. And it gave clear notice not to expect him at the farm tonight.

Yes—somewhere underneath, something was different. But what had happened to cause the change? Last night, as we fell asleep in each other's arms, he'd been attentive, loving, even teasing. His best self.

Today, he took every opportunity to talk to anyone who could pull his attention away from me. He discussed irrigation lines with a man who didn't seem particularly interested. He told a woman at one table about a new citrus supplier he might try.

As our meal arrived and we ate, he asked me about Paris—if there were any set location trips in the planning. When I mentioned my injury, he waved it off as if it would heal without question and I'd continue with my life as before.

He quizzed me about the actors I worked with—which ones I enjoyed the most, which were the biggest pains. Did I have a favorite director? I nodded and responded where it made sense, but it felt like we were playing roles—him the dependable small-town businessman, me the film and television writer home from her glamorous life abroad. It was almost as if last night had slipped through a crack in the floorboards. As if we'd both quietly folded it up and put it away where we wouldn't trip over it.

Maybe he was simply being cautious. Maybe he needed time to figure out how he felt about everything—about Poppy, about me, about the way the ground had shifted beneath us.

And honestly, I needed to have the same conversation with myself. Maybe I was asking too much of him. More than he was ready to give. More than I was ready to give in return.

I picked at my pancakes and bacon more than I ate them. My stomach felt too tight with worry and unspoken things.

Asa ate his meal with gusto. For some reason, I found that irritating.

"You okay?" he asked again, eyes on my mostly untouched plate.

"I will be when my—our—daughter is back safely in my arms," I said softly.

He held my gaze a second longer than necessary, then nodded, as if that was all that needed to be said.

We finished breakfast that way—circling everything that mattered and never quite touching down on any of it.

Back upstairs at his place, we moved through the small apartment like people packing up after a long weekend. I made his bed out of habit, then folded the robe he'd lent me and laid it at the foot before straightening a corner of the quilt—just to have something to do with my hands.

"So you won't be at the farm today?" I asked.

"I really have a lot to do," he said. Even his tone felt like an excuse. "I need to get a few things done before my week starts tomorrow." He met my gaze. "But if you need me for any reason, just call."

My mind screamed, *I've always needed you—you've just made me see how much.* But I kept my expression neutral. "Of course."

I tried to read his expression, his body language. I'd honed my skill as a studio writer by reading the room. But in this room, I found nothing but a thoughtful reserve that was really beginning to annoy me. No blame. No anger. But no easy intimacy either. It was as if he'd flipped off the sweet and loving switch.

My bag was on my shoulder, keys in hand, when his phone rang.

He glanced at the screen. "Hold on—this is the River House Inn calling."

Hope surged—maybe Julian had arrived early.

Asa answered. "Hey, Stella. Everything all right?"

A pause. His gaze sharpened and flicked to mine.

"She's right here," he said. "I'll put you on speaker."

He set the phone on the counter and tapped the button.

"Maggie, honey?" Stella's voice filled the kitchen, breezy but edged with something that made my skin prickle. "I didn't have your cell number, or I'd have called sooner. I didn't want to worry your mama in case I've made a mountain out of nothing, but… we've got a visitor."

"What kind of visitor?" I couldn't imagine why she'd call me about one of her guests.

"Well," Stella said, "the kind of guest who looks like she stepped out of a fashion shoot. Arrived in a limo from Atlanta. Can't imagine what that five hour trip cost. Expensive luggage—expensive everything, really. Shoes, clothes, the whole package. Calls herself Isabella. And when she found out Julian wasn't here, she asked for directions to your place."

The room tilted slightly.

"Isabella," I repeated. "As in the Viscountess Isabella Montford."

"Not sure about the viscountess part," Stella said, "but she said her name was Isabella Montford. Sweet as can be, but strikes me as a little uppity."

My mind scrambled to put the pieces together—Katrina's call, Isabella's confession, Julian's theatrics, Poppy in the middle of it all. She must've hopped on a plane as soon as Katrina called her.

"Okay," I heard myself say. "Thank you, Stella. I'm on my way to the farm now."

I ended the call and looked at Asa.

"I'm coming with you," he said before I could ask.

Relief slid through me. "Thank you."

"I'll drive. I'll bring you back for your car later."

"I can drive."

"Maggie, you look like you've seen a ghost. You ride with me."

The drive out of town felt shorter than usual. Maybe it was the way my thoughts crowded in on themselves, leaving no room for scenery. Maybe it was the way Asa's truck—steady, familiar—felt like the only solid thing under me right now.

"She must've come after Katrina called her."

"Tell me everything Katrina said," he said quietly as we turned on State Road 84 and headed for the farm.

I pulled together everything Katrina had shared that morning—Isabella's love for Julian, the engagement and her hesitance, the unfair tug-of-war over a man who seemed perfectly willing to use a child's affection as leverage. Isabella's inability to have children, and the wound she carried so deep she'd rather cut Poppy out of their world than live with the reminder.

"That's what Katrina thinks, not what Isabella told her." Saying it all out loud made it sound even more twisted.

"So Julian's here to force her hand," Asa said finally. "To prove he has options if she doesn't commit."

"That's Katrina's theory." I stared out the windshield. "She reminded me that Julian always did like grand gestures."

"And you?" he asked. "What do you want?"

The question hovered between us like something fragile.

"I want my daughter home and safe," I said. "After that… I want us to figure out our lives. There's so much I need to fix. So many conversations I should have had years ago."

He simply nodded. Didn't say *you're not alone in this*, even though I felt his presence. But for the first time, I felt his judgment. Guilt swam like a circle of piranhas in my stomach, nipping at my insides in sharp, lethal bites.

We pulled into the farm's drive ten minutes later. The sight of the house—white paint, gray shutters, deep porch, the grove of pecan trees in front standing like sentries—usually soothed me. Today, it felt like stepping onto a stage where someone had rearranged all the props.

A woman I recognized from one brief meeting and countless society-page photos sat in one of Mama's front-porch rockers: Viscountess Isabella Montford. She looked as if she'd been born right here in Pines County. Her royal blue dress was simple but, if one recognized fashion, too perfectly cut not to be designer. Her hair was swept up in an effortless French twist that would take me more than an hour to achieve. On the table beside her sat a glass of sweet tea and a plate with a half-eaten slice of Mama's pecan-orange pound cake.

Barbara McAllister, hostess extraordinaire, chatted about the orchard as if she'd known this woman for years, not minutes.

"There they are," Mama said when she spotted us. "I was just saying you'd be home any minute. Maggie, darling, look who's come for a visit."

"Yes, look," I muttered under my breath.

Isabella rose gracefully, smiling broadly. "Maggie. It's good to see you again—and so special to see you in your home environment. This place is… charming."

"Thank you," I said, aware my voice sounded thinner than usual. "Stella called to say you'd arrived at the inn. So you know Julian isn't in town at the moment."

A corner of Isabella's mouth lifted. "Yes. After a bit of

back-and-forth, she finally admitted he wasn't expected back until later today. I had to give her my best concerned fiancée performance to get even that much information out of her."

Mama eyes widened. "Fiancée? Well how about that."

"Yes, it seems Julian and Isabella are engaged," I said. "It is wonderful news."

I swear I heard Asa chuckle under his breath.

We all sat on the porch, though *sat* felt like a strange word—me, Asa, Mama, Isabella. Four people linked in ways that made my head spin.

The conversation refused to dip below small talk. Weather. Travel. The endless mystery of American biscuits versus British scones. Mama asked Isabella about London and Milan; Isabella asked Mama about the orchard. When my hiatus from work came up, I felt Asa's attention sharpen beside me, though he said nothing.

Isabella noticed. Of course she did. Her gaze flicked between us, something speculative in it, but she let the topic slide.

I checked the time. 1:58.

My heart began counting seconds instead of minutes.

"Julian said he'd be here by two," I said, more to the air than to anyone in particular.

"Julian says a lot of things," Isabella murmured, almost too softly to hear.

Two o'clock came and went.

2:10.

2:17.

I pulled out my phone and sent a new text.

*Checking in. Everything all right?*

It spun for a long moment and then… nothing.

No *Delivered*. No *Read*.

I tried again. Same result.

My throat felt dry. "It's not sending."

"Could be the signal," Mama suggested. "You know how spotty it gets out on the highway."

"Or," Isabella said lightly, "he's turned his phone off. He can be dramatic that way."

I called him. The call dropped before it even properly connected.

"Why would he turn off his phone?" A sick, sliding feeling started up in my stomach.

"I'm calling Joleen," I said, already scrolling.

She answered on the second ring. "Hey. Everything okay?"

I put her on speaker so everyone could hear and so I wouldn't have to repeat myself. "Julian's not back," I said. "He said two o'clock. My texts aren't delivering. My calls are going straight to voicemail."

"Okay. Breathe," she said. "First—don't assume the worst. Second, it sounds like he may have turned his phone off. Or…" She blew out a breath. "He could've pulled the SIM card. Some people do that when they don't want to be tracked or bothered."

"Who does that?" The words came out sharp and judging, exactly how I felt.

"Oh, I do," Isabella said brightly from her rocker, that same odd, amused detachment in her eyes. "When I'm tired of everyone expecting me to answer. I pick up one of those cheap phones—they call them drop phones in the movies—and suddenly the world is very quiet."

I stared at her, torn between outrage and the hysterical urge to laugh. "This isn't a weekend retreat, Isabella. My child is with him."

"She's his child too." Something flickered across Isabella's face—real worry breaking through the polish. "I know he's upset you. He can be incredibly callous sometimes. I don't like what he's doing any more than you do."

Joleen's voice cut back in. "Katelyn just sent me an update. Julian checked out of the hotel at eleven on the dot. Right on time to be back at the farm by two."

My mind raced through maps without really seeing them. "So he left with her. They're on the road."

"If they are, it's in another vehicle," Joleen said. "Katelyn just confirmed that the Maserati is still in the hotel garage. Whatever Julian's doing, he's not using that car."

The ground shifted beneath my feet.

"Asa," I whispered.

He moved closer, his hand hovering at my shoulder as if waiting for permission. I leaned into him without thinking.

"Joleen," I said, forcing the words through a tightening throat. "What can you do on your end?"

"I'll put Simon on it," she said. "But this is more complicated now, Maggie. Two people in a big state, no clear destination—it's going to take time. Needles in haystacks don't show up fast."

Time.

Time Julian had already stolen without asking.

Time scraping against my nerves with every passing second.

I ended the call, my world narrowing to the grain of the boards beneath my feet, the creak of the rockers, the distant hum of a semi passing the farm.

I'd wanted this to be the day everything began to mend —Poppy back home, hard truths spoken, some kind of path forward with Asa.

Instead, the pieces were scattering further apart.

I turned to Isabella. "Does he know you're here? Are you communicating with him?"

"He doesn't." She hesitated, then nodded. We have been in communication, but not since I arrived in the Sates."

Asa stayed close to me, a steady presence at the edge of my vision. Isabella watched the road as if she could will a car into existence. Mama's walked and stood behind me, her hand found mine and held tight, warm and sure.

And somewhere out there, my daughter was on the move with a man I no longer trusted to put her first. My thoughts were so scrambled I couldn't hold a straight one for more than a few seconds.

Fear rose sharp and wild in my throat.

Julian had promised he'd bring her back.

But as I stared down the empty road, I finally admitted what I hadn't wanted to face—Julian's promises were never just promises. There was always something beneath them. Something shifting. Something I had never quite trusted.

## Chapter Thirty-Three

### ASA

Asa had the uneasy sense they were about to be sideswiped. No one said it out loud, but everyone felt it—braced for impact.

They still hadn't heard from Julian.

Worse, Maggie still hadn't heard from Poppy.

Not a word.

No voicemail.

No text.

No explanation.

Nothing.

Every time Maggie's phone buzzed, she jerked like she'd been shocked. Every hour it stayed dark, another thread seemed to snap inside her.

She stood at the kitchen counter with a dishtowel twisted between her fingers, staring at the window, but Asa knew she wasn't seeing a thing beyond it. The sink was empty, the counters wiped down, the coffee pot washed and set to dry. Asa had rearranged the barn, mucked the stalls, cleaned the tack room.

They'd finally run out of things to clean.

"I know he wouldn't hurt her," Maggie whispered.

Asa moved closer, braced his hip against the counter. "So that ought to give us some peace, right?"

It sounded hollow even to his own ears.

He said words he didn't feel, hoping to calm her. A man who put a woman through this kind of worry for no good reason deserved a horse-whipping. And even though Asa would never whip a horse, he wasn't at all sure he wouldn't unleash his pent-up fury on Julian if given the chance.

Maggie swallowed, her eyes still fixed on some middle distance only she could see. "It's just… Julian shifts his moods so fast. He can be all charm one minute and cold the next. I'm thirty-three, and there were days I could barely keep up." Her voice thinned. "How is a nine-year-old supposed to? She must be wondering why she isn't allowed to call me. She must be confused and worried."

Asa didn't tell her he agreed. Didn't say out loud that Julian's erratic behavior—so familiar to Maggie, so new to Poppy—was its own kind of harm. The kind that didn't leave bruises, but settled deeper. He didn't let himself sit with that thought for long. Anger came too fast when he did. Horse-whipping almost felt too kind.

Her shoulders shook, and she buried her face in the dish towel clenched in her hands.

Asa pushed the anger aside and slid an arm around her shoulders, pulling her in. She came willingly, pressing her forehead to his chest, fingers clutching the front of his T-shirt as if she might drift apart if she didn't hold on to something solid. He held her while her breath hitched, felt the damp of her tears soak through the cotton.

Something inside him tightened.

Because he couldn't stay here like this. Not indefinitely.

He'd let his assistant handle the store this afternoon, but tomorrow the deliveries would come in, and he didn't have the staff to cover both the floor and the shipments. Schedules needed setting. Invoices were piling up. Produce would spoil if no one was there to mind it. His life—his real life—didn't pause just because Maggie's was in crisis.

And neither did hers.

When Poppy was safe again, Maggie would return to Europe. To her work. To the life she'd built without him. This—whatever this was—would loosen and slip away, just as it had before.

Asa felt it happening anyway. The pull. The dangerous ease of holding her, of letting her lean into him like he belonged here. Like this was permanent.

He couldn't let himself fall any deeper.

Because if he did—if he gave her all of himself again—he wouldn't survive watching her leave this time.

So he stayed still. Kept his arms around her, but his heart braced. Loving her quietly, carefully, the way a man does when he knows the ending is already written.

Barbara was on her third unnecessary load of laundry and her seventh unnecessary task. Asa knew because he'd started counting—anything to keep his mind busy, his hands off his truck keys, and himself out of trouble.

When Barbara didn't know how to fix something—especially when it involved her daughter—she cleaned. At the moment, she was stacking already-clean mixing bowls, then rearranging them by size, then clanging them back into the cabinet with more force than any bowl deserved.

"Lord, grant me patience," she muttered as she closed the cabinet. "Because mine's wearing thin with that man."

She meant Julian. She'd stopped calling him by name, as

if naming him would give him more power than he already had.

Joleen's update sat heavy in Asa's mind: Julian had checked out of the hotel right on time. But his Maserati was still in the garage. Whatever he was doing now, he was doing it in a different vehicle.

Men who switched cars and turned off phones weren't just taking the scenic route.

Asa was using his thumb to wipe Maggie's tears and searching for words to steady them both

when the crunch of tires on gravel cut through the kitchen.

Maggie stiffened against him.

Barbara's dish towel stilled mid-swipe over an already spotless counter.

They all turned toward the window at the same time.

A black SUV rolled past the kitchen window, its paint catching the afternoon light. Asa recognized it from yesterday.

"Well," Barbara said quietly, hope and worry braided tight in her voice, "maybe the Viscountess comes bearing good news."

It seemed a reasonable assumption. Why else would Julian's fiancée visit again?

The SUV came to a stop. The engine cut off.

Asa stepped closer to the window.

A moment later, Isabella stepped out same rental, same ease in her movements, as if stepping into a Pines County afternoon in a silk blouse and tailored slacks was the most natural thing in the world.

She lifted her sunglasses to her head and looked toward the house. For a second, her eyes met Asa's through the glass. Something unreadable passed over her face—calculation, fatigue, resolve. Maybe all three.

"She must have heard from Julian," Maggie said, already moving toward the door.

Barbara wiped her palms on her apron and followed her daughter, her expression smoothing into that practiced McAllister hospitality that had greeted governors, preachers, and door-to-door Bible salesmen alike.

Maggie opened the door and warm air rushed in. Isabella was halfway up the steps. She looked up, took one look at Maggie, and paused—her serious expression shifting into a composed smile.

"Please excuse me dropping by unannounced," she said. "I hope I'm not intruding."

"It's fine," Maggie rushed on. "Have you heard from Julian? Is that why you're here?"

Isabella must have noticed Maggie's shaky tone, thinned with worry. Her expression softened. "I'm sorry. I have not."

"Come on in out of the heat," Asa said, reaching around Maggie to open the door wider.

Isabella's gaze flicked to his as she passed—quick, assessing, sharp.

"It's warmer than it looks," Isabella admitted. "I'd forgotten how… committed the weather in the South of the U.S. can be."

"Georgia doesn't do anything halfway," Barbara said with a small, genuine smile.

They stood in the foyer, staring at one another. No words came to soften the moment.

Barbara inhaled a quick breath. "Well, you're just in time. I was about to start supper. You'll stay?"

Isabella hesitated a fraction of a second—just long

enough for Asa to catch the calculation behind her eyes—then inclined her head. "If you're certain it's no trouble."

"It's no trouble," Barbara said firmly. "It's the South, after all. Feeding people is what we do in a crisis."

Asa surmised the viscountess wouldn't stay for supper without a reason.

## Chapter Thirty-Four

MAGGIE

Tuesday afternoon settled over the farm, and everywhere I looked there was something I should have been doing.

The fence along the north pasture needed mending. Empty feed buckets sat by the barn door. Mama had fed the chickens and my horse while I showered—let Sugar out to pasture—but I still needed to muck her stall. My computer in the front room waited with its lid closed, my schedule of six hours of writing looming like an accusation I didn't have the heart to answer. Lunch, then supper, needed planning—vegetables to be picked and washed, a dozen small tasks that usually kept my hands busy and my mind quiet.

Instead, I sat in the rocker on the porch and waited.

Two days earlier, Isabella had arrived without warning. She hadn't heard from Julian—not a text, not a call. He'd cut her off as completely as he had me. He didn't even know she was in Loblolly—she'd made that clear, almost defensively, as if his ignorance somehow softened the blow.

She'd admitted she no longer understood his motives. That his silence felt deliberate. Controlled.

The word had settled between us like a warning neither of us wanted to examine too closely.

Isabella returned to the River House Inn afterward, and according to Sue Ellen, she was still there. I couldn't imagine she'd linger much longer. Loblolly wasn't her kind of place.

Me?

I waited for Julian's car to turn up the drive.

I waited for Poppy's beautiful smile to come running toward me, for the feel of her arms circling my neck the way she always did when we'd been separated for more than a few hours.

I waited for my life to return to its shape—familiar, imperfect, but whole.

The house felt too quiet, so I sat on the porch.

When I became too frustrated with myself and my inability to act, I went inside, paced the kitchen with my phone in my hand, stopping every few steps to check the screen even though I already knew it hadn't changed. I couldn't call Joleen again. My calls were becoming a nuisance, and she'd promised to call as soon as Simon had any news, no matter how small.

Asa had all but abandoned me. It was unfair to feel abandoned—he had a business to run—but still, his absence felt like more.

Poppy should be in school. And I should be preparing to walk the driveway to meet her school bus, walk her home, hear about her day.

The thought lodged in my chest and stayed there, heavy and immovable. She loved school—loved knowing what came next, loved routine, loved telling me what she'd learned before bed.

She had to be missing me by now. Yet Julian had chosen

to ignore all of it.

Was this punishment? For me—for bonding with Poppy? Or was it, as Isabella suggested, control? My heart told me Julian's drama had nothing to do with building a relationship with his daughter, which only deepened my anger into fury.

Mama joined me on the porch. "It's a little cooler today, don't you think?" she said.

"A little, maybe."

"How are you holding up?"

I shook my head. "I want to hate him. So why can't I?"

She settled into the rocker beside me. "Hate's a strong word. But I think I know what you mean. Why do you think that is?"

"I don't know. I've been sitting here trying to figure it out. I should be furious with him—for being careless with Poppy, with me. But—"

"Guilt's a funny thing," Mama said gently. "It excuses a lot of life's messes."

I considered that. "Maybe."

She started a slow rock. "I think it's also because he was there for you when you needed someone most."

My thoughts drifted back. "Those first couple of years, he really was a doting father. And for a while, a loving husband. But the more successful my career became, the more he pulled back. Or maybe that's the version I told myself. I was busy. I was exhausted. And it was easier to believe everything at home was fine than to admit I wasn't fully there. Julian wanted all of me, and I can't fault him for that. But I only ever gave him fragments, because my heart still leaned toward Asa—even when I refused to name it. Then Julian met Isabella, left for Rome, and within a month, filed for divorce."

"And did you mourn your marriage?" Mama asked. No judgment. Just curiosity.

"No, not really. It required adjustment. I had to find a live-in nanny, but once that was handled, my life went on. Julian leaving was actually a relief. He was no longer there to make me feel guilty about the hours I worked, the travel."

Mama nodded, as if that answered more than I realized. "I suspect you don't carry hard feelings because you never truly loved him. And somewhere deep down, you understood why he left. You're grateful—for his help during a difficult season, not for the life you shared. And somewhere inside, you understand why he's angry—for the truth you withheld about Poppy's father."

It all sounded so reasonable. So obvious. And yet I'd never really examined my relationship with Julian. It had been enough to have Poppy, my career, my friends. I'd been happy in Paris—sometimes lonely, yes—but far too busy to dwell on what I didn't have. Not until my injury sent my career careening off a cliff.

I had never once allowed myself to believe Julian wasn't Poppy's biological father. And now I was paying the price for burying that truth deep in my heart.

Mama pushed herself up from the rocker. "I'm a little tired," she said. "I think I'll take a nap."

The quiet she left behind pressed in, thick and restless.

Sitting with my thoughts only made them louder—sharper. I had to do something or I was going to lose my mind. I couldn't just sit on the porch and rock, hoping Julian would come to his senses.

I rose, walked into the house, and into the kitchen. I scrolled my contact list until I found Caleb's number. I needed facts. Laws. Boundaries. Something solid to hold onto.

He answered on the second ring, but before he finished his greeting, I jumped in.

"What can I legally do?" I pressed my forehead to the kitchen window. "There has to be something I'm allowed to do to find my child."

He was quiet for a moment. Each silent second sliced a little deeper.

"Caleb—something. Anything. Please." My voice broke.

"I know this is hard," he said gently. "But the truth is, there isn't much I can do that Joleen isn't already doing. If we had proof he'd taken her across state lines and you had legal primary custody, I'd call in the FBI. But you have joint custody, and he's her father. The water is very murky."

Joint custody.

The words echoed long after we hung up.

If I'd faced the truth—been honest, tested for parentage—my life might have been harder. But it would have been true. Honest. And so many people might have been spared this heartache—Asa, Julian, but most of all, Poppy.

I stayed at the window, watching my reflection blur against the fields beyond. I barely recognized the woman staring back at me—eyes rimmed red, shoulders drawn tight, braced for impact without knowing where it would come from.

I checked my phone again.

Nothing.

Not from Julian.

And not from Asa.

That absence hurt more than I wanted to admit. It shouldn't have, not with everything else pressing in—but it did. Asa was steady. Asa showed up. The quiet felt deliberate now, not circumstantial.

I told myself he was overwhelmed. Anyone would be.

Fatherhood arriving without warning. A relationship trying to reassemble itself under pressure. The looming possibility of courtrooms and tests and truths that couldn't be taken back once spoken. And now my ex taking off with the daughter he'd just realized he had.

Still, no word seemed unlike Asa.

I called him.

He answered on the third ring. "Maggie."

His voice was calm, controlled—but thinner somehow, stretched taut.

"I can't keep waiting like this," I said. "I'm going to hire a private investigator."

I heard movement on his end—papers sliding, a chair shifting. He didn't respond right away.

"You should talk to Caleb," he said finally. "He'll know who to trust."

That was it.

No offer to come by. No suggestion we meet together. No reassurance beyond logistics.

"I've talked to Caleb—" I started, then stopped. I didn't know how to finish the sentence without sounding unsteady.

"Maggie, I'm sorry, but I've got to go," Asa said. "I'm in the middle of something."

The line went dead.

I stared at the phone, my chest tight.

Asa pulling away cracked something I'd been holding together, and the panic rushed in—sharp and sudden. I cried for him, for Poppy, for everything I couldn't control.

The doorbell rang an hour later.

Caleb stood on the porch with Joleen beside him, both of them radiating competence and a calm that, no matter how much I tried, I simply couldn't summon.

"Can we come in?" Caleb asked.

Inside, Joleen got straight to the point. She explained again about Simon—how he worked, why he was effective, why speed mattered more than formality right now.

"Simon is already on the trail," she added. "He'll find Julian, sooner rather than later."

I noticed Caleb watching me carefully.

"You talked to Asa," I said.

"Yes," he replied. "He's wound tight."

That felt true. He just didn't want to be here with me.

Joleen laid out the next steps. After forty-eight hours, Savannah PD could act once Poppy missed three consecutive school days. If necessary, Joleen would go to Savannah herself—she still had friends on the force.

As they were leaving, Caleb asked about Joleen's kids and whether she could actually make the trip to Savannah if necessary.

"I have a nanny and a new minivan, thanks to my husband," she said. "I'll load the kids and the nanny into the van and take them all with me."

"A road trip with two two-year-olds," Caleb said with a snicker. "Now that should be fun."

Joleen smiled. "Hollis and Porter were racing trucks across the kitchen floor last night. Hollis decided he wanted to trade for Porter's truck and Porter wasn't having any of it. And Addie—" She paused. "She just looked at me like it was my job to be the arbitrator. She usually steps in as the mother figure, but last night she didn't try to manage anything. Just… let go. That's real progress."

Something in my chest cracked at the story—the light on Joleen's face, the quiet care in Caleb's eyes. I'd missed the true camaraderie of friendship. The way people showed up. How they rallied around one another like family.

Suddenly, I realized just how much I'd missed Loblolly.

After they left, the fear rushed back in, stronger for having been briefly contained. My mother tried to comfort me, but there was no comfort to be found. I called Isabella.

"No. I haven't heard from him." She sounded genuinely surprised at my call. "I think it's time we discussed a plan."

Her response surprised and pleased me. The it sliced another nick in my heart. If she was this worried, what did it mean?

Within the hour, Isabella showed up at the farm. We talked through options—investigators, money, next steps. She offered to pay for a private investigator without hesitation.

"It's not about the money," I said, skirting the truth until I finally admitted I didn't fully understand Simon myself. Only that Joleen trusted him—and that had to count for something.

The phone rang. I recognized Joleen's voice and put the call on speaker.

"Got an update from Simon," she said. "He located a car service pickup paid for in cash. A man and a little girl were dropped at a Tybee restaurant. The driver thought it was odd—dropping them at a seafood place on the beach with their luggage." She paused. "Simon did too. And it lined up with another lead—a burner number that booked a VRBO Saturday night. One week. Prepaid card. The house is only a block from the restaurant. I think this is it. Katelyn sent her guy to check it out. As soon as we confirm, I'll text you the address."

"If this was Julian—and with luck, it is—why all the cloak and dagger?" I said. "Why remain in state, switch vehicles, pay in cash?"

Joleen exhaled. "Could be he's deliberately avoiding a

line that would trigger something bigger—crossing the state line makes this federal. Brings in the FBI."

The thought chilled me. Was he really that calculating? Had he researched the laws—knew exactly what I could and couldn't touch here, what wouldn't hold up in court? Like taking Poppy across state lines.

The question lodged in my chest, sharp and unanswered.

My hands shook as I thanked Joleen, hung up, and called Asa. Straight to voicemail. I left a rushed message, recapping Joleen's call, my words tumbling over one another.

I left Isabella on the porch, went inside, found Mama, and brought her up to date. I grabbed Poppy's blanket from the couch and pressed it to my chest. The familiar scent—laundry soap and something uniquely hers—undid me.

Joleen called back. Katelyn's man spotted Julian at the house but didn't approach—deemed it too risky. But all my heart knew was that Julian had rented a beach house on Tybee Island, and as of twenty minutes ago, he was still there.

I was shoving the blanket and Poppy's favorite stuffed animals into a tote when Asa's truck pulled into the drive.

He stepped inside without calling my name. His presence filled the living room, steady and contained. His eyes went first to the bag, then to the counter where Poppy's blanket was folded, to Isabella, who sat with folded hands at the kitchen table, then finally to me.

Not searching. Not questioning.

Assessing.

"I'll drive," he said.

It wasn't urgency that sharpened his voice—it was

resolve. The kind that comes after decisions have already been made, privately and without ceremony.

He lifted the tote with deliberate care. His focus had narrowed—not away from me exactly, but toward something singular and immovable. In the back of my mind, I waited for him to touch me. A hand at my back. Fingers brushing my arm. Something that said *we*.

He didn't.

Poppy was our first priority. Everything else fell away.

Like me, his attention had aligned around her—planning, measuring distance, anticipating resistance. His jaw tightened, just slightly. A familiar tell.

A fleeting thought surfaced—that he was bracing himself for a future that didn't include me—and something quiet shifted inside my chest. Not panic. Not anger.

Acceptance.

Some wounds needed time before they could even be named.

Finding Poppy could not wait. She was our only focus now.

Isabella stepped forward. "I should come." She held up a hand to stop any argument. "I'm the only one with a chance to make Julian listen. I can convince him to give up this fight without taking prisoners as the saying goes."

Mama stepped up. "I agree. Take her with you."

Asa stood for a moment, considering the idea, then nodded. "I agree." Practical. Clear-eyed.

He turned toward the door, already moving, already focused on what mattered most.

I followed him—not because everything between us was settled, but because for now, the future could remain unresolved.

All that mattered was bringing our daughter home.

# Chapter Thirty-Five

## MAGGIE

The drive to Tybee took three hours, but it felt like one long, held breath.

Asa offered Isabella the front seat without hesitation, as if it were the most natural decision in the world—practical, polite, inevitable. Which left me in the back with Poppy's tote bag hugged to my ribs like a life raft, watching Asa's shoulders from behind. No chance to reach for his hand. No casual brush of my fingers against his arm. No quiet reassurance I could borrow.

By the time we merged onto the causeway, I was jittery—too much coffee, too little sleep, my thoughts looping faster than I could rein them in. And that was when it hit me how much I'd come to rely on Asa's calm to keep me centered. When he was near, the noise inside me softened. Without him beside me, everything felt sharper, harder to manage.

Soft jazz drifted from the speakers—something smooth and old, saxophone and brushed drums—music meant to calm you down in a dim restaurant where nothing bad ever happened. It did nothing for me now. Every mile marker was another reminder that my baby girl was somewhere ahead of us, in a house we didn't know, with a man who'd decided the rules of shared parental decency no longer applied.

The farther we got from the farm, the more the landscape flattened into pine forests and then rivers and marshland. The sky had that pale, washed look it sometimes wore in fall, as if even the sun had been wrung out. I kept checking the GPS on my phone, watching the distance tick down even though I already knew the estimated arrival time—thirty-two minutes.

Joleen texted to confirm that the man Asa insisted be posted at the house until we arrived had assured her no one had left—not since Julian and Poppy returned from a brief lunch at a local diner. Knowing Poppy was still there gave me something just short of peace, but it steadied my breathing enough to keep going.

Isabella faced forward in the front seat. I couldn't see her expression clearly, but her voice stayed composed, measured—as if we were headed to a business meeting rather than to retrieve an abducted child from a man clearly unraveling. She'd slipped on oversized sunglasses before we pulled away from the farm, and though I only caught glimpses of her in the rearview mirror, they did little to hide the tension in her tone when she spoke. Every so often, she leaned toward Asa, murmuring something low—an observation about traffic, a billboard, our ETA—and Asa answered in the same clipped, contained cadence he'd used with me back at the farm.

He drove like he always did—steady speed, both hands on the wheel, minimal movement. When he changed lanes, he did it decisively, like the road had already informed him what lay ahead.

I pressed my forehead to the window and tried to keep my breathing steady, my heart at a reasonable pace. I failed on both counts. We stayed on I-16 until Savannah swallowed us whole, then peeled off toward the city streets that would eventually funnel us east—toward U.S. 80 and the islands beyond. Traffic thickened immediately. Less open land. More cars. More buildings. More people.

And still, we weren't there yet.

I rolled down the window, craving fresh air, and the damp river smell that clung to the city rushed in—sharp and familiar. I didn't mind it. That smell meant salt water. It meant we were getting closer to Tybee.

We passed streets I could once have taken blindfolded, from summers spent on the island through the years. The closest beach to Loblolly always was Tybee—at least one local family renting a cottage, offering a borrowed place to land. As teens, it was a porch we could crash on, towels draped over railings, salt still drying in our hair.

I caught a glimpse of the skyline through low-hanging clouds, historic homes flanking palm-lined streets. Then we veered toward the water, toward the ribbon of causeways that led east—away from the city's brick and wrought iron and straight into marsh.

The marshes opened like a wide, breathing thing. Brown grasses waved in the wind, dark water threading through them in narrow channels, catching the light like scattered coins. Egrets stood motionless at the edges, patient and bone-white against the green-brown sprawl. The sky felt bigger here. The world quieter, even with the hum of tires and the steady pull of the engine.

We crossed the first bridge, then the second—long

stretches of marsh unfurling between them—as if Tybee wasn't an island so much as a decision you made slowly, step by step.

I thought about Poppy and her love of routine. Her school mornings. Her backpack. Her insistence that her shoes be tied the same way every time. She was the kind of child who wanted to know what came next—who asked *after this?* as if certainty were a blanket you could wrap around your shoulders.

Sometimes I wondered if she needed that reassurance because I traveled so much. Because there were goodbyes she'd learned not to question, and nannies who came and went. If routine was the one thing she could count on when I couldn't always be there.

Julian had taken that from her without asking.

My stomach tightened, and I had to swallow hard to keep my head from spinning.

Isabella must have sensed it, because she shifted in her seat and turned slightly, her sunglasses reflecting the pale daylight.

"You'll see your little girl soon," she said, her voice soft. Not reassurance. Not quite. More like a claim she needed to make out loud.

I didn't answer. I couldn't. If I opened my mouth, something raw would spill out.

Asa glanced at me in the rearview mirror. Just a flick of his eyes—quick, controlled. Then his gaze returned to the road.

No touch. No gentle question. Just that single look that said he knew exactly where I was—and how close I was to coming apart.

We reached the island, and the scenery shifted, like we'd stepped into another decade.

Low houses with tin roofs and sun-faded paint. Palms and live oaks bending slightly in the coastal wind. Old motels that looked like they'd been built when families still piled into station wagons with coolers of sandwiches—when vacations were simple and cheap and sunburn was a badge of honor.

Tybee had always been that way—half beach town, half time capsule. It didn't try to impress you. It simply existed, stubbornly familiar, a little worn around the edges and oddly charming because of it.

Asa followed the GPS through narrow streets lined with cottages and rental houses. The closer we got to the address, the more my skin prickled with awareness, as if my body sensed an electric current connecting my heart to Poppy's—something instinctive and undeniable. Maybe it began long ago, when my heart lay inches from hers. I'd never thought much about the wonder of a mother's bond before now.

We passed Pier Road, and I caught a glimpse of it through the trees—the long wooden stretch reaching toward the ocean, weathered and steady. The beach itself was hidden behind dunes and fence slats, but I could smell it: salt and sand and that faint metallic tang that always made me think of summer storms.

Asa slowed as we turned into a small neighborhood—a quiet residential stretch where the houses sat close enough to hear a neighbor sneeze, but far enough apart that everyone pretended they couldn't. Faded spring wreaths hung on doors. A string of lights sagged along a porch rail, leftover from Christmas a few years ago. Someone had painted a driftwood sign that read *BEACH RULES HERE* in cheerful blue and rusty red letters.

It would have been quaint under different circumstances.

Now it felt surreal.

Asa rolled past the house, then parked a half block away beneath the shade of a live oak and turned off the engine. The jazz cut out mid-note.

For a moment, none of us moved.

The silence inside the truck thickened. My breath sounded too loud. I gripped Poppy's tote bag so hard my fingers ached. I reached for the handle and opened my door.

"Wait."

Isabella swiveled toward me and slid her sunglasses onto the top of her head. Her eyes were clear, steady. She looked at Asa first, then back at me.

"Let me go in first," she said.

"No." The word came out sharper than I intended. "Absolutely not. She's my daughter."

Isabella didn't flinch. "I know. But if we all go up there—if you storm the door—Julian will dig in. He'll turn this into a scene. And Poppy will remember that scene for years."

Emotion pressed behind my eyes like a rising tide. She was right, of course, but I blurted the first thing that came to mind. "He already made it a scene when he took her without telling me."

Asa inhaled slowly, the way he did when he was sorting through words to find the truth. When he spoke, his voice was quiet, firm.

"She's right, Maggie," he said.

My gaze snapped to him. "Asa—"

He turned in his seat and met my eyes straight on. His expression was set—resolved in that maddening way that made it clear he wasn't going to be moved by emotion alone.

"We're not here to win an argument," he said. "We're here to get Poppy out without scaring her."

"I am her mother," I whispered, the words trembling with everything I was holding back. "I need to know—"

"I know," he said, softer now. "I know. But we have to put her first, right?"

His voice was like a caress to my heart, but he still didn't reach back to find my hand or squeeze my shoulder. The only part of him that touched me was his gaze.

And that hurt in a way I didn't have time to name.

Isabella opened her door. "I'll keep it simple," she promised. "I'll get her to the door. Then you take over."

I watched Isabella walk up the sidewalk, her posture straight, her arms swinging with each step. She looked like someone who belonged in glossy magazines, not on a cracked concrete path in a beach neighborhood that smelled faintly of shrimp boils and sunscreen.

Asa got out of the truck and stood beside it, watching the house like he was assessing angles. Escape routes. Threats. Control points.

I slid out more slowly, clutching the tote bag to my chest, then tossed it back into the truck. If Poppy needed her blanket and Mr. Bunny, she'd have them on the ride home. My legs felt unsteady. The world tilted, then righted itself.

We followed Isabella at a distance, our bodies not touching. Close—not enough to look like an ambush, but close enough that I could reach her in a few strides if something went wrong.

The rental house was a pale blue two-story with a wide porch and rented beach chairs stacked beneath an overhang. A sign tacked beside the door read *SALTY BUT SWEET.* I had a sudden urge to rip it from its nail.

Isabella knocked.

Once.

Twice.

My heart pounded so hard I felt it in my throat.

The door opened.

Julian stood in the threshold in a white linen shirt, sleeves rolled, hair slightly tousled as if he'd been running his hands through it. He looked like he belonged on Tybee. Like he'd spent his life in salt air rather than on the beaches of St. Moritz or fox hunting in Cornwall.

He took in Isabella—not cautiously, not defensively. As if he'd been waiting for her to find him.

Even from ten feet away, I saw something in his face ease—soften in a way I'd never witnessed, or if I had, it was so long ago I couldn't recall it. Relief, unmistakable and immediate, passed over his expression. A quiet kind of happiness lit his eyes.

If I'd ever wondered, there was no question now—he loved her.

And suddenly, everything aligned. His rushed departure. The cash payments. Tybee instead of Paris. Poppy spirited away like a secret instead of a daughter. His reason stood right in front of him.

He hadn't come to the States for Poppy.

He'd come for this.

Something I'd suspected but never wanted to believe—that he could be so callous as to use Poppy for his love dramatics.

He'd come for Isabella.

He'd come to test her love.

And with her arrival, she'd given him the proof he needed.

He must have sensed us then—a shift on the sidewalk,

movement in the air—because his gaze slid past her shoulder and found us.

For a fraction of a second, something flashed across his expression: surprise, irritation, calculation.

Then the performance settled in.

"Maggie," he called, as if I were an unexpected guest who'd arrived early to a dinner party.

As soon as we reached the first step leading to the porch, Isabella called, "Poppy," her voice bright and warm. "Sweetheart? Can you come here a moment?"

She'd usurped Julian without effort—and received no rebuttal. I realized then she knew him far better than I did.

I held my breath, my eyes searching beyond him for a glimpse of my baby girl.

Then I heard it—the light patter of feet, the sound of her moving across hardwood.

Her sweet face appeared. Her eyes widened. "Mommy!"

"Poppy," I whispered, dropping to one knee, arms open.

She scooted past Julian and sailed down the steps into my arms, her hands wrapping around my neck. She was wearing her pink hoodie with the tiny embroidered horse on the chest—the one she'd insisted on wearing to school last Friday.

Alive.

Whole.

Here in my arms.

I held her at arm's length and for a heartbeat she just stared at me. Her hair was in a messy ponytail she'd probably done herself, her cheeks rosy as if she'd been outside. A plastic seashell bracelet circled one wrist. A faint smear of chocolate lingered at the corner of her mouth.

Her face crumpled and lit up at the same time. "Mama!"

She launched herself back at me, arms squeezing so hard she nearly knocked me over. I clutched her, feeling the warmth of her through her shirt.

"Oh, baby," I whispered into her hair, breathing her in—soap, salt, childhood. "Oh, Poppy. I've missed you."

She laughed against my shoulder. "You came."

"I came," I said, fighting tears, fighting rage, fighting the urge to look past her and scream at the man who'd used my daughter to win a battle with his lover.

Her arms tightened, and for a moment the world narrowed to the simple miracle of her breathing.

Then she pulled back just enough to look at me, eyes wide. "Mama, we went to the beach. I found a crab shell, but Papa said we had to leave it there."

My stomach twisted at the word *Papa*, but I kept my voice steady. "That sounds like fun."

"It was fun," she insisted, earnest. "But I missed you."

"I missed you too," I whispered. "So much."

Behind me, I felt Asa step closer—not touching, but present. Like a second pillar.

Poppy's gaze slid past my shoulder and found him.

Her face changed again—softening, brightening.

"Coach!" she squealed, wriggling out of my arms and running to him.

Asa crouched instinctively as she barreled into him. The moment she hit him, something in his face loosened—like tension he hadn't realized he was holding slipped free.

He wrapped his arms around her with careful strength, as if afraid she might disappear if he held her too tightly.

"Hey, Peanut," he murmured, voice thick. "Did you have fun?"

"I did," she said, nodding fiercely. "Papa took me to the

beach and there was seaweed and I got sand in my shoes and I didn't like that, but I liked the pier."

Asa's mouth curved, small and involuntary. "The pier's always fun. Did you fish?"

"No, but I want to go back. Will you take me?"

"Sure," he said softly. "But not today."

"Okay. But can I have a riding lesson when we get home?"

His eyes flicked to mine for a split second—something warm and conflicted there—before he looked back at her.

"Of course," he said. "You've already missed two, so we have a lot to catch up on."

Her face beamed. "I'll work really hard."

"I know you will," he said, his voice turning tender. "Right now, let's get you home. You can tell us all about your beach vacation on the way." He said it like this had been nothing more than that. No drama. No damage. "Sugar's probably wondering where you are."

Poppy nodded solemnly. "She misses me."

I wanted to memorize that moment—Asa with her, his heart visibly softening, his entire world narrowing around her.

And I wanted to mourn it too, because I could already feel the distance he was building—quietly, carefully—like a wall he meant to stand behind.

Julian cleared his throat from the doorway.

"I think," he said mildly, "we can have this conversation inside."

Isabella glanced back at him, unreadable. Then she looked at Asa.

Asa didn't move. "Poppy," he said calmly. "Do you want to go grab your shoes?"

Poppy nodded and darted down the hall, chattering as she went.

"Pack up your backpack, sweetie," I called, buying us a few more minutes.

I stepped onto the porch, muscles coiled and ready. Asa stayed a pace behind me.

Inside, the rental house smelled of lemon cleaner and ocean damp. Beach towels hung over a chair. A half-finished puzzle sat on the dining table. A plate of peeled shrimp rested on the counter—as if this had been an ordinary little getaway.

It made me want to throw something.

Poppy scampered down the hall. When the sound of her footsteps faded, Julian lowered his voice. "I didn't think you'd come with her."

He was speaking to Isabella.

"You didn't think she'd come for her child?" Isabella asked coolly.

Julian's laugh was quiet, indulgent. "I didn't think she'd find me this fast."

"She has powerful friends," Isabella said. "Judges. Sheriffs. And Asa."

A pause.

Then Julian, softer. "Why are you here, Isabella?"

"I'm here," she said, "because you made a terrible mistake leaving Italy and coming here."

Asa went still beside me—not rigid. Alert.

My anger stirred, slow and steady, like a match being struck.

Julian's gaze flicked to Asa, then back to Isabella. "You know why I left."

"Don't," Isabella said. "Not now."

Julian stepped closer, his voice dropping into something

intimate. "You're registered at the inn," he murmured. "I called after your last text. It's a charming little place on the river, isn't it? You could stay a few days. We can talk about where to go from here."

I watched Isabella's expression shift—the way it did when a truth landed somewhere unexpected.

"I can stay a few days," she said after a beat. "But I need to be in Paris by Thursday. I have shopping to do before the weekend hunt in the Cotswolds. It's the hunt of the year. We don't want to miss it."

Julian's mouth curved, pleased.

"You could do with a few things as well," Isabella added, all practicality.

"Perhaps," he said. "We'll see if we come to an understanding."

Poppy ran back with her shoes in one hand and her backpack in the other, entirely unbothered—as if this were a simple change of plans.

I breathed out slowly, grateful for a child's ability to normalize what was anything but normal.

"Ready?" Asa asked.

Poppy nodded. "Mama, can we have hot chocolate when we get home?"

"Yes," I said. "All the hot chocolate you want."

She grinned and took my hand—then stopped, turned back, and went to Julian.

He hadn't noticed her. She tugged his pant leg. "Hug me goodbye, Papa."

He bent and hugged her, held her at arm's length, kissed her cheek. "I'll see you soon."

Out of earshot—near the steps while Poppy examined seashells in a flowerpot—I leaned toward Asa.

"She seems… okay," I whispered. "Like she doesn't even realize—"

"That's the best outcome we could've hoped for," he said quietly. "Let it be that."

Emotion tangled in my chest—relief, fury, gratitude, shame.

Before we left, I turned back to Julian. "I need to speak to you before you leave for Europe."

"I'll be in touch."

"Don't leave the States," I said, keeping myself between him and Poppy. "Not before we talk."

His eyes narrowed. "I don't need a lecture."

"No lectures," I said. "Just the truth."

Something old and hard flickered across his face—then vanished.

"We'll be back in Loblolly tonight," he said, already turning to Isabella. "We'll talk."

Katrina was right. He and Isabella seemed made for one another.

Asa ushered us toward the truck. Poppy climbed into the front seat between us, humming to herself. I handed her the tote I'd packed and she pulled out her blanket, and hugged it like a prize.

Asa started the engine. The jazz returned, soft and smooth, as if nothing had happened.

But everything had.

We pulled away from the rental house, from the island, from the ocean smell that had soaked into my nerves. The causeway opened again, marsh stretching on either side like a witness.

Poppy leaned against me, her eyes drifting closed, murmuring about horses and seashells and Sugar waiting at home.

I closed my eyes, letting the rhythm of her voice steady me.

Asa drove.

And beneath my relief, beneath my exhaustion, I felt it —the unresolved future waiting just past the headlights.

Everything between Asa and me wasn't settled.

But we set it aside because Poppy needed to come home.

She was what held us together.

And for now, that was enough.

# Chapter Thirty-Six

## MAGGIE

The solarium at the River House Inn was empty, late morning light filtering through tall windows and casting pale reflections across the tiled floor. The world outside felt muted—as if the inn had decided privacy was part of the service.

Julian sat across from me at a small round table, his posture relaxed, his expression unreadable.

This was our second meeting. The first had more than a few harsh words between us, but in the end, we'd come to an agreement, so I knew to say it quickly—without preamble, without another apology—because there was no apology that could wipe away what I'd done.

I'd tried explaining that as impossible as it might seem, I didn't know until I came back to Loblolly that Poppy was Asa's child. But now, that was water under a dirty bridge as mama would say. No reason to go back.

The wronged person rarely cared about intent, but I drew in a breath and said it once again anyway.

"I'm sorry," I said. "I don't know what else to say

except that I truly didn't know. Or perhaps I did and refused to see it—I'm not sure which. But the deceit wasn't intentional. I know that hardly matters. Still, I am sorry. And I'm grateful for the love you've given Poppy over the years."

It felt like the bare minimum. He deserved that much, and probably more—but I knew better than to offer too much. Julian had always known how to take advantage of generosity.

I slid a large manila envelope across the table.

He didn't react. Not at first. Not even when I let the silence stretch.

"The blood test is inside," I said. "It states unequivocally that Poppy is Asa's child."

Julian wrapped both hands around his coffee cup. He didn't lift it. Just stared into the dark surface like it might offer commentary.

"And I suppose he'll fight for his parental rights?"

I studied his face but couldn't read the emotion behind his bland expression. He might as well have asked if the sun were shining. "I hope it won't come to that... but yes, he will."

"Not surprised. He seems the sort who likes to make claims."

"It's me you should be angry with, not Asa."

He huffed a laugh. "Well, I can't say I'm shocked." He frowned. "After seeing you with him—and him with Poppy—and knowing you came running back here at the first sign of your injury. Makes sense there's unfinished business between you."

I nudged the envelope closer. "There's a copy of the blood test inside. And a notarized release." My voice stayed even, though my chest felt tight. "If you sign, you're released from all parental responsibility. Financial. Legal. Everything."

His gaze flicked up then—not startled, just alert. Calculating. The Julian I'd always known.

"And Asa?" he asked.

"Will be listed as her father. Legally." I watched his face carefully. "But we're not telling Poppy yet."

Julian nodded once. "That's probably wise."

No hesitation. No bargaining. No wounded pride. Just acceptance.

Of course he cared for Poppy. He may not have been the world's most attentive father, but he did love her. Even now, though it felt less like a parent's love and more like that of an estranged uncle—fond, distant, and already loosening its hold.

The pen moved with quiet finality, like this was something he'd already resolved privately—likely after a discussion with Isabella.

When he slid the papers back toward me, he leaned into his chair. "Isabella and I set the date," he said. "September."

I absorbed that quietly.

"We'll be leaving before Poppy gets home from school today."

The words landed heavier than I expected. Not for me—for Poppy. "You don't want to see her? Say goodbye?"

"Better this way, no?" A faint smile touched his mouth. "You know I never liked hard farewells."

I searched his face—for regret, for doubt, for some flicker of uncertainty—but found only resolve. The same resolve that had always allowed him to walk away cleanly.

"Goodbye, Maggie," he said, standing.

"Goodbye, Julian."

He left the solarium without looking back.

The door closed softly behind him—no slam, no echo. Just the quiet finality. The same way he'd ended our marriage.

Without regret.

Julian had always been able to walk away as if nothing tethered him to the moment he was leaving behind. No backward glance. No visible cost. Just a smooth pivot into whatever version of himself suited the next room, the next city, the next woman.

I used to think of him the way people thought of Holly Golightly in *Breakfast at Tiffany's*—effortlessly charming, endlessly adaptable, drifting through life on borrowed light and good manners. But beneath that polish was something brittle. Someone who couldn't stay still long enough to face reality, or sit with the damage he left in his wake.

Watching him turn back toward Isabella, already reshaping himself to fit her world, I understood it more clearly than ever. Julian didn't leave because he didn't care.

He left because caring required a kind of staying he'd never learned how to do.

---

The days after Julian left Loblolly, our life returned to normal, and time seemed to soften again. But before long, our days began moving more swiftly.

Poppy returned to school with her backpack swinging and stories tumbling out before the bus driver pulled away from our drive. When I told her Julian had gone back to Paris, she barely paused—just nodded, as if the information fit neatly into what she already understood about their world.

She didn't ask when she'd see him again.

Which made me look back in time and realize she never had.

Asa came to the farm several times a week—sometimes after school, sometimes near dinner. Always for Poppy. Always careful with me.

We talked easily enough, but there was space between us now, deliberate and respected. As if we were both standing on opposite sides of something unnamed, aware of it without needing to define it.

The paperwork was filed quietly. Asa listed as her father. Official without being emotional.

Nothing changed.

And everything did.

I returned to my job in earnest—eight hours a day, sometimes ten, working before Poppy woke for school, and long after she went to bed. I was disciplined and focused. My hand protested, but not sharply. More like a warning. A reminder that healing wasn't something you rushed or assumed.

Between writing sessions, I worked the farm. I did as much as I could, but unless I sold my Paris apartment, I couldn't spare any more savings to tackle the bigger repairs—mending fences, installing new irrigation, putting a roof on the barn. I made lists of what was within my power to fix. I didn't strictly need them, but they steadied me, proof that I was still useful.

Katrina and I had slipped back into our old rhythm—daily video calls that sometimes stretched through the afternoon. It almost felt like being in the office again, except for the absence of actors, directors, and location chaos. All of that now fell to Katrina, and I knew it wasn't fair. She was carrying the weight of the travel, the negotiations, the on-the-ground decisions—because I wasn't there.

I couldn't keep straddling two lives.

I had to decide, one way or the other, and soon. Even Claire, my boss, was losing patience with my indecision. She'd given me a deadline to be back in Paris and that day was drawing near.

Mama healed steadily, though she still napped twice a day, settling into the armchair by the window like it was her second bed. I noticed that as the days wore on, those naps became shorter, turning into thirty-minute power naps before she was up and moving again. In the evenings, she reclaimed the kitchen, cooking with quiet satisfaction.

She took over homework duty with Poppy while I worked, her voice drifting down the hall—gentle corrections, encouragement, the steady rhythm of reliability. It seemed she enjoyed playing the role of teacher again.

Our days found a pattern.

It surprised me how much I needed that.

One afternoon, Asa stayed longer than usual.

Poppy had insisted he help her with a science project—cotton balls and cloud formations—and by the time they finished, the sun was already lowering over the fields.

I found him at the sink afterward, rinsing glue from his hands.

"Thanks for staying," I said.

He nodded. "She asked."

"I know." I hesitated. "Still."

He dried his hands on a towel, folding it carefully, like he needed something to do with them. "She seems really good," he said. "Settling in here."

"She does."

The quiet stretched—comfortable, but weighted. I knew

he likely wanted to ask about my plans. How long his daughter would be with him. But he said nothing more. Our quiet was the kind that invited honesty if either of us leaned too far forward. He didn't. And I hadn't yet made my decision about how our future would look.

"I'm glad she's here," he said finally. "With Barbara. With all of this."

I met his eyes then. "So am I."

For a moment, I thought he might reach for me. The space between us felt charged with everything unsaid.

Instead, he stepped back.

"I should go," he said gently. "It's getting late."

Poppy barreled into the kitchen and wrapped her arms around his waist, breaking the moment cleanly in two. Asa laughed, hugged her back, and a second later the quiet was gone.

But after his truck disappeared down the drive, I stayed on the porch longer than usual, aware of the feelings he'd left behind inside my heart.

---

The next day, Katrina called. "So," she said, skipping pleasantries, "are you going to meet Claire's deadline?"

"Maybe," I said.

"Maggie."

"I know," I said softly. And I did.

The following Saturday, Joleen and Tally arrived just before noon, bringing with them the kind of chaos only close friends could.

Joleen climbed out first, already mid-instruction. The nanny followed with the twins, who were bouncing and squirming, while Joleen's daughter Adaline—who had the nickname Addie, which she gleefully pointed out rhymed with Maddie—brought on a laugh all around. She spotted Poppy at the barn and took off running.

Lola spilled out behind Tally, and within moments the girls had disappeared inside the barn, seeking the new litter of kittens we'd inherited when a stray decided to call the barn her new home—all without my knowledge. A collusion between Poppy and her Nana. I fussed about cats being underfoot every chance I got, but secretly I loved that Poppy would have the experience of raising animals on the farm.

After thirty minutes of playtime with the kittens, then hugs and reminders, the nanny loaded the twin boys, Hollis and Porter, back into the car, citing the need to cart them home for an afternoon nap.

Mama went inside for her afternoon rest, and the remaining adults took our iced teas onto the porch and commandeered the rockers.

"So," Tally said, folding her legs beneath her. "Are you ready?"

"For what?" I asked, though the answer hovered between us.

"To go back," Joleen said gently. "To Europe. To your life. Barbara told Sue Ellen that you work with your writing partner every day, and your boss has issued a deadline."

I looked out across the fields—the long lines of patience and work. "I don't know if I'll ever feel ready."

"But Sue Ellen says you're running out of time," Tally said. Not unkindly. Just honest. "It seems to me that doing nothing is making a decision. Do you want to stay here in Loblolly?" She waved her hand to encompass the pecan orchard. "Be a farmer?" She held up a hand. "Don't get me wrong, I love it here. But I wasn't the one attending the

Oscars and being nominated for best screenplay. I'm just not sure I understand how you can give it up."

I'd argue her point, except it was true. As much as I loved the farm, if I were honest, I loved writing more. "I'd miss writing if I don't go back," I admitted, stretching my fingers in and out. "And I won't really know if I'm healed unless I try to keep up with the schedule again."

Joleen studied me. "And Poppy?"

"Mama and I talked last night. I'm considering letting her stay here, at least until Christmas, but maybe longer. It seems unfair to uproot her, and Asa is just getting to know her and spend time with her."

Both women went still.

"I just can't take her away from Asa so quickly." My voice turned shaky. I attributed it to the thought of being apart from Poppy, but I knew there were unsaid words between Asa and me—at least on my side. He seemed perfectly happy to go on as we were. Friends, sharing Poppy, nothing more.

"Taking Poppy away from him so soon feels cruel," I added. "And I've been cruel enough to him. Ten years of not acknowledging him as her father. And I need to know if my hand can even handle the crazy schedule we have this season."

"And the farm?" Tally asked.

"I found a manager I can afford," I said. "But only if I keep my job."

Joleen leaned back, exhaling. "That's a lot of uncertainty."

"I know." I smiled faintly. "By Christmas, maybe things will be clearer. Maybe I can convince Mama to spend part of the year with me in Europe." I'd figure out a way to get

Poppy back into her school in Paris. Maybe appeal directly to the headmaster. Claim extenuating circumstances.

"Maybe," Tally echoed. "I can't quite picture Barbara in Paris."

The girls' laughter drifted back toward us, bright and unburdened, the opposite of my heart.

That evening, Mama and I sat at the kitchen counter shelling peas, the radio humming softly between stations. She loved her music; maybe for Christmas I'd spring for surround sound throughout the house.

"You've been quiet," she said.

"I'm thinking."

"That usually means you're deciding something you already know the answer to."

I smiled. "You always say that."

"And I'm usually right."

She slid a bowl toward me. "Christmas will come faster than you think," she added, casual but precise.

"I know." I sighed, exhaling all the reservations in my heart. "You really don't mind having Poppy here that long?"

Mama's hands never stopped moving—shelling, tossing the hull, shelling another. "I raised you, didn't I? I can manage my granddaughter for a few months."

"It could be for the whole season," I said. "I'll come home on our holiday break, but if I don't take Poppy back to Paris now and settle her in school, she won't be allowed to start mid-term. They have rules and have refused to make an exception—I got an email from them today. They turned down my request to start mid-term. And honestly, I don't know if I can be away from her for an entire school year."

Mama placed her hand over mine. "Let's just plan until Christmas. You can go back to Paris and focus on your career without worrying. And if everything works out and your hand is healed, or you figure out how to work around it, I'll go back with you after the holidays—live with you, homeschool Poppy."

"Homeschool?" I blinked. "Where did that come from?"

She huffed a breath, picked up another pea, and ran her finger down the seam, spilling the contents neatly into the bowl. "I taught school for twenty years, didn't I?"

"You taught high school English, Mama."

She shrugged, eyes twinkling. "Well then, by the time she reaches sixth grade, they may have to let her skip a year or two. She's smart as a whip and loves to read."

She glanced at me, and her expression softened. "You don't have to know how everything turns out yet, Maggie. Just the next step."

"And if what comes next changes again?"

"That's life," she said simply.

Later, when I tucked Poppy into bed, I asked if she'd like to stay in Loblolly while I went back to Paris to work.

She scrambled upright. "Can I?"

Her reaction caught me off guard—it made my heart soar and break all at once. "I think it would be best until I get resettled with my job. We don't have a nanny, and there is a lot of traveling scheduled for the fall. But I'll come back on my holiday break. Christmas isn't that far off," I said, to myself as much as to her.

I guided her back beneath the quilt. "So, how does that sound?"

"I'll miss you," she said. "But I love it here." Her voice softened. "And if I went back to Paris with you, Sugar and Mr. Asa would miss me."

"Yes," I said quietly, tucking her in. "They would miss you indeed."

It seemed only fair that it be my time to miss Poppy—fair to let her father have space to know his daughter at last. I reminded myself for the hundredth time that he'd been deprived of that joy long enough. Taking her now, when they were just beginning to bond, would be far too cruel.

Outside, the air had shifted—cooler, edged with inevitability.

The season was turning.

And whether I was ready or not, my life was about to turn with it.

# Chapter Thirty-Seven

## ASA

Asa arrived early on the chance he could steal a few quiet minutes with Maggie after Poppy's bus left and before she got a start on her day.

Over the past few days, his friends had ragged him. Even his Aunt Sue Ellen had reminded him—gently but firmly—that Maggie in Loblolly wasn't a forever thing. They were only saying what he already knew: if he was going to say something, he needed to do it now.

After another sleepless night, he decided they deserved one honest conversation about their future before she left town—one where he was honest without making her feel cornered. Without turning it into an ultimatum.

Even though part of him wanted exactly that. To draw a line in the sand and be done with the waiting.

*Be careful what you wish for,* his mother's voice surfaced, soft and familiar. Ultimatums rarely landed the way you imagined. And the outcomes almost never worked in your favor.

But the conversation had to be had, and he was tired of the unsaid words eating a hole in his gut. So here he was.

He heard her on the phone with her writing partner as soon as Barbara let him inside. She'd explained last week that she worked ten hours a day—sometimes more—because her mind needed constant use, and without it, she feared the one gift that truly defined her—writing fiction—might slip away.

He stood for a moment and listened. She sounded animated. Happy. Laughing and planning. In all the time she'd been home, this was the first time he'd heard her so relaxed—so fully in her element. It was a video chat, and he hesitated, unsure whether to interrupt.

"I can't believe we've been nominated for another BAFTA."

Maggie let out a laugh that came close to giddy. "What's Claire saying?"

"She's saying you need to get yourself back to Paris."

"I know. I made my flight reservations today," Maggie said. "After Monday, you'll no longer have an office to yourself."

Maggie's revelation hit him square in the chest.

"Great," Katrina said. "You can go to Milan on Thursday. Alexander is adamant that we have a sit-down with the talent before the rewrite. He wants us to see them in action, nail down—"

Asa let the words wash over him, then settle deep in his gut. He turned and walked out of the house. She hadn't noticed him. Wouldn't. Better this way.

He'd always known Maggie's career was the kind that made stars. But what he hadn't fully understood was the scale of her talent—or maybe he hadn't let himself think about it because it hurt, knowing she'd never give it up.

Shouldn't give it up. Her gift wasn't something that could be shaped to fit a place.

It required space. Reach. A life larger than one small town could ever hold.

Loblolly lived in her—the land, the people, the history—but what lived in her head stretched far beyond this town.

It took her returning to Loblolly for him to realize that Paris hadn't changed her. It had simply met her where she already was.

That realization settled with quiet finality. To ask her to give up her career—to ask her to choose against it—would cost her too deeply. Maybe not immediately. Maybe not loudly. But slowly, the way erosion worked. The way something vital wore away until only the shape remained.

He knew in his heart she loved him, and she might stay if he asked. She might try a life together.

But she would never be whole.

And if she stayed because of him—because he asked it of her—he would witness that loss every day. In the stillness. In the hesitation. In the lack of light that never quite found its way back to her eyes.

He loved her too much for that.

By the time he pulled away from the farm, he'd forced down the searing, gut-wrenching realization: all he'd ever have of Maggie was Poppy. And that would have to be enough.

He would pull back. Create the space she'd need to tell him her decision. And when she left again, it would be her choice—never knowing that the price of asking her to stay had been too high even for love.

---

Poker night at Jackson's had evolved into something halfway between a tradition and a survival tactic.

Tonight the over-the-garage man cave smelled like pizza, fresh sawdust from Jackson's newest project, and whatever cologne Tanner had grabbed in the dark that morning. A battered poker table dominated the center of the room, scarred with the history of bad bets and spilled beer.

Jackson dropped into his chair and dragged a hand down his face, the legs of the table screeching slightly against the concrete.

Caleb pulled out the chair beside Jackson. "Nice playground you've got in the backyard. I'm in the market—you game?"

Jackson reached for a slice of pizza, folded it in half, and shook his head.

"I was hell-bent on building the jungle gym myself. Three hours of sawing and measuring later, I admitted defeat."

Caleb stacked his chips into neat towers, a smile playing at the corners of his mouth. "Let me guess—you called Bud?"

"Yep." Jackson took a bite, chewed, then added, "Bud and his helper."

Tanner flicked a poker chip across the felt toward the pot. "Smart man."

"They finished the whole thing in under two hours." Jackson leaned back, staring at the ceiling like it had personally betrayed him.

Tanner smirked. "There's a lesson in there somewhere."

Jackson pushed his chair in with a foot and reached for his beer. "The lesson is that pride has no place in parenting."

Asa reached behind him and opened the window. He always chose the seat closest to the window to control the smoke, then passed around cigars before lighting up.

Caleb stuck an unlit stogie in his mouth and shuffled the deck with practiced ease. Tanner lounged back, sniffed the cigar like a connoisseur, then racked in the pot—evidently here to add commentary and take everyone's money.

Caleb began dealing another hand, then stopped, a card hovering midair as a grin spread across his face. "Okay. I need to man-share." He gave them all a sweeping stink eye. "That means it doesn't leave this room."

They all nodded in unison.

All but Tanner, who simply lifted his beer. "If this is about us siding with you on the dumbwaiter being installed from your bedroom to the kitchen, we've already vetoed the idea."

"Nope." He continued dealing, then looked at Tanner. "But that was a really good idea." He finished dealing, looked at his cards, and announced with a somber face, "Is it too early to buy my boys Falcon jerseys and stuffed footballs?" He tossed his cards on the table. "I fold."

Jackson froze, his fingers gripping his stack of chips. "Dude. It's never too early for football."

Caleb rocked the legs of his chair forward, palms flat on the felt. "I figure it'll be their going home from the hospital outfit. I haven't told Tally, so keep it zipped for now."

Tanner snorted, tapping his cards against the table. "Yeah, we'll see if Tally's on board."

Caleb shrugged. "I painted the nursery blue."

Tanner pointed a chip at him. "And you think that's an even trade off?"

Caleb's smile vanished. He pointed right back. "Absolutely."

Jackson lifted his beer in surrender. "Being a judge, I'm excellent at referring marital discourse."

Asa assessed his hand, decided he might be able to pull this one off. "I'll put down a twenty that he loses that argument."

Caleb slapped his hand over his heart. "I'm hurt."

Jackson snorted as he gathered the pot. "Yeah, I can tell."

That brought on a round of laughter.

The game picked up pace—cards slapped down, chips clinked, beer bottles thudded against the table. Tanner studied Asa over the rim of his bottle, eyes sharp despite the casual slouch.

Asa looked up, met his gaze. "Something on your mind?"

"Actually, there is," Tanner said, drawing out the word as he tossed in a chip. "Kind of miss seeing the Viscountess floating around the Inn."

Asa snorted and checked.

"I bet." He glanced up. "Does Stella share that sentiment?"

Tanner barked a laugh. "I'm smart enough not to ask. Just saying—she did class the place up."

Asa tossed a chip into the pot without looking. "Good riddance. Too much baggage."

Caleb peeked at his cards, then glanced between them. "Heard Maggie's heading back to Europe."

That slowed everything.

Jackson leaned back, chair creaking. "Heard she's leaving Poppy here?"

Asa flicked another chip forward. "With her grandmother." And me, although he left that part out. But the fact that Maggie was unselfish enough to consider leaving their daughter for a few months didn't go unnoticed. He knew how close they were and what it would cost her.

Silence stretched. The cards lay untouched.

Jackson finally sighed. "Okay. So I'll address the tiptoeing elephant in the room—how do you feel about that?"

"Fine." Asa checked. "Great, actually. It gives me time with Poppy." He pushed back the sudden sadness threatening to escape.

Jackson's brows lifted as he tossed in his chips. "What'd you say when she told you? Did you tell her?"

Asa frowned, genuinely confused. "Tell her what?"

"That you don't want her to go."

Tanner nodded, tapping the edge of the table. "Yeah. That."

Asa scoffed, folding. "Why would I ask her to squash her dreams?"

Caleb slid another chip forward. "Maybe those aren't her dreams anymore. People get new ones."

Jackson stacked his chips slowly. "You two looked like you were destined to pick up where you left off. But lately you treat her more like a sister."

"Yeah. A sister you don't particularly like," Tanner added.

Asa stared at his cards a few seconds longer than necessary. Now that he looked again, he had nothing worth playing—and nothing worth saying. He let the silence stretch, the way he always did when he didn't want to lie.

Finally, he tossed his cards face down. "I'm not a glutton for punishment."

They waited.

After a long, uncomfortable beat, he added, "I learned

my lesson the first time. Long-distance doesn't work. Not when one of you always has one foot out the door."

Caleb nodded, thoughtful. "So you're protecting yourself."

Asa gathered his chips into a tighter stack. "I'm saving what little sanity I have left."

Tanner frowned. "Still seems like a hell of a thing to walk away from." He racked in the pot and began dealing the next hand.

Asa met his gaze. "I didn't walk away. I stepped back."

There was a difference.

"Maggie's going back to her career," he said, tapping the felt. "That's who she is. I'm not standing in the way of that. But right now?" He glanced at his new cards. "I've got a daughter."

Caleb leaned back. "Yeah, but maybe she's ready to give it up—if only someone would ask her."

Asa scoffed softly. "I don't think so. She's back writing with her partner, planning to accept some big European award. That doesn't sound like someone thinking about walking away." He shook his head. "She belongs in the big leagues. Always has. She knows it. I know it. And her studio sure as hell knows it—they let her take four months off and are welcoming her back with open arms."

Jackson's expression softened. "That sucks."

"She's coming back for the holidays." Asa gathered his chips. "Between now and then, I've got ten lost years of being a father to cram in."

Caleb grinned. "No pressure."

Asa huffed a quiet laugh, rubbing the back of his neck. "Tell you the truth, I'm knocked sideways. Terrified. Excited. All of it."

Jackson lifted his beer. "Welcome to fatherhood."

They played on, the room settling into familiar noise.

And for the first time that night, Asa felt steady.

Whatever came next—with Maggie, with Paris—could wait.

Right now, he had winning cards in his hand, friends at his back, and a daughter waiting for him tomorrow.

## Chapter Thirty-Eight

### MAGGIE

Paris welcomed me back the way it always had—with efficiency, beauty, and a kind of indifference reserved for the world's most beautiful cities.

Katrina sent our new driver to the airport with an effusive apology for not being able to meet me herself. The car service was a new perk, along with a generous salary increase that came with the award nomination—and, evidently, a newly renovated and much larger office. Stewart, our driver, carried my suitcase inside, set it just beyond the apartment door, and bid me goodnight, promising to pick me up in the morning at 7:45.

I stood in the foyer for a moment, keys still in hand, listening as an unfamiliar hush settled around me.

The apartment smelled faintly of beeswax polish and fresh flowers. My favorite lilies were arranged on the sofa table in the living room—likely orchestrated by Claire's assistant, Lesley, as a welcome-home gesture. Lesley had volunteered to water my plants and collect my mail while I was away. In return, she'd had use of the apartment.

She'd jumped at the chance to escape her cramped flat and annoying roommate a few days a week and promised no wild parties. Since everything was exactly where I'd left it, it appeared I'd made a good bargain. Where Lesley found white lilies this time of year was anyone's guess. A hothouse, surely.

The apartment looked almost unlived in. The throw was folded neatly over the arm of the sofa. No stray toys. No half-finished puzzles. No big and small shoes kicked off wherever exhaustion had finally overtaken my baby girl and me after a long day.

This was my life. The one I had chosen. The one I had worked for.

I told myself the old, familiar euphoria would come once I'd rested. Showered. Eaten something. Settled back into the rhythm I knew so well.

I set my suitcase aside and moved through the rooms slowly, touching nothing, as if the apartment might startle if I disturbed it too quickly. After checking each room, I finally crossed to the wide main window in the living room and pulled back the curtain. Paris unfolded beneath me—gray rooftops and pale stone, a thin slice of blue sky breaking through the clouds.

Beautiful. Eternal. Unchanged.

So why did it feel as though I'd arrived late to my own life? A world I'd spent years shaping to my satisfaction. I sank into the sofa and melded into the melancholy I'd tried shrugging off ever since kissing Poppy and Mama goodbye.

The next morning, not quite well rested but eager to get on with my life, the studio welcomed me back with its usual efficiency. There were warm handshakes in glass-walled offices, cheek kisses from colleagues I hadn't seen in months, quiet congratulations on my recovery. After my first story meeting, the executive producer clasped my shoulder and smiled, clearly pleased.

"Excellent work," he said. "Your instincts are sharper than ever. The rewrite sings."

High praise, coming from him.

My hand held steady as I worked. Strong. Responsive. No pain. No hesitation. The injury that had once threatened everything now felt like something I'd imagined rather than lived.

I met the days demands easily. Even I had to admit it. There was an old belief in the industry that the best work came from emotional fracture—that when something broke open inside you, the writing found its way onto the page without resistance.

I moved through the first weekend the way I always had—long walks through familiar neighborhoods, stopping at cafés I'd loved for years. But now I sat alone at small round tables with espressos and a book I barely read, watching the city drift past. Couples leaned in close over shared plates. Friends laughed too loudly, unconcerned with the space they occupied. Families navigated narrow sidewalks with strollers and sticky little hands clutching lollipops, moving with the choreography born of love and fatigue.

Once, that vibrance had reminded me I was alive—part of the pulse of the city I'd come to call home. I struggled to find that feeling now. It came, of course, in fleeting moments—but then my thoughts would circle back to Poppy and Mama and, always, to Asa. And I would settle into the quiet longing that now lived just beneath the surface of everything.

As the weeks wore on, in the evenings, I met colleagues from the studio for dinner. There was wine and teasing and talk of upcoming projects. They told me how good it was to have me back, how indispensable I was, how lucky Paris was to claim me again.

I nodded. I laughed. I agreed.

I told myself the hollowness I felt was Poppy-shaped.

That explanation fit neatly. It didn't demand further scrutiny. I'd left my daughter behind—temporarily. Of course things felt off. Of course the apartment felt too quiet, the weekends too unstructured, the nights too long.

But the truth pressed at the edges of my thoughts, refusing to stay quiet.

I'd been here before—alone, driven, fulfilled. This life had once felt electric, like standing at the center of something rare and brilliant.

Now it felt… distant.

As if I were watching myself live it from a few steps away.

After a day of back-to-back meetings, Katrina caught me as I was leaving and insisted we cap off our "day from hell" with a very dry martini. I was exhausted, but when she promised we wouldn't discuss work—not even one word—I let her drag me to one of our favorite haunts: a small restaurant near the Seine, one of those intimate places with low lighting and an impossibly long wine list. We'd been coming here for years, celebrating contracts and triumphs and near-misses that eventually turned into victories.

---

We asked for a corner table and settled in.

"Paris missed you," she said, smiling as she squeezed my hand.

I smiled back. "Did it?"

Katrina's eyes lingered on me a beat too long, as if she'd

noticed the delay between the smile and whatever was supposed to come after.

She insisted on choosing the wine, mentioning a new red she'd been wanting to try. In truth, I knew she'd never trusted my palate. Too American, Julian used to tease.

"We need something indulgent," Katrina said.

We busied ourselves with the small talk of catching up—in he end discussed work and upcoming projects as I knew we would. We move on to books and films I'd missed while I was away.

She studied me over the rim of her glass the way she always did—professionally, perceptively, with affection threaded through the analysis.

"The studio is thrilled," she said. "Absolutely thrilled. Your recovery is a nonissue. The buzz is already building."

I nodded. "Good."

"You don't sound excited."

"I am," I said quickly. Then paused. "I think."

Katrina didn't rush to fill the silence. It was one of the things I liked about her. I realized, not for the first time, that she shared that quality with Asa.

"You seem… different," she said finally.

I laughed softly. "That's vague."

"I know." Her expression softened. "You're not unhappy. But you're not lit up, either."

I stared at the candle between us. "I don't think it's my work."

"No," Katrina agreed. "Your instincts are intact. More than intact."

"And it's not the studio," I said. "They're wonderful. And yes—I'm writing well."

"Exceptionally."

I exhaled. "I just don't feel the way I used to."

The sentence lingered between us, heavier than I'd intended.

Katrina leaned back slightly. "Tell me what that feels like."

"It feels…" I searched for the right words. "Quieter. Like the praise happens somewhere else. Like I'm grateful—but not transported."

I looked up, almost apologetic. "I used to feel like I was standing inside something magnificent."

"And now?"

"Now it feels like a job I'm very good at."

Katrina studied me. "And Loblolly?"

The name settled between us, uninvited but inevitable.

I didn't flinch. "It felt full. But it wasn't sustainable."

"Wasn't it?"

I shook my head. "It was temporary. A pause. A version of myself I don't get to keep."

"And Asa?"

My fingers tightened briefly around my wineglass. "Asa was never a plan."

"Ah," Katrina said gently. "But he was happiness."

I swallowed. "For a moment."

"I chose this life," I said quietly. "I don't regret it—but it comes with a cost."

Katrina reached across the table and squeezed my hand. "You're allowed to want more than one thing."

"Not always at the same time," I said. "And I'll always have a part of him in Poppy. They are so much alike."

We sat with that.

Later, as dessert arrived—mine untouched—Katrina cleared her throat.

"There is something else."

I smiled faintly. "And why am I not surprised?"

"I have a friend," she said carefully. "An American. Businessman. Recently relocated."

I lifted an eyebrow.

"He's single. Handsome. Insufferably persistent." She smiled. "He calls me at least twice a week asking if I'll make an introduction."

"That's flattering."

"I think he's quite taken with the idea of you," Katrina said. "Which is different from being taken with you—but still."

I laughed despite myself.

"I'm having a small dinner party Friday," she continued. "Very casual. No pressure. He'll be there. If you get on, wonderful. If not—claim a headache, an early meeting, whatever you like."

I considered it. The idea didn't spark excitement—but it didn't repel me, either.

"All right," I said. "I'll come."

Katrina smiled, satisfied. "Excellent."

I lifted my glass. "One problem."

"What's that?"

"I have nothing to wear."

Katrina laughed, her brown eyes sparkling. "Well then. That sounds like a shopping trip. Tomorrow?"

"Sounds perfect."

Back at home, the laughter had faded, and the familiar ache returned.

Paris was beautiful. My career was intact. My future was secure.

This was the life I had built.

And now, it was time to live it—even if part of me still longed for a place where life felt messier, closer, and more like home.

# Chapter Thirty-Nine

## ASA

Thanksgiving at the River House Inn had become something close to a town tradition—less about family trees and more about chosen ones.

If you didn't have relatives nearby, or if the idea of sitting across a table from them felt like too much work, you came here. Stella threw the doors open every year and let the town fill the space with noise, collected gratitude, and appetite. The restaurant was usually closed to the public, but on Thanksgiving—and a few other select holidays—she made exceptions. "No one should be alone on the holidays," she'd said too many times to count.

Asa arrived early, as he always did since his parents had passed. Spending the day quietly at home no longer appealed to him, and he refused to let his Aunt Sue Ellen do all the cooking just so she could insist she wasn't tired afterward. So he'd loaded her into his truck and brought her along—one of the few days a year when she was served instead of serving others. Besides, all his friends were usually here. It just made sense.

This year, he'd also invited Poppy and Barbara.

All four of them walked in together, Poppy mumbling about having been forced to wear her coat for the short walk from the car to the front door. "Why do I have to wear it?" she argued with Barbara. "I don't need it inside."

It made sense to him, but Asa stayed out of the tussle. He'd learned early on not to intervene in disagreements between two determined women—even if one of them was only ten, going on thirty.

Once inside, all of Poppy's attention pulled toward the solarium, where sunlight spilled across white tablecloths and polished floors. Barbara followed just behind them, taking in the room with the practiced eye of someone who understood both hospitality and legacy.

Sue Ellen lingered near the door, pausing to survey the buffet with open approval. "Well," she said, hands on her hips, "the Colonel's certainly outdone himself this year."

The buffet ran the length of the room—turkey carved thick and glistening, cornbread dressing fragrant with sage, green beans snapped fresh, sweet potato casserole crowned with pecans that Asa suspected came from Barbara's orchard. The Colonel ruled the kitchen with theatrical authority, issuing commands while sneaking tastes when he thought no one was watching.

Stella moved through the crowd like she owned every inch of it—which she did—greeting guests, directing staff, laughing easily. Tanner Sutton hovered nearby, relaxed but watchful, a mayor who knew when to lead and when to stay out of the way. He caught Asa's eye and raised a hand in greeting, the silent language of long friendships and shared poker nights.

Caleb and Tally, her body bulging with twin boys, arrived not long after, Lola already a step ahead of them, her curls bouncing as she laughed and scanned the room. Harper—Tally's twin sister, in from New England with her son Levi—lingered just behind them. Levi became promptly transfixed with Poppy. Asa watched him with the solemn attention of a boy encountering something entirely new.

Levi walked over. "My aunt says you speak French."

Poppy replied in French, her voice soft and smooth.

Levi grinned so wide Asa almost laughed out loud. Even to the young, French appeared to be the language of love.

Poppy's fingers slipped from Asa's hand and followed Levi across the room to join Lola. The three children formed a loose circle near the dessert table, their appetites apparently already sticky with anticipation.

Joleen and Jackson came in next, managing a small parade of limbs and voices. The twin boys, Hollis and Porter, bounced with uncontained energy, while the little girl —Adaline, or Addie for short, as pretty as her name, with blonde hair and big brown eyes—held Jackson's hand with quiet determination. Joleen looked radiant—and tense. Very tense.

Lola spotted Addie and ran to her, grabbed her hand, and dragged her toward the kids' corner, where Stella had set up a smaller table with name tags just for them.

Asa nodded at the table as Stella passed. "Looks like the kids table is a hit."

"Not my first rodeo," she said, slapping him on the shoulder as she passed. "Good to see you with your girl. Always knew you'd make a fine daddy. Now we just need to find the right woman."

Asa lifted both hands in surrender, then nodded toward Tanner. "You might be careful with the love strategies—that can work both ways."

Stella gave him a long look. "Good point. Maybe we

both need to get busy." She all but cackled and moved on to the next group.

Joleen walked over with one twin on her hip. "This is our first public outing without the nanny," she announced to no one in particular. "I've accepted that chaos is inevitable."

Jackson followed with the other twin, smiling at her like a man who had learned to measure life in small victories.

Asa shook his head. "I have to take my hat off to you two. They're doing great in this crowd."

"Might be because their feet haven't touched the ground yet," Joleen deadpanned.

Asa glanced between the boys. They were definitely identical. "Can you tell them apart yet?"

"Nope," Jackson said without a trace of shame.

Joleen rolled her eyes. "Most of the time." She blew a long breath. "Okay. Sometimes."

The conversation drifted naturally toward the children—how they were adjusting, how quickly routines formed, how early spring would bring a federal trial in Atlanta that could change everything. Joleen kept her voice steady, but Asa could hear the strain beneath it.

Loving children who might not stay in your life required a special kind of courage.

Sue Ellen and Barbara claimed their seats near one of the windows, heads bent together in laughter, trading stories that spanned decades—diners and orchards, weddings and losses, a life built in overlapping chapters. Sue Ellen caught Asa watching and smiled.

The Colonel emerged briefly from the kitchen, apron dusted with flour, to accept applause like a monarch granting favor. "Eat," he commanded. "Then go back and eat again."

Asa found a seat near the edge of the room, and Poppy joined him.

"You don't want to sit with your friends?" he asked.

"No. I want to sit with you."

Her fingers were sticky with pie filling. Just this once, he'd okayed dessert first. He appreciated that when he was around, Barbara deferred to him on all decisions. If it confused Poppy, she never mentioned it. As her father, he reckoned it was his right to grant her wishes—if she wanted pie before turkey once in a while, it seemed like a reasonable request.

He watched the room—the laughter, the easy affection, the way people leaned toward one another instead of away.

Maggie wasn't here. Paris held her tonight, her life unfolding somewhere far beyond the river's bend. The space she would have occupied lingered anyway, quiet but undeniable.

Asa didn't reach for it. He let it be.

Outside, the river moved on, steady and indifferent.

Inside, lifelong friends gathered, and for this one evening, it was enough.

# Chapter Forty

## MAGGIE

By the third week, I'd cancelled my morning driver pickup and walked to work. For those twenty minutes, at least, I saw the sun and people living their lives. Most days, when I left the office, night had already descended. Morning people carried a different energy—an anticipation for what the day might bring. At night, people were either tired or searching for more. I found the streets of Paris haunting and sad then, unsettling in a way they never used to be.

But in the mornings, I knew which café would have its windows fogged with steam, which flower stall on Boulevard Saint-Germain would be open, which stretch of sidewalk always smelled faintly of espresso and damp stone.

Mornings I loved.

I moved through the streets like someone who belonged. I had changed since returning—not dramatically, not all at once, but through small, daily rituals that slipped past my defenses and settled into my bones. My mind stayed half-anchored to the evening video calls with Poppy—hearing about her day, her riding lessons, school gossip—checking in with Mama, occasionally catching a glimpse of Asa moving through the background of the farm.

I told myself his presence there made sense. He was spending as much time with Poppy as he could before she and Mama joined me in Paris. Still, the distance he'd put between us before I left lingered, dull and inexplicable, like a bruise I couldn't remember earning.

This morning, the air outside my building on Rue de Grenelle carried that damp winter chill that wasn't quite rain and wasn't quite fog—just Paris breathing. I hurried past the corner bakery as the door swung open, warmth rolling out with it: butter, yeast, sugar. The scent followed me down the block.

I walked east toward Boulevard Saint-Germain, scarf pulled high, hands tucked into my coat pockets. Café terraces woke in slow motion—chairs scraping over stone, metal tables wiped clean, a neighbor greeting me by name as I passed. Cups clinked. Steam rose in pale ribbons. The city sounded like work being done beautifully.

Everything here was deliberate. Even the ordinary.

And still—beneath the beauty—my thoughts returned to a place across the ocean where nothing was curated and everything mattered.

Georgia.

Poppy.

Mama.

Asa.

I tried not to think his name. I really did.

But it arrived with my thoughts the way an abandoned idea resurfaces mid-draft—uninvited, inevitable, perfectly timed.

I told myself it was because he was taking care of Poppy. Each conversation seemed to confirm it. Just yesterday, she'd begged to stay with him while Mama went on a short trip with her Sunday School class. Mama had hesitated, careful as always, but I'd agreed without pause. Asa was her father. How could I say no?

Still, I couldn't stop imagining her inside his apartment —her shoes kicked off by the door, her voice filling the space.

I shook the thought away and turned into the entrance of Aurore Films & Télévision.

The building never failed to humble me. Aurore occupied a renovated nineteenth-century structure tucked along a quiet Paris street tourists rarely found unless they were lost. Iron balconies and arched windows softened by age bore witness to its past. Once, it had housed a publishing firm—ledgers and ink instead of film reels and scores.

I liked that lineage. Stories had always lived here.

Inside, the space was all restraint and light. Original beams crossed the ceiling. Floors bore faint scuffs, left intact as if acknowledging the lives that had passed through before. Nothing felt staged. Nothing needed to be.

Aurore didn't manufacture worlds the way Hollywood did. Their films were shot where life already existed—borrowed kitchens, real cafés, apartments where someone had loved or argued or died and left something unfinished behind. Crews traveled lightly, capturing places as they were instead of reshaping them into something else.

I had loved that from the beginning.

My writing didn't have to compete with spectacle. It lived beneath footsteps on worn stone, beneath cups clinking in cafés, beneath overheard conversations. My sentences weren't meant to announce themselves. They were meant to settle quietly alongside real lives unfolding onscreen.

The door closed behind me, and alignment settled in.

This place made sense. The work. The rhythm. The quiet devotion to craft.

On most days, it was enough to convince me this could be my complete life.

I headed straight for the studio, shedding my coat, my bag, my thoughts. The schedule ran ahead of me—most of the day spent with Katrina developing a new series, deadlines looming, another late night likely.

Inside our writing space, I inhaled the familiar scent of rosin and varnished wood. Pale winter light fell across the floor and our oversized partner's desk. It was easy—too easy—to disappear here, to believe a life that looked complete must be complete.

My hands held steady. Strong. Responsive. No pain. No hesitation. That still felt like a miracle. I typed for hours, imagining scenes clearly before translating them to the page.

But between dialogue and description, my thoughts drifted.

Always to the same place.

Sometimes the image of Asa surfaced so vividly it stole my breath—his capable hands, his steady presence, the way he lifted Poppy as if the world weighed nothing when she was in his arms. Paris refined everything. Loblolly remembered what mattered.

The contrast hit hard enough to sting.

I wrote through it anyway.

By the time I shut down my computer, night had swallowed the corridors. I lingered long enough to print my pages and let the silence settle. Somewhere beyond these walls, people were meeting for dinner, children were being tucked into bed, lives were unfolding.

Outside, Paris gleamed under streetlights, washed in pewter.

Katrina caught up with me on the front steps.

"Wine?" she asked.

"Yes," I said easily. It was easier than going home alone.

"And something light to eat," she added. "I'm starving."

I wasn't.

We walked toward Le Marais, crossing Rue de Rivoli where shop windows glowed warm and gold, like tiny theaters staging perfect lives. We passed the long stretch near the Hôtel de Ville, its façade lit up against the deepening dusk, and then turned down narrower streets where the air smelled of damp stone and perfume and roasted chestnuts from a street cart.

Paris at night was not loud. Not in the way I remembered New York or even Savannah during tourist season. It was a murmur—footsteps, scooters, a burst of laughter slipping out of a doorway, then swallowed again.

We chose a small wine bar tucked off Rue Vieille-du-Temple, narrow and dim with chalkboard menus and shelves of bottles climbing the walls. The room smelled of red wine, citrus peel, and something faintly herbal—rosemary, maybe, or thyme. There were candles on the tables, their flames steady as if they welcomed us.

Katrina sighed the moment we sat down.

"I'm tired of working all the time. And I'm tired of always being alone," she said, blunt as a joke gone wrong. It was as if she'd read my mind and spoken the words out loud.

"If you're alone, it has to be by choice," I said.

Katrina was beautiful and had achieved in our world the promenance that few women or men achieved. She was quiet and reserved in a way that made men look twice and women assume she had life easy. But I knew from experience that loneliness didn't care what you looked like. Nor did loneliness negotiate with charm.

Our wine arrived, and we sipped, studying the half-empty room, making certain we recognized no one before continuing our conversation.

"Yes, I'm lonely and I'm tired of pretending I'm not," she added, fingers circling the stem of her glass as if she could generate warmth by friction.

I didn't rush to answer. Sometimes the most generous thing you could do was let someone say what they meant without trying to fix it.

She watched the candle a moment, then looked back at me. "Every man I date only wants fun. None are interested in roots. No one wants to stay monogamous."

The words landed with an odd weight because—without meaning to—I pictured Asa again.

Asa wasn't fun-and-games. Asa was the opposite of games. He stayed. He showed up. He didn't rely on grand gestures—he proved himself quietly, day after day.

Just not with me.

After our one night, he'd pulled back as if we'd crossed a line neither of us had named. I tried to tell myself it had been about timing, about caution, about Poppy. All the drama that Julian had brought with him. But the question kept circling: had it been nothing more than old familiarity dressed up as longing?

It didn't feel like that.

But his distance suggested otherwise.

It was startling how quickly my mind reached for him like a railing. How I measured every man against him. Had I always? Maybe without realizing it? No, that was ridiculous.

Katrina took a sip of wine. "I'm thinking of taking Stuart up on his standing offer." She gave me a small smile. "I know I said I'd never go back to him, but . . ." She shrugged. "I'm lonely. What good is it to be rich if you spend all your time alone?"

I hadn't expected this. Never dreamed Katrina would consider going back to her ex. "But didn't he want you to start a family. Give up your career?"

"He's coming around to the idea that woman can have it all, as long as we have a full-time housekeeper and a nanny for the children." She laughed. "I honestly think he means it. He's like a puppy in love, sending roses, tickets to a new play, invitations to weekend retreats in Spain and Portugal."

"Maybe you should," I said quietly. "He's a lovely man."

She gave me a sharp, questioning gaze, then leaned back in her chair, a knowing smirk on her lips. "And what about you, Maggie McAllister?" She leaned in. "What about Luc?"

Luc.

Even his name sounded expensive.

"Luc Beaumont," I said, because saying it out loud made it seem more real than it felt.

Katrina's eyes gleamed. "Yes. Him. He's crazy about you."

I shrugged. "We've gone out a few times. Dinners. A concert. It's… fine. He's fine."

"Fine?" Her tone made fine sound like a crime.

"There's no spark," I said. "No magic click."

Katrina laughed—low, disbelieving. "That's not what he says. I hear you have a whirlwind trip planned next month."

"He has a trip and he inivited me. I haven't committed."

"Really, Maggie." She set her glass down with care, as if

she were about to deliver a verdict. "Luc Beaumont is what you American women call tall, dark, and handsome. Rich. Very smart. Divorced. And—this is the truly miraculous part—his children actually like him."

"Which is shocking," I agreed, because teenagers were hard to please in any language.

"They're thirteen and fifteen," she went on, "so the kids are not in the way. They live with their mother in California." She appeared delighted by her own case. "Do you know how rare that is? A man who can remain civilized through his children's adolescence?"

I smiled, but my mind had already betrayed me again.

Thirteen and fifteen sounded like a different universe. Asa's world had suddenly turned to ponytails and missing socks, school lunches, bedtime stories. I would love to be a fly on the wall watching it all. Poppy didn't merely occupy his life—she shaped it. He didn't orbit around his child. He brought her home and made her the center.

Katrina tilted her head. "So what's the problem with Luc Beaumont? You can't keep ignoring these men looking for perfection. There is no perfect man. You have to take a chance."

I lifted my glass, buying time.

She lowered her voice. "You don't have to marry him. Just… have an affair. See where it goes. Isn't that what Paris is for?"

I laughed—a real laugh, quick and startled, as if she'd suggested I rob a museum. "Katrina. Really. Why don't you follow your own advice?"

"I'll tell you why," she said, unrepentant. "Because I have no Luc Beaumonts chasing after me. And Stuart isn't tall dark and handsome, although he is well positioned." She sipped more wine. "You keep returning home night after night alone. You act like you're waiting for permission to live."

Permission.

That word found a tender spot.

Because the truth was—I wasn't waiting for permission. I was waiting for clarity. Waiting to feel something clean and certain. Waiting for my heart to stop splitting itself in two.

Waiting, perhaps, for the one person who made everything feel less complicated without even trying.

I shut down my thoughts and sipped my wine, motioning for the waiter to bring another. He brought the bottle to the table and topped off both our glasses.

I looked down at my wine. The candlelight painted it dark and velvety, like a secret.

"I don't know," I said honestly. "Luc is kind. And he does seem… interested. But when I'm with him, we don't connect."

"Connect how?" Katrina asked.

"He talks and I listen," I said. "For a while. Then my mind starts to wander."

"Wander where?" she pressed, amused. "Give me an example."

I didn't answer right away. I didn't say Poppy, even though she lived in my chest like a second heartbeat. I didn't say Asa, even though his name surfaced whenever everything else went quiet.

Instead, I said, "He reminds me too much of Julian."

Katrina stilled, her knife hovering midair.

"How so?"

"Smooth. Charming. Handsome as sin," I said. "And very good at *appearing* busy without actually doing much of anything."

She studied me for a beat, then said, "Unlike Julian, Luc has financial security."

"Yes," I said. "But it's family money."

She lifted a brow. "And what, exactly, is wrong with family money?"

"Nothing," I said quickly. Then I hesitated. "I just—I don't know. I think I relate better to men who make their own way in the world. That's all."

Men who showed up. Men who built something. Men who didn't coast on what had already been handed to them.

Katrina leaned back, considering that, then reached for a slice of thin bread and smeared it with foie gras d'oie. "You, my friend, are a conundrum."

She leaned forward, lowering her voice. "You think very carefully about what you want your life to look like. If Loblolly—and Asa—are part of that picture, then go. Write screenplays. You have the résumé. You have the contacts. Writers can live anywhere."

I sighed. "I have to admit, the idea has crossed my mind."

"I can't imagine leaving Paris," she said thoughtfully. "I'd be afraid of losing myself. Paris is as much a part of me as the blood coursing through my veins."

I nodded. "I know what you mean."

And yet, even as I said it, I felt the quiet truth settle deeper than the words: Paris had shaped my career—but it wasn't where I belonged anymore.

We left the bar later than usual. We'd ordered more tapas and more wine and decided it was enough for dinner. The cold air had turned biting and sharp. Paris shimmered under streetlamps, the stone buildings glossy from a light mist, the sidewalks reflecting gold. We walked past Place des

Vosges, the square calm beneath its arches, trees bare and elegant like sketches against the night.

Katrina hugged me goodbye at the corner and turned off toward the Métro. I continued alone, my boots clicking softly as I crossed streets that felt both familiar and foreign.

The city was beautiful enough to make you believe it could replace anything. There was nothing quite like Paris when it began dressing itself for the holidays.

Shop windows glowed with candlelight and velvet; mannequins in wool and silk posed beneath garlands and gold stars. Strings of lights crisscrossed narrow streets, reflected in wet stone and café windows. Carolers gathered on corners, their voices lifting into the cold air—familiar hymns threaded with accents from everywhere and nowhere. Chestnut vendors worked small braziers along the sidewalks, the scent drifting between bursts of laughter and clinking glasses.

Paris dressed itself for Christmas the way it did everything else—with elegance, confidence, and the quiet assumption that beauty was enough.

But when I unlocked my apartment door and stepped inside, the quiet met me with the same practiced precision as Paris itself—orderly, composed, untouched.

I set my keys down. Hung my coat. Turned on the small lamp by the sofa.

And then I did what I always did.

I checked the time and waited for my phone to ring.

Poppy called to video chat at the same hour each night, like she was keeping me tethered. When her name lit up the screen, warmth spread through me so quickly it startled.

"Mama!" she sang, bright and breathless. "Guess what!"

I sank onto the edge of the sofa, smiling at her beaming face before I could stop myself. "What, sweetheart?"

Her stories tumbled out—school, a spelling word she'd nailed, Sugar stealing sugar cubes from her pockets. And then, like always, she mentioned Asa.

"We're making cornbread," she said. "And he let me stir the bowl even though I got flour everywhere."

Although it was only her face on the screen, in my mind, I could see the scene perfectly, as if writing it in my mind: Asa's kitchen, the lamplight, Poppy's earnest concentration, Asa pretending not to notice the flour dusting the counter because the point wasn't the mess. The point was her.

I heard Asa in the background then—his voice low, teasing. "Tell her you're the chef. I'm just your hired hand."

Poppy giggled. "He says he's my hired hand!"

My throat tightened, swift and unwelcome. I swallowed it down. "Sounds about right."

Asa came into view briefly—just long enough to let me know Poppy was fine and he was keeping to her schedule, bedtime at 8:30 and homework before TV. He said she'd been helping him in the store and loved it. He sounded excited. We didn't talk long—just long enough to make my apartment feel less empty with the simple steadiness of his tone.

When the visit ended, I set the phone down carefully, as if careless handling might break whatever thread connected me to them. I'd made the right decision. Asa deserved time with Poppy, and one day, when she was older and could understand, we'd tell her that Asa—not Julian—was her father.

I stared out my window at the Paris rooftops—slate and chimneys and a slice of night sky. Somewhere in the distance, a siren wailed faintly and then faded. The city moved on without me. And I did as Katrina asked, I thought hard about my next career move. In the end, I decided to hold off until after Christmas, it was a huge decision to give up what I'd worked so hard to build—a position a million writers only dreamed of having.

Our holiday break was less than two weeks away.

I would fly home, and we would have four weeks—four weeks for me to face whatever was waiting on the other side of all this distance, all this restraint, all this careful not-yet. Four weeks would be enough time to pack up Mama and Poppy and travel back to Paris if that was my decision in the end. Four weeks would be enough time to decide what the next phase of my life would look like.

When I returned, I'd have my family and I wouldn't be lonely. I'd have no need for Luc Beaumont. But maybe I'd hold that thought… wait and see how I felt about Luc in the New Year.

But a realization arrived quietly, uninvited, and more honest than I was ready to say out loud: Luc wasn't the question.

He was only something to look at while I tried not to stare straight at the answer.

And the answer—steady as a downbeat, certain as a finished scene—kept sounding like home.

# Chapter Forty-One

## MAGGIE

As a kid, Christmas in Loblolly had never announced itself all at once. It crept in quietly—one wreath at a time, one string of lights hung a little crooked, one shop window dressed by someone's aunt or a teenage son after school. Winter didn't arrive with any certainty, either. One day called for gloves and a scarf; the next, you could get away with short sleeves and flip-flops. That unpredictability had always felt like part of the magic—never knowing what you'd need when you stepped outside.

By December, the courthouse square glowed with white lights wrapped around the magnolias, and the old lampposts wore red bows that faded a little more each year but were never replaced.

I knew that downtown would smell like pine and sugar and coffee brewing too early in the morning. Storefront windows holding mismatched displays—ceramic Santas beside antique ledgers, hand-knit scarves draped over mannequins that had seen better decades. Someone always set a speaker outside the hardware store playing the same scratched Christmas album, and no one complained because it meant the season had officially arrived.

People stopped to talk. Really talk. They stood in the cold—or what passed for cold—with gloved hands wrapped around paper cups, asking after mamas and surgeries and kids who'd grown too fast. Loblolly didn't sparkle so much as it glowed—from inside the buildings, from the windows of the bakery, from the easy way everyone seemed to belong exactly where they were.

It wasn't beautiful because it tried to be.

It was beautiful because it remembered who it was.

Maybe we'd take a drive downtown and visit the bookstore. I needed a few stocking stuffers for Mama and Poppy.

Maybe I'd invite Asa to join us to decorate the tree when he came later this morning for Poppy's riding lesson. I tucked the thought away, unsure what I wanted from it just yet.

In Paris, mornings announced themselves with precision—alarm tones, scheduled meetings, the muted hum of traffic far below my apartment windows. Here, the day arrived softly. Pale winter light filtered through the curtains. The house creaked as if stretching awake. Somewhere beyond the window, Sugar and Finn—Poppy's new horse, an early Christmas present from Asa—snorted, followed by the low, steady hush of wind moving through bare branches.

Buying another horse when she was leaving for Paris had seemed excessive. And a little heartbreaking. Maybe that had been the point—not to hurt her, because that wasn't Asa's way, but to give her something to come back to.

Mama said he'd already begun talking about Poppy spending the summer in Loblolly. I'd agreed to it when we worked out our parental sharing arrangement. Back then, summer had felt distant. Now it hovered just beyond the holidays.

For a moment, I stayed still and imagined waking up this way—rooted, unhurried—permanent. A quieter life, free of rushing to the office and adhering to rigid schedules made by demanding bosses and directors. Maybe, just maybe. I tucked that thought away for later, too.

I slipped from the bed and went to find my family.

Christmas sat only a few days away, and I'd already begun cataloging ways to make it special. The tree we'd buy in town this afternoon. Or maybe we'd go into the woods and cut one ourselves, if Mama insisted. The ornaments I'd brought back from Paris, wrapped in sweaters and tucked carefully into my suitcase—delicate glass bells, a tiny Eiffel Tower Poppy had begged for two years ago, just to remind her of home. We'd join them with Mama's ornaments, all the memories of my childhood.

I imagined setting them out one by one, telling stories about where each had come from. I imagined laughter. Warmth. Traditions braided together until they made sense. I imagined the happiest Christmas we'd ever known. Maybe we'd always come back to the farm for Christmas—a new tradition for us.

I padded into the kitchen to find Poppy already awake, seated at the table in her nightgown and socks, swinging her legs while Mama moved around the stove making bacon and pancakes studded with chocolate chips.

"Morning, jet-setter," Mama said, sliding a plate onto the table. "You got home late last night."

I hugged Poppy, holding her a minute longer than she wanted. She squirmed, but when I released her, she was beaming.

"You're home for real."

Calling the farm home didn't escape me, but now wasn't the time to correct her. "I am. And I can't wait to put up our tree today."

I turned to Mama. "Plane was delayed in Atlanta." I yawned as I poured myself coffee. "I finally got into bed around three."

We sat down to breakfast—cheese eggs, bacon, grits, and chocolate chip pancakes—the kind of sugar rush I'd probably need to make it through the day on four hours of sleep. It was the sort of meal that felt solid, grounding. The kind I hadn't had since leaving the farm for Paris.

I took a sip of coffee and began outlining our return to Paris, my quiet way of reminding Poppy—and myself—that we had a home an ocean away, and that in three weeks' time, we would return. No matter what I decided about remote work, I had an apartment in Paris. A life. And I owed it to my boss, Claire, to discuss the future face to face.

"When we go back to Paris," I said, "we'll take Nana ice skating near the river. Remember that little café with the green chairs? They keep their Christmas lights up all winter. And Nana's promised to stay with us until summer. We can take weekend trips to the country."

Poppy poured syrup on her pancakes with great concentration.

"She'll live with us," I added. "In the apartment."

Her hand stilled.

"I don't want to live in Paris anymore," she said.

The words were calm. Not dramatic. Just… final.

I took another sip of coffee, buying myself a moment. "Let's talk about this a little later."

She shook her head. "I don't want to."

Mama forked a bite of eggs, her movements slow and deliberate. She didn't interrupt.

"You won't have to go to school," I said gently. "Nana will be there, and she'll teach you your lessons. Won't that be fun? You love when she reads to you at night. Just think —no school. Just Nana and me every day."

Poppy looked up then, her eyes serious in a way that always caught me off guard. "I don't want to leave Asa. And now I have two horses. They're my responsibility."

The air seemed to thin.

I was glad Mama and Asa were teaching her about responsibility. I just hadn't expected it to come back to me so soon.

"Nana wants to stay here, too," Poppy went on, as if explaining something obvious. "And if I leave I won't see Asa. Or Sugar. Or Finn. Or my friends." She said it again, softer this time.

I looked at Mama. "Nana wants to come with us, don't you, Mom?"

She smiled. "I wouldn't want to let my girls go anywhere without me." She set another pancake on Poppy's plate.

Not exactly the resounding endorsement I'd been hoping for.

"I want to live here," Poppy said. "On the farm. With Nana and Asa. And you can visit us." Her voice wavered, tears pooling in her eyes. "Why can't Asa be my daddy?"

I froze.

"Lola says Mr. Caleb adopted her," she went on. "Why can't Asa adopt me?" Her tears spilled over her cheeks. "Will you ask him, Mama?"

There it was—the conversation I'd thought we still had time before us, suddenly pulled into the here and now. And not one I could have with Poppy without Asa.

I reached across the table and softly wiped her tears with my napkin. "We can talk about this later," I said, reaching for a tone that felt reasonable. Steady. "I just got home, and Christmas is coming. Today, let's just enjoy being together, okay?"

Poppy studied me for a moment longer, then nodded once. She went back to her pancakes. "It's okay. I'll ask him."

Mama looked down, but not before I saw the smile on her face. She rose and refilled our coffee cups. "Sometimes wishes come true," she said quietly.

She quickly issued a reminder of a riding lesson, and Poppy hurried upstairs to get dressed. Maybe I'd wait on the porch and squeeze in a moment to tell Asa that we might not have to wait to let our daughter know the truth.

"She's got a willful streak," I said, lifting my mug.

Mama huffed out a chuckle. "Wonder where she got that from." She smiled, but her eyes stayed thoughtful. "You'll likely need Asa's help to talk her into going back to Paris without a fight."

I didn't answer, but my heart told me she was right. I was grateful for the closeness Asa and Poppy shared, even as I feared it might eclipse my sole parental place in my daughter's life. There was no room for selfishness—she needed us both. And Asa was easy to love. Riding lessons. A new horse. Cornbread baked on Sunday afternoons. He deserved easy. And Poppy deserved to have a loving father who doted on her every whim.

I told myself three weeks was plenty of time. Time to remind her why Paris mattered. Time to reframe it as an adventure again. Time to bring her around.

"I'll check on Poppy, make sure she remembers to layer. It's a little cooler today." Mama paused at the door, then turned back. "I've made up my mind to stay in Paris if that's what you want."

I looked up, startled.

"This farm is your legacy," she said gently. "But if it's not the life you want, we'll save it for Poppy. She may love it, or she may not. We won't know for years." She smiled then, soft and steady. "But you're my daughter, and you need me now. So for as long as you want me with you, I'll stay."

She stepped closer. "All I ask is that you examine your heart and make sure it's the life you want to give your daughter. Just know—I'll support you, whatever you decide."

And with that, she left me sitting with a cold cup of coffee and far too many thoughts swimming in my head.

Fifteen minutes later, when Asa pulled into the drive for Poppy's riding lesson, the morning conversation felt safely tucked away. Manageable. Something we'd have to talk about, just not today.

Poppy ran out the door, tugging on her gloves as she went.

"Wait until you see him," she called back, barely containing her excitement.

I followed more slowly, the cold air sharp against my cheeks. Asa stood by the fence, tall and easy in his jacket, one hand resting on the lead rope of a handsome chestnut gelding. He wasn't handsome in a polished, leading-man sort of way. There was nothing cultivated about him at all. He was solid. A little rugged. The faint creases at the corners of his eyes only made him more so. His hair never held gel or spray, his nails were clean but never buffed, his clothes pressed but practical.

So different from the men in Paris.

I let my eyes linger longer than necessary, my heart doing something foolish and warm in my chest.

"Come to meet Finn?" he asked, smiling at Poppy. "This

girl wants to learn to jump, and Sugar doesn't have it in her anymore."

Sugar watched from the paddock, unimpressed. I walked over and stroked her mane. "Looks like we're both on the outside of this love affair, my Sugar-girl."

Asa helped Poppy mount, adjusting her stirrups, tightening her helmet strap, murmuring instructions I couldn't quite hear. They moved into the arena, and I settled onto the fence rail, content to watch. Poppy rode with confidence, her posture good, her smile bright. It was obvious how much time he'd spent with her while I was in Paris.

When they approached the small jump, I felt a flicker of nerves. Asa nodded, clucked softly. Poppy urged Finn forward. She cleared the first jump easily, sitting tall, graceful and sure.

Asa guided her around again.

The setup was the same, but this time Poppy leaned forward too soon.

She rushed.

Finn's cadence broke. He hesitated. Poppy tipped forward and fell hard—the soundless impact cracking the air.

I was off the rail and running before I realized I'd moved.

Asa reached her first, dropping to his knees, lifting her with careful urgency. Poppy didn't cry. She didn't move.

My heart stopped.

"Poppy?" Asa said, his voice tight.

She stirred, a small groan escaping her. Her eyes fluttered open.

"My head hurts," she whispered.

That was all it took.

Asa carried her to his truck, calling for me to grab her

coat. He laid her carefully across the backseat, and I climbed in beside her.

He yelled for Mama to call the pediatrician to meet us at the emergency room, and then drove with one hand steady on the wheel, his eyes flicking between the road and the rearview mirror.

I kept my hand flat against Poppy's chest, reminding myself not to let her sit up until a doctor checked her.

"I'm okay," she murmured, trying to lift her head to take off her helmet.

"Not yet," I said softly, keeping my hand firm. "We're almost there."

Asa pulled into the hospital parking lot and was out of the truck before it fully stopped, lifting her into his arms. I followed, my legs numb, my thoughts scattered.

The automatic doors slid open, and Asa rushed inside with Poppy held tight against him, while I trailed behind—praying, bargaining, and knowing deep down that nothing about my life would ever feel simple again.

# Chapter Forty-Two

## MAGGIE

Poppy was home from the hospital by lunchtime, cleared of anything more serious than a mild concussion and a bruised ego. No riding for a week, no running at recess for a few days, and strict instructions to tell an adult if her head hurt again. She accepted the verdict with solemn seriousness, as if she'd been handed a sacred responsibility.

"I'll be careful," she promised the nurse, then looked up at me. "I really will, Mama."

I believed her.

By midafternoon, the house had settled back into its familiar rhythms. Poppy was curled on the sofa with a stack of Christmas books, her eyes drifting closed, then popping open again. I estimated another ten minutes before she'd be fast asleep.

Through the window, I could see Sugar and Finn standing in the paddock beyond the fence, close enough to be watching, as if waiting for their girl to join them. I slipped on my coat, shoved a few carrots into my pocket, and joined Mama outside, needing air, movement—something to quiet the lingering tremor in my chest.

I gave the horses their treats, then Mama and I walked the perimeter of the farm slowly. The winter sun hung low and bright, lighting up freshly painted fencing, garden beds newly turned and waiting for frost before winter greens were planted, and a barn roof that no longer sagged in the middle.

"It's never looked better," I said finally, turning in a slow circle. "The new farm manager really measured up."

Mama laughed, soft and knowing. "That man was a waste of time and money."

I stopped. "What do you mean?"

She waved a hand. "He worked two days—or barely worked—then never showed his face again."

I turned fully toward her. "What? Then how—"

"Asa," she said simply.

I blinked. "Asa?"

"He took over without a word. Sat down with me one morning, made a list of what needed doing. If he couldn't do it himself, he hired a crew and oversaw the work." She smiled, still a little amazed.

"Oh." I swallowed. "I'll talk to him. Get an accounting, pay him—"

"Don't you dare." Mama stopped and pointed a finger at my chest. "I tried that. Hurt his feelings something awful."

She shook her head. "He told me when a gift is given out of love, you don't get to turn it into a transaction."

My chest tightened.

"He said one day this place would be Poppy's," Mama went on. "And he wanted it to be a home she'd be proud of."

I didn't trust my voice.

"And you listen to me," she added, wagging that same finger again. "Not a word to him about money. You hear me, Margaret Elizabeth McAllister? Just tell him thank you. And that the farm looks beautiful. Because it does—more beautiful than it's been since long before your father died."

We stood there a moment longer, the land quiet around us, before Mama reminded me that Poppy's class Christmas party was tomorrow afternoon. Apparently Asa would be there too, and she suggested that would be a good time to thank him.

The next morning, I wandered through the house with far too much time on my hands, Poppy's class party never far from my thoughts. I planned to pick out a tree before coming home and decorating the house from top to bottom. Mama's words echoed, along with the memory of how many boxes she'd had me drag down from the attic.

I walked Poppy to the end of the driveway to catch the school bus, and when I returned, Mama reminded me—again—that Asa would be at the party that afternoon.

As if summoned by the thought, my phone chimed.

"Poppy tells me you pinky-swore to attend her class party," Asa said when I answered.

"She doesn't play around when it comes to pinky swears," I said, smiling despite myself.

"Would you mind stopping by the store around one?" he asked. "There's something I'd like to talk to you about."

"Sure," I said. "I'll see you then."

After we hung up, my stomach fluttered in a way I refused to name. I dressed with more care than necessary, finally settling on winter-white pants, a matching sweater, red flats, and my hair twisted into a loose knot—understated, festive.

I told myself it was for a room full of fifth graders.

I didn't believe that for a second.

I arrived at Asa's store ten minutes early, only to have him intercept me a few steps inside the door.

"Mind if we walk?" he asked. "Through the park?"

I nodded. He looked jittery, which only made me more aware of my own nerves.

We walked a wide circle, talking about nothing important—my horrendous flight from Paris, his cashier out with the flu, the Loblolly Christmas parade on Saturday. I tried to thank him for the work he'd done at the farm, but he waved me off, clearly uncomfortable, and I let it go. I was far more interested in what he wasn't saying.

When we reached the gazebo, we slowed. It stood just as it always had, framed by winter-bare rose bushes, the old swing tucked inside.

Memories pressed in all at once. I wondered if Asa felt them too—if he remembered the last time we'd sat there together.

"Let's sit," he said, ushering me toward the swing.

We settled side by side, the space between us familiar in a way that made my chest ache. The air felt charged with nerves—the kind that came with either very good news or very bad.

He cleared his throat. Rubbed his palms over his thighs. Leaned forward. Stopped.

He sat back and drew in a breath. "Poppy asked me to talk to you about something," he said finally. "A few things, actually."

My chest tightened. "What kind of things?"

"Well, the biggest thing was that she asked me to adopt her. Like Caleb did Lola."

I wasn't surprised after our breakfast conversation the day before, but before I could respond, he continued.

"And she says she doesn't want to live in Paris anymore. She wants to live at the farm. With your mama." He glanced at me, then smiled softly. "And with me."

I looked away, the ache in my throat sudden and sharp.

"She explained that if I lived at the farm, I'd be near the horses and wouldn't have to drive out every day," he added. "And that she couldn't live with me at my apartment even if I adopted her because she couldn't leave her Nana alone. So I had to move in with them." He shook his head. "She had it all worked out in that pretty little head of hers."

I swallowed. "She wants to live with you and Mama?"

"What she really wants is all of us," he said gently. "You. Me. Barbara. A family, living at the farm." He noticed my expression and reached for my hand. "She just misses having a father around, Maggie. Don't make too much of it. Right now, the farm feels safe to her."

He hesitated. "But it got me thinking. I wanted to ask if you'd be all right with me coming to Paris in a couple of months. I don't want to be away from her for five months and—"

"Of course you can," I said quickly.

I tightened my grip on his hands. Enough. Enough denial.

"I'm going to say something," I said quietly. "And I don't know how it's going to sound. I'll probably mess it up, but just hear me out."

He waited. Just like he always did.

"I'm tired," I said.

"Tired?" His brow furrowed.

"Of my life," I admitted. "Of writing all day and sometimes into the night and flying city to city, then writing long hours on the road. I'm tired of hotel rooms and empty dinners. Of letting other people raise my child while I chase something I thought I needed."

My voice wavered, but I pressed on. "I'm tired of pretending I don't know where I belong. Of measuring every man I meet against you and finding they never measure up. And I'm tired of pretending I'm not madly in love with you."

The color drained from his face.

I felt exposed all at once. "You don't have to say anything," I added softly. "I just need to stop lying to myself. And for once, face the truth of my life."

He pulled me forward an inch, then two, then suddenly I was in his arms.

His mouth covered mine—urgent and sure, as if he'd been holding back for years. He kissed my cheeks, my eyelids, my mouth again, his hands framing my face until the rest of the world fell away.

"I've never stopped loving you," he said against my hair. "Not for one day, one minute, one second. And this time—no matter what harebrained idea you come up with—I'm not letting you go again."

He leaned back just enough to look at me. "But what about your writing career?"

"If you mean my career as a studio writer, I'll have to give them my notice when I return to Paris. I'll need to sell my apartment, pack up a life I worked hard to build." I let out a breath. "That part scares me. But leaving the studio doesn't mean I'll stop writing. I'll always write. For me it's like breathing."

I smoothed the crease on his forehead. "I'll write for myself now. And if I sell something, I'll sell it directly. I know how the business works."

I looked around the park. It wasn't Paris, but it was beautiful—and it was mine. "I think it's time to see just how far my talent can take me."

Asa sat with that, then reached into his pocket and pulled out a small box.

Inside was the diamond I remembered from his mother's hand.

"You planned to propose today?" I asked.

He laughed. "No. I'm not that brave. I swore years ago the next time, it'd have to be you doing the asking."

"Fair enough." I nodded at the ring. "The why do you have it?"

"I was going to ask if it was too soon to give it to Poppy for Christmas," he said quietly. "Before she leaves, I wanted her to know she belongs here. That she had roots."

Something in my chest finally unclenched. I took the ring, held it to the light, then slid it onto my finger.

"What a wonderful idea," I said softly. "But you're forgetting something. I distinctly remember your mama saying this ring would be worn by your wife first."

His breath left him in a rush. He laughed. "Well," he said, nodding toward the courthouse, "I happen to know a judge."

"Probably better that we wait on the diamond for Christmas anyway," he added. "Since I'm picking up the prettiest little black-and-white puppy on Christmas Eve."

"Asa Griffin," I said, shaking my head. "You're in charge of training."

He saluted. "Got it."

He didn't rush us toward the courthouse or mention marriage again. Instead, we sat shoulder to shoulder, his thumb brushing the inside of my wrist.

“You know,” he said softly, “we don’t have to do anything today. Or next week. Or even next month.”

I let his words settle.

“What if,” he continued, “we did this our way? After Christmas, when you come back from Paris for good, we can elope somewhere quiet. Somewhere warm. When we return home, we’ll be married.”

I pictured it—no guest lists, no expectations. Just us.

“And then,” he said, “after Poppy has time to adjust… we’ll take another trip. All three of us. Call it a family honeymoon.”

I leaned into him, the idea taking root. “I like that idea.”

The late afternoon light slanted across the square, the courthouse bell chiming the hour. I thought of the farm waiting just beyond town—the horses in the paddock, the barn standing straight again, my daughter safe inside a house full of warmth.

For the first time that I could remember, I wasn’t torn between lives.

I was coming home—to the farm, to my daughter, to the man who had always been waiting.

## More by Veronica Mixon

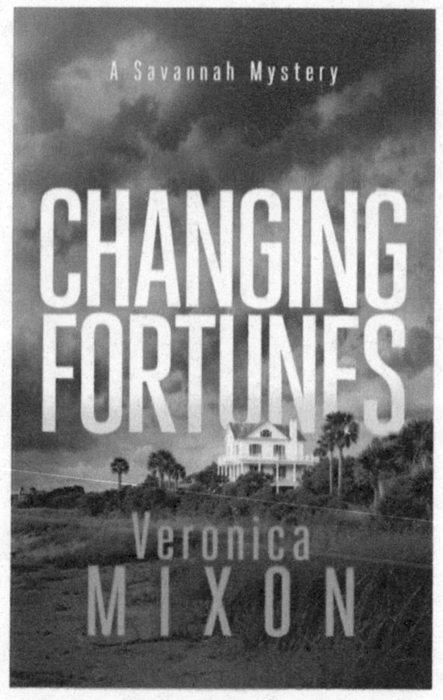


vinci-books.com/ChangingFortunes

**One living, one dead—and the truth won't stay buried.**

When Kate's husband vanishes with their son, and a woman tied to him turns up dead, she's forced back to Savannah for answers. Guided by Tess—a ghost determined to expose the truth—Kate uncovers a deadly criminal network and a secret that could destroy her.

Turn the page for a free preview...

## Changing Fortunes: Chapter One

### TESS

The first thing I noticed was the quiet. Not peaceful—the opposite, really. It was the kind of silence that settles after something violent. The kind that makes your skin go tight, your instincts flare. Something had happened. Something bad.

I stood frozen in the hallway. My hands hovered in front of me, fingers twitching like they'd just let go of something. Something important. But whatever it was had already slipped away.

A sliver of light spilled through the cracked bedroom door, faint and trembling. And then—I heard it.

Breath.

Sharp. Shallow. Ragged.

Adam.

I moved toward the sound, more drift than step, like the floor no longer mattered.

The room beyond looked like the aftermath of a nightmare.

Because it *was*.

A lamp had fallen, throwing long, jagged shadows across the walls. The bed was a tangle of sheets, kicked and twisted like someone had fought their way out—or been pulled back in. Blood soaked the edge of the mattress, dark and spreading.

And Lena—dear God.

Lena.

She was half-curled beside Adam, her body twisted at an angle no living person could hold. Her hair clung to her face in dark, wet ropes. A ribbon of blood had soaked into the pillow and dried at the corner of her mouth. Her eyes were open. Wide. Still.

"No," I whispered. "No, no, no."

I stepped inside. "Adam."

He didn't move. Just stared at Lena. Not blinking. Not breathing.

"You have to get out of here," I said. "This is a setup. The police will think we killed Lena."

He didn't react. He looked straight through me, like I wasn't there.

His hand moved toward her shoulder, then stopped. Trembled. Pulled back.

So much blood.

"What the hell happened?" he whispered.

I couldn't look away. Something about Lena's jaw was… wrong. Tilted at an unnatural angle, like it had come unhinged. The side of her skull—caved in. Blunt force, not once but twice. The kind of damage that says *finality*.

I stepped closer, half-expecting her to stir. To flinch. To breathe. Something.

But she didn't.

She was gone.

And the strangest part? My body didn't react. No jolt of

panic. No bile rising in my throat. I hated blood—got light-headed if I cut my finger. But now, even with it pooling beneath Lena, staining the sheets, matting her hair... nothing. No racing heart. No shaking hands.

Just a strange, weightless stillness. Like I was floating above it all. Watching through the wrong end of a telescope.

Removed. Distant.

"I told you," I whispered to Adam. "I warned you both."

I wasn't even sure why I whispered. Maybe because the room felt... *off*. As if sound didn't belong here anymore. Like speaking too loudly might break something fragile. Or maybe because Lena was—

Gone.

The stillness had weight now. Heavy. Watching.

I took a step toward Adam, my voice low, urgent. "We have to go. Right now. The cops are going to come and find her like this and think we did it. That *you* did it."

He didn't flinch.

Didn't blink.

Just kept staring at the floor, eyes glassy, his hands covered in—

God. *Her* blood.

"Adam, listen to me," I said, louder now. "We don't have time."

Nothing.

Not a flicker.

I moved closer. "Get up. Please. We need to move her—we need to figure this out before someone knocks on that door."

Still nothing.

My pulse should've been racing. My hands should've

been shaking. But there was nothing. No pounding in my chest. No sweat. No breath.

Just cold logic and rising dread.

I waved a hand in front of him.

He didn't react.

I snapped my fingers. "Adam."

He looked straight through me.

"I warned you both this would happen." But warning someone and saving them weren't the same thing.

And now it was too late.

Lena thought she could confess her way to freedom—gather records, flash drives, tidy rows of digital breadcrumbs—and walk. She thought if she handed the truth over first, she'd get to decide how the story ended.

"She's going to get us all killed," I told Adam two nights ago. "You think they'll let her talk? You think they'll let you walk if she does?"

Our employers—the ones with the galleries and private islands and the taste for stolen Modiglianis—didn't like complications. They liked obedience. Predictability. No witnesses. No loose ends. Our bosses might deal with stolen art and false names, but are always in control. Precise, brutal control. They didn't do the cleanup themselves. They hired people who left no noise, no struggle. Just results.

Lena hadn't understood what it meant to be a liability.

Adam sat at the edge of the bed, head in his hands, fingers digging into his scalp. He moved on instinct, like his body remembered what to do, even if his mind hadn't caught up. He pulled on his jeans with shaking hands, as if clothes could make this real, or undo it.

I turned toward the hallway, trying to breathe.

Nothing happened.

No inhale. No flutter in my chest. Just the quiet,

crawling panic of stillness. I felt *present*—but wrong. Unmoored. Like I'd been cut loose from my own skin. Shock. I must be in shock.

That's when I saw her.

Not Lena.

*Me.*

Crushed against the wall, not three feet from the front door. One arm reaching out like I'd been trying to claw my way forward. My hair soaked in blood. My eyes—wide, blank, glassy.

"No—no, no. That's not—"

I backed away, reaching for the wall. My hand went straight through it.

I didn't stumble. I didn't fall. Gravity forgot me.

"Please," I whispered, "this isn't real—"

But it was. It *was*, and some part of me deep down—below the fear, below the mind-scream—*knew it.*

The memories came like aftershocks, jagged and out of order:

Lena on the phone. Crying. Saying she'd had enough. She had the evidence that would keep her safe. Enough that would allow her to walk from *them.* She had to think of more than herself now.

Me promising to come. To talk it through. Begging her to wait until I drove across town to her house.

Me using the key Lena kept under the flower pot. Unlocking her door.

The hallway stretched longer than it should have.

A cold that had nothing to do with air conditioning.

A shadow behind me.

The pain. Blinding. Sharp.

Then dark.

Then... this.

I turned back into the bedroom, frantic now. "I tried," I said to Adam, my voice cracking. "I tried to warn her. Sloane said I'd be too late, but I had to try—"

Sloane, who'd once been part of the Collectors' cleanup team—one of the quiet ones who made inconvenient problems disappear. But like the rest of us—me, Adam, Lena—she wanted out. She'd seen too much, done more than she could live with, and by the time she whispered her warning, we were already out of time.

Adam stood and stumbled into the hall, dazed, disoriented, barefoot. He moved like he was underwater.

And then he saw me.

Saw *her*—the body I used to wear.

He froze. "Tess?"

His voice was cracked glass.

He dropped to his knees beside me. Pulled me—*her*—up, his arms going rigid around my lifeless weight. "Oh God—no—Tess—"

His shirt turned dark where my blood soaked in. My hair clung to his fingers as he tried to push it off my face. He was crying now. Loud, ugly sobs.

Not because he loved me.

Because we were friends. Because I was Lena's friend. Because I didn't deserve *this*.

I moved toward him, desperate to touch his shoulder, to say something—*anything*—but I couldn't make contact. My hand passed through him like smoke.

And then, a shiver that didn't come from the air.

A presence—just behind me. Watching. Waiting. Not human.

The room dimmed slightly, like someone had turned down the volume on the light.

A whisper moved across the base of my skull. Not words. But *awareness.*

I wasn't alone.

Not in this house.

Not in this state.

I wasn't even the only one dead.

Adam eased my body back to the floor and reached for his phone, hands shaking. He dropped it. Picked it up again. The screen lit his face—hollow, pale, smeared in blood.

He stumbled back to the bedroom, sat on the bed, staring forward, unaware that no matter what he did, they already had all the evidence they needed.

They'd planned it perfectly.

Lena was the target. I was the buffer—the warning system.

They killed me first.

Now Adam—Lena's lover, a man with a record of bad decisions and worse nights—was the fall guy. A woman dead in his mistress's hallway. And his lover dead in her bed.

The police would walk into this scene and see everything they needed.

Motive. Opportunity. A body in the hallway.

A bow tied up in blood.

And a scapegoat already wearing it.

And behind me, something stirred in the silence. Watching. Waiting.

The dead don't sleep.

*We remember.*

## Changing Fortunes: Chapter Two

### KATE

Adam slouched in the corner chair, freshly showered but still unraveling. His shirt was buttoned wrong, half tucked into sleep-rumpled pants, like he'd gotten dressed without thinking. A half-empty glass of scotch hung from his hand, the bottle teetering on the edge of the rug behind him.

He kept rubbing his palms against his thighs, again and again, like he couldn't get them clean. His eyes were restless, tracking shadows instead of meeting mine.

I stayed near the window, arms folded, trying not to speak first. Not because I was afraid—because I was tired. So damn tired.

Too many nights spent away from home only to return to Adam's silence—his anger simmering just beneath the surface, waiting. Too many days spent trying to patch the cracks in a marriage that had long since collapsed under its own weight. And far too many years pretending I still loved a man who hadn't earned my admiration, much less my devotion. The exhaustion wasn't just in my body. It was in my bones, in the quiet corners of my mind where hope and love used to live.

"Where did you go last night?" I asked finally. If he noticed my clipped tone, he didn't show it. He didn't even look up.

"Just out."

"You left Owen with the sitter."

"I waited until he was asleep," he muttered. "Read him a story. Let him beat me at Mario Kart."

I almost laughed. It was the kind of line meant to soften me. Years ago, it might've worked.

"Do you remember calling me?"

He blinked. Like he didn't remember. Or didn't want to.

"I got three calls between midnight and two a.m…" I stepped closer. "I texted you after each one. Told you I had an early flight. That I was in bed. Yet, you kept calling."

"I was just checking in." He lifted his shoulder. "Just wanted to see how your trip was going."

"You weren't checking in," I said. "You were checking *up*. Making sure I was where I said I'd be." Or making sure I wouldn't arrive home earlier than expected.

He slammed the glass down harder than necessary. "I just—wanted to talk."

"Since when?" I shot back. "We don't even talk when I'm *here*. I walk in, you walk out. We orbit the same house on different schedules—let's not pretend that's an accident."

He flinched. That one hit. He stood, started pacing—tight, anxious circles that didn't go anywhere. His hands kept moving, wiping at his thighs, like nerves were crawling under his skin.

By now, Adam's usual move would be to storm out—angry that I'd questioned him, or suddenly busy with some imaginary errand or a "can't-miss" real estate deal that never led anywhere. But tonight, he didn't leave. He just unraveled right in front of me. And my chest ached—not with anger, but with the quiet, familiar grief of everything we'd built… and lost.

But I didn't cry.

I'd already cried my last tears for Adam.

"You left Owen alone," I said again. "He had breakfast with the sitter. Again."

"I needed air," he snapped.

"No," I said. "You didn't leave for air. And if you're not going to be here when I'm away, then I'll handle the sitter myself."

He stopped, turned toward me, eyes sharp. "You're never here, Kate. You're gone most of the week."

I nodded. "You're right. I've been gone too much."

His expression flickered. That wasn't the response he expected.

"I built a career I thought would give us something solid. But it cost us something else."

I looked down at the floor, then back at him.

"I stayed with you because I thought at least one of us was showing up for Owen. But if I have to do this alone—I *will*."

He stepped closer. "Don't do this. You think I don't love him? I—"

"I'm not saying you don't love him," I inhaled a breath and softened my tone. "I'm saying you're not showing up. The sitter's here more often than you are when I'm gone—and that's not the deal we made when I agreed to stay in this marriage."

His face twisted, defensive, wounded. "You like the travel. The power. The attention. Don't act like you're some martyr."

I met his eyes, steady. "Maybe I do like parts of it. But it doesn't matter. Because I'm done pretending this marriage works."

The silence thickened between us.

Outside, the lake shimmered, still and silver in the twilight. I turned back toward the window, blinking hard. My voice was softer now. Honest.

"I used to want to fix us. But now I just want to be okay. For me. For Owen."

And just like that, I knew.

I'd cut back on travel. I'd tell my boss I was a single parent now. I'd build something stable for my son—even if I had to start over to do it.

And I'd stop carrying the weight of a marriage that had been broken for years.

## About the Author

Veronica is an Amazon chart-topping Florida girl living in a Georgia world—specifically the scenic Low Country—where she has realized her lifelong dream of writing fiction. Known for her gripping tales navigating the shadowy depths of Savannah's haunting allure, Veronica pulls her readers into a labyrinth of mystery and suspense, making it impossible to put down her books until the last twist is revealed.

In her downtime, Veronica enjoys a fulfilling life with her husband, her steadfast partner in love and adventure, and their lively Australian Labradoodle, Fiddler.

www.ingramcontent.com/pod-product-compliance
Lightning Source LLC
La Vergne TN
LVHW030915080826
845145LV00013B/2909
* 9 7 8 1 0 3 6 7 3 3 7 1 1 *